MOTHERS AND OTHER STRANGERS

MOTHERS AND OTHER STRANGERS

COREY ANN HAYDU

LITTLE, BROWN AND COMPANY
New York Boston London

The characters and events in this book are fictitious. Any similarity to real persons, living or dead, is coincidental and not intended by the author.

Copyright © 2026 by Corey Ann Haydu

Hachette Book Group supports the right to free expression and the value of copyright. The purpose of copyright is to encourage writers and artists to produce the creative works that enrich our culture.

The scanning, uploading, and distribution of this book without permission is a theft of the author's intellectual property. If you would like permission to use material from the book (other than for review purposes), please contact permissions@hbgusa.com. Thank you for your support of the author's rights.

Little, Brown and Company
Hachette Book Group
1290 Avenue of the Americas, New York, NY 10104
littlebrown.com

First Edition: March 2026

Little, Brown and Company is a division of Hachette Book Group, Inc. The Little, Brown name and logo are trademarks of Hachette Book Group, Inc.

The publisher is not responsible for websites (or their content) that are not owned by the publisher.

The Hachette Speakers Bureau provides a wide range of authors for speaking events. To find out more, go to hachettespeakersbureau.com or email hachettespeakers@hbgusa.com.

Little, Brown and Company books may be purchased in bulk for business, educational, or promotional use. For information, please contact your local bookseller or the Hachette Book Group Special Markets Department at special.markets@hbgusa.com.

Book interior design by Marie Mundaca

ISBN 9780316597470 (hc) / 9780316603034 (int'l)
LCCN 2025942947

Printing 1, 2026

LSC-C

Printed in the United States of America

To the friends you get to know when you become a parent — and the magnificent few who stick around for the rest of it too.

To Lauren Nita and Anna & Chloe Casey and Patty.

MOTHERS AND OTHER STRANGERS

PROLOGUE

SYDNEY CARRIES THE baby as Mae always suspected she would—as a sweet little bundle attached to her otherwise sinewy frame. It goes without saying that Mae's pregnancy is less contained, parts of her body that she never thought would change suddenly rounding, stretching, straining.

Instinctively, Mae pulls her hair up, neatening herself as much as possible in the moments before saying hello to this person she hasn't seen in years, someone who is both a stranger and her most intimate friend. She wishes she'd worn something different—her stepmother, Catherine, had sent her a care package filled with tea and Tums and compression socks and modest maternity dresses in muted tones, the sorts of things women are supposed to wear to let the world know they are the right kind of pregnant.

Mae, in a sports bra and overalls, is the wrong kind of pregnant.

She reaches into her tote and takes out a sweater in the hope of pulling it over her head before Sydney catches sight of her. But it's too late. As Sydney closes the distance between them, her eyes find

Mae's belly first, then the rest of her. The look is something trapped between wonder and worry, fear and fragility.

They lock eyes and so much melts away—time and hurt and unfamiliarity, gone so fast they are immediately rearranged, redrawn. Mae is stumbling around in a feeling so wide and raw and brilliant that it nearly topples her, gathers tears to her eyes. She will try to paint it later—lavender and gold, smooth and spiky. But it's too big a thing for canvas.

Mothers, both of them. At once. Impossible and true.

Just like the rest of it.

THEN

MAE WAS GOING up the slide and Sydney was coming down it at preschool pickup that first day. They were both in pink leggings, sporting bowl haircuts and big smiles, and at that age, that's really all you need to become best friends. Sydney liked Mae's sparkly headband. Mae liked Sydney's unicorn T-shirt. By the time their mothers picked them up in the sweaty afternoon sun, they were holding hands and begging to go to an entirely different playground together.

Mae's mother, Joni, said yes in the same sleepy breath as Sydney's mother, Beth Ann, said no, and for a moment the disagreement felt charged, uncomfortable, like something they would all have to work to find their way out of. Difference was like that sometimes — thick and strange and creating distinct paths forward. It was a kind of tension not unlike when the working moms went back to the office after a few months of stretchy, impossible, beautiful newborn days. The stay-at-home moms dug in their heels and said goodbye to the women who had taken the shape of friends for that brief period, women they promised to stay in touch with but wouldn't. And a small group of moms lived in between—work-from-home administrators and freelance writers and wedding photographers and struggling actors whose auditions were drying up but were not gone, not entirely. Moms who could go to the occasional baby-and-me music class but also lived in the impossible push-pull of work and children, the desire to succeed for them and in spite of them and because of them.

The first moment between Joni and Beth Ann was like that, a sort of reckoning: *What kind of mother are you? What kind of woman does that mean you are? And what does that mean for our ability to sit at the playground side by side and watch our children navigate who gets to go first on the slide, who can go higher on the jungle gym, whose hair is longer, whose doll needs to be fed more pine cones?*

But it was only for a moment. A big breath that took in the way their daughters leaned toward each other, seemed to sparkle a little in each other's presence, looked easy, tantrum-less, not poised to demand snacks at the loud decibel three-year-olds were known for. In that breath Joni and Beth Ann saw the same thing—that their girls looked the way they themselves recalled feeling as children, at least when they were remembering the best of childhood—the messy-haired, scraped-kneed, dancing-to-scratchy-records-in-the-den, squealing-at-the-perfect-hiding-spot-for-hide-and-seek, eating-popcorn-from-a-big-bowl-and-finding-barely-an-unpopped-kernel-at-the-bottom parts of childhood that were so sweet and boring and nostalgic that it was easy to wonder if they'd ever existed at all.

So much could happen in a breath between three-year-olds and their tired, trying, taut mothers.

"It's a little windy for the playground, isn't it?" Beth Ann said, partly to herself, partly to Joni, partly to Sydney in the conspiratorial way she was often saying things to her daughter. Beth Ann, Joni would come to understand, was always trying to make Sydney agree with her about things like the weather.

"We hate wind," Sydney said. Beth Ann nodded, not so much in agreement but with pride that Sydney had said the right thing, knew her script so precisely.

"Okay," Joni said, looking for the right response, "well, I guess I've never given it much thought. Have you, Mae?"

"Poop!" Mae said with a smile so wide and buoyant it seemed to be willing itself to overflow right off her face. She laughed then, a sound that reminded Joni of all things light and airy and delicious — pink cupcakes and fluffy clouds and enormous puffs of spun-sugar cotton candy.

"Well," Beth Ann said, an admonition, surely, of Mae's exclamation, maybe even of Mae's unleashed laughter, so big and bold it had wrapped Sydney up as well. Sydney was giggling now too while glancing up at her mother to see if it was okay.

Sydney looked, Joni noted, extremely unbothered by the wind.

"There's a nice playground right around the corner," Joni said, her insistent sunniness poking its way through the unsettled feeling between the two mothers, breaking the breath, bringing them all back to the moment. "I've never noticed it being especially windy there. And I have an extra scarf if you need it." She dug in her canvas tote and pulled out something she'd knit herself — yellow-and-blue-striped, soft, imperfect.

"Oh," Beth Ann said, smiling thinly. "Pretty." She pulled her lilac fleece jacket tightly around herself, zipped it all the way up. She tried to tuck her dark blown-out hair behind her ears but it kept flying around in the wind, undoing her prim part, making a mess of what was supposed to be neat and elegant and smooth.

Joni's light brown hair was braided and pinned up like a suburban milkmaid's, and there was something about her skirt's length (long) and style (patchwork floral) that seemed designed to make the other mothers uncomfortable. Mothers in Sommersette wore expensive jeans and navy-blue fleece jackets over tailored T-shirts. They made casual feel practiced. Safe. Uniform.

Joni's skirt, braids, and lacy shirt exposing her bare shoulders were a middle finger to the Sommersette dress code, a fuck-you, honestly, to the other parents at pickup, implying she knew something they didn't. For the first of a thousand times to come, Beth Ann considered asking Joni why in the world she'd moved here, to a place that she so obviously didn't belong in. A place that Joni—Beth Ann could tell from the way she started every other sentence with the phrase *In the city, we used to*—didn't even seem to want to be. By the end of the afternoon, Beth Ann would learn the names of three bars in the East Village, a great French bistro in SoHo, "the best" thrift store in Brooklyn.

Beth Ann would never go to any of these places.

"Didn't they essentially just spend the whole day at a playground?" Beth Ann asked, gesturing to the redbrick preschool and its front yard—the shiny slide, the overly elaborate climbing apparatus, the swings that didn't squeak yet but inevitably would someday soon. There was a list of things Beth Ann had planned to do this afternoon. Mail something at the post office. Stop by the ballet studio to see if they took kids Sydney's age. Enlist Sydney's sticky hands to help make something for dinner.

"So one more hour is probably harmless," Joni said with a shrug that covered up the rest of the things she probably wanted to say but was choosing not to.

"*Harmless* isn't the same as *enjoyable*," Beth Ann said.

"No," Joni agreed. "It's not." She shrugged again. There was a lot about being Mae's mother that wasn't exactly enjoyable but was more or less harmless. Living in this town, for instance, pretending it was enough, pretending it was anything other than a place where people spent money and showed off and bitched about one another's parking skills and haircuts and garden designs.

Joni and her husband, Graham, had once upon a time discussed living in Portland or staying in New York City. She'd made a play for Paris or Amsterdam or buying an RV and adventuring around the country. It had all seemed so possible back in the day, back when they had been mapping out their lives together lying atop the quilt Graham's mother had made him for his college dorm and that had become an integral part of his bedroom aesthetic in the years since then, charming Joni and probably a dozen girls before her, because who didn't love a guy who unabashedly loved his mom?

But then there was Mae.

Joni had been the one to bring up leaving the city, a fact that stunned her city friends, who were all raising their children in tiny apartments, hauling strollers up three flights of stairs, buying plastic storage bins that stacked on top of each other in whatever closet spaces were available, abandoning the idea of a backyard and claiming that a rooftop or a terrace or the neighborhood playground was enough.

And maybe it was.

But Joni had had her eye on Sommersette from the moment she felt a lurch in her stomach and a soreness to her breasts that would someday, somehow, turn into Mae.

"I thought you hated suburbs," Graham had said, suspicious of the house listings she'd sent him, the remarkable way Joni seemed to suddenly know everything there was to know about suburban school districts and finished basements.

"I'm trying to be less judgmental," Joni replied. "Sommersette is artsy. For suburbia, at least. Their movie theater shows indies. I know a children's-book illustrator who moved there a few years ago. There's a bar that plays pretty good jazz, apparently. A lot of transplants from the city."

Graham adjusted his glasses like maybe they were the problem. But nope, it was still Joni in front of him. She was asking him for something he'd always sort of wanted, so who was he to fight against it? Before they got married, his father had warned him about the way people changed over the years and how marriage was about hoping you'd grow together and not apart. And perhaps it had happened, Graham thought, just the way he'd hoped. Joni had changed, but in a good way, a way that made their marriage stronger, their lives more in sync.

So they bought the house with the tall ceilings and the window seat that Joni fell a little in love with, and she promised Graham that the window seat would be enough for her. She liked the lushness of the backyard and the quiet of the street. And she did love that window seat, wide enough for her and her belly and her cats and a pile of books. They did a major renovation of the kitchen, the primary bedroom, all three bathrooms. It took longer than expected, the way these things often do, but they did it, and by the time they arrived there, Mae was old enough to take a pile of picture books up to the window seat herself and flip through them, making up stories, repeating memorized phrases. She did it often, and each time it gave Joni a bit of hope that they were in the right place, that they'd done the right thing.

Sommersette wasn't the city, with its shrieking sirens and possibilities, but it was fine. Joni was fine. Sommersette wasn't special, but it was harmless.

So it felt strange to Joni that Beth Ann was saying that *harmless* wasn't the same as *enjoyable*. Of course it wasn't. She wondered if Beth Ann's life was limited to things she enjoyed, if she hadn't made the sorts of compromises that Joni had in motherhood—if somehow Beth Ann's version would fit Joni better, even though it looked sadder, more stripped of personality. She would've asked her, but Beth Ann didn't seem like a woman who responded well to questions about how she was doing and what she felt and what it meant to live in a beautiful home and have a beautiful child and feel unmistakably wrong in it all.

Maybe, Joni thought, Beth Ann had other things that made her life feel fuller, more anchored. A job. A time-consuming hobby. An affair.

The idea made Joni smile.

Beth Ann was pretty in a conventional way, but brusque, and Joni knew that really any sort of woman might have an affair. Any sort of woman might have any number of secrets. She hoped that Beth Ann had a few.

They hadn't reached an agreement about the playground, their conversation having halted as the girls chattered on in the way three-year-olds did, in a sort of cobbled-together language that was filled with slurry sentences and odd grammatical errors and heartbreaking little stutters and repetitions and struggles to get out the right words in the right order.

Out of that cacophony, however, the girls sang a squeaky *Pleeeeeease* in desperate toddler harmony, and the mothers, both of them in different ways and for different reasons, fell in love with the way Sydney and Mae were together, the way each of them bent and unbent their knees like they might leap off the surface of the earth at any moment; the way their hands were clasped so tightly together that the naked eye could see the strain, the effort of it; the way neither ever wanted to let go of the other. They both had strands of baby hair in their eyes and grass stains in the strangest places—chins and shoulders and stomachs—and smiles that straddled the line between darling and devilish. Smiles that Joni and Beth Ann both loved and feared.

"Who knows, maybe it will be a little enjoyable after all," Joni said, because this was when mothering in Sommersette didn't feel like a lie or a burden or a sad shadow of the way things had been in her head. Mae's joy—at watching the gymnastic stylings of monkeys at the local zoo; at the feeling of dirt under her fingers when she worked in the garden with Joni, overwatering hardy plants that would probably not survive her exquisite love; the rush of *Daddy, Daddy, Daddy* that erupted from her when Graham came home—was a sort of drug. Mae's joy made the hard days better, made the decision to live here feel sturdier.

And maybe that was true for all parents. Beth Ann smiled at Joni, her eyes crinkling in the corners briefly before she seemed to correct them. "Playground it is," she said, reimagining dinner as a cheese-and-apple sandwich and a small salad, the sort of meal her husband, Barrett, would grudgingly accept but have some questions about: *Why such a simple dinner, what were you up to, did you forget to do a grocery run, wasn't Sydney in school today, are there any leftovers?* It would be hard to offer *We went to the playground with that artsy woman who finally moved into that house down the street that was bought a few years back and her daughter, who is now, apparently, Sydney's best friend* to her husband, but he also wouldn't stay on it for long. He never did.

The girls ran off as soon as they arrived at the playground, and Beth Ann started to settle onto a bench.

"Can we move over here?" Joni asked, pointing to another empty spot. "Farther away from the trash cans—bees are always hovering by the trash. I'm allergic." She smiled like it was something whimsical and tragic about her. Joni had a way of making every fact about herself seem meaningful. Profound. Beth Ann would find herself surprised to be jealous of Joni's allergy to bees, her preference for butter rather than cream cheese on her bagels, her collection of beat-up bookstore tote bags, how she used a regular mug instead of a travel one when she went for a walk in the mornings.

Beth Ann had the opportunity to take note of every tiny thing about Joni, because within days, Joni, Mae, Beth Ann, and Sydney had entered into a new routine, carpooling to school in the mornings, going to the playground after school. It was harmless. Or enjoyable. Or something in between, shaded with the anxiety of befriending someone new and wondering what exact role that person might end up playing in your life.

The slurpy *r*'s and swishy *s*'s of the girls' speech drifted into the women's homes, cars, backyards, lives. Always, Mae and Sydney were talking.

When they were three, Sydney and Mae talked mostly about princesses.

When they were four, it was witches and monsters.

And when they were five, it was the dollhouse.

For years and years after, it was mostly the dollhouse. Even as teenagers Sydney and Mae spent whole afternoons with that dollhouse. Not that they would ever have told their friends, who smoked cigarettes and kissed boys and, later, had sex with those same boys or slightly different ones from better or bigger or more Catholic schools in the backs of used cars.

The dollhouse lived in Sydney's home, but it was Mae who made it something special. Mae had an ease with things like glue and paint and scissors and knew instinctively where a tiny couch fit best in relation to a tiny armchair.

"Already an artist, isn't she?" Beth Ann asked Joni once when the two women were enjoying coffee while their seven-year-old girls fought over what color carpet to put in the tiny plastic baby doll's room. Over the years, Joni and Beth Ann, too, had fallen into an unexpected best-friendship. It wasn't a friendship grown from interests or even connection, but it was, by the time the girls were seven, a friendship that felt large and stable and familial and right. If asked, Beth Ann would have said, with a self-deprecating laugh, that, yes, Joni, the one with the skirts and the nose ring and the messy yard, was her best friend. Joni would have said the same, shrugging in a sort of surrender to the way things were in a place like Sommersette. Beth Ann wasn't exactly cool. Or even necessarily interesting. But she was easy to be around and made a great cheese plate and didn't judge an early-afternoon glass of wine or Mae's way of ever so slightly bossing Sydney around, poking her, shoving her once in a while, hitting her a few times. Beth Ann bought Joni's favorite brand of tea to always have on hand, and read the paper and even a novel here and there, and still invited Mae over for playdates even after she cut the hair off Sydney's favorite doll, broke a delicate vase, experimented with the word *bitch* on one occasion.

Some evenings, Graham laughed, bemused, at stories Joni told about prim and proper Beth Ann, but he was happy Joni had found someone to spend time with. It was only Barrett who was prickly about the friendship. But then Barrett was prickly about a great many things, from overdone steaks to un-ironed shirts to the way that both Sydney and Beth Ann left wet towels in the bathroom, spent too much money on manicures and fancy dresses, preferred watching movies on the couch to hiking the nearby trails that Barrett was always dragging them to.

Beth Ann had been in the middle of complaining about one such hike when seven-year-old Mae came to Joni's side with a bit of paper upon which she'd painted a tiny still life: apples and oranges in a bowl. She was making a frame for it with pipe cleaners and wanted to show her mother her accomplishment. It was always this way, Mae making something surprisingly perfect, then bouncing into the room to show it off, while Sydney slogged behind, ready to show some other, much lesser item.

The mothers gave the requisite compliments and sent the girls on their way again, but before they were completely out of earshot, Beth Ann couldn't stop herself from saying, again, "What a talent. She's an artistic prodigy, that kid of yours."

"Well, you know, apple and tree," Joni said. It always felt like she had to remind people that she was the real artist in the family, not her precocious child, who from the age of four had been getting outsize attention for her coloring, gluing, renderings of mermaids and family members and gardens, and, every so often, when things were unraveling, feelings.

"Right," Beth Ann said, "of course."

But Beth Ann didn't ask Joni what she'd been working on in the backyard or compliment the new painting that surely by now she'd caught sight of in the front hall. She didn't extend the compliment of artistry to Joni herself, even though, as Joni saw it, Mae's abilities were simply extensions of her own genetics — proof of her own prodigious talents, her own undeniable artistic identity.

"It must be fun to see her shine," Beth Ann said instead, another way of drawing attention only to Mae, only ever to Mae, who was slight and scrawny but still managed to take up so much space.

"I'm glad we have something in common," Joni said, trying again to carve out her own importance but getting only a tight-lipped smile from Beth Ann in response. Neither woman was working in those days, and it made them both unsteady, though they'd never say it out loud. Instead, Beth Ann was in the habit of listing all the tasks she had to get done in a particular day, as if she needed to prove her worth through errands, and Joni found moments to remind Beth Ann of all the jobs she'd once done, or could be doing, or would someday do again. Artist. Waitress. Writer. Administrative assistant. Music therapist.

"Sydney has other talents," Beth Ann said at last, worried momentarily that the girls might be hearing their conversation.

"Oh, of course," Joni agreed.

And they were both sure this would someday be true.

Upstairs, though, the girls were not listening at all, were never listening to the goings-on of grown-ups in the house. They'd moved on from paintings and pipe cleaners to address more pressing matters. There was currently the issue of how to carpet the baby's room in the dollhouse. Sydney liked a pale blue with stripes and Mae was arguing for a golden paisley pattern, and they had reached an impasse.

"It's my dollhouse," Sydney said after Mae had given an impassioned speech about how golden paisley was special and blue stripes were boring. "So it's really my choice anyway."

"You usually say it's ours," Mae responded. "That we share it. That's, like, your favorite saying." Mae didn't mind a fight. She was good at them—sure enough about almost anything to take a stand, and she liked the rush of adrenaline, the way her brain would shut off and her mouth and limbs and heart would take over, shouting and shaking and drumming. Even at seven, she sometimes hunted for something to explode about—an unflattering haircut, a disgusting dinner food that her mother knew she hated, a playground injustice involving a missed turn or an ignored rule.

While Mae liked the explosive feeling of provoking and defending and demanding, Sydney liked the simpler, cozier feeling of being the victim. She liked the stillness of it, the way she could close her eyes and sigh and have everyone worry about her.

"I mean, it's ours, but really it's mine," Sydney said. She let her shoulder shrug, her eyes lower, like maybe it was embarrassing to have to have this conversation at all. "I mean, it's here. My dad bought it for me. So I guess it's ours, but he'd probably be really upset if you made all the decorating decisions. Because, like, he did buy it for me, you know?"

"Your *dad* would be upset? About the dollhouse?" Mae's eyebrows spiked. She scoffed. Her own father barely knew what toys she owned, let alone where they were or what was done with them. She found it hard to imagine that Sydney had some entirely different kind of father, one who was monitoring a dollhouse, one who was invested in miniature chairs, miniature pizza, miniature people living miniature lives.

"It was expensive," Sydney tried.

"I *know*, obviously, that's why I want it to look good!" Mae was not backing down. It felt good to be right and to make that rightness known.

Sydney stormed to the other side of the room and sat in grumpy silence.

"You always do this," Mae said. "You always change the rules to get your way. I hate that striped carpet. It's stupid. If you use that carpet, I'm never playing with the dollhouse again."

"Good! Then I won't have to listen to all your stupid ideas!"

"*Your* ideas are stupid!"

"No, yours are!"

It was at this stage, then and always, that the mothers appeared. Beth Ann and Joni used to wait before trudging up the stairs to mediate, but waiting it out had proved too dangerous over the years. Once, Mae punched Sydney in the arm. Sydney screamed and kicked her in the shins. Joni was frankly relieved that Sydney was showing signs of fight. Beth Ann was horrified at the act, but Joni tried to telegraph to Sydney that it was okay, good, even, to fight back if you were pushed too far. It was something she would need to know.

Joni suspected, for a variety of reasons, that Beth Ann was missing that fight.

But after the shin kick and an incident involving a remote control thrown against the wall, Joni and Beth Ann tacitly agreed to intervene as soon as the girls' voices were loud enough to make one or the other of the mothers wince.

"Enough dollhouse," Beth Ann said. She had a tired hitch to her voice and wanted nothing more than to finish her coffee in peace. She had been wanting nothing more than to finish her coffee in peace for the seven years since Sydney was born, and yet, almost always, she ended up with half a cup of cold coffee forgotten on the counter.

"But Mae thinks—" Sydney started.

"I said enough. You can try again another day."

"You girls should play outside," Joni said. Children were supposed to do well in the sunshine. They were supposed to need it and like it and play in it.

"Play what?" Mae asked. She crossed her arms over her chest.

"Yeah, play what?" Sydney asked, imitating her friend's stance. And just like that, they were on one team again. They wouldn't play outside, but they wouldn't fight anymore that day either. They picked up a stack of *Archie* comics and settled on opposite ends of the couch. Over the course of an hour, they migrated to the center so they could peek over each other's shoulders to see something funny Jughead did or what cool thing Veronica was wearing.

By the time the sun set, they were ready to eat burgers and spinach salads with their mothers at the kitchen table, and they were sunny and sweet and exactly the kind of daughters their mothers had envisioned when they'd first learned of their pregnancies. Sydney and Mae giggled. They leaned against their mothers' shoulders. They said "Thank you" for scoops of chocolate ice cream and "I love you" when Beth Ann and Joni agreed to a sleepover.

That night, just before eleven, Beth Ann listened to them whisper their way to sleep. She was overwhelmed by Mae and Sydney's closeness—the love and the rage and how big it all was, how subject to change, moment by moment. Who knew what they would be like when they woke up in the morning, how they might feel about each other after a night of dreaming, and what new joys and small tragedies would befall them that day.

It wasn't like that with her and Joni. They sometimes shared something intimate—a strange thing an ex had once asked for during sex, the hit of pain from not receiving Mother's Day wishes from their own mothers, a buried memory of the embarrassing way one had acted on a long-ago date with a guy who was a little too handsome, a rude thing one had said to a stranger in the supermarket who was taking too long to find the exact right avocado.

But there was a deeper-down closeness that they never found. Beth Ann was sure that if Joni ever convinced Graham to move back to the city or if Barrett took that job in Florida and moved everyone there, she and Joni would never speak to each other again.

Joni, meanwhile, figured they'd be together forever, even if their relationship seemed ill-fitting and strange, even if no one else understood it.

That night, when the girls were asleep in Sydney's bedroom and Joni was down the street and probably reading tarot cards or drinking green tea or painting indecipherable abstracts that she showed in the gallery in town from time to time, Beth Ann would have liked to talk it all over with Barrett. The push and pull of having a best friend like Joni, the wanting and not-wanting her around. The wishing Joni would do something normal, like join a book club or get a manicure. She even would have liked to lie next to her husband and stare at the ceiling, worrying and then deciding not to worry about the water damage, the cracks, the places that looked like the whole house might come tumbling down if they weren't careful.

She would have liked to talk about Sydney and Mae and the things they said to each other and the way the love still sparkled and settled around them like dust, like sunbeams, like the powdery snow everyone was always waiting for.

She would have liked to tell him about the job she'd impulsively applied for—nothing fancy, just a job at the local paper editing announcements about the Halloween parade, writing obituaries, remembering to put on coffee for the rest of the office.

She would have liked to tell him all about it.

But he still wasn't home.

So Beth Ann lay in bed remembering that day four years before when she'd met Joni, when Sydney met Mae. It had seemed so small then, the decision to take the girls to the playground, the way Beth Ann and Joni hung back and let the girls fight over who went down the slide first. It had seemed a small thing to ask Joni where she'd grown up and to tell Joni she had one sister and two brothers. It could have been just one day that never turned into any other day. But instead, somehow, that one day had become her whole life.

NOW

Sydney

SYDNEY TOOK THE dollhouse out of storage as soon as she found out she was having a girl. The nurse had left a voicemail notifying her of her baby's sex, which seemed oddly informal for such enormous information. Sydney had listened to the message five times, worried that she'd misheard. It was strange to have concrete answers, to see a bit of the future taking shape. *Okay,* she thought. *There will be tea parties. And dolls. And princesses. And the dollhouse.*

There was only one way to bring up a girl, in Sydney's opinion, only one outcome to this news, and that was a replication of her own childhood. The good parts, before the bad parts came. *There will be a best friend. She'll be artsy and bold and they'll fight but they'll also love really hard. They will hide away on winter afternoons in a basement or an attic and emerge with ideas and dreams that could only have been baked up between the two of them. It will be beautiful and ugly and strange and familiar.*

The dollhouse, more than anything else, seemed like a vital part of the whole equation. It was in a storage unit across town filled with

Sam's old furniture that over the years Sydney had slowly rejected. It had some signs of wear, Sydney noticed when she got to the storage unit. Carpet peeling off the floors. Shingles falling from the roof. A bed with a broken leg. A mom doll but no dad doll.

Not that there's anything wrong with that, Sydney thought. But she immediately took out her phone and searched for a dollhouse shop to buy a new miniature dad. He would have to be tall. Preferably bearded. Dark-haired. It would be nice if he wore a sweater. *A perfect dad.*

Sydney looked around the space as if someone could hear her thoughts. Was Sam's broken IKEA lamp listening in? Was the velvet armchair his ex-girlfriend bought him taking notes on who Sydney's ideal man was and how he was nothing like her actual husband, the true father of her future daughter? Possibly. The armchair was a nearly neon yellow and seemed capable of just about anything. Maybe it was reporting back to Sam. Or his ex-girlfriend! Her name was Ember and she was rich and into fashion, and in addition to the armchair she'd also bought Sam a watch he still wore, a suit he brought out for special occasions, and, he admitted to Sydney one very drunk night, a new chin.

Sydney had tried to forget these facts. Avoided photos of his former, weaker chin and the way it made his pale face seem ever paler, his blond hair thinner, his narrow nose even skinnier. Photos of Sam's old chin were probably tucked into all kinds of boxes in this unit, underneath high-school trophies and college diplomas and framed baseball jerseys and cheap pots and pans that Sam refused to get rid of and Sydney refused to use, all of it forgotten but still costing them a few hundred dollars a month to store.

What is he hanging on to? Sydney wondered, then told herself to forget. *When would he ever need these pots unless—*

"Shut up, Sydney," she said out loud, sounding a little like her own mother on a bad day. Maybe she would let the storage unit's bills go unpaid. She'd heard that eventually things left in storage places like this one got auctioned off, curious bidders standing outside the unit looking in, imagining what each box might hold. She'd heard about the practice on a podcast or from a friend, and the image had stuck with her. She liked the idea of these hopeful bidders, the kind of people who believed in fate and good things coming to those who wait and in taking chances.

Sydney was not one of those people, but she wanted to become one. Lately, ever since she connected with the women of LillyLou, she had felt she could be any kind of person. Maybe, like Ivy Miller had promised, Sydney would surprise herself. Maybe it was *Sydney* who should bid on a stranger's storage space. She wondered what Ivy Miller would think of that and made a mental note to post it on the forums.

Better yet, she would ask Ivy Miller when she met her in person. The prize dangled in front of her—in front of all of them—every day. LillyLou emails emblazoned with Ivy Miller's face reminded her every morning, every evening, that if Sydney could sell enough units or, alternatively, bring enough new women into the business with her, she would get face time with Ivy Miller. A sit-down lunch in Los Angeles would be offered to a dozen women who'd proved they were ready for more.

Sydney was ready for more.

Ivy Miller might not like Sydney getting the dollhouse, though—she was always encouraging the women of LillyLou to put their pasts aside, to be something new.

"Inside us all," Ivy Miller said, "is a map of the places we always return to. It's a wretched map, isn't it? Wrinkled and old and hard to read in some places, torn on the folds. We don't need it, do we? Shouldn't maps be followed to new locations, new parts of ourselves? New futures? I want you to fold up the old maps and imagine new ones. Stop going again and again to those old tired places."

There was always applause after she said this. The phrasing was sometimes a little different, the images shifting, but the message was the same: The past, especially those tired old parts you kept poking at, was done. It was time to move forward.

Sydney very much wanted to agree.

But the dollhouse had always been intended to live—well, where exactly? In the baby's room? In the living room? Or would she finally persuade Sam to move them out of Park Slope and back to Sommersette, where the baby could have a whole room filled with toys and Sam could have a garage and Sydney could have whatever it was she wanted. She wasn't entirely sure yet what, but something.

Something.

A room for her business was what she always said. "I need storage for the clothes, the mailing supplies, all of that," she'd told Sam just yesterday when he got home from work and she got home from an Empowerment Now conference.

"We're not investing any more of ourselves in your scarves," Sam had said.

"Pashminas," Sydney said. "They're very all-season. That's part of what makes the business so viable."

"It's not a business," Sam said. Here he took an especially big bite of the grilled chicken she'd made for dinner. It felt aggressive, though Sydney couldn't say why exactly.

"I work at it. It makes money. What would you call it?"

"A scam," her husband said. Sam had been cruel about Lilly-Lou. He'd supported Sydney when she became a Pilates instructor and when she started her Etsy store. He'd encouraged her passion for photography, gifting her with an expensive camera last Christmas and offering to send her to graduate school if she wanted. He liked her social media posts about self-confidence, valuing oneself, learning to be brave, lifting up other women. He didn't necessarily remember to comment on each post, but at the end of the day, if she sent him a reminder, he would eventually write *I love you!* underneath her uplifting statements and allegedly makeup-free selfies. But something about LillyLou crossed a line for him, and that line only made Sydney want to try even harder to prove him wrong.

"You don't get it," Sydney said. "I just want an office. In a house. Somewhere with a backyard. And if you suggest Kensington again, I will scream. Ivy Miller says big houses make room for big dreams."

"Playgrounds are the backyards of the cities."

"Why can't I want a nice life for my kids?" Sydney felt tears climbing up, begging to come out, but crying would be blamed on pregnancy, on hormones, on all sorts of things that let Sam see the feelings as not hers, not real. But she had always wanted these things. The beautiful life, the pretty one in the house that looked like her old house but without the mess going on around it. She wanted to try again. She needed to.

"Maybe when we have a second baby, we'll move," Sam said finally. "We can fit one kid here. Happily. Comfortably. It's bigger than the place I grew up in."

"Well, we want better for our kid than your mother's—"

"Don't, Sydney."

"I love your mother, but her apartment is—"

"I said don't."

The conversation had continued. Sam spoke about all the ways his mother was a perfect mother, and Sydney brought out the LillyLou paperwork, mentioned the check for eight hundred dollars that she'd gotten last month. Sam asked how much she had spent on inventory; Sydney told him how many followers she had online; Sam told her he loved her photographs and hated these scarves; she said she could do both, and, Jesus Christ, they were *pashminas;* he said she was hormonal and they should talk about it when that wasn't so clearly a factor; Sydney reminded him that she'd be hormonal until she stopped breastfeeding, which would be in, like, two years, five years if they had another kid right away, so now was the time, now was the only time, life was a rushing river, and they were letting it move them along instead of climbing into rowboats and deciding how to manage the current. Just like they'd warned her about at Empowerment Now.

This was where the conversation ended, and where it always ended, because when Sydney started spiraling out into what the next five years meant for her body, herself, her life, she'd inevitably begin crying and talking about Empowerment Now and quoting Ivy Miller about maps and rowboats and magical futures that everyone deserved, and Sam would say she sounded like her mother, and Sydney would cry harder—would sometimes, without Sam seeing it, dig her fingernails into the tender skin of her palms, as if maybe the pinch there could make the things he was saying untrue.

"I'm not my mother," she would say—sometimes a whisper, sometimes a scream, sometimes something else guttural and rough.

"Then let's just stay here and live our lives," Sam replied, like it was just that simple.

The dollhouse was maybe a little heavier than something a ten-weeks-pregnant woman was supposed to be carrying, but Sydney chose not to care. She covered the whole thing in bubble wrap, taking the time to individually bundle each miniature piece—a tiny porcelain bathtub, a tiny refrigerator and the tiny apples and pizzas and steaks it housed, a tiny marble fireplace, and a tiny tricycle. A tiny coffee mug with the tiny words *World's Best Mom* on it. She wondered who'd bought that—was it her own mother, subliminally signaling something to Sydney? Or was it Sydney's father, who sometimes bought little joke accessories for the dollhouse family: a tiny poop for the tiny toilet that her mother visibly stiffened upon seeing, a miniature set of golf clubs, an itty-bitty copy of the Bible even though they were not a churchgoing family. "Who's to say what the dollhouse family believes?" her father said in that big booming voice he had. "Let them figure it out for themselves!"

Sydney's mother had laughed and Sydney laughed now, remembering it, but at the time she hadn't really understood the joke, hadn't known much about Bibles or God or what her family believed as opposed to what other people believed. The idea was a little frightening, in fact, that the family she was nurturing in her dollhouse might believe other things, have different values and thoughts and operate in its own mysterious ways. Because of that, she'd hid the tiny Bible in the top drawer of the tiny dresser in the primary bedroom and never let the dollhouse family see it.

Sydney loaded the dollhouse into the back seat of the car and listened to the message from the nurse again. And again. The words were as clear as day. Sydney and Sam were having a little girl. Someday she would explain to this little girl everything about the tiny Bible and the mug and even the miniature poop. She would explain how her father was funny but forgetful, how her mother never once left the house in anything but an official Outfit and how that had mattered to Sydney so much until it hadn't anymore. She'd tell her daughter about the girl who had been her best friend, little Mae Dawn Dyer, with her straight nose and crooked teeth and messy blond hair, and how girlhood was made for friendships like that, for dollhouses and miniature pizza and also regular-size pizza eaten on the couch while watching *Drop Dead Fred* and *Girls Just Want to Have Fun*, and for telling secrets about crushes and other kids and what they thought about in the dark and what they noticed shifting and changing in their bodies and what they thought other people might think of those changes.

Sydney's phone rang as she drove and thought and dreamed of her little girl and the life she would live. It was Beth Ann calling. It was always Beth Ann.

"Hey, Mom," Sydney answered, a little tired already by the conversation that had yet to happen.

"Sydney. Sweetheart. I told you to post every two hours. Every two. It's been five, almost six, and nothing from you. I want you to meet your goals, sweetheart, and you're never going to get there this way. How can I support you better?"

Inquiring *How can I support you better?* was a tenet of LillyLou, a primary question they were always supposed to ask the women working below them. It sounded both familiar and uncomfortable coming from Sydney's own mother, who had never asked Sydney such a thing in her childhood, when maybe it would have been more welcome.

"I'm planning something for later," Sydney said, trying to sound thirty-three and grounded in her own self-worth. Trying to sound like she, too, was wearing an official Outfit.

"I thought you wanted to meet Ivy. I thought that's what we were working toward. I'm telling you how to get there, Syd, and you're just ignoring me."

Sydney strained to hear her father half-heartedly defend her in the background.

"I'm not ignoring you, I'm doing it my own way, Mom," Sydney said. She knew the phrase would not sit well with Beth Ann.

"Oh. Well, okay, then. Your own way. Nothing to learn from me, I guess. Nothing valuable here at all."

"Not what I said." Sydney sighed. And it wasn't what she thought either. She'd joined LillyLou because of her mother, hadn't she? She'd picked the wedding dress her mother liked, she'd chosen the carpeted venue with the big windows that her mother wanted instead of the industrial space with the wooden beams she wanted. She was wearing her hair short and wispy after going to her mother's stylist. She was even considering a scheduled C-section, something Beth Ann obsessively asked her to plan on, for the sake of her marriage.

Maybe, Beth Ann had been known to muse after a third glass of wine, it was the vaginal birth that did it, the long recovery, the ways her body was never really the same. Maybe Sydney and Sam could make different decisions and have different outcomes, if they were lucky, if they listened to everything Beth Ann had to share about where her life had gone right and where it had gone wrong.

Sydney thought for a moment about her mother's rage when she and Sam announced they'd be going to Peru for their honeymoon. At first, Beth Ann looked almost like she was going to laugh about the choice, but then laughter folded into something else, something raw and unfinished. She'd begun to cry, and Beth Ann wasn't one for crying, really. "Peru," Beth Ann had said through tears, directing the word not to Sydney but to Barrett. It sounded like an accusation, and he hung his head in response. Later, Barrett asked Sydney to reconsider the location, but without getting an explanation as to why, Sydney didn't. It had felt important not to give in to Beth Ann now that she was getting married. Sydney was certain her marriage would make her stronger, more separate from her mother and, more important, her mother's marriage.

Her parents' marriage was at once a thing of mystery and a thing she knew far too much about. It was a bit of white noise in the background of every conversation she had with her mother, every beat of every phone call, including this one. It was there in the way her father didn't ask to be passed the phone, the way he never joined Beth Ann on her weekend visits, the way he communicated with Sydney mostly by sending internet memes she wasn't convinced he fully understood.

"You'll see. You'll have this baby and you'll see," Beth Ann said, making some sort of promise for Sydney's future. Sydney didn't know what to say, so she didn't say anything.

Sydney would tell her daughter about the dollhouse and Mae and long afternoons picnicking behind their house and eating pretzels at the mall and learning how to put on eye shadow they bought by the bundle at CVS and wondering why it didn't look on them the way it did on the models in *Seventeen* magazine.

She would tell her daughter so much about what it was like to grow up with a friend like Mae Dawn Dyer.

But not everything.

Definitely not everything.

NOW

Mae

MAE WANTED TO keep the dresser. It was dark brown with silver knobs and tiny peg feet painted dark red, a strange combination that someone had Frankensteined together over the years, and Mae liked the reminder that the dresser had had a life before it made its way into her apartment with Leo. The chaos of its design was a promise, too, that it would have a life after them as well.

Leo had never liked it.

"Greg. Up here," he called to a friend who used to be a shared friend but, Mae supposed, now belonged to Leo alone. Enough of her friends had broken up that she knew the rhythm of it. At her age, everyone was either getting married or breaking up, and Mae was now squarely in the second camp, even though just a month ago she'd been researching what stones besides diamonds made for good engagement rings.

Sapphires, it turned out. But not amethysts, her birthstone. They were weak. That shouldn't have been a surprise, but it was. And somehow learning that took the wind out of her sails almost as much as learning that Leo had messaged no fewer than three girls from the personals section of the local paper's website when he took that directing job in Colorado this past summer.

The situation played over and over in her head, an endless loop she was forcing herself to watch.

If he'd been looking on a legitimate dating website or even some sort of classy escort service, Mae supposed she could probably have talked herself into accepting and understanding the revelation. She had done it before, forgiven him for briefly breaking up with her to pursue a barista with a shaved head and, she learned later through a series of unfortunate and regrettable conversations, a nipple ring. She'd managed to forget the way he looked at her cutest, bustiest friends when they met up on Saturday nights. And she'd successfully convinced herself not to care that he spoke about beauty as if it were something that belonged to other people, not to her. "Really beautiful people are always crazy," he'd said soon after they got back together following the barista dalliance. "Fun, don't get me wrong. Intoxicating or whatever. But crazy."

"I'm not crazy," Mae had said, smiling at the way the conversation felt flirtatious and sweet, slipping herself into the label of a really beautiful woman like she'd simply needed him to confirm it for it to be true.

"Right, exactly," he'd said, and something essential in her had wilted. "That's what I mean. People like you and me shouldn't be with super-beautiful people. Not worth it. Right?"

Mae had been stunned into silence. It was strange, the way he was insulting her but also insulting himself but also saying it so casually that it would be impossible to respond with any sort of heat or vigor. He'd said it the way you'd say any sort of fact, like her lack of beauty was as inarguable as her height, her zodiac sign, her allergy to penicillin. So she hadn't gotten mad at him, and when he said it a second and third and ninth time over the years, she'd just shrugged and nodded and tried to un-hear it. But of course, by then, it was a thing living inside of her, a few words strung together that had come to define her.

She didn't forgive him for all that so much as decide it didn't need forgiving. It was a true thing he believed, which meant it was probably a true thing that everyone knew, and so she had to live with it.

But hunting for someone to occupy his time or even just his thoughts through a local paper's low-tech website—the kind of place where people go to find used couches and shitty roommates and part-time jobs that never work out—was different. It was cheap and ugly and base. It was an undeniable litmus test of how he was never going to change, of how truly unable to be committed to her he was. He'd been in Colorado for the summer, and the week before he came back, she showed up to celebrate his birthday with him. He was still sleeping when she turned on his computer to check her email, and the personals page was right there on full display, as if he'd hoped she'd come across it.

Men Seeking Women, the top of the page announced, like it wanted to make sure she understood. He'd favorited a few choices—girls with toothy smiles and straight hair and the kind of freckles that bragged about having spent afternoons outside in the sun instead of behind a desk or in a coffee shop. Girls who looked easy, carefree, the way people in Colorado all looked, maybe, like things were going to be okay as long as they could fit in a nice bike ride. The girls Leo had favorited, these Colorado girls, wore T-shirts and ponytails and tiny denim shorts. They wore fitted sweaters and sometimes the perfectly placed, extremely tiny nose stud, so small you had to wonder at first if it was a freckle.

These girls weren't messy and worn, the way Mae felt. They were fresh and neat and probably that certain kind of *good* that Mae could never quite pull off.

"Well, fuck," she said to the screen of pretty women.

Her voice shook when she asked him about it, and he stumbled over explanations that involved how he was just looking out of boredom and loneliness, how he'd messaged three of them but of course he would never actually meet up with any of them, how it was just a silly way to pass the time.

And for seven weeks, Mae tried to accept it. She didn't tell friends, tried not to let her mind wander back to those images, the straight hair that required no product, the pink lips and cheeks that looked untouched by any sort of makeup. The quick descriptors she thought she hadn't really taken in but clearly had, because they wouldn't stop popping up in her mind, dancing around, taunting her. *Christina, twenty-seven, nurse. Bella, twenty-five, journalist. Eve, twenty-nine, horticulturist.*

She was something more like *Mae, thirty-three, almost-artist and sometime grad student, cocktail waitress, waiting to be something else but no idea what that something else might in fact be.*

And after seven weeks and one day, Mae was tired of trying to make it okay, tired of trying to believe something that seemed, ultimately, pretty unbelievable. Some women, she was sure, could forgive Leo. Some would maybe even view it the way he had—a nonevent, nowhere in the universe of infidelity. But Mae was not one of those women.

She'd called her dad's wife, Catherine, hoping for her agreement. Catherine had always liked Leo, but still, Mae assumed she'd stand up for her stepdaughter, maybe even call Leo to admonish him herself.

It was what Joni would have done.

But Mae would have to settle for the thought of Joni haunting Leo. It was comforting, sort of, until she realized that Joni probably had too long a list of hauntings to make time for her daughter's ex-boyfriend.

"Sometimes it's good," Catherine said in her slow, thoughtful way, "when someone makes it obvious that you shouldn't be with them."

"So you think I shouldn't be with him?" Mae hadn't exactly determined what her next steps were, only that she was humiliated by the ordeal and suddenly questioning a great number of things, like her hair color, the fit of her jeans, the worthiness of her whole self, the trajectory of her adult life.

"No, honey, no," Catherine said. "Don't you want someone to choose you, every day? Isn't that what we all want, really?"

Mae was stumped. It was certainly what Catherine wanted. And, Mae supposed, what her father wanted too, and finally had. Probably it was what Mae wanted, but to know for sure, she'd have to really talk it out with someone, and that someone couldn't be Catherine. She and Catherine were already circling too close to the unsayable things, the histories they both preferred to look away from.

For the millionth time, Mae wondered what it would be like to talk to Joni about Leo, about love, and about how you line up love with things like hope, hurt, history.

"He did you a favor," Catherine said. "Imagine if you had married him, started a life with him. This is for the best. Say thank you to him and walk away."

It was quintessentially Catherine to want to say thank you to the people who were the most hurtful, caused the most wreckage, were the most unpredictable. She'd said it to Joni, even, on the day of her wedding to Mae's dad. Said it to the memory of Joni, at least. Catherine was the sort of woman prone to speaking to memories, personality traits, bad habits, dead first wives.

When Mae told Leo it was over, she did not say thank you. And he did not say sorry. He said she didn't understand him, that she wasn't perfect either, that he had nowhere to go, nowhere to live, that he was homeless and she'd done that to him. "All you want to do is punish me for one mistake!" he yelled so loudly that the apartment's silence seemed to expand in response to the sound.

"Okay," Leo said now, a week after he'd stomped out and gone to stay with a friend. "Who's getting what?"

As far as Mae knew, there wasn't much to talk about. Most of the furniture in the apartment was hers, Leo having sort of slid into her life and her heart and her one-bedroom place as if she didn't really have a choice. And though he came with a lot of shit—ex-girlfriends and stories about sexy actresses he knew before they got famous, an unfinished degree from an arty Chicago college, a penchant for the personals in local papers' websites, a solid T-shirt collection, and a lot of thoughts about what kind of life he deserved, what kind of woman he wanted—he did not come with dishes or tables or, as it turned out, rent money.

"You take your shit, and I'll keep mine," Mae said.

"What about shared stuff?" Leo was tall, his torso soft, but he carried himself like he was built solidly, compactly. Mae used to love that about him. The strange way his body moved—a delicate bend to his arms, a perfect straightness to his back aside from a forward slope in his shoulders, like he didn't want his height to unnerve anyone. It made her believe him to be kind. He wore his hair long and it curled at the ends. In the winter it was light brown but in the summer he looked nearly blond. She wondered, for a moment, if he'd ever looked at her with that same kind of precision. And she wondered how she would hold up under that much scrutiny.

Mae liked that he wasn't the kind of man other people would find exceptionally good-looking. She had, over the years, dated mostly jocks—high-school football players and men who liked running on Saturday mornings and, once, right after college, a very religious accountant who went on to win a handful of bodybuilding competitions. Leo had, for a while, seemed like the perfect antidote to this string of ill-fitting partners. Mae was an artist, or at least had a bank account with some real money in it from the moment when everyone thought she was an artist. She was not—she told herself a dozen times a day—an artist like her mother had been, just dabbling and pretending and only very occasionally selling something in a Sommersette gallery to a random neighbor who didn't know the first thing about art. No. Mae wanted to be the real kind of artist, different from her mother in a hundred vague and meaningless ways and a few very important ones. And if she was going to be a real artist making her way in the city, she should be *with* an artist, she'd thought.

She had, of course, been wrong. "What would you consider shared?" she asked.

"The things we bought together," he said. "The record player. The kitchen console. The dresser."

The record player had been an impulse buy after a crummy day when they'd fought about what to eat for lunch and why the Wi-Fi was such shit. They liked the ancient buzz of the records, the grainy quality of the music. It gave them something to define themselves as: the kind of couple with a record collection. The kind of couple who read novels on the couch and let their feet touch and took turns picking the soundtrack.

The kitchen console was a strange and perfect piece. It was made of wood and metal and painted an unexpected neon pink on the sides, had hooks to hang pots and pans on and a cupboard for storage and a block of wood for cutting vegetables or, more often, letting mail gather until one or the other of them gave in and separated junk from bills. They'd found it together on the street and had fallen in love with its awkward perfection.

The dresser, however, she had bought on her own. They had shared it, sure, as two people living together share a dresser—him taking the top drawers and her taking the bottom ones—but it was hers. It was all hers, in her mind. They had bought things like the record player and the console and the chair *together* in the sense that they had both been in the store at the same time, and there had been unkept promises of stops at the ATM to reimburse her. But that wasn't the same as both of them owning those objects, was it?

"I mean," Mae started, wondering how much to nitpick over who paid for what, how starkly to remind him that he owed her probably thousands of dollars between unpaid rent and unpaid promises. "I guess you can take the kitchen console?"

"And the record player," Leo said. "And of course the records. You don't need records if you don't have a record player."

Joni, Mae thought, would have spat in his face at this. No—she would have upended the record player and smashed the records so that neither of them could enjoy this small pleasure they'd once shared. Joni had known how to blow something up, how to make it unusable, how to break it in the most definitive way. Maybe Mae did too, but Catherine's voice was ringing in her head. And some days she thought it would be nicer, wouldn't it, to be a Catherine than a Joni. So she'd tried, imagining Catherine's Lululemon leggings, her loose-knit sweaters that covered her ass, her tasteful beige flats. Her sunny, unfettered smile.

"I could get a new one," Mae said, and in even that statement, she supposed, she was giving up custody of the record player, letting him have it.

"I doubt you will. It was really more my thing."

Mae wasn't sure that this was true, but he said it so confidently, she figured it must be.

"Fine," Mae said, but she hoped she would someday get a new record player, be that person again—listening to Ella Fitzgerald, reading novels, stretching out on the couch, just without Leo.

Leo nodded to Greg, who started unhooking pans from the console, unloading plates from the cupboard. Mae's heart zinged. It had not been a perfect relationship. Or even, honestly, a good one. But that strange piece of furniture in the kitchen had felt homey and sweet, the sort of thing married people had, the sort of thing that pure struggling artists in big bustling cities owned to make their lives feel small and simple and cozy. And there were Greg's clumsy hands just undoing all those delicate moments.

"I'm going to the café," she said. It hadn't been the plan. But she didn't know what else to do with her body in this moment. "Be done by the time I get back."

"When will that be?" Leo asked.

"How fucking long does it take to carry, like, two objects down the stairs? I'll be a minute. I'll read a chapter of a book. Don't forget anything; you won't be coming back here."

Fuck it, Mae thought. She didn't own beige flats or the right kind of sweaters. She would never be Catherine anyway.

"I wanted this to work," Leo said, hearing, probably, the crack and splinter of her voice.

"You had a weird way of showing it," Mae said. It felt good to slam the door behind her. It felt good to stomp down the four flights of stairs, to make each step bang and echo. It felt good, until it felt bad.

The second the outside air hit her, the sun made her squinty and sad, and there were things about Leo that suddenly seemed irreplaceable. The way he said her name, overemphasizing the *M* at the beginning so that it became practically its own country. The way he read parts of books out loud to her at night, sometimes even waking her up when she'd drifted off to share something especially evocative or strange or funny or sad. He liked things that made no sense together — wrestling and knock-knock jokes; gardening and karaoke; Sylvia Plath and volleyball.

That was irreplaceable, wasn't it? That was something to make sacrifices for, perhaps.

She was desperate to know what Joni would have thought and

also certain that whatever Joni's opinion was, it would have been infuriating enough that she wouldn't have listened to it. What a privilege it actually was to get the chance to know what to do because of how you felt about what your mother told you to do.

"Mae-Mae!" her neighbor Georgie called out before Mae could spend another minute stuck contemplating her mother's legacy. Georgie was a pretty girl—no! Woman! *Woman!*—around Mae's age whom Mae had befriended only recently when they'd both been on their stoops around midnight with mugs of coffee that were actually wine. They'd passed each other on the street hundreds of times with barely so much as a nod, but for whatever reason, that night, Mae motioned toward the mug and asked, "Tequila?" and Georgie grinned and said, "Chardonnay, I'm classy," and Mae grinned wider and said, "I've got you beat. Prosecco." They'd laughed about how hard it was to get away from the people you lived with. Georgie had two roommates, one an old college friend and one a stranger with a penchant for playing opera at full blast and cooking fish with the windows closed. Mae had told her the bare bones of her latest fight with Leo. Nothing about Christina the nurse or Eve the horticulturist. But she told Georgie about the way Leo pouted when she'd said she was going to California to visit friends, as if it were her job to always stay home and his job to always leave.

Georgie had listened and not given any kind of advice and called her Mae-Mae, which felt sweet and intimate, and they'd started meeting on the stoop at weird late-night hours once a week when Leo was asleep and one of Georgie's roommates was cooking something disgusting or the other one was listening to something ear-piercing or they were both calling her out for some mundane infraction like putting the big plates on the shelf meant for the small plates.

She was, in some ways, the perfect friend for Mae.

"Hey, Georgie," Mae said.

"You headed somewhere?"

"I—coffee, I guess. But I'm trying to decide—I might head back upstairs."

Georgie squinted. It wasn't from the sun. "What's up there?" she asked.

Mae shrugged. "Leo. His friend. He's moving out. But I—I don't know. It's so final. And maybe—"

"I could go for coffee," Georgie interrupted.

"We were talking about rings. I mean, fuck, what am I doing? We're in love. And, like, he's—he's really smart. I like Sundays with him. They're calm. We listen to records. We read."

"I love records," Georgie said. "And reading. And Sundays. I even make pancakes. Let's get coffee."

"I want to get married," Mae said in a small voice, surprising even herself. It wasn't the sort of thing a person like Mae said, or even thought. And it definitely wasn't the kind of thing she should be saying right now. "I'm like a hundred and I want to be married and do all of that even though I know *all of that* is literally the worst, but I want a ring and a dress and a whole thing. I want the whole thing. And if he leaves, then I'm starting from scratch and the whole thing is even further away."

"Mae. Seriously. Do you want to marry Leo? Do you want to bear his pouty, grumpy, seven-foot-tall babies? Is that what you actually want, for real, more than anything else?" Georgie's body was only a shiver away from Mae's now, too close to feel natural, but Mae didn't want to lean away from her. She wanted a sip of that certainty. She wanted to be okay with having pancakes with Georgie on Sundays. She wanted to be ready to wait for something better. She wanted to be as sure of anything as Georgie was that Mae shouldn't marry Leo.

"Coffee it is," Mae said.

"That's what I thought."

* * *

They stayed at the coffee shop for less than an hour. They didn't talk about Leo or whoever it was that Georgie was dating or not dating or thinking about dating. They talked about painting, which Georgie was taking a class in, and she wondered if Mae would look at her stuff.

"I'm not, you know, good," Mae said. Years ago, she'd been one of thirty under-thirty artists to watch. A particular painting of hers had been in a particular gallery, and the paper of record, the *Times*, had written an article about her and the painting and what it was to be a young female working on art about things that other artists dismissed: families, friendships, femininity. People had loved the painting and the article about the painting and even the picture of her in the paper, looking like someone's idea of an artist. There had been more articles. More cover photos. More almost-fame, of the kind people capture and struggle to hold on to in the city.

And because of all that, the painting had sold for a great deal of money. It was purchased by an anonymous buyer, and sometimes, but not too often, Mae wondered who the buyer was, thought she'd like to write them a polite thank-you note or send some flowers, grateful for the unexpected safety net.

But she would have been embarrassed to say what she'd done with that freedom, because since then, she'd barely painted anything at all. She was the very definition of *wasted potential*, and she knew it.

"I like that painting you have in your living room. Of the girls on the beach. The sisters," Georgie said. She'd been in Mae's apartment only once, when Mae had run out of wine and Georgie had joined her in getting a refill.

"They're not sisters," Mae said. "Just friends."

"You'd paint them differently if they were sisters?" Georgie asked. It made Mae laugh. And think. The painting was a portrait of herself and her long-ago childhood best friend, Sydney, her attempt to capture everything about what used to be between them. She'd set the painting at the beach. There was a pile of sea glass and pebbles between the girls, and the sun was setting, indicating their work was done, they'd collected all they needed, and they could now enjoy the sand, the pink-gold sky, their gathered treasures.

She'd painted that years ago, and it still made her heart do something solemn and quick.

Most of Mae's paintings, including the famous one, were of herself and Sydney. Most of them were at the beach. But she had stopped knowing what it was she wanted to say about Sydney or the beach, so she'd stopped painting altogether.

"Maybe not," Mae answered. "I guess I don't know. I've never had a sister."

"Well, I have one. Looks the same," Georgie said with a shrug like it didn't really matter, it was just small talk, but once Mae started thinking about Sydney and sisters and making art, she couldn't stop.

Maybe, with Leo gone, she'd get to painting again.

She and Georgie drank too-hot coffees and talked about not much and Mae tried not to think about weddings that would never be and friendships that ended even though you didn't really want them to and moms who left the earth before they were supposed to and the spot in her apartment where the record player would no longer live.

Maybe she'd get a plant.

"I'm coming up with you," Georgie said when they'd walked back to their stoops. It sounded like it'd be awkward, for Georgie's second time up there to be her watching Mae's life fall apart, watching the apartment shift from a home to just a place where Mae lived. Making friends in your thirties was challenging. It couldn't happen naturally. It happened with effort. It was nothing like meeting and befriending Sydney thirty years ago had been, that sloppy, fated, accidental way that three-year-olds make friends. Standing too close to each other. Fighting over and then deciding to share a toy. Finding a shared rhythm on the swings, then laughing about it in the full-throated, delirious way of childhood.

Mae wished it felt like that with Georgie, with anyone, but it didn't. It never would again.

"I'm fine, you don't have to come up," Mae said.

"Oh, I know I don't have to," Georgie said. "But I'm worried that guy's still up there and you'll end up down on the stoop tonight telling me all the things he said to get you back, all the promises he made that you're going to wait around to see if he'll keep. And I'll have to nod and pretend it's a good idea. And I mean, shit, I am a really bad liar. So I'm coming up. Just in case."

Mae started to say she was fine again, but Georgie told her to shut up as if they were sisters, as if they *had* met on a playground thirty years ago. It was the way Sydney and Mae used to talk to each other growing up. Intimate. Sharp. They hadn't needed to be nice. They'd been something better than nice. Something Mae had been missing with a vague sort of thumping desire, unidentified. Until now.

They climbed up the four flights of stairs, neither of them out of breath at the end, exactly, but both breathing a heavy sigh of relief anyway. *We're here. We've arrived. The climb is over. We can see what's inside.*

"It's probably a mess," Mae said, opening the door.

"Oh, whatever," Georgie said, grabbing her hand. Things were disorganized, clearly having been moved around and taken out and sorted through, but there were no cans of soda or beer on the coffee table, no remnants of yesterday's lunch on a plate on the kitchen counter. No unidentifiable smells or alarming number of magazines piled up in the corner.

Leo, however, was gone. Mae felt a cry asking to come out and told it not to. She stilled her body to try to understand the new reality of the way things were. Maybe the apartment looked sunnier. Maybe it was quieter. Maybe she could be happy, someday, here.

She had felt this before, the sudden shift of reality, the way a familiar life became an unfamiliar one. The way a room, absent of the person who used to occupy it, was more of a graveyard, really.

Mae and Georgie walked through the kitchen/living room hybrid into the bedroom, where things were pretty and cream-colored and organized.

Except for the pile of underwear, pajamas, and T-shirts on the bed. It looked like dirty laundry that hadn't yet been put in the machine or clean clothes that needed to be folded and put away.

"What the *fuck*," Mae said. Georgie couldn't place the object of her ire—the laundry, she supposed. Maybe Leo was supposed to have put it away for her? Maybe he moved it from the laundry bin for some reason? "My fucking dresser, what the *fuck*." Mae sounded angrier than the first time, louder, like she was on the verge of tears that had been building up all day or maybe all year or maybe really forever for someone like Mae, someone who was so determined to be fine and fine and fine, fine, fine.

"I don't see a dresser," Georgie said. She wasn't usually quite so slow, and before the words were all the way out, she got it that, yeah, that was the problem, that was the reason Mae's face was twisting and turning pink and bug-eyed. There was no dresser.

The dresser was gone.

THE PAINTING

ALL OF THE paintings were of two girls: The one she kept in her apartment that Georgie had commented on, the one in the storage nook behind the stairwell of her building, the one she'd gifted Graham and his new wife on the occasion of their wedding, a piece of her artwork that surely he had kept but somehow she'd never actually seen in his home. And, of course, the painting she was famous for.

The Painting, as she came to think of it.

She first painted a rocky shore, then two girls contemplating its snaking shape. Then she'd started playing with the light. Maybe that's what made all the difference. She made the day gray but also golden. She let the sun come in from two sides so that both girls were aglow in it. At first there were only the forms of them, their faces still featureless, the particular shapes of their bodies still nebulous. She simply knew she wanted them to be equal forces in the Painting, equally important.

If the Painting sounds beautiful so far, it wasn't. Not in the way of sunsets and waterfalls, not beautiful the way blooming flowers and young brides are beautiful. The Painting was interesting. It was arresting. It was emotional.

She painted sunbeams that reached like daggers to the girls' arms. She made the ocean on the verge of a gigantic wave, too big for anyone to survive. She repositioned the girls so they were looking at each other instead of at the ocean, instead of at all they should have seen coming.

She painted the wave dark blue, stormy. It looked wild on the edges, torn. It collided with the sun.

People looking at the Painting would feel that it was coming for them too.

And who knows, maybe it was.

THEN

JONI WAS THE one who said they should take a vacation together. Joni knew how to make a decision and stick with it, knew how to sculpt a life out of scraps and scrambles in a way that the rest of them didn't.

"It's because I'm an artist," Joni said when Beth Ann looked skeptical about the idea of a family vacation. "I have a vision. The girls are five. They'll remember this summer. We're the ones painting the picture of their childhoods. We create it and they live in it. You know?"

Beth Ann wasn't sure what she knew. She wanted to be a good mother. She wanted to feel the way Joni did—inspired and creative and alive with the responsibility of making a beautiful childhood for her kid. But that feeling was always getting dulled by the uninspired way Barrett kissed her in the mornings, by the times Sydney dumped a bowl of pasta on the ground or vomited on an especially delicate smocked dress or, more often than Beth Ann would like to admit, hit her in the face or kicked her shins with a passion Beth Ann could never seem to muster for anything.

"You make it sound nice," Beth Ann said. "But Sydney gets carsick. And hates the water. And she's in this really difficult phase where she—"

"Art is messy," Joni said, waving the rest of it away. "Motherhood is finger painting, not, you know, stenciling."

"I mean, okay, but I hate finger painting," Beth Ann said, to which Joni laughed. It wasn't funny, though. "What are you thinking for this vacation? Disney or something?" The words came out accidentally. Beth Ann knew what Joni thought of Disney. What she thought of all things pink and princess and commercial and narrated by squeaky-voiced cartoon characters, Elton John songs, shiny roller coasters, sweaty ice cream sundaes.

"Camping, maybe," Joni said. "S'mores and scary stories and skinny-dipping."

"The girls or us?" Beth Ann asked.

"Whoever's in the mood," Joni said.

"I'm not much of a camper," Beth Ann said, skimming by the suggestions of nudity, the way Joni smiled sneakily, knowing, as she did, how much more fun she was than Beth Ann, how much more free.

"Lake house?" Joni suggested.

"There are really beautiful properties on Nantucket," Beth Ann replied, trying not to draw attention to the fact that Nantucket was not near a lake, was not a campsite, would not fit what Joni had surely intended. Had Joni brought up her ideas in front of the husbands, Barrett might have pushed Beth Ann in the direction of Joni's suggestions, as unappealing as they were to her. He always said he'd love to take them camping. But he had never planned a camping trip, had never even researched tents or sleeping bags, so how much did he really want it anyway? "Nantucket is gorgeous. You'd love it."

"Oh," Joni said, resigning herself quickly to everything that would come next—booking fees and grocery-shopping lists and flipping through a book on Nantucket from the bookstore in town that she was somehow both surprised and unsurprised to learn did not have a poetry section but had three travel guides to the fanciest beaches in Massachusetts. It wasn't what she'd had in mind, but it was something, it was a compromise, maybe, between the two women whose friendship was filled with little compromises, little shifts they made in who they were supposed to be so that they could fit more neatly into the friendship their girls insisted on them having. And that, at least, was pure. There was almost a religious rightness to watching Sydney and Mae wrap their lives together.

Sydney and Mae were so close that even Joni, who'd birthed Mae, who'd breastfed her for almost two years, sometimes couldn't distinguish between their voices, couldn't guess at whose laugh was whose or accurately determine if it was Sydney or Mae who was asking for more cookies or to stay up later. She'd like to know which ideas belonged to her daughter and which to Sydney, but there weren't beginnings and ends to these thoughts and demands, not the way Joni was used to with Graham. With Graham, Joni was almost always the person with the ideas. It was her idea to put a hammock between the two tired trees in their backyard. It was her idea to let Mae draw on the walls of her room as a form of self-expression and maybe a sign of Joni's own exhaustion at having to say no over and over.

And of course it had been Joni's idea to be here at all. She was thinking about it again, the way she often did when she was in Beth Ann's kitchen and feeling a little outside the rhythm of her own life.

When she'd confirmed the pregnancy, she started telling Graham about a little house in Sommersette with a window seat. It needed some work, they wouldn't be able to move in right away, but it would be worth it. He'd been surprised at first, skeptical, but eventually excited when it became clear that she really was serious. It wasn't, Joni thought, that unlike this moment now, with

Beth Ann. A resistance, followed by a giving over to the process, an accepting of what their life would become. He'd never asked how she happened upon the house with the window seat to begin with, never wondered aloud how she'd heard about Sommersette. He'd probably assumed that women were simply born with a radar that pointed them toward idyllic domestic settings.

Joni, of course, had no such thing.

She really had only the belief in finger painting. A messy confidence that meant creating something swirling and strange and, some would say, ugly, but art wasn't only the beautiful still lifes, the Degas ballerinas.

She was sure of her rightness on this, but she was perhaps the only person in Sommersette who understood it. She was aware, lately and always, of the shadow life behind the one in Sommersette—a life of eating croissants from French bakeries with her preschooler while crossing busy streets, of squeezing a desk underneath a lofted bed in a cramped two-bedroom, of hiking a child's scooter up four flights of stairs and feeling the sort of exhaustion that came from negotiating the chaos and community of city living. Sometimes she found herself wanting to answer questions about why there were rats running around the subway tracks or wishing at night that there were little windows across the street filled with light and silhouetted bodies and the occasional wistful dog peering at them. She wished Mae knew the way those windows lined up, each of them a tiny snapshot of life.

She tried painting her memory of those night windows, starting again and again on a large canvas, painting a brick facade and a dozen windows with different people and animals peering out of each one. It didn't look the way she wanted it to, though. It was in the style of a cartoon, not a piece of serious art. Still, she kept at it. What was art if not the re-creating of something you missed, longed for, chose to leave without fully understanding the consequences?

She had a few sketches of Sommersette too—not the way it actually was but the way it had looked in her head when she'd first thought to move there. The idea that had formed after she'd heard the name: rosebushes and American flags and frog ponds and herself, barefoot and laughing, in the middle of it all—happy.

She looked at the sketches late at night and early in the morning when she was confused about where she lived and why. She returned, when she needed to, to the way she'd hoped it would be, the reality she was trying to create.

Lately, she'd been thinking she could have another baby. Another girl, hopefully. Maybe one who would look like Graham. He'd like that; he was always pleasantly teasing her about Mae's light hair, tiny nose, spunky personality, all the things about her that were nothing like him. Another baby would be good for him. For them. For the way her life felt unmade and ever so slightly imaginary.

The next time she spoke to Beth Ann about the vacation, when she was having coffee at Beth Ann's kitchen counter before bringing Mae home after a playdate, she tested the idea out on her. "Who knows, this could be our only year to have a family vacation with just the girls. Next year there could be more babies."

"There could?" Beth Ann asked. Joni was struck again by how little they actually shared of themselves. They spent many afternoons together, every week, but questions like *Do you want more kids?* and *How's your marriage?* and *What do you think, really, of this whole motherhood thing?* never came up.

"Why not?" Joni asked. The girls were out on the deck, and Joni looked to see what they were doing. Beth Ann had set long reams of paper out there, taped the ends to the light gray wood, and squirted blobs of finger paint onto paper plates for the girls to experiment with.

Finger painting.

But it was finger painting the way Beth Ann could tolerate it—

outside, controlled, the girls approaching the paper cautiously, clearly having been told not to make a mess, not to mix the colors, to draw something concrete with their fingertips rather than letting the whole of their palms sink into the color and pushing the paint around the way Joni would have done.

Beth Ann did not answer the question of why not have more babies. Joni wanted to know if Beth Ann and Barrett ever talked about it, and if they did, what exactly they said. But Beth Ann's mouth was pursed and Joni knew not to push too hard.

"Look at this," Beth Ann said, abandoning conversations about babies and husbands and art, opening a drawer and pulling out a one-sheet, like real estate magic. It was a beautiful home in Nantucket, near the ocean, with an in-ground pool and even a tiny gazebo out back. "The gazebo made me think of you," Beth Ann went on. "I know you love them." She said it as if it were a strange thing for someone to like, a fun and quirky fact about her friend. When they'd first met, Joni had pointed to the one in the center of town and told Beth Ann, "When I saw that gazebo, I decided we could live here. Nothing more romantic than a gazebo." And Beth Ann had laughed and said she'd never thought of it that way. Then over the next three years she brought it up like a sort of inside joke, a thing particular to them and no one else.

"It's beautiful," Joni said, which was entirely different than *I'd like to stay there*, but Beth Ann wouldn't note the space between the two statements.

"I'll book it tonight!" Beth Ann said as if a question had been asked and answered and certified and solved.

"Tonight. Okay. It's — Graham will love it, I'm sure."

"Barrett will hate it, but deep down he'll love it, you know?" Beth Ann smirked about something Barrett had said or done, some bit of the past that Joni wasn't privy to. Joni didn't like the way she was shut out of even that glimmer of information.

"Is Barrett not a swimmer?" Joni asked, trying to piece together whatever it was Beth Ann was saying and not saying about her husband. Joni stored up facts about him like she might be quizzed on them later. Maybe Beth Ann did the same with Graham, but she didn't seem as interested in knowing about him.

"Oh, he's a fine swimmer. He's just not a person who enjoys things. Anything. He likes work and roast chicken and vanilla ice cream and reading the newspaper. He likes quiet."

"I like quiet," Joni said, not defending Barrett, just maybe defending silence, defending the way it feels to wake up at five in the morning and have two hours of time before Graham's too-loud yogic *oms* and Mae's screeching about how she liked bananas and not strawberries or strawberries and not bananas.

Beth Ann tilted her head like she was trying to imagine a quiet version of her friend. "Well. You and Barrett can stay behind and be quiet together," she said, the knowing smirk, the remembering of something Joni would never know, reaching her mouth again, "and Graham and I can go have oceanic adventures with the girls."

"Deal," Joni said.

And it was. Because as soon as they arrived at the sprawling Nantucket property, Beth Ann grabbed buckets and sunscreen and told the girls it was seashell-collecting time. Barrett sighed at the prospect.

"Can't we get settled?" he said. "I want to unpack. Figure out the layout of this place."

"Stay," Beth Ann said. "It's fine. I'll take them."

"I wouldn't mind checking out the ocean," Graham said. "Joni? Should we join the adventure?"

Joni and Beth Ann exchanged a glance. A decade later, Beth Ann would remember that look in an entirely different light. She'd see the sparkle of Joni's eyes, the way they were a little bit too blue. She'd recall that Joni's shirt fell off her right shoulder and that she wasn't wearing a bra. She'd be sure there had been a glance in Barrett's direction, as if Joni were trying to decide something, and then, in a moment, it was decided. A decade later, Beth Ann would be sure of all of that. She would be sure she'd seen the moment when Joni and Barrett decided to ruin everything. It was easier to swallow, somehow, if it could be pinned to a single moment, a solitary, clear decision made in the ocean air.

Of course she was wrong about the moment. The moment was not then at all. The glance wasn't a decision; it was something else entirely.

And anyway, at the time, with two five-year-old girls fighting over who got the pink bucket and who got the purple bucket, none of that registered, none of that even existed, and Beth Ann thought only of the conversation she'd had with Joni about the quiet. And she thought of it as a little gift she was giving to her best friend and her husband. Joni could lie out on the deck and think the sorts of thoughts Joni thought—about crystals or horoscopes or, who knows, Picasso or something. Although maybe it was silly to think that Joni's thoughts were large and ranging and creative, that they weren't about, say, whether her daughter's bowel movements were happening too often or not often enough or about how one taught a five-year-old to stop herself from telling the neighbor that she looked wrinkly or weird. Still, Beth Ann felt certain that Joni didn't think of these things, didn't think of anything so pedestrian or real, and when she left the house with Joni's husband holding the hands of both girls, the ocean air hitting her face with a salty slap, she was just happy to be outside, to be here, to be the architect of a perfect summer holiday.

When Beth Ann and Graham and the girls returned, it was not to a quiet house, it was not to what Beth Ann had been promised.

They arrived to Joni and Barrett on the deck together, cocktails in hands, legs bare, heads flung back, laughing about something that they couldn't properly explain to their questioning spouses. Still, they had made enough martinis for Graham and Beth Ann, they'd set out cheese and crackers and put cushions on the outdoor furniture and generally made the house feel like a home. Mae and Sydney took handfuls of cheese that they immediately said was disgusting, too salty, too crumbly, not real cheese. Graham responded not by admonishing them for their rudeness but by digging into a cooler, pulling out hot dogs and hamburgers ready to be grilled, and asking them to show Barrett and Joni their seashells. It would be hard, impossible really, to recall this version of Graham later.

Mae and Sydney bubbled with enthusiasm, recounting the story of a woman on the beach who'd asked if they were sisters, an idea that filled them with such pleasure, they were practically drunk on the joy of it, giggling, wishing it into existence. They went on to tell elaborate stories of how they'd found each shell, recalling their walk down the beach in the style of a page-turner: *And then, and then, and then.*

"I thought this one was a rock," Mae said, holding up a black-and-white shell that was jagged and wind-worn, "and then I picked it up just to see, and it's actually a shell that looks like a rock, and I think it's my favorite one, because it was secretly cool, and it's a secret that I found all by myself. This is the kind of shell that someone finds and throws away and then someone else, like me, finds, and it changes everything." There was a pause as the adults took in the beautiful way Mae spoke about the world, the poetry of it. Even Barrett, who so often only half listened to everyone, smiled at the words.

"Wow," he said. "I'd like a day in your brain, Mae."

Joni beamed with pride and something else. Mae, she was sure, would live a life entirely different from her own. One with clear-eyed decisions and a sturdy sense of herself. Mae would live in the city. Maybe New York or maybe a different one, like Paris or Mexico City, and she would have a dozen friends with piercings and green hair and hand-sewn sundresses and tattoos of trees or birds or skeletons stenciled on their backs, their arms, the soft curves of their hips.

She'd always known it, and now it seemed Barrett saw it too.

"This one's pretty," Sydney said, holding up a pink shell curled into a tiny fist. She didn't have a story like Mae or even a particular appreciation for the shade of pink or the unusual furled shape of the shell. Still, Joni picked the shell out of Sydney's hand and held it up to the light, just as she'd done with Mae's, with the same level of reverence and interest. Joni was so much better at caring about nothing than Beth Ann was, and for that, too, Beth Ann felt a twinge of envy.

"Beautiful," Joni said. "That's just lovely, Sydney." There was no irony in the way Joni spoke to Sydney, no bit of laughter in her voice, just genuine affection. "Let's line them all up on the railing." She pointed them to the porch's railing, a basic wooden fence with a flat top that went the whole way around the house. Sydney nodded and placed the pink shell in the prized position, the very center of the porch railing, and Mae followed, subtly trying to push her shell into that central space. No one really won or lost in the silent battle, and soon the girls were taking each shell gingerly out of their buckets, making a tiny parade of their collection. Over the week, sea glass and pine cones and lost treasures like toy boats and abandoned jewelry would find their way to the railing. It became an important part of the end of each day, sorting through the buckets and picking the best treasures to line up, the adults listening to the girls' tales of finding each piece, and all six of them leaning back to look at the collection, the way it told the very story that they were currently living.

They did other things too. They used the pool, of course, blowing up a rainbow raft and a dolphin raft and a swan raft and trying not to wince when the girls jumped from them a little too wildly with a little too much enthusiasm. They played with the waves, all of them but Barrett, who hung back and snapped pictures, which Beth Ann fell a little more in love with him for. She already knew she'd make a triptych of the best ones—action shots of Sydney leaping in the air, grinning at the sky, kicking one perfect pointed foot into a bubbly froth of a wave. He was a good photographer, good with anything artistic, had an eye, it seemed, for color and shape and form in a way that Beth Ann could barely grasp.

Like Joni.

They ate outside and let their ankles be devoured by mosquitoes; they slept late in the mornings and made pancakes before going blueberry picking. They blued and purpled their tongues with ripe berries and filled baskets with the swollen fruit. They made pancakes again, this time with the blueberries, and they worried about getting sick of the taste, but it stayed delicious, stayed sweet and tart and decadent. They lined a few blueberries up on the railing and watched them change under the sun.

They all changed in the sun, their skin pinking and browning and freckling, but the rest of them shifting too. Barrett laughing a little harder, his blond hair getting blonder still. There was Joni getting drunker than she would at home, Beth Ann not washing her hair for three days in a row, and Graham taking extra delight in the girls, suddenly speaking their language, coming up with imaginative play, making them laugh before they had a chance to grow angry at a change in schedule or a disappointing rule.

"This is the life, huh?" Graham said on the last full day, kissing Joni's neck in a way that made Beth Ann uncomfortable, made her own husband try to kiss her neck, but she lifted her shoulder before he could reach the skin, too scared of what might happen from showing that side of themselves.

"Summer at its finest," Barrett said after the rejection. He poured more wine into Joni's glass, watching as Sydney and Mae sprinted across the perfect green lawn, playing some sort of two-person tag. He wondered who was winning and if the rules were set or changing. He hoped the game would last past bedtime, that Beth Ann would let it unspool past nine, past ten, until the girls were ragged and panting, surprised to be awake at such an hour. He wanted that for them, the way summer evenings could sprawl in the moonlight. He remembered it from his own childhood, and Beth Ann rarely let it happen, always worrying herself about bedtimes and wake times as if Sydney were still an infant and not a young girl. Beth Ann had never fully let go of those early motherhood days, still monitored how much milk Sydney was consuming, as if calories from anything else didn't quite count, still worrying if there were too many blankets on her bed, checking to make sure she was breathing before she finally fell asleep herself. He loved and hated this about his wife.

Barrett loved and hated a lot about her and them and parenthood and even this moment right now — where she was smiling at him but telling him not to touch her, where he was enjoying the company of their friends and also feeling a hazy something else about the way Joni's body loosened on her third glass of wine, the way she sometimes sang to herself under her breath, the way she, too, wanted the girls to experience the feeling of staying up past bedtime and going to sleep sticky and unclean and wet-haired and sandy-toed.

There was the pang of the life he wasn't living and the one he was and the battle between the two. And underneath it all, the girls, running, screeching, making a beautiful mess of everything. They ran the same way, maybe one of them imitating the other, a sort of prance-run that looked supernaturally graceful for kids their age, long strides that bounced, arms that moved through the air like ballerinas'.

"I'll be sorry to leave," Beth Ann said.

"Next summer," Joni said. "We'll be back next summer."

Barrett smiled at Joni, and Beth Ann tried to smile at Graham, but he was looking somewhere else, hand playing with the graying parts of his dark beard, and for a moment she felt a thick sort of loneliness and was startled by it. She gripped her own thigh for stability. She'd been so sure the loneliness wouldn't be able to find her here.

It started to rain right then, a warm summer rain that they lingered in for a while, letting the girls linger too. The grass slickened, the girls started slipping, falling over themselves with giggles and screams. But eventually Beth Ann felt the wind coming in, and though no one else seemed to really notice the force of it, the wildness of it, the way it promised to knock you around, twist you up, make a mess of everything you had put together, Beth Ann knew that the wind meant the night was over, the holiday done with, the summer practically finished as well.

She called everyone inside, and even the adults obeyed, either because they thought she was right or because they were too tired to tell her she was wrong. The parade of treasures, the shells and glass and toys and coins and berries still there on the railing, lasted a few minutes into the summer storm until the wind turned even more violent, the rain whooshing sideways instead of just downward. The rain and the wind dispatched pieces this way and that until all that was left by morning was Sydney's tiny pink shell and Mae's white-and-black one, the two shells so much like the girls themselves, pretty and messy, perfect and unruly, ideal and seemingly mundane.

"It's gone?" Mae said when she went onto the porch in the morning after refusing to help her mother pack, refusing to eat anything but a handful of berries and a spray of whipped cream. "Just like that, it's all gone?"

"That's what happens," Barrett said, reading his newspaper, enjoying the distant ocean noises and the way the world smells after a summer storm. "Sometimes, that's just how it goes."

NOW

Sydney

SYDNEY PUT THE dollhouse in the living room to give Sam the news of the baby being a girl. If Sam wouldn't let her live in a real house, well, then, fine. The perfect picture of a real house would be right here until he gave in.

Sydney had never meant to live in the city, was never the sort of girl who anyone expected to live anywhere but Sommersette or somewhere like it, somewhere with beige houses and neatly cut lawns and concerts in the town square on the Fourth of July and New Year's Eve. She was here because of Mae and then because of Sam, but now it was time to live somewhere because of her. Or if not because of her, then because of what was growing inside her.

Sam didn't know yet that the baby was a girl and that Sydney had already decided on her name and where she needed to live, which was upstate, maybe on the river, or maybe in a suburb of a different city, a smaller and cleaner city, like Boston, with its cobblestones and fleece everything and cold, crisp way of talking and being and feeling.

Or Sommersette itself, if Sydney could put some memories aside. It was still a beautiful town in spite of everything.

Sydney set up the dollhouse family in order to communicate all of it to Sam. She wanted it to be perfect, but the dollhouse was unfinished, the result of years of ideas and arguments with Mae — some rooms beautifully decorated, some wildly undone. She thought about what LillyLou's latest newsletter had said: *Be yourself! People want to get to know YOU, and that's how you make connections. That's how you grow your business. Not by being perfect but by being authentic.*

Perhaps it was good that this dollhouse was so strange. *If everything in your home is perfect, you aren't relatable,* she remembered the newsletter telling her. *Be aspirational but not out of reach. Your plates don't all have to match. You can forget mascara some mornings. Don't be afraid to show an occasional blemish, a flaw that actually makes you more you — more beautiful!*

The dollhouse had blemishes. The dollhouse mom was in some bizarre outfit that she was pretty sure Mae had created for her one afternoon when they were bored. The dollhouse dad was still missing, and the closest store that might sell a new one was way downtown and not open on Mondays anyway. She wondered where he could have gone. She remembered him as a sort of fumbling-looking dad, more like Mae's dad, Graham, than her own father, though it turned out Barrett was the one who was blundering, fucking it all up, really, in spite of his neat haircut, his tailored suits, the way he cut vegetables so perfectly, in uniform sizes and shapes, onion rings the same thickness, peppers in neat little lines, cucumbers in perfect circles, never slipping with the knife the way other fathers — other people — seemed to do.

The missing doll and the weirdly dressed doll both felt like Mae's fault. She was always changing things around in the house, making it reflect some angst she was in or some book she was reading or some experimental art whatever that she was trying out.

Not for the first time, Sydney had the urge to call Mae and chew her out for the past, yell at her for the ways—large and small—that their friendship was still seeping into the life she was trying to make for herself here and now. And maybe she would have if there weren't also, always, Joni's tragic death hanging over it all, a thing that made Mae a victim too, an uncomfortable brand of grief that made the rest of it hard to square.

Ivy Miller would tell her followers to share that anger. She would say that people come together over what is beautiful *and* what is difficult. And memories of Mae Dyer and Joni Dyer were difficult. *Connect to your community of contacts,* LillyLou insisted, *share yourself. You are incredible. Let the world see it!*

But also, Sydney reminded herself to stop thinking of the past. *Do not get lost in the map of the places you always return to,* she heard Ivy Miller say in her head, like a song that gets caught there, keeps you up at night with its exhausting rhythm. *Start a new path. Draw a new map.*

She was not, it turned out, much of a cartographer.

Sydney was ready for the crown jewel of the tableau she was creating, the girl baby doll, wrapped in a tiny soft pink blanket. "There," Sydney said, the way she often spoke to herself when she was trying to get something just right. It was the same way she spoke to herself when she was doing a photo shoot for LillyLou, stacking pashminas on top of each other in just the right rainbow sequence or draping one or another of them over her back so she could shoot herself from behind, peeking over her shoulder, like a pashmina was a delicious secret someone just might let you in on.

This tableau, even with the missing father, was perhaps the most perfect thing she'd ever done, Sydney decided then and there. It was better than a hundred pashmina photo shoots—the doll people in their beautiful home, the dollhouse in the living room, Sydney's makeup fresh and glowy, her thick brown hair swinging and smelling a little like jasmine, their compact Park Slope apartment cleaned to within an inch of its life, shining and white and sparse and new. It wasn't a town house, no. It wasn't old and charming and elegant the way the homes of the rest of the LillyLou Brooklyn contingent were. But there was something to be said for a condo in a new development with a gym and an extra-large stainless-steel fridge and a built-in bookcase. And yes, maybe the best blocks in the neighborhood were those with the brick town houses, the concrete stoops. But her home had large windows and clean floors, and that was something too, wasn't it?

And maybe it was even good not to have a dad doll. Maybe she was making space for Sam to be the ultimate father. She didn't need a dad doll. She had her husband, with his low, smooth singing voice and stylish socks and ability to make a great cup of coffee.

Blessings don't look like blessings until you look through the right lens, Ivy Miller said when someone complained about her business not going as well as she'd thought it would, when someone else mentioned that the new colors of pashminas weren't quite seasonally appropriate, when a third woman cried about losing customers. Sydney was determined to look through the right lens.

She stood next to the dollhouse when she heard Sam's key in the door. She wanted it to have an impact, all of it—the message she was trying to send about what their life needed to look like (a house in Sommersette, not a cramped apartment in a too-loud city) and the new information about their baby girl and what that would look like too.

Her phone was set up, of course, ready to film the whole enterprise. She was certain this was the sort of content that could catapult her into that other realm, the one where it wasn't just fellow Lilly-Lou moms liking and commenting on her posts but actual strangers who just wanted to watch her beautiful life unfold.

And then buy her pashminas. Or, even better, learn to sell them, with her guidance. Her heart pounded. It was all happening. She had three credit cards she hadn't told Sam about, and now she'd never have to. The bills would get paid and the problem solved before he had a chance to worry. They said a baby didn't fix a marriage, but in the world of LillyLou, a baby could fix your business.

Ivy Miller was coy about it. *We like to know about your life. Make sure your life is one worth knowing about. People like weddings. They like love. Beauty. Vacations. And babies. So don't hold yourself back from the things you want. If you want more babies, have them. Ignore the people who say you can't have a business and a baby. In my experience, your business thrives when you have both! This is about getting what you want. This is about a life that resembles the life you dreamed up when you were ten and wistful and hopeful and ready. Be that girl.*

In Sydney's favorite video of Ivy Miller, someone from the audience asked a question about how to connect with her ten-year-old self and also throw away the map to that old self, and Ivy Miller paused and nodded, just like she always did.

"The new map can go to old places," she'd said, the words practiced and rote but still infused with her signature inspirational lift. "Two things can be true at once. A hundred things can be." She raised her eyebrows at the question-asker, a friendly admonishment that her thinking was still limited, her mind operating in black-and-white instead of the hundreds of grays.

Sydney knew she was like that question-asker. She had always been so literal. It was exhausting.

But the dollhouse was metaphorical. It was a bridge from past to present. And it photographed beautifully. She was finally getting it. She was.

"Hello, hello," Sam called out upon entering the apartment. Sydney wanted Sam to come home and put his things in the hall closet, take off his jacket, loosen his tie, unbutton a button, and sit down for dinner. She wanted him to ask her about her day and be proud of her sales and whatever meal she'd made—pasta with pesto or steak in a pepper sauce or slow-cooked chicken in apple cider served atop a bed of rice. She wasn't any sort of amazing cook, but she did her best and she wanted him to notice.

Just notice.

Maybe it was silly to want this old-school version of marriage, something her mother had tried and failed at, but wasn't that what all the women her age were doing, really, trying to live up to their mothers somehow? Her workout buddy Lisette went to med school because her own mother had dropped out when she got pregnant with Lisette. Sam's best friend's wife, Anita, was trying to open a vegan bakery because her own mother, who died five years ago, taught her how to make cookies when she was a kid and it was Anita's only good memory of the otherwise erratic and unkind woman who raised her. Wasn't each and every one of them just a reaction to her own mother? Mae, too, Sydney was sure of it, was off doing or not doing art entirely because of the art Joni did and did not do. Maybe Mae was breaking apart a family. Or starting one. Either repeating or undoing the past, either mirroring or exploding it.

Mae just happened not to have Joni sitting there watching her do it all. Sydney hated how, for a moment, not having a mother sounded like an enormous relief.

But Sydney didn't know how to say all of that, so if anyone asked, she just shrugged and called herself *traditional*, trying to say it like it was something hip and edgy, now.

She had even looked into renting the house in Nantucket. She would like to return there. Hunt for sea glass on the beach. Eat burgers on the porch. There had been perfect summer weeks spent there, times that felt full and easy and alive.

She wanted that time again, the time before she'd learned that a family can become only the secret it's keeping.

Tell your own story of who you are. You are the main character in your life. Tell the story to yourself so many times that you come to believe it. There's not much difference, is there, between believing something to be true and it really being true?

Sydney had written that particular question down in one of her LillyLou Empowerment Now notebooks, and she toyed with it, letting her brain sort of squint at it the way someone might look at an optical illusion, trying to find something solid in the shifting images.

Sydney snapped a selfie. The light was good and she had been practicing a certain type of knowing smile for just this kind of moment. *About to do something fun… and life-changing. Stay tuned!*

Ivy Miller reminded them not to dull down their lives. To make the most of small moments. *Women undersell their joy. Don't say, "I'm happy," say, "I'm overjoyed, everything has shifted into place." Don't make yourself smaller; the world will do that for you. Make yourself bigger.*

Sydney was working on making herself bigger. She watched the space underneath her post, waiting for someone to like it. A heart appeared, from Genevive Lett. Genevive ran her Small Group. She had the biggest engagement ring Sydney had ever seen and posted short videos about her skin-care routine that made Sydney herself go and buy new eye creams and expensive serums. Genevive was without a question the perfect person to like the post first. Sydney beamed. It was an important time to be doing the right thing.

At long last, LillyLou was developing some new products. "Pashminas are our staple," Ivy Miller said at the last conference from a stage lit in a soft purple, "but we are more than that. The LillyLou woman is more than that. We want to appeal to the kind of wives who don't just look beautiful at a charity event or out to dinner at the club or on a lovely vacation to Paris. Those same wives are more than that. We want to remind them of how much more than that they are." Ivy Miller had paused meaningfully.

Sydney had been at the conference. She was at all the conferences—Las Vegas, San Diego, Chicago, the North Fork. In Ivy Miller's pause, Sydney held her breath, wondering what the new items would be. Purses, maybe? Or—oh!—briefcases? There'd been some bad press about LillyLou marketing and how they were a bunch of stay-at-home moms taking advantage of other stay-at-home moms, as if *stay-at-home mom* were an insult of the highest order, as if it meant something about who you were and how you were placed in the world. A briefcase would be smart, Sydney thought, because it would show the world that they were reaching working moms too. Or working people in general. Not just moms! Or maybe LillyLou was going to do some sort of accessory for men? Ties? That could work.

"Lingerie," Ivy Miller had declared with a wide smile. "Bras. Panties. Eventually some even sexier garments for special time with your husbands. Everything a LillyLou woman could want."

Sydney remembered watching the slideshow of the products in development with a thumping in her chest. She didn't care about lingerie, but the room was thrumming—there was loud music like the kind she remembered from nights clubbing with Mae when they were young, and there were gasps from the crowd, and there was Ivy Miller with her hands on her hips, like she had arrived, like they had all finally arrived. And in that soup of sound and energy and the perfect symmetry of Ivy Miller's face, Sydney had found herself excited about the lacy bras, the sheer panties, the color palette of muted pink and periwinkle blue.

Not for the first time, she felt the squeeze in her chest. She needed the bras. She needed the sexiest ones, the laciest, lowest-cut ones, the ones that would get her ever so slightly closer to who she was supposed to be. Someone like Ivy Miller. Or at least like Genevive Lett.

Someone unlike Beth Ann, unlike Sydney herself, really.

But the bras weren't ready yet, so Sydney was just Sydney today.

"I'm here," Sydney said, even though Sam already knew, was currently looking at her like she was a carton of milk on top of the washing machine instead of in the refrigerator, where it belonged.

"Oh!" Sam said, and then, seeing something new taking up room in their limited space, "Oh. Huh." He kissed her temple and then her shoulder. Every day, he chose a different part of her to greet. Her wrist and cheek on Thursday. Her thumb and nose on Wednesday. The back of her neck and her lips when he was in the mood on Tuesday. She looked forward to this mapping of her that he did so easily, so unthinkingly, this tiny way of saying *I love you.*

It was strange, then, wasn't it, that it didn't often feel like enough.

"What's all this?" Sam asked at last, fully in the room now, standing in front of the dollhouse.

"A dollhouse," Sydney said. "My dollhouse. From childhood. I've mentioned it before, the one I had with—"

"Right, right, yeah, with Mary."

"Mae."

"That's her name? Mae?"

Sydney nodded. They'd never met, Sam and Mae, probably never would. Beth Ann kept tabs on both of the remaining Dyers, a task she seemed to have charged herself with, either as penance or as some sort of revenge; it was hard to tell which.

Beth Ann reported on them annually to Sydney, who was always surprised that her mother didn't want to forget about them entirely, leave them to the past.

Mae was living in Brooklyn, Beth Ann said, probably one of "the bad parts," going to school yet again, that one painting that everyone had been so impressed with all those years ago was now no longer even a blip in the art scene, Mae's name practically forgotten in the gallery world—as if Beth Ann knew anything about art or galleries or talent. Graham lived on a farm with his new wife, Catherine, who really wasn't new at all anymore, the two of them having been married for well over a decade. He had moved on with a startling quickness, a fact that Sydney found simultaneously repulsive and brilliant. If she could, she wouldn't mind starting over too, picking a new friend on the playground, unknowing everything she'd ever known.

Sydney had attended the wedding, held on Graham and Catherine's farm, not as a part of the celebration, exactly, more as a buffer for Mae, who needed someone there with her, someone who could also snark and mourn and stand in awe of how life had changed in a way that mere years before would have seemed impossible.

Sydney had worn gray satin and thought the entire time about Joni and what she would have said about the pink floral arrangements, the cold weather, the meal of fried chicken and pie that the bride had made herself, of Graham singing—*singing!*—"You're Beautiful," a song that had been popular years ago and that sounded awkward and incorrect in Graham's tepid but ultimately on-key voice.

Maybe it was because of the wedding that everything changed. Sydney was preoccupied with thoughts of Joni afterward, and she was too young and too weak to hold them in, so eventually she let them out.

Mae moved out less than a week after the event.

It was for the best, even if it had been a catastrophe at the time. Now Sydney promised herself that her daughter would be friends with daughters of other LillyLou moms. LillyLou was safe. No one in LillyLou had long, tangled hair or tattoos or wry smiles. The women in LillyLou wanted the same things Sydney wanted—renovated kitchens and shiny hair and a way to be both a mom and something else too. LillyLou was the something else.

Still, in spite of it all, Sam should know Mae's name. Sydney had told Sam stories about Mae hundreds of times over the years, stories about watching fireworks and liking the same boy and taking prom pictures and getting sunburns and writing their own picture book when they were eight years old about a woman named Addie who was somehow killed by a purple polka-dot scarf.

That one had made Sam pause. "Doesn't sound like you," he'd said. "What were you, like, goth?"

"I was not *goth* when I was eight years old," Sydney had said, laughing, but she didn't know how to describe what or who she was when she was with Mae.

Now she said, "Anyway, look closer, you're missing it." She picked up her phone to get a better shot of Sam and the dollhouse and whatever his reaction would be. She needed a perfect follow-up to her selfie, something that would show his excitement about their growing family, something that would make people stop and comment, *Oh, that Sam, he's going to be a great dad.* Or *Congratulations, you two, this is so freaking cute!*

Sam took a closer look.

"Do these tiny books actually have writing in them?" he asked, taking a volume, *Great Expectations*, from the dollhouse's bookshelf.

"Of course," Sydney said, smiling. "Only the best for this family."

"I had no idea — wait, there's miniature glue sticks? A miniature garlic press? Is that a tiny stapler? Does it work?"

"No, that one's a fake, unfortunately," Sydney said. She did find things like the not-working stapler and the glue stick without any glue inside depressing. Mae had thought it was fun just to have the representative objects. Sydney longed to give her dollhouse family the real thing. "But look closer."

"Closer?" Sam said. He squinted. "I don't think I can get any closer than these tiny Q-tips." He'd found one of Sydney's favorite objects, a glass jar in the bathroom filled with Q-tips so small, it was hard to even pick one up between her fingers.

Would other husbands have noticed the tiny baby-girl doll right away? Would other husbands know what this all meant? Sydney was always doing calculations about this, trying to understand her life, her husband, her choices, in relation to other people's. When she graduated from high school, she'd studied Mae's face to see if she felt the same way Sydney did. Was Mae feeling an odd mix of sadness and thrill? Was she wondering what would happen next while wishing she could relive everything that had just happened but do it right this time? When Sydney was planning her wedding, she looked not just at bridal magazines but also at all the photographs online of her friends and acquaintances getting married. She watched their bodies to see how the bride and groom held each other. She looked at the first kisses to determine what a normal one looked like. She tried to count guests, to calculate how many guests the happiest-looking couples had and whether those guests were wearing cocktail dresses or formal wear, whether they were inside or outside, how they seemed to be dancing and smiling and eating and being. She was sure, always, that if she could just do things the way everyone else did, she would someday, surely, start to *be* like everyone else.

Sam sighed. The guessing game was getting old. "What am I looking for here, Syd?"

She hated being called Syd but didn't know how to tell anyone without sounding prissy, so she just accepted it as this awful side effect of her name. She paused, hoping if she just gave him a little more time, he'd get there.

"Syd. Can we wrap this up? I'm starving."

"Sure. We can wrap this up. No problem. We're having a girl. Congratulations."

It was like this more often than Sydney would admit. Always the goal was to make something beautiful, and often Sam was too impatient for it or too tired for it or too hungry for it or just not actually interested in making small moments lovely and meaningful and special.

"Hey, okay, all right, a girl, wow," Sam said. His gaze drifted for half a second to the kitchen to see what Sydney had been cooking. He didn't smell anything simmering or baking. Sydney held her phone loosely at her side, playing with one of the buttons.

"I worked hard at this," she said, gesturing at the dollhouse.

"It's beautiful," he said, but it sounded flat. She was glad she'd stopped the video; she wouldn't have to edit this part out later.

"This is a big moment. This should have been a big moment." Her voice was shaking. She was getting ready to cry, and still Sam wasn't entirely sure what he had done wrong. Hadn't they already performed a whole reveal for finding out Sydney was pregnant to begin with? He'd done better with that, since the shock was real and Sydney had been able to capture it all on video to post later for everyone. *Sleepy daddy-to-be can't believe the big news!* she'd captioned it. It was her most popular post, over a thousand likes, and she went to look at it and the comments whenever she felt blue. Looking at the quadruple digits, the higher-ups at LillyLou sending little baby and heart emojis and dozens of exclamation points, made her feel anchored to something real, something good.

Sam was less thrilled with the aftermath. His brother had started calling him Sleepy Daddy-to-Be. *Hey, Sleepy Daddy-to-Be, you want to shoot some hoops? Hey, Sleepy Daddy-to-Be, have you called Mom lately, she's complaining about you not calling. Hey, Sleepy Daddy-to-Be, Tania asked that Sydney stop posting photos of our kids online to, and I'm quoting her here, "hock her wares." Can you pass that on, please?* Sleepy Daddy-to-Be hadn't exactly wanted his bleary morning face up on social media, but Sydney was so excited about it that he hadn't pursued the fight that was right there, waiting to happen.

"I'm just happy you're happy," Sam said now.

This was the wrong thing to say.

"*You're* supposed to be happy! You! You're supposed to care! You're supposed to respond!" Sydney wasn't a very good shouter; her voice was naturally soft and the strain of shouting made it shaky and raspy and strange—you could hear the effort of it, how poorly anger sat in her throat.

"I just *said* I was happy."

"You said you were happy *for me*." Sydney was turning pink around the edges, shaking her head so violently he worried her neck might seize. "You should be happy for you! This is your baby too. This isn't just my baby. This isn't just my experience. This is ours. This was supposed to be ours."

"Not every day needs to be a production," he said. "Some days we can just eat dinner. Watch a show. Not even talk much, just be together. You know?" He meant it gently, like she could take a break from the hard work of all this.

"I'm so sorry that I want our lives to matter," Sydney said.

And with that, she stormed out of the living room and into the bedroom, where, Sam supposed, she would be for the rest of the night. He considered following her, but instead he made himself a peanut-butter-and-jelly sandwich that he ate over the sink in four enormous bites. He made another sandwich. And another after that. And that last one he brought to Sydney, who was stewing in their bed, red-eyed and frowning so deeply, her features all seemed to slope downward.

"So," he said, "a girl."

Sydney nodded and accepted the sandwich.

"Well, as long as she's as pretty as you, we sure will be lucky," Sam said.

It was, again, wrong.

But Sydney didn't know how to explain that to him. She didn't even know how to explain it to herself. Her prettiness was well documented, was the only thing she was ever better than Mae at. Mae was better at art and making friends and telling jokes and being strong-willed and precocious. She was even better at being tragic, at having to overcome difficult things at a young age. Sydney was better at having nicely brushed hair and soft features and wide eyes and a smile that strangers complimented her on.

Beth Ann was always talking about her prettiness, reminding people of it, like it might be forgotten otherwise. Beth Ann glowed like a sunrise when people said they looked alike. Sydney wasn't entirely sure how to feel about it.

"You're like your mother, and Mae is like hers," Barrett had said to Sydney once when the families were all together and he was a few drinks in and so was Joni.

"That's how it goes," Beth Ann had said proudly, the only one in the room happy with the comment.

"You think girls take after their moms, not their dads?" Joni asked, and the words came out intense, like the question was an important one.

Barrett grimaced, shook his head, and poured himself another drink.

"Sure," Beth Ann said, and Joni looked like she had follow-up questions, but they didn't get asked, because Mae and Sydney had caused a bit of chaos involving the vacuum cleaner and Play-Doh, and the conversation halted and forgot to restart. So many conversations were like that in those days and would be again soon for Sydney and Sam and whatever friends they made, she supposed.

"She'll look however she looks." Sydney's voice was sore and her mind was tired. Sam would nod along to whatever came out of her mouth and apologize for whatever she said he'd done, but none of it would mean anything, because he wouldn't actually hear her, not really, not the way she wanted to be heard.

She wanted to tell him how prettiness hadn't done much for her, hadn't protected her from anything. Prettiness didn't help Beth Ann either, even though she was pretty too, hers a restrained, polite variety. This baby needed to be something else, something better than pretty, with its sad limitations, its broken promises, its disappointing heft.

Special was better. She knew that now. Talented was good too. Mysterious. Different.

All the things Sydney and Beth Ann had never quite managed to become.

NOW

Mae

IN THE PLACE where the dresser used to be, Mae set up an easel.

It wasn't a sound decision, easels being great for holding paper and canvases but completely unable to hold such things as socks and T-shirts and jeans that were a size too small but would maybe someday fit. Her clothes were now stacked up in the corner of her bedroom, separated into piles by category and cleanliness. The sort of thing that might have been okay when she was twenty-two, but when she was twenty-two, she was living with Sydney, and Sydney never would have allowed such disorderliness.

But Sydney wasn't here, of course. Hadn't been in ages.

And at least Mae was painting.

It was the first thing she mentioned when Leo texted and asked if she wanted to get coffee. *I'm painting again. Thanks for the debilitating heartbreak.*

Coffee sounded safer than drinks, so she said yes. But of course that was wrong. Getting coffee with Leo that day reminded her of getting coffee with Leo a hundred other days. Saturday mornings after sex; Sunday mornings hungover but telling each other they'd definitely get to the gym; in the middle of the day on a Wednesday when she was in grad school and working part-time at the comedy club and forgetting entirely about painting and how she was supposed to be someone and had failed to become that person and instead was becoming like every other art major in Brooklyn except with a stash of money in the bank from that one painting that she couldn't find a way to replicate or build on. While she was floundering in her own waitressing-and-grad-school-going way, he was directing an all-female production of *Romeo and Juliet*. He would interrupt her while she was trying to come up with the perfect sentence to compare Jane Eyre to Hillary Clinton for her expansive thesis on the way literature tells us how to view women, knowing that his work was more important, more meaningful, more intellectually profound than whatever it was she was doing.

Sometimes she wished she could paint a picture of her ideas instead of writing them out, but she'd failed at that, hadn't she? Wasn't that pretty much why she was getting a master's in English? So that she could someday turn that into a PhD and then turn that into a whole other career as a professor at a cozy college somewhere? The money from the Painting hadn't dried up yet, wouldn't for a long while if she was careful with it, which she was. But now the money was more a proof of her failure than a reminder of that long-ago success.

"What if they didn't speak?" Leo had said one Wednesday morning back then. They were at the café and the light was coming in harsher than she liked. She was sensitive to it, light, always bending away from it, wishing it could be hazy and muted all the time and not so *bright*.

She had just finished writing a ten-page section on Anna Karenina and Monica Lewinsky and was taking a scalding sip of a fresh cup of coffee.

"Who's not speaking?" The coffee was really too hot. Her tongue was struggling to understand what had happened. The drink swished around as her mouth tried to un-burn itself.

"The actors. What if it's a silent production of *Romeo and Juliet*?" Leo tapped his pen on the table when he was excited about something, and he was tapping away now, frowning. He frowned when he wanted to be taken seriously.

"You want to take the words out of Shakespeare?" Mae tried to say it gently, but sometimes the instructions she gave her mouth weren't followed very closely.

"Shakespeare is about the story," Leo said. Sometimes Leo got prickly about the fact she was in grad school and he hadn't quite finished college, even though he was—according to him but also to anyone who met him—brilliant. The prickliness made Leo come up with Big Ideas, the sorts of things, he said, that come only from being a truly freethinker, a person not beholden to fancy degrees and student loans.

"Shakespeare's brilliance is *story*." He was speaking a little loudly, so Mae looked around to see who might be listening. "You don't need the words," Leo went on. "The words are...decorative."

Mae's eyebrows shot up. Shakespeare wasn't her current focus, but she'd considered writing her thesis on his works, then felt boring for even thinking about it. Shakespeare's words being called *decorative* by a guy in a wool sweater and thick glasses whose hair had recently gotten long enough to be tied into a messy bun seemed wrong. "I think most people consider Shakespeare's words to be... kind of the whole thing," she'd said. To her left, a girl in a corduroy blazer smirked.

"Well, my production would be challenging that." Leo took a deep breath. Tapped his pen. Frowned even more severely. "My own thesis, if you will."

I most certainly will not, Mae thought. "Huh," she said.

Leo didn't know it, but *Huh* meant *What is it like to be a man in the world whose ideas are always treated like treasures, who feels able to say anything about anything and assume it will be met with respect no matter how stupid what he's saying is? What is it like to call your crappy off-Broadway show a thesis when your girlfriend is writing an* actual thesis?

Maybe if Mae were some dude, she would think her oil paintings piled on top of each other in the kitchen were worth having someone look at. But they felt incomplete to her, the way all her work had since the article in the *Times*. Nothing lived up to that one painting that everyone loved, that everyone said meant she was the next big thing.

She could practically hear what Joni would have said had she been here to see Mae's rise and eventual crash in the art world. *You're supposed to be an artist, Mae, not a professor.* She felt sure that Joni would have sent out the rolled-up paintings Mae had made when she was five and eight and thirteen and eighteen, adding notes about what made them special, what made it obvious that Mae was destined for something more. Joni was preoccupied with Mae's art, with her own art, with some idea of the two of them as better than, different than, everyone else in the small town she and Mae lived in.

Mae's sternum ached at the thought of Joni, at the idea that maybe her best mothering would have been now. Mae felt Joni's mothering was its own sort of unfinished painting, something that looks a bit off when you begin, when you don't know where it's going, but slowly comes together with time. Joni, Mae thought, had probably been working toward something, with all her fun and wildness and ability to say yes to Mae's whims. And now that Mae was in her thirties, Joni would have told her what it all meant, would have unveiled a spectacular conclusion that showed Mae how to be an artist, how to be the person she was supposed to be.

Joni would have hated Leo, Mae thought, looking at him in the coffee shop. Then he leaned forward in a nearly imperceptible way, put his shoulders back with reckless certainty, and Mae reassessed. Joni would have hated him or loved him, nothing in between.

"You wouldn't get it," Leo had said then about his idea, as if that were the only reason a person might disagree with him about wordless Shakespeare. Mae turned back to her work, he turned back to his, and seven months later his all-silent production of *Romeo and Juliet* met with harsh criticism. The *New York Times* called it "dripping with hubris." *New York* magazine put it on its grid in the Highbrow and Despicable square with the tagline *Taking the Shakespeare out of Shakespeare and calling it art.*

Mae's painting had once made the grid, in the Highbrow and Brilliant square. The clipping was still hanging on her refrigerator, proof of something vital and true. Her breakup with Leo wasn't all that long after his appearance on the grid. Maybe that's why it had been so ugly.

Now they were back at that same coffee shop where he'd had the idea.

It was a bare-bones sort of place. Before living with Leo in Windsor Terrace, she'd been in the East Village, and the café she frequented there was cozy and stylized: Little chandeliers hanging from the ceiling. Pale pink and yellow seat cushions and coppery tables. Stained glass over one of the windows, which mercifully stopped the sun from making its full assault.

She missed that place, even though she liked this one too, with its black chairs and white tables and perfect pastries. She was glad that in the aftermath of their breakup, this café was hers. He was now a visitor here, the baristas raising their eyebrows in surprise at seeing him.

"How's the new apartment?" Mae asked.

"Cheap," Leo said. "Roommates are weird."

Mae nodded. She wasn't about to apologize for her no-roommate existence. She'd signed the lease on her own. She'd lived there alone when he was off directing in various places. He'd never given more than a quarter of the rent in any single month, so he didn't exactly have a claim to the apartment and couldn't have afforded it on his own.

"Cocktailing still keeping you busy?" Leo asked, something snide and tight slipping into the otherwise casual question.

"I want to see it. The new place," Mae said instead of answering the question. She had promised Georgie she would not do this, but she couldn't seem to help herself. Mae was prone to boredom, and she was bored with the gloominess of the breakup, bored of not painting and not fucking, bored of the things she knew Joni would have thought about the life she was living, bored of missing her mother all these years later—even grief, it turned out, became mundane. Even the grief around Joni's death, with the questions that poked up every once in a while if Mae let her guard down—*Why was Joni in the woods and where was her famous tote bag and what did the secret Sydney had kept all these years have to do with it, did it have anything at all to do with it?*—had grown tiresome. The questions were, legally speaking, answered, so Mae needed to stop asking them.

Joni had never let things get boring. She'd take Mae out of school and they'd go to a Broadway musical or a pottery-painting place for the afternoon. She'd force everyone out of bed early to see the sunrise or let Mae stay up late to watch stars in the front yard. And then she'd tell Mae to make art about all of it, and Mae would. Joni would too, and she'd brag to anyone listening about their artistic bond, imagining a future where they had a studio, owned a gallery together.

Fuck everyone who harped on all of Joni's mistakes. In her own ways, she was perfect, she was undeniable.

And now Mae was desperate to make another painting as dynamic and arresting and evocative as the famous one before, and

Leo was the only person in her world who made her feel a mix of emotions potent enough to promise that.

"So you're painting?" he asked on their walk to his new place in Flatbush.

"I am."

"Painter Mae. Never got to know that version of you."

"She's spectacular. What are you working on?"

"Just started rehearsals for a new play. Experimental."

"Of course." It went unsaid that Leo was asked to direct only experimental work since his wordless-Shakespeare fiasco. It also went unsaid that Leo had always hated experimental theater.

"How's your thesis going?" he asked.

"Almost done." She tried to say it humbly but then said it again proudly, because why the fuck did she have to undersell her own accomplishments just because he directed experimental theater?

"Then you'll be beautiful *and* be a doctor of English *and* be a painter. Again. Quite a catch." Leo never called her beautiful. Always cute. Mae couldn't help her internal response, which was immediate and swirling and intense. *He thinks I'm beautiful.* Followed by an admonishment: *He's an asshole, who cares what he thinks, beauty is a construct, it means nothing.*

"I always thought so," Mae said. "I always thought, you know, what kind of idiot would cheat on a beautiful woman with a graduate degree in English? And a one-hit-wonder painter too, no less? With a cute one-bedroom apartment with its very own breakfast nook?"

"A real fucking idiot, I guess."

"The kind of guy who grows a breakup beard."

"The kind of guy who tries switching to green tea because his ex-girlfriend told him he needed to get healthier."

"The kind of guy who would steal a dresser," Mae said. It was a test. If he stormed off, she'd know their breakup had been for the best.

But Leo smiled. "I stand by the dresser," he said. "But we could work out a custody agreement."

"If I could at least store my underwear in it," Mae said, remembering when he'd left all her cheap lace bras and underwear on the bed as if he'd never traced the patterns with his index finger, as if he'd never called them sexy, as if she hadn't bought the most uncomfortable ones especially for him.

It was a risk, saying the word *underwear* to her ex.

"I could live with having your underwear in my bedroom again," Leo said.

"What would your roommate think?"

"Let's find out."

His apartment was a twenty-minute walk away and by the end of it they were holding hands, something they rarely did when they were actually together. She'd seen the place on social media, but it looked different in person, like it was trying hard to be something respectable. The guys had gotten patterned rugs and a broad leather couch and a table for the record player that was really half hers. It was tidy. And it smelled like vanilla, courtesy of a scented plug-in that someone's mother or maybe the broker had put in. His bedroom was familiar: A throw she used when they watched *The Sopranos* together, both having somehow missed it when it originally aired. The same abstract art hung over the bed—three paintings with red stripes and black backgrounds and bold scribbles in primary colors that Leo loved and Mae hated, wishing that Leo wanted *her* art above the bed, waiting for him, always, to love one of her paintings enough to ask if they could put it there. The same photograph of his family on his bedside table. The same pile of socks and towels in the corner, as if he thought they might someday just get up and wash themselves.

And, of course, the dresser.

She went right to it. Gave it a hug. Leo laughed, but not hard. "I don't want to hear it, Mae," he said. "I'm sure you have a new dresser by now."

She didn't tell him that no, she did not. She had an easel and a pile of clothes and a reason to believe she might make art that mattered again.

"If I hear the word *dresser* one more time from you, I will literally explode," she said instead.

"Well, then, let's stop talking."

Leo's seduction lines were always a little much and also a little sexy because of the way they rubbed up against the rest of him — the awkward way he occupied his tallness, the soft, un-muscled torso underneath his ill-fitting shirts and chunky cardigan sweaters, his glasses, his thick, curling hair, his knowledge of chrysanthemums and perennials and compost. She could never tell if she was attracted to him in spite of or because of the strange way it all fit together.

And it didn't really matter, because then his hands were on her waist and in her hair and up her shirt and down her pants, and his bed smelled the way he had always smelled and his skin was soft where it was always soft with patches of hair lazily appearing here and there. Then she stopped doing the math of attraction, and she let it happen, let it be enjoyable, let it be not a mistake but a choice, a thing they were doing because they could, because why not, because they weren't kids and they weren't with other people and the sex had always been good and the heartbreak had been shattering, and hurting like that was the same as being alive, and on the easel back home right now was a canvas with an outline of his back, the way it was a little lopsided, his hair just past his pale shoulders, and her hand reaching out to touch the shoulders or the hair, who could say, so why not, why not, why not be here in this bed, knowing it hadn't worked out and would never work out but that somehow this was still good.

"Oops," she said after, before starting to get her whole body out the door, out of the apartment, out of this moment that was maybe a mistake or maybe just a thing that had happened, as long as she never mentioned it to any of her friends.

Luckily, she didn't have many friends.

"Oh, well," he said. "Guess we had one more in us."

"Guess so." She smiled. She wouldn't tell anyone. There wasn't any reason to. She didn't feel conflicted or turned around about it. She didn't want him back and she wasn't ashamed that they'd done it, and he wasn't saying he'd call her, and it was all so light and easy and friendly, especially compared to everything that had been before. "Our little secret, right?" she said.

"I always liked a good secret."

"You sure did."

And then she was out the door, and it was a little cooler than it had been on the way over but still nice, really, still enjoyable, and she hugged the park the whole walk home, not going in but peeking at the bare trees, the grass, the promise of summer, someday. She unzipped her jacket halfway and remembered how much she loved when winter turned to spring, when summer turned to fall, when the hardest, most intense seasons softened and became something less sure, less understandable, less boundaried, less harsh.

It was spring, at last, or almost, and who knew exactly what that meant anyway? Sometimes it snowed in April. Sometimes you could wear a sundress in March. And wasn't that at least a little bit beautiful?

She thought she would add snow to the new painting, the one about Leo and what it was to love someone who was also terrible, to be debased by someone you are better than. A blizzard in a bed full of crocuses, she thought. Spring and snow and lust and hate and the life of an artist, the way she'd promised Joni when she was a kid. Not that that mattered, of course. Not that's why she painted. After all, Joni wasn't here to see what she had become, would never know about the one painting everyone loved and the years of nothingness after. There was unbelievable grief in that. But relief, too, a little, when she was honest. It was her life. Not her mother's. It was her canvas. Her painting. Her exquisite heartbreak.

Joni had had her own.

SOMETIME BETWEEN NOW AND THEN

ANYONE WHO HAS worked in a gallery can tell you there is a lot to learn about people from the way they consider a painting in front of them—the stances they take, the expressions on their faces.

At the show featuring Mae Dyer's singular painting, for instance, anyone watching can see the way a nose sharply inhales, lips grip together, when a person is holding back the sort of comment that most often comes from jealousy. There's the head tilt, the open mouth, the turned-out foot, the heavy hip of someone trying to determine what it is that makes one painting spectacular and another simply proficient.

And then there is the other thing: The way the man who comes in on an overcast Thursday morning looks at the work. A hand accidentally lands near his collarbone; he swallows in a way that looks like it hurts. The small and sharp squint of eyes, the brief feeling of time falling away. Wonder, the gallerist knows, is a quiet thing.

The gallerist is patient. It will be a good day if she can wait out the wonder. If she can let it take hold. Let it change the course of things. Which it always does. Wonder changes the course of anything in its path.

So of course, she does just that. She waits until the man is ready. Until he has had his fill.

It takes quite a long time.

THEN

"WHY ARE YOU putting them there?" Mae asked. Sydney had put the mom doll in the primary bedroom and the dad doll on the couch.

"It's bedtime," Sydney said.

"Right." Mae always sounded just like her mother when she said this word. It was a long word when the Dyer women said it. Long and dripping with judgment, waiting for the other person to change her mind.

"Where do *you* want them to sleep?" Sydney asked.

"In the same bed," Mae said. She laughed. "Why would the dad sleep on the couch?"

"It's more comfortable," Sydney said. She tried to sound as sure as Mae did about everything. It came out strained and made her throat hurt. "His back bothers him. And she gets hot."

"She gets *hot?*"

"This is my dollhouse. Not yours."

Mae didn't reply. She would never have a dollhouse. Her mother made comments about the kinds of things Sydney's parents bought her: The dollhouse. The pink dresses. The ballet lessons. The shirt with the words *Daddy's Princess* on the front in rhinestones. Even the play kitchen was, according to Mae's mother, "some real shit parenting if you ask me."

Lately, Joni was making a lot of comments about Beth Ann's parenting in particular, but Mae didn't understand. Beth Ann was nice, and Barrett was even nicer, always complimenting Mae's drawings, Mae's outfits, Mae's crisp speaking voice and confident handshake.

"I'm glad your mom taught you that," he'd mused in this voice that sounded like it wasn't really meant for her. "It's important. A girl with a strong handshake."

So now Mae shook Barrett's hand whenever she entered his house, just to get that poke of pride. She'd tried Sydney's handshake and found it weak. Loose-wristed. Wrong.

Maybe that was what Joni meant with all the talk of bad parenting. Maybe not teaching a strong handshake was just the tip of the iceberg. Mae wanted to know and also didn't want to know more about this very topic.

"I don't like what the mom's wearing," Mae said now, thinking the doll looked dull, like a character in a picture book from her mom's old collection, dated and sad and beige. "She looks ugly."

Mae was not supposed to say words like *ugly*. Not about women, at least. Not about herself either. Sydney's mother wouldn't mind about the word *ugly*. Mae was sure about that, because she had heard Beth Ann call people ugly before — their second-grade teacher, for instance. The girl at the mall who worked at Hot Topic, where Sydney and Mae liked to buy glittery nail polish. Her own image in the mirror when she was patting her skin with lotion before she covered it with makeup.

"Anyone who says they look good without makeup is lying," Beth Ann had said that day Mae saw her painting herself in the mirror.

"My mom doesn't wear makeup," Mae said.

"Oh, well, your mom is different," Sydney's mother said then, like she'd forgotten, for a moment, who she was speaking to. "Joni lives in her own world."

"She sure does," Barrett said, and Beth Ann had swatted him for the remark.

The dollhouse mom wore blue jeans and a red-and-white-checked shirt tucked in at the waist. She had short brown hair that kind of looked like a hat. She seemed to Mae like the sort of mom who helped run things at school, someone who brought really good cookies to the bake sale but also didn't mind throwing a ball in the backyard with her kids. She looked like she probably walked briskly and had a loud laugh and threw fun pizza parties.

She didn't look anything like Sydney's mom or Mae's mom. Sydney's mother liked tight black pants and T-shirts with deep V-necks in an array of colors. She curled her dark hair every morning even though Mae thought it looked nicer straight. She had pink-pink lips, and even her sneakers seemed sort of fancy and like they were trying to tell everyone something, but Mae wasn't sure what.

Mae's mom liked ripped jeans and long skirts and T-shirts that she'd owned for years or maybe even decades, since that mysterious, weird time before Mae was born. She had a big collection of cozy cardigans and hand-knit scarves, and Mae liked the way she looked in the winter because of them—transformed into a walking blanket, someone you might want to cuddle into.

The dollhouse mom, though, needed to be a different kind of mom than Sydney's or Mae's. Mae wanted to see what other kinds of moms there were, what other kinds of women.

"Let's make her something new to wear," Mae suggested. "We can cut up some old clothing. Something no one would miss."

"Don't you want to just, like, watch a movie?" Sydney asked. But she knew the answer. Mae never really wanted to watch a movie. Mae wanted to make a castle from an egg carton. She wanted to braid their hair into elaborate new structures. She wanted to make a collage from Sydney's mom's magazines or make friendship bracelets for the dollhouse people or make a sidewalk-chalk masterpiece in the driveway. Mae wanted to make beautiful things or weird things or really anything that required her two hands and a little bit of focus and magic.

Mae made the world make sense through her projects. It must be nice, Sydney thought. Sydney herself was never able to make the world make sense, though she kept trying. (She'd assumed, back then, that she'd figure it out by the time she was fifteen or twenty-two or thirty. She did not know then that this particular feeling—of being sure something was fine and then understanding, suddenly, irreparably, that it was not—would haunt her forever. It would be the feeling she felt more than any other, more than joy or fear or rage. She would look to Mae for things to make sense, then to Sam. Then to Ivy Miller. And still, nothing really would.)

"Okay," Sydney said. "All right. My mom has a sewing kit that she fixes stuff with. It's in the attic. And then we can figure out the fabric, I guess. But you're sure? That this mom isn't—she's wrong, you think?" Sydney turned the doll around, trying to see whatever it was that Mae was seeing. Trying to understand why this mom wasn't good enough, what about her needed changing.

Mae tried to give her the answers. "This doll's too perfect," she said. "She needs to be more interesting. More noticeable. Otherwise, she's, you know, like, just a mom."

Mae had stopped herself from saying *like Beth Ann* because she could see that might hurt Sydney's feelings, and Sydney's hurt feelings would put a stop to the project of the dollhouse.

Sydney nodded and showed Mae the string to pull the attic steps down, warning her to be careful, just as Beth Ann was always telling her when she wanted to adventure up there. Once up the wobbly steps, they grabbed the sewing kit, and Mae carried it carefully back down.

"I think we should look in your mom's closet," Mae said.

"You want to use my mom's clothes?" Sydney asked.

"I've seen stuff she never wears," Mae said, her voice getting a little loud with its insistence. "Dresses from weddings and parties and stuff, but she told us she wore them once and can't wear them again. Remember? She said once you're in someone's wedding album in a dress, that's it, you can't be seen in it again."

Mae remembered the things Beth Ann said. She lined them up against things Joni said and tried to make truth from the way they wound around each other.

"Stop being so obsessed with us," Sydney said, and maybe it was a joke or maybe it was something else, a worry about the way Mae hung around all the time, a nervousness about how much her own mother admired Mae's talents, how her father called Mae *precocious* and *old soul* and *charming*, words that he never said about Sydney.

"I'm not obsessed with anyone," Mae said, but she blushed. The rosiness of her cheeks was a tacit admission that Sydney had, in fact, called her out on something real. Mae liked being around Barrett and Beth Ann, their tidy kitchen, their perfectly organized craft closet, their polite way of talking to each other. "Come on. Your mom won't care."

On this, Mae was right. Beth Ann wouldn't care. She wouldn't even notice.

There was so much going unnoticed in those days.

Once they'd chosen dresses from Beth Ann's closet and gone down to the basement, Mae took charge. "I want the mother to be cool and pretty but also, like, sort of princess-y? But also not princess-y." The girls had recently given up princesses, more or less, after an offhand comment from Joni during last summer's Nantucket trip about the silliness of them and a hearty agreement from Barrett that spurred a spat that was Joni and Barrett versus Graham and Beth Ann. The girls didn't like when the teams split this way. It was fine when the couples were battling it out against each other. Or when it was moms versus dads. But this alliance—more common than anyone liked to admit—was wrong, was all mixed up and upside down in a way that made the girls grumpy. So because of that, it seemed easiest, *smartest*, really, to simply stop caring about princesses altogether, to avoid another awkward showdown.

"Okay, but she definitely isn't a princess," Sydney said.

"No, totally, she's not going to be a princess. But she'll be, like, romantic."

"Like in love?"

"No. Like, just, I don't know, she'll be really pretty and into dresses but also really cool about it."

"Like my mom?" Sydney asked, hope streaming through the words. It was true, after all—Beth Ann was pretty and loved dresses.

Mae considered it, then sort of laughed in a way that made Sydney's insides gasp. "No," Mae said, "your mom's, like, trying to be perfect and cool and stuff but she's actually... you know."

Sydney nodded because she agreed that her mom was almost right but not quite, but she didn't like that other people knew it too. She didn't even like that she herself knew it. "She's really pretty, though," she said, wanting to defend Beth Ann (in a way that she would again many times, for years, even when she was all grown up). "And nice." It seemed like those were important things to be, for a mom. Sydney wanted it to matter.

Sydney wasn't sure that she could be much more than pretty and nice when she someday grew up and became a mom. But maybe, maybe—if she listened really carefully to Mae and let her jeans fray, let her hair grow longer than she really liked it; if she watched the way Joni moved around a room, threw her head back, laughing, licked the drippiest part of the ice cream cone like she didn't care who saw—maybe then Sydney could thread that needle and be perfect *and* noticeable, pretty and nice *and* special. Maybe. She let herself believe it was possible.

Mae just shrugged and pulled out a sparkly purple dress they'd taken and Sydney chose a red slinky one. Immediately, Mae knew just what to do with them, how to fit them together into the perfect outfit for the dollhouse mom, who was primed for a makeover: A strip of purple on top. A strip of red on the bottom. The skirt would be long. The top would be short and tight.

The mother doll would be spectacular. She would be something greater than a mom.

Mae did the cutting and the sewing. Sydney did the watching and the suggesting. She did the complimenting too — of Mae's tiny, straight stitches and the way the dress actually looked like a dress. Under every strange fight the best friends had, every shove or screech or dismissive *whatever*, there was a stream of love and admiration and the beauty of knowing each other so, so well.

Sydney snuggled close to Mae. They sat on the floor, leaning against the basement wall, Sydney's head on Mae's shoulder, for what might have been hours or maybe minutes but could have been days too. It could have been forever. Mae's hands sewed slowly. They were stitching what was and what would be.

And when the tiny doll dress was done — the dollhouse mother a reimagined idea of womanhood, sparkly and chic and also, maybe, a little awkward in all that glitz, her doll-hair bob out of place with Mae's creation — Sydney and Mae both hesitated to put her back in the dollhouse.

"What's she going to do in there, wearing this?" Sydney asked.

"Maybe she's having a fancy dinner with her husband?" Mae suggested. "My parents have done that before."

"Oh. Yeah. Mine have too," Sydney said. But they hadn't.

"Okay, let's do that, then," Mae said. They didn't have a nice suit for the dad, but they didn't care so much about what he wore or did. They gathered plates and forks and knives in the tiny kitchen and set them up with miniature steaks and green beans so small they might have been mistaken for lint.

They had the dolls make small talk for a while—about the deliciousness of the steak and the saltiness of the beans.

"I'm worried about Melinda," Sydney had the doll mom say. Melinda was the name they used for the little-girl doll. Parker was the boy. And the baby they simply called Baby.

"You are?" Mae as the doll dad said.

"Yes," Sydney said. "She seems sad."

"She does?"

"And she's put on some weight."

"Melinda? No way."

"Yes. You haven't noticed. But it's true."

"Well. That's... I'm sure she's still—"

"It's ugly."

"Melinda has never been ugly. She's as beautiful as her mother," Mae said, then giggled. It was the sort of thing she'd heard her dad say to her mother before, and her mother would tell him to shut up, but she would also smile at herself in the mirror, so maybe she liked it.

"Well, then, I must not be very beautiful," Sydney as the doll mother said. Her voice hitched. For a moment, Mae thought it was just a stupendous acting job. But when she looked up, she saw it was Sydney's face that was wilting, Sydney's eyes that were filling.

"Hey," Mae said in a whisper. "Why are you crying? What's wrong?"

Sydney's gaze found the ceiling. Her fingers did a quick dance across her face to get rid of the tears. It seemed, for a moment, like they were going to settle in for a long talk, or maybe put on a movie they both loved to drown out whatever was happening. Mae was going to suggest *Anne of Green Gables*, which was long and perfect and also reminded her of herself and Sydney. Sydney was sweet and pretty Diana, of course, and Mae was strong and willful and romantic Anne, and it made her feel warm to watch a friendship like their own on-screen, knowing all the twists and turns and beats it would take.

"Your idea was stupid," Sydney said instead, though. "Rip apart my mom's dresses and then just make them have dinner at home? It's boring and it's stupid and I don't like it. I don't like playing this." Sydney's voice wouldn't stop shaking no matter how hard she tried to keep it calm and prevent the tears.

"What's wrong with you?" Mae asked.

"This isn't how families are," Sydney said. "I like the dollhouse to be real. This is stupid. You can't play with the dollhouse if you're going to make it all weird."

"What am I doing?" Mae was nearing tears now too. "What's weird?"

"It's *my* dollhouse. You always forget and try to make it yours, and it's mine."

"You said it's ours." When Mae cried, she didn't sound as shaky as Sydney because she didn't try to hold it back. She let the tears come. She cried and let everyone know she was crying.

"Louise does things in normal ways. I could have a friend like Louise, you know," Sydney said. She knew she wasn't making much sense to Mae, but she didn't care. She'd run into their classmate Louise yesterday in the grocery store with her mother and had felt something—a sort of longing. Louise was always going to swim class or art class or the children's museum. Sydney thought it sounded boring and nice, like the sort of thing normal friends did together.

She wanted Mae to apologize—for what exactly, she wasn't sure. For not being Louise. For making the day feel tight and hot and swirling. For being her friend in the first place. For tangling their families up together in ways that had felt innocent and fine at first but were beginning to feel confusing and expansive and impossible to ever untangle, like two thin silver chains left too long in a drawer together, now a mess of knots that no fingers were small and nimble enough to separate.

Her parents kept having fights in which Joni's name came up. The fights were always late at night and they were always hushed, but still Sydney heard them.

"Fine, then have a friend like Louise," Mae said.

It was not how the day was supposed to go.

Mae left and Sydney didn't know what to do then. She could call Louise, but Louise probably wasn't home and didn't really need a friend like Sydney anyway. And Sydney certainly didn't need a friend like Louise, as nice as it sounded. There wasn't room for another friend.

Still: "Can we take a break from the Dyers?" Sydney asked over dinner that night, a vegetable pasta in need of more garlic, more cheese.

"A break?" Beth Ann asked, smiling at the absurdity of the question. "You and Mae having a disagreement?"

"Sort of. I don't know. They're just around all the time. It's annoying."

"Family's like that," Barrett said. He had a look of bemusement too, like the ins and outs of Sydney's feelings were a bit of silliness, really. "The Dyers are family."

"But they're not," Sydney said.

"Chosen family," Beth Ann said. "Joni drives me crazy some days too. That's just how it goes."

"You girls need to get along," Barrett said. He rarely had this much to say about the things Sydney worried about, so the comment sounded like a demand, like something Sydney couldn't ignore. She nodded.

"Sometimes I think I have more in common with Louise Horace," Sydney said in a small voice that maybe no one would hear anyway.

"Mae's your best friend," Beth Ann said. "I probably have more in common with Cindy Horace too, but she's not my best friend."

It didn't feel like a solid explanation but Barrett nodded firmly like it was, and no one suggested that maybe the Horaces could come over one day for burgers or ice cream sundaes or a long, sunny afternoon in the backyard. No one thought there could be Joni and Mae *and* Cindy and Louise.

There wasn't room for the Horaces.

The following morning Joni and Mae came over and the girls went on their bikes and the moms drank coffee on the front lawn, and Graham stopped by to say hello, and when the girls came back, Barrett filled Mae's tires with air and the morning turned into afternoon, which turned into cocktails and an old movie that Beth Ann loved when she was little and a sleepover and a bottle of wine split among the grown-ups and breakfast cereal in the morning and the whole thing over and over again, the Horaces long forgotten about, the destinies of Mae's and Sydney's families seemingly cemented in place, unbreakable.

Inevitable.

NOW

Sydney

AT LUNCH, SYDNEY ordered salmon and her mother ordered salad, dressing on the side, and neither of them ordered a drink. It was a ritual, though one not spoken about or acknowledged directly: Whoever ordered first ordered the least caloric thing she could find, and the one who ordered next would find a way to make her dish even more spare, even less filling.

Sydney found herself doing it with other people too, but they didn't play the game like Beth Ann did. So the other woman would order a burger and Sydney would order leek soup and feel incensed at the person enjoying actual food.

Today, though, Sydney pointedly scraped all the sauce off her salmon before taking a bite, and maybe she hadn't won, exactly, but she was still in the game.

Without sauce, the salmon tasted like fish. And Sydney actually hated the taste of fish.

"This is when it starts," Sydney's mother said.

"I don't know what that means," Sydney said. Her mother was

always beginning sentences in the middle of thoughts, a conversational tic that both exhausted and infuriated her daughter.

"The pregnancy. It's when things get—well. You remember. With your father." Beth Ann took the smallest bite of cucumber, then placed a hand on her stomach as if to say, *Oh, gosh, I'm so full now.* The thing about lunch and the game they played was that Sydney's mother always won.

"I—well, no. I don't remember the time when you were pregnant with me, Mom," Sydney said, and watched her mother's face take on a sort of surprise.

"Oh, that's right. I just think of you as always there," she said. "Well. Things changed then." Beth Ann's hair blew a little in the wind. She hated sitting outside, which was exactly why Sydney had chosen an outdoor table. She watched her mother try to push her hair into formation, her slight flush at the realization that she wouldn't be able to fully control it.

"I thought nothing happened until I was, like, eight," Sydney said, not offering her mother the hair band around her wrist or the seat less affected by the slight breeze.

"Six. But you'd be surprised how those six years fly by and how all the DNA for how it will be later is already there in the way things are during the pregnancy, during those early months and years."

"Sam's good. I'm good. No one's—"

"Of course. Of course. Sam is great. And you look—you look so healthy."

Sydney remembered that Mae was the first person who'd pointed this out, back when they were teenagers: "Your mother uses the word *healthy* as an insult," she'd said after Beth Ann commented that Sydney looked "healthy" in a mismatched stripes-and-florals two-piece. It was impossible not to notice now, and even being pregnant didn't protect Sydney from the impact.

Sydney thought of Louise Horace and the times she had tried to convince her mother to let her be friends with that girl and her simpler, easier family. Often, especially lately, Louise's name was at the tip of her tongue around her mother, a bit of ammunition to use if she ever needed to. An *I told you so.*

"Let's talk business!" Beth Ann said. She took out the small pink notebook that she used for business but that looked better suited to a long afternoon playing MASH like Sydney and Mae used to do when they said they were doing homework. Memories of Mae were always there. Sydney had heard women say the same after break-ups with boyfriends—that there was a constant battle to hold off the most potent memories. She assumed this was true, though she herself had never been through a breakup. Sydney had met Sam at twenty-four and he was her first real boyfriend, and she'd attached herself to him ferociously, desperate for a certain kind of closeness in the wake of her falling apart with Mae the year before.

So Mae was really her only experience with a breakup, aside from, of course, her parents' separation starting when the girls were fifteen. And though she hadn't seen Mae in ten years, she was still walking around in a world colored by Mae, as if her particular tint was too bright and vibrant to fully scrub off. Mae was that red sock that pinks all your whites, and though you put those whites through the machine again and again, trying to rid them of the rosy hue, they never return to their original shade.

Trying to forget about Mae for at least a moment, Sydney took out a notebook of her own. She'd chosen this particular notebook because of how much it didn't look like her mother's. It was brown leather and heavy with thick pages and had the feel of an unwritten classic novel. The notebook took her life seriously. It would, when she eventually used it, make her concerns, her grocery lists, her reflections and mantras and business notes, feel weighty, serious, practically literary.

Though she wasn't sure, actually, where to start. Ideas for social media posts, maybe? Lists of people to call to gauge their interest in high-quality and brightly colored pashminas? Reminders to herself about what an excellent businesswoman she was? Sometimes Sydney felt that her work for LillyLou was both difficult and nonexistent. It occupied huge parts of her mind and her time and certainly her space, what with ten boxes of product piled in the corner of their bedroom. But she also didn't know what else to *do*, day in and day out, aside from photograph herself draped in the fabrics, remember to include the right hashtags, and engage with anyone who commented that she looked cute. Perhaps, when the bras and panties Ivy Miller had promised them were finally released, her work would somehow be clarified, would crystallize into something that felt to her the way it seemed to feel to other women at LillyLou.

Women like Beth Ann.

Beth Ann had met Ivy Miller in person already. She reminded Sydney of this fact often, her face smug and flushed, like she had a secret she wasn't ever going to tell.

A good secret, not the kind Sydney had swallowed down for all those years.

Maybe, if Sydney could meet Ivy Miller, she'd know what it was like to have that kind of certainty, that sort of sureness that you were doing the right things, following the right paths, making all the right choices.

She hoped the baby would bring that too. A shape and sturdiness to her life. A check mark saying *Yes, yes, this is it, you made the right choices.* So far, though, pregnancy didn't feel that way. The getting pregnant had been good. Not the sex, exactly, which was fine, but the planning of the sex and the study of her ovulation and tracking of her cycle. She had focused her energy with scientific precision on the task of getting pregnant, and it had given time a definitive shape and purpose, something that she was currently missing now that her task had been accomplished. These days there wasn't much to do but look every week in her pregnancy app to see what size fruit her baby was now. Allegedly, her body was doing a bunch of very intricate work to make this little girl inside her, but Sydney felt distinctly outside of the effort.

She put her hand on her stomach, waiting to feel something more.

"How are your sales looking this month?" her mother asked. Beth Ann's pen was poised above the page, and Sydney supposed that was one thing to write in the notebook, how the people she had recruited were doing. It wouldn't take up much space for Sydney, who had managed to recruit only Sam's coworker's wife, Annie, and her young cousin Tess, a recent college graduate. Her mother, though, had thirty people under her, childhood friends and empty-nester friends and friends of friends, anyone she ran into at the grocery store or the salon or on one of her long walks around the neighborhood, pumping her arms. Beth Ann was able to talk all of them into the genius and ease and profound meaning of LillyLou.

Everyone in Sommersette—everyone *everywhere*—knew what had taken place between Joni and Barrett. Not at first, of course. Not while Joni was alive. And not immediately after her death, when things were shaky and strange and police were asking questions that were by turns accusatory and apologetic about who knew what about the bees in the back woods, Joni's allergy, where her EpiPen was stored, what her plans were for that day. It had been so, so many years, and still those questions made her feel ill, some of them. (*Why would she have been in the woods? Why didn't she have her usual tote bag? How could something so awful happen in Sommersette, of all places?*)

When the case was closed, the police declaring Joni's death a terrible, tragic accident, Beth Ann started telling everyone who would listen about what had happened for all those years, right under her nose.

Sydney wondered if she was the only one who found it strange, how Beth Ann wore it as a badge of—maybe not honor, but of something. It was a defining characteristic, a thing she was: a scorned wife, a duped best friend, a forgiver of a philandering husband, a survivor of the impossible.

It was probably even how she had been able to convince Sydney of the future that LillyLou would provide for her, the kind of safety Beth Ann could never have imagined, had never had before. "I had to stay," Beth Ann was always saying. "You need to protect yourself so that you can leave if you want to."

Sydney hated the implication of it, that her life was unstable, that things might happen, unexpected and awful things.

"They're—I mean, my sales are okay. I've sold a few things. Whenever I see someone talking about going to a wedding or any sort of event, I make sure to reach out and ask what they're planning on wearing. I guess I've sold, maybe, like, three or four items from that?"

"Three or four? Syd, that's nothing."

"Well, I've been helping Annie and Tess get on their feet. Training them, you know? So that took a lot of my energy."

"And they're on their feet now? Are you able to let them fly a bit?"

"They're—yeah. Flying. And on their feet. All of that."

"You need to set the tone, Sydney. You need to show them the potential. Like I do. I sold thirty-seven items this month. And that's not even a huge month for me. You have to have that hustle. It gives your team hustle. And then you start to see your life change." With a swift, practiced motion, Beth Ann tucked her hair behind her ears and leaned toward Sydney. The smell of lunch was on her breath, and coffee too—also the slightly raw, rancid smell that accompanied a person who never really ate enough. But that wasn't what Sydney was supposed to notice. She was supposed to notice the tiny diamond studs in Beth Ann's ears. They weren't much to write home about, except for the sparkle, which was significant. Still, her mother beamed, turning her head back and forth so that Sydney could admire them properly. "This is what I want for you," her mother went on. "To be appreciated and seen. To be given more than you ever imagined you deserved. You know they sent me these?" She pointed to the earrings. "Out of nowhere. They just appeared in the mail, with love from the Girls."

The Girls were Ivy Miller's colleagues, the three women who had joined LillyLou underneath Ivy, each prettier and shinier than the last. They presented themselves as your friends, sending letters in the mail and little gifts if you hit certain goals. The Girls weren't shy about sharing their life stories either, just like Beth Ann herself. Letters from the Girls might come with photos of a child's kindergarten celebration, a pashmina tied proudly around the child's mother's shoulders. Or a recipe for detox soup. Or a piece of stationery with a favorite poem printed on it. Sometimes a secret they said they'd never shared before—eating disorders, alcoholism, or a marital infidelity that they had chosen to forgive. Sydney found herself startled that she knew the names of all their children—ten among the three of them—and the approximate square footage of each of their homes. She knew where they had last vacationed and often even bits and pieces of an argument they'd had with their husbands, their wives, their kids' teachers, their ministers.

Sydney's mother loved the Girls and called them weekly to check in. "The Girls are worried about you," she said now. "That's what I really wanted to talk to you about today. They asked me to reach out and dig deep to figure out why you're holding yourself back."

The thing about getting into LillyLou in its infancy, as Beth Ann had done, was that it gave you a direct line to the Girls, if not to Ivy

Miller herself. Beth Ann had met one of the Girls and later even Ivy Miller herself, when she was involved in HigherLife, a supposedly progressive not-church (as it labeled itself) that she had joined around the time of Sydney's graduation, when she and Barrett were still separated. She never left HigherLife, just sort of stayed until it became something else, a social network and a business opportunity and a consuming way of life. Eventually, Ivy Miller renamed the company LillyLou.

Sydney remembered the way Mae used to ask critical questions about HigherLife. Mae had a lot of theories about Beth Ann starting at the beginning of her separation from Barrett; she posited that Beth Ann had a diet-pill addiction, that Barrett was in trouble for money laundering, that Beth Ann was secretly in love with Joni. Sydney didn't let on about the truth, even though each vicious hypothesis was more fraught than the last, and the work of keeping Joni and Barrett's secret to herself felt heavier and heavier as time went on.

When the girls were in New York, Mae continued to poke fun at Beth Ann, at HigherLife, at the life she was continuing to live after Joni's had stopped. When Beth Ann and Barrett got back together, Mae seemed relieved, happy that something had returned to the way it had once been.

If she'd known, Sydney thought, Mae would have had questions about the timing of their reconciliation, so soon after Joni's death. Sydney herself had a few.

But Sydney had promised not to tell Mae about Joni and Barrett. For a while, she believed it was her duty to Joni's memory, a way to honor her. So she didn't tell and didn't tell and didn't tell.

Until she did.

"Am I?" Sydney asked her mother, tolerating another bite of salmon. "Holding myself back?" The people at HigherLife had said that same thing about her when she decided to defer college. They told Beth Ann that Sydney would never go if she didn't go right then, and Sydney was adamant that she would, that she just needed a break, that she was reeling after Joni's sudden death, that she and Mae would gather themselves in New York and figure out what steps were next in their journey.

The fact that the people at HigherLife had ultimately been right was something Sydney tried never to think about.

Her mother nodded deeply, regretfully, like she wished she didn't have to deliver the terrible news, but there it was anyway. "I don't want you to be just a mother," Beth Ann said. "I want more for you. Maybe it seems like now is the time to step back, but Sydney, it's not. It's the time to push forward. To prove yourself and your worth before there's a little baby screaming at you all day long. Besides, motherhood is an avenue to more business. People love pregnancy. And babies. You should be posting constantly, all your little updates. Meeting other moms. Bringing everyone on this journey with you. Don't get trapped the way I did. All I had was you. And then Joni, who snuck her way in. I was so desperate, I let that woman befriend me, let her take over our lives. You have no idea what you'll do, who you'll spend time with, when you're a mother. You've never met the mother version of you. But let me tell you, she's weak. She's small and desperate and ready to cling to anyone who comes along. You have to show her who's boss."

Beth Ann was worked up now, flying through her sentences, gripping Sydney's arm so tightly it had begun to hurt.

"I have to battle it out with my mom-self?" Sydney asked, genuinely confused. "What does that even mean?"

"It means focus on you and your passions and your connections and your path. Focus on more. Okay? More."

The word *more* was a mantra at LillyLou, just as it had been back when LillyLou was HigherLife. A word that was chanted at manifesting meetings, repeated in Ivy Miller's speeches, glued onto vision boards, used as a caption on photos about abundance, about next steps, about the life they should all dream about and make happen.

The word felt heavy now, though. Like a terrible secret Sydney had been keeping since finding out she was pregnant. The double line on the drugstore test was supposed to be the goal, but almost immediately, Sydney found herself wondering what was next. Surely there had to be more to pregnancy than this? She got the urge to look up more things one could do to ensure a healthy baby. What foods to eat. What exercises to do. She could make a spreadsheet of names. She could pick up sewing or knitting or crocheting and make something lovely and pale pink for the baby.

"You do everything halfway, Sydney," Beth Ann said. Her tone was casual, like this was a neutral comment about who Sydney was and not the exposure of Sydney's greatest source of shame about herself. "You are so tentative. So unable to follow through. I keep waiting for you to be bigger."

"Better," Sydney said, tired of the way Beth Ann always used euphemisms for her disappointment in her daughter.

"That's your word, not mine," Beth Ann said. She didn't exactly argue, though. "For instance, you posted your pregnancy announcement and gender announcement, which was fine, but then there was no follow-up. Get that look off your face, I'm telling you this for your own good. You need to be independent. You need to have drive in case things fall apart."

In case things fall apart was a constant refrain of her mother's, another sort of mantra. It was a strange warning, because from Sydney's perspective, she had already been there for things falling apart. It had already happened — her whole perfect childhood shattered, her friendship with Mae lost, the shape of the world twisted and unsteady and, most of all, wrong.

She didn't say any of that, though. Next to her mother, Sydney knew only how to be small. Obedient. Apologetic for how things had ended up.

"What do you mean, follow-up?" she asked, poising her pen over her notebook, willing herself to care about the answer.

"Follow up with the people commenting. They're not going to see you're pregnant and then just buy a pashmina, Syd. I mean, think about that, right? They see you're pregnant, you're having a girl, and it opens a door to conversation. Every single person congratulating you is saying, *Hey, I want to be a part of your life,* even if it's someone you haven't connected with in a while. They're letting you know that the door is open. And for some reason you haven't been walking through that door. You haven't even peeked through it. Do you understand?"

Three years ago, Sydney's mother barely used her own email account for anything aside from forwarding chain letters that HigherLife sent her — *Send this to ten people and your energy will shift. What's the best advice your mother ever gave you? Write it below and send it on to twelve other amazing daughters of wonderful mothers.* Back then, Beth Ann was on Facebook only to look at photos of other people's grandkids.

But now she was pitching herself as some kind of social media expert, and maybe she was. Sydney watched her mother's online presence with curiosity and discomfort. Online, Beth Ann was breezy and kind, upbeat and engaged. She used exclamation points excessively and called everyone *lady* and *babe,* words that Sydney had never heard her speak.

People seemed to like it, though, and maybe that was the point. They even called her a role model. Sydney fidgeted in her chair. She could never quite get a handle on whether Beth Ann was a warning or a goal. She always left these lunches hazier than when she'd arrived.

Sydney ate another piece of salmon. It was dry. At least the wind was picking up, rattling Beth Ann, making her nudge her chair this way and that to avoid it. Sydney looked at the pregnancy app on her phone. Her baby was the size of a nectarine. She thought about telling Beth Ann that but was fairly sure Beth Ann wouldn't care.

"You need to use the skills you have," Beth Ann went on, leaving no space for Sydney to say much at all. "You have your handsome husband and your beautiful hair and no one's ever been mad at you, so all your connections are open." None of these things sounded quite like skills to Sydney, but she was stuck on the last phrase, which she knew from her LillyLou training booklet. Connections could be open or closed, and LillyLou advised its ambassadors to focus on their open connections rather than wasting their time picking at closed ones. Open connections were people who had simply drifted from your life but still wished you a happy birthday online, were still disposed to be friendly toward you. Closed connections were friendships that had gone awry, ex-boyfriends, people you had rubbed the wrong way, people you argued with about politics or religion or veganism.

"Not all my connections are open," Sydney said. It was true that her former coworkers from the café and the PR firm and the bridal shop and the guy she'd been on three dates with before Sam had all congratulated her on the pregnancy and were all therefore open connections she should be harvesting. But there was one person missing from the list, and her mother knew as well as she did who that one person was.

"Hmm?"

"Not all of my connections are open."

"Well, most, Sydney, certainly. All the important ones."

"Except Mae."

Sydney observed the change in her mother's form and supposed it was what she had been looking for. She had said the unsayable name. Her mother cleared her throat and sipped at her empty glass of water. She let out a heavy sigh. Then, as quickly as she'd darkened, she shook her head and shoulders, like a dog trying not to be wet, and put a smile back on her face.

"Haven't thought about that name in ages," she said, like Mae was her fifth-grade teacher or the boy who always got lost in the back of the class photos — someone incidental and far away, someone who had barely mattered to begin with.

Except Mae was what was left of Joni. And Joni was not, would never be, incidental.

There was a scar on Beth Ann's finger from where she'd broken a glass while drinking too much wine with Joni one night, and there was her diamond-studded wedding ring, a gift given after Beth Ann threw her old ring into the river on a hiking trip with her HigherLife friends. Sydney and Beth Ann both still cringed when a bee buzzed around a flower, lazy and harmless. Sometimes Beth Ann found herself strangely drawn to a long floral skirt, trying it on before realizing who it was meant to belong to. Sydney had, more than once, wandered into a SoHo gallery, looked at the paintings, and wondered if Mae had made anything else, waiting for another painting that would show her something important that she needed to know, the way the Painting had all those years ago.

She wondered how Mae would paint her now — her slightly swollen belly and wondering eyes and so much time gathered up between them. Would she be rounder, sadder, more hopeful, less shy than she'd been portrayed in the Painting? What would Mae see that Sydney simply couldn't? It felt sometimes like the Painting was the definitive portrait of Sydney, but that made no sense now, when so much had changed.

Back home after lunch, she took a dozen selfies, a dozen different angles of her face, her body, the light in her house, the soft corners of the couch. She didn't capture anything special.

Still, she posted the photos online.

Which one is the most me? she wrote, making a poll for her followers, then spending the rest of the evening watching the numbers rise, no conclusion being reached, no winner being spectacularly revealed. According to her followers, she could be any of these versions of herself. According to the people left in her life, she wasn't really distinctly anyone at all.

NOW

Mae

GRAHAM CALLED MAE constantly but never had anything to say to her. Quickly, he'd pass her off to Catherine, which was how Mae had formed a relationship with her father's sweet, easy, uncomplicated wife. It wasn't exactly out of desire on either woman's part, but they did things like trade recipes that Mae never made but Catherine always did and bring up various popular books, movies, TV shows, with the same tepid "So have you checked out…" neither truly that interested in the other's reviews of literature or film. These routines weren't born of desire but of function, or, in the case of Mae and Catherine, politeness.

Every so often Mae would try something new, like ask after her father, whose gruff *Miss you, come visit* before he handed over the phone was the extent of the emotional content of their conversations. She didn't know what he was up to—which did he like better, the chickens or the horses on their farm, did he make his way into town much, did he have friends, did he ever, late at night, think of Joni and the way her skin, her throat, her whole self must have become inflamed in the woods? Did he consider her terror, her aloneness, the way she had never actually enjoyed the woods behind their house, had a great many times refused to so much as venture in there alone to retrieve a too-exuberantly kicked ball. Mae wanted to know if her father was still gripped, as she was, by the impossibility of Joni dying a terrible, cinematic, painful death the very day Mae had graduated from high school.

Mae didn't ask after Graham today, but she tried sharing something small with Catherine in the hope that she would be primed to share bigger things. She liked Catherine, after all, liked the way she cooked chicken with lemon slices on top and liked that she knew how to hem pants and play tennis. She liked that Catherine herself never crossed the invisible line between *father's wife* and *mother figure,* a line that neither woman had drawn, exactly, but that was indisputably thick, solid.

"I'm painting again," Mae said as a test. "Portraits still. But not of kids anymore. I'm working on something about what happened with Leo. Which — we broke up. I can't remember if I mentioned it."

There was a startled silence on the other end of the line. "Well. Oh. I'm sorry, Mae, I know breakups can be—"

"No, no, it's been good. It's been — I hadn't been painting and now I am. So it's really for the best."

In spite of all the years that had passed, Mae still, somehow, always, expected Catherine to morph into Joni. Joni would have focused on the painting. She would have asked what sorts of brushes Mae was using and if she'd thought anymore about watercolors.

Catherine didn't know about watercolors or brushstrokes. She certainly didn't know what it was to work one's way around heartbreak by spooling it out onto a thick canvas in greens and grays and shimmery blues.

"You're such a lovely painter," she said, as if it were exactly that simple.

Mae nearly contradicted her, but instead she let herself sink into the compliment as if it might mean something real. She let herself feel loved by someone easy, someone whose care for her was straightforward in its own way.

"That Luke didn't deserve you anyway," Catherine said, sounding distracted by something in the background—her father's grumping about a hard-to-reach light bulb or some other small thing that made up their life without Mae. Mae didn't correct her. It was close enough, wasn't it? It was almost what she needed.

They said goodbye just as Mae approached the bar where she would be meeting Leo. She had hoped to arrive bolstered and strong, but instead she was something else. She was always, really, something else.

Leo's favorite story was one about this minor celebrity he'd made friends with working on some play years ago, before she'd become a minor celebrity. He'd talk, starry-eyed, about how they both liked run-down amusement parks and seasonally clichéd activities, so they'd ride shaky roller coasters and go to pumpkin patches and Leo said she'd sort of changed his life, but he never specified how.

At first it had given Mae an uncomfortable zoom of jealousy—Mae didn't particularly like roller coasters or holiday traditions and she knew enough about the celebrity to be aware that she was beautiful and made raunchy jokes on cultish podcasts and was cast in TV shows in roles that featured her body—weepy strippers, lifeguards, ice-skating champions. So Mae worked hard to file it away under Cool and Interesting Things About My Boyfriend That I'm Totally Okay With, Actually, and also as an entry under Reasons I Must Be Good Enough for Him (because he could probably be with her if he wanted but he's with me).

Over time, she'd gotten used to stories about the minor celebrity. Even began to believe what Leo said, that their dynamic and deep friendship had made him the guy he was today, a guy who asked smart, soul-stopping questions about Mae's mother, always wondering what songs she used to sing to Mae when she was little and which season made her seem the happiest. A guy who showed her ancient movies starring glamorous movie stars and explained to her why and how to fall in love with them. Who bought her a bouquet of umbrellas instead of flowers one Valentine's Day because she was always losing or breaking hers.

Still, even though she had gotten over hearing about the minor celebrity and even though they would never be together again, it was not what she wanted him to be talking about when she met him for a drink after getting off the phone with her father and his wife.

But Leo had rushed right in, hugging Mae like she was his old pal, all flushed and vibrating. "I saw her. Just now. She's here. She lives right here!" he said instead of a greeting. "God, I never thought I'd see her again because she's, you know, getting more famous and will probably forget all about me eventually but we really had a special connection, you know? I mean, we were *close*, I don't know if I ever told you, but I helped paint her apartment. I met her parents. We took them out for pancakes when they visited and I was there when she got the call booking her for her first commercial. I was sort of part of her whole ascent, you know? It was — it was incredible, actually. And I guess I always wanted something to happen and she did too but we both had hang-ups — "

"Hey, can you take a breath? I'm not Greg, you know? I don't need to hear all about how in love with some hot C-list actress you are."

"It's a part of my *life*," Leo said, shaking his head adamantly. "You always make things—anyway, she's building something. Not everyone just lucks into fifteen minutes of fame and then wastes it."

Mae startled, her inhale sharp. Leo was always so clever at finding the most painful thing, the achiest bruise, the hottest shame. With Herculean effort, Mae stayed silent. He could say what he wanted. She had a different kind of power now.

Leo went on, not noticing her prickly quiet. "We were big in each other's lives, her and I. I'm not going to apologize for that because it makes you feel—"

"I hope you're very happy together, Leo."

"Look, I came to be nice. If it's going to be like this, I don't need to be here." Leo started to gather his things. It was interesting to observe him now from this new perspective. Not as her boyfriend whom she loved and not as her boyfriend whom she hated and not even as her ex whom she still had to work shit out with. He wasn't really any of those things anymore. She was looking at him as a person, as a person in her life.

"Stay. I need to talk to you," she said. She could have blurted the news out then—stopping him in his tracks, stopping whatever high he was currently on. Whenever Leo talked about other women, the ones he'd loved or fucked or never got a chance with, Mae sized herself up, just as she'd done since she was on the cusp of teenagerdom, done with Sydney a hundred times, more, for years, until they stopped being friends altogether. If she wasn't happy with what she saw, she'd change outfits, put on lipstick, try her hair up in a messy bun or down around her shoulders or twisted into braids. She'd stay in front of that mirror until she looked a way that she could tolerate, until she looked a way that felt like enough.

She never had the allure of the minor actress or the togetherness of Sydney or the easy prettiness of her mother or the hard-won perfection of Sydney's mother. Mae was something else—plain but trying, just like Leo had always implied—and she hadn't turned the Painting into some beautiful career, she hadn't figured it all out. She wasn't, as it turned out, special.

What Mae hadn't understood at the time all those years ago when she was first talking to Leo was that she would never in fact change into the person she imagined someday being. The way you wish you looked at twelve is too big a wish to ever come true.

"Please just stay," she said again.

"I'll stay," he said. "I'll even get you a drink. Rioja?"

"Sure."

"Let's be cordial. We're just two desperate artists trying to make our way, you know? Imperfect, longing, left behind, moving on." When they were together, Mae had liked when Leo sounded like he was speaking in poetry.

Things were different now, though.

And there was always something Leo was trying to tell her about who he was and therefore who she was that she never quite grasped but that always made her feel a little bit ill and a little bit awful. With Leo, she was always too cute and not cute enough, and it was disorienting, a map she kept turning around and around, looking desperately for that red star—You Are Here—but never actually locating it.

She watched Leo now as he leaned on the bar the way someone confident might, but there was always something spiky and aware underneath. His shoulders slumped when the bartender passed him by to take someone else's order. Mae took out the pencil she kept tucked into her purse, a long-ago mandate from Joni, who used to give her tips on what she would need to do were she to become an artist. She followed those little snippets of instruction, out of respect, she supposed, or maybe just habit. She wished there had been more instruction. Especially now.

She sketched Leo's slumped shoulders on a cocktail napkin, and they looked like question marks or parentheses—they looked like grammar, like a certain kind of uncertainty or aside. She had thought the people who would hurt her most would have spines like exclamation points, would remind her of words written in bold, underlined, italicized.

How, she wondered, would she draw the way it felt to be undone by someone like Leo?

Or was that maybe what the Painting had already captured all those years ago. Sydney wasn't exactly a person in Caps Lock either.

Still, she wasn't staying with Leo, she wasn't letting his interest in other women, his quiet contempt for her, become her whole life. It felt good to know she didn't have to conform—wear Ann Taylor cardigans, for example, and renovate a kitchen and stay in a marriage to a man who wanted other people. That was for women like Beth Ann, another person made of question marks, ellipses, uncertainty. Mae quickly sketched her too, trying her shoulders, at least, her overly bouncy hair.

"We get it, you're an artist," Leo said when he sat back down, and Mae remembered why she had stopped doing art when she was with him. She kept her pencil poised above the napkin, hoping to capture, somehow, the next moment.

"I'm pregnant," she said. "It's yours. I'm keeping it."

Mae put her lips in a certain position that she imagined made her look untouchable. For reasons she couldn't quite identify, she thought of the mom in the dollhouse that she and Sydney had spent their childhoods playing with. She wanted to be like her, not like striving Beth Ann or dreamy Joni. She thought for a moment of Catherine. Then she put that thought away. Catherine wasn't right either; none of them were.

"Hey," Leo said. "Whoa, okay. All right. You're—and how do you know—and you want to—"

"Let's talk about what you want. Or what you need. Time? You probably need time, right? To figure out what you want from all this?"

Mae let her pencil move, watching Leo's face. It was the sort of thing they did in art school, draw without looking, without lifting their tools, without worrying. She willed the pen to trace Leo's shock, the moment of his world changing.

He looked lost. Mae had felt that way too, watching the days pass without her period arriving, walking to the pharmacy, getting the test, then sitting on the bathroom floor and waiting for it to reveal its answer, which it did in the form of two parallel red stripes.

Leo drank. Looked around. Looked at her. Drank some more.

"You don't seem pregnant."

She couldn't help laughing. "Leo."

"I mean, are you sure? Is this like a premonition or an assumption?"

"Why would I bring you here and tell you this because of a premonition? Have you ever known me to have premonitions?"

"So you took some kind of test."

"A pregnancy test, yes."

"And it said—"

"Pregnant."

"I thought you were on—"

"I got off it, remember? It was making me all—"

"Crazy, right."

"Hormonal," Mae said. "Not crazy." It was the shadow of an old fight.

"And it's mine?" Leo asked. A not-small part of Mae wished she could say she wasn't sure, make him think that there had been other people since their breakup, to signal that she had moved on in the exact way that would hurt him the most. But of course, there hadn't been anyone else.

Mae picked up her Rioja, then set it back down. "It's yours. I am one hundred percent sure."

Leo's mouth did something in that moment that made Mae's insides scream. His mouth battled a smirk. He was, as she'd known he would be, smug. Proud. He had won. She could see him figuring out a subtle way to let her know he'd fucked other girls already.

"I thought you'd be the first one to move on," he said at last.

"I've moved on," she said, too fast.

"Well, I thought you would be the first to move on... with someone else."

"Okay," Mae said. She wanted Leo to sit with his own words, to see the absurdity of what he'd chosen to focus on. So she waited.

It seemed impossible now that she had ever loved this person in front of her. The end was always like this for Mae. By the time something was over, she'd already spent so much time deciding that it *should* be over and planning how to end it that there was no longing, no missing, no heartbreak, really.

Except with Sydney. It had been years—ten of them—and she still wasn't sure. It still felt too abrupt, too jarring, too impossible, to have let that go.

Leo was no Sydney.

She watched as his eyes scanned the room. They settled on a girl with dark hair and big earrings. "Well. I'm really glad you've found some nice girls to sleep with, Leo, but we're here to talk about having a baby," Mae said in a cool, measured tone.

He swallowed and looked away from the girl.

"So you're keeping it," he said. She tried to determine if he sounded disappointed or at peace or something else, but the sentence was neutral, and for this she was grateful. He was a lot of things. A lot of terrible things. But in this one way, he wasn't a total asshole.

"I'm keeping it," she said for the second time. It was still such a new sentence; it felt thick in her mouth. She'd thought of telling Georgie, considered letting Catherine know. A strange part of her had woken up at three in the morning today wanting to call Sydney and tell *her*. They hadn't spoken in years, though, not since those early, heady, terrible New York days. Mae had muted her on social media, so they were technically friends online but Sydney was shrouded in invisibility and had been for ages. She could be anywhere, doing anything.

But Mae was short on friends, and when she was lost, Sydney still felt like a sort of lighthouse, a person who knew Mae in the real ways, the ways no one else was ever allowed to.

"Okay," Leo said at last. "So, a baby."

When they were little, Sydney and Mae talked about raising babies together. For years, the idea was that they would get pregnant or adopt, that they would live together as single mothers, helping each other with the kids, cementing their friendship as the most real thing.

Leo's face was lemon-sucking pursed lips, and he kept scratching his head.

"You don't have to be involved."

"Seems like I already am, though."

"You know what I mean. You don't have to, like, be some dad or whatever."

Leo squinted. "You really think I'm trash, huh?" he said.

Mae didn't know what to say. *Trash* wasn't the right word. But she wasn't about to tell him that he was not cut out for the role of father in any way aside from having accidentally impregnated her. "I think—I think you're a person I was ready to let go of. I was sort of—excited for you to be in the past. But I don't think you're trash."

It was as kind a comment as she could muster.

"And now I'm not in the past," he said. "So you and I could maybe—"

"Oh. No. We aren't—this is about you and this baby. And what you want to be to them. I...I already know what you are to me."

"And what am I to you?" He leaned close. Again, he seemed to be poised for something intimate with her, still maybe grasping at whatever had happened not so long ago in his bed.

"Just some guy I used to love," she said at last. "Truly. If this weren't happening, you'd never see me again."

"I don't know about that." His eyebrows waggled. Maybe Barrett used to talk to Joni like this, to Beth Ann too. Maybe he had waggling eyebrows and a smirking mouth and a way of making them question everything, even the most obvious things. Again, Mae let herself feel a surge of pride at not falling for it. At being not Beth Ann or Joni but that dollhouse mom, unflappable and sure.

"I'm only here to ask if you want, like, updates," Mae said. "I'm around if you want to talk about your role with the baby. But otherwise, you know, we're done." It felt so good to say. She was not imitating anyone; she was squarely being herself.

She looked down at the cocktail napkin she'd been blindly drawing on.

In one sense, it was entirely scribbles. A mess of markings.

In another, it was a web of the way things were. She could see, in the spirals, the jagged stripes, the impossible patterns, Leo's sharp elbow, his grimace at the idea of fatherhood. And she could see also how Sydney was wound in there too, her wide eyes and the way they watched Mae for answers Mae never had, her hand squeezing tight at moments when she was holding something back.

She folded the napkin. Put it in her purse. It was ugly, but it was art too.

"I'm going," she said to Leo, standing up.

"I'll call you. Soon," he said. He looked like he almost meant it. "It's just the life of an artist, you know? Doesn't pair naturally with parenthood. I'm going to be traveling a lot for work. And work is—work is my whole life. I don't see that changing. I'm not you. I can't give it all up, you know?"

Mae did not know.

She headed out. The cocktail napkin in her purse felt stupid now. Like a dream of a kid, a wish made with a coin tossed into a well, a penny no one would ever find again. He was right, for once. She thought of Joni's sad, heartless paintings and her shed full of sculptures that no one wanted even after her funeral. Graham and Sydney and even Barrett discussed what to do with them and agreed eventually to donate them to...someplace that wanted subpar art; Mae couldn't think of where that might be. Whatever promise of artistic glory Joni had was gone once she had Mae, once she moved to Sommersette, befriended Beth Ann. All her artistry was used up making Mae's own childhood. Construction-paper garlands on the tree and stenciled valentines every February and the magic of the tooth fairy and summer vacations and Saturday-morning breakfasts. For Joni, even everyday life—remembering to tell Mae to brush her teeth, figuring out what was giving Mae a rash on her left arm, deciding what to say when Mae was caught shoplifting tampons from CVS—took a surge of creativity that must have, Mae was sure of it now, depleted her artistically.

Leo's back was straighter than usual, she saw as she left the restaurant. He took a beat-up copy of *Othello* out of his back pocket. He had always been the kind of guy who carried Shakespeare around where other men kept credit cards and condoms.

He would direct a hundred more plays. Some would be terrible, but surely some would be good or even brilliant.

And Mae? She had the beginning of a new portrait, years after her singular success. And she had this cocktail napkin, an art-school exercise gone wrong, a bit of nothing. Leo would be an artist and she would be a mother, and Mae's sudden certainty of this future made her chest tighten; she leaned her body against a brick building, waiting for the shock and horror of what was happening to pass.

Meanwhile, Joni—Joni wouldn't get a chance to be or see any of it.

THEN

THE FIRST TIME Sydney noticed, they were eleven. *Everything happens at eleven*, they'd say later, when they were thirteen and sixteen and eighteen and making new friends who had their own stories of being eleven and realizing such things as *My mother had a nose job; My father drinks too much; My mother hides cigarettes in the bathroom; My father watches porn; My mother isn't nice to waitstaff; My father hasn't hugged me since I started growing breasts.*

It was Memorial Day weekend, and their fathers were grilling. Their mothers were sitting on the grass. Beth Ann had a blanket with more than enough room for Joni, but Joni was flat on her back in the blades instead. From where Sydney and Mae were sitting, it was possible to see the grass stains inching up her shorts, but still, she made it look good, made it look fun, even, like the better way to be. Because of that, both girls sat in the grass, eschewing the purple-striped picnic blanket Sydney's mother had set up for them under one of the big trees. She'd made it special with a vase of flowers in the middle and new pink-rimmed juice glasses and floral-patterned china and a spread of cheese and crackers to start.

Sydney's mother was always trying to make something normal into something special, but never in the ways that Mae and Sydney wanted.

"We're not babies," Sydney had said upon seeing it. "We don't need, like, a princess tea party."

"I thought it looked grown-up," Beth Ann said, knowing as the words came out that it wasn't worth defending. Sydney's mind was made up. Trying to change it would only make Beth Ann look more desperate, more pathetic.

"Calling something *grown-up* is babyish," Sydney said with a vocalized sigh and a twist of her hair around her middle finger. Lately, Beth Ann barely recognized her.

"That's sort of true," Mae said, stretching her legs.

"Well, I certainly don't want anything to be babyish," Beth Ann said, wondering if any of her hurt came across, unsure if she hoped it did or hoped it didn't. "You two are not babies. Or even kids. You're practically adults. That's why you're out here with us. With the adults."

"Okay, Mom," Sydney said, and the words sounded cutting, cruel, even though there was nothing to them. The cruelty was in how Sydney didn't linger on the interaction, how quickly she turned to Mae to continue their conversation about a boy named Jay and a girl named Olivia as if Beth Ann had never been there at all.

The first time Beth Ann noticed, she was forty-five. It was that same Memorial Day; her husband, Barrett, was flipping burgers, Joni's husband, Graham, was watching, arms crossed, commenting on which ones needed more time, which ones were ready for a single slice of American cheese. Beth Ann had always hated American cheese, but that wasn't the sort of thing you said in the middle of a party, even if the party was just you and your best friend and your families. She knew saying she hated American cheese would make her sound silly and high-maintenance and impossibly uncool. Lately, she had become aware of a list of things that were impossibly uncool about her. Things Sydney and Mae pointed out (her pink lipstick, her French manicure, her purple capris, her bangs) and things her husband pointed out (her unwillingness to wear thongs, her way of calling him at exactly 5:15 every day to ask when he'd be home, the fact that she wanted to celebrate their anniversary with something as mundane as dinner at their favorite Italian place, which was apparently no longer his favorite Italian place).

Joni pointed things out too, not with words but by the way she chose the opposite of everything Beth Ann wanted to choose or do or be. They'd have lunch and Beth Ann would order a coffee and Joni a martini. They'd go for drinks and Beth Ann would wear a cute gray dress and a ponytail and Joni would wear old jeans and a top that looked like lingerie and have her hair in mysteriously intricate braids on the top of her head. And today—today Joni was in the grass, barefoot, drinking a beer, not going anywhere near the prosecco Beth Ann had brought out in an ice-filled bucket. From time to time, Joni would raise a foot to the sky, stretching or inspecting her bare toenails or maybe just showing off the length of her legs, the careless shapes her body was able to take.

The folding chairs Beth Ann had unearthed from the garage were empty, unwanted. Even Barrett stayed standing.

If he sits, I'll know everything's okay, Beth Ann said to herself. It was something that had worked when they'd first started dating. She'd stay by her phone and will it to ring—*If he calls me by eight p.m., I'll know it's real*, she used to say in her head.

He almost always called by nine.

"Nothing like a long weekend," Beth Ann said, then bit into a burger, making sure the juice didn't dribble down her chin.

"It's really so—I mean, burgers on Memorial Day. It's really—we're really doing the thing, huh?" Joni replied.

"The thing?"

"The suburban thing. The family thing. We could have done anything, right? We could have, like, gone to Peru or meditated in the woods or learned how to make, I don't know, chocolate croissants or something, right? But here we are, making burgers on the lawn like we have some kind of Americana checklist we're working our way through."

"What's in Peru?" Beth Ann asked. She was tired of conversations like this. Joni had lived in town for eight years and still acted like it was a place she was visiting. Joni made observations about suburban life as if she were a sociologist and not, in fact, a mom of a kid who went to soccer and liked the mall. As if she were not married to a man in a polo shirt that matched exactly the polo shirt of every other man in the neighborhood on the weekends. Beth Ann had tried to ask her a few times how she ended up in Sommersette, and Joni always talked about the gazebo, the window seat, pregnancy hormones making her hate the city. She said she liked the name, how it sounded cozy and sweet, and how it seemed like the weather was always perfect.

But the thing was, Joni loved rainy days. She was always going on about it.

"I mean, who knows what might be in Peru — that's the point, right?" Joni rolled from her back to her stomach. Her bracelets jangled; her hair fell around her face; bits of grass stuck up and out and all over.

"I'd love to go to Paris someday," Beth Ann said. "Barrett and I talked about going maybe for our anniversary. October — right, honey?"

"What's that?" Barrett asked. He looked startled to hear his wife's voice. He and Graham hadn't been involved in the conversation, had instead been passionately talking about the girls' softball team for which they were coach and assistant coach, respectively.

"Our anniversary. October. Paris," Beth Ann said.

"Paris. Right. Yeah. Or somewhere else. Everyone does Paris for anniversaries, right? We should go somewhere we don't know so much about. Somewhere we haven't seen in everyone's photo albums already. Like Peru or something. I'd love to go to Peru."

Beth Ann's head jerked toward Joni, who was blushing. She caught the blush, the way Joni turned her head and lowered her cheek to the ground as if she were suddenly exhausted and ready to take a nap right there. But before Joni's face fully turned away, Beth Ann saw it, the beginnings of a certain kind of smile. A secret smile.

A shared dream of Peru.

And Beth Ann just knew.

It was different for Sydney. She didn't see the Peru moment, as Beth Ann would forever call it. She saw something much clearer later that evening, when cleanup was happening and the adults were starting to droop, the way they always did at the end of days like this. A combination of booze and sun. There had been a rousing game of charades, which Beth Ann dominated, and an impromptu dance party when "Lady Marmalade" came on the radio. Sydney hated the way her mother tried to shimmy. She'd turned Mae away from it, as if awkward sexiness was passed down from mother to daughter and Beth Ann's uncomfortable attempts would mean something certain and ugly and unsexy about Sydney herself.

It was different with Joni, who didn't dance the way Christina Aguilera did but who was so deeply in her own body that it didn't matter that she was off the beat or doing something strange and trance-like with her hands. Joni's hips moved and her eyes closed and her head hung back, and that was all that mattered. Sydney watched Mae to see if she was embarrassed the way Sydney was of her own mother, but of course Mae wasn't, she was never embarrassed.

Eventually, Graham started a fire in the firepit, and Beth Ann brought out ingredients for s'mores, all laid out on a tray, and Sydney was caught between pride and disgust at the useless perfection of it. Joni and Barrett both liked their marshmallows burned so black they looked like charcoal, like something diseased and wrong. Eating them that way was a risk — to get them so black, you had to let the flame attack the marshmallow, you had to listen to it melt and bubble before bringing the fire to your mouth to blow it out.

Joni couldn't wait.

She bit in and screeched, threw her creation on the ground, and rushed into the house. Sydney watched her father follow Joni, abandoning his own s'more, his own child and wife and the moon he'd only just been admiring. "I'm an expert," he said. "I've done that exact same thing a million times. Nothing a little ice can't fix." The rest of them started to clean up, taking Joni's burned mouth as a cue that the night was over. Wasn't it even sort of a relief when something happened that let everyone transition elegantly from *We're having so much fun!* to *Okay, that's enough, though?*

There were plates and utensils and cups and abandoned sweatshirts and blankets and board games that had never gotten opened and bottles of wine and beer that had, and everyone got to work gathering it all up. Sydney grabbed the cooler, figuring she'd take a big-ticket item and maybe get away with fewer trips back and forth. She heaved it into her arms and leaned against the back door to push it open and bring the cooler inside.

When she did, there was an explosion of movement from Joni and her dad, a hopping away from, a tripping backward, a flurry of breathy explanations. Sydney didn't hear them. She was still processing what she'd seen in the single instant before the leaping away of limbs.

Her father's face had been nestled in the crook of Joni's neck, his hand on her waist — tense, desperate, wanting more.

What she'd seen was just enough to know it was something.

"Sydney, the cooler, what a big help, is everyone packing up and getting ready to go?" her dad said at the same time as Joni said, "Oh, wow, it's late, gotta take care of this burn, you know it feels almost like a bee sting—with my allergy, a bee sting feels awful, this horrible burn but then my whole body—well, this isn't that, I guess. This should just need Neosporin, right, Barrett? No EpiPen necessary! That's what you recommend? Were you able to see any, um, anything that would be a, um, problem? Thanks for giving it such a thorough—"

"Everyone's cleaning up," Sydney interrupted because she didn't want to risk hearing anything more, and Joni rambled when she was flustered. Sydney's brain was already trying desperately to make sense of the moment, to make it mean something different than what it felt like it meant. Because it felt like a collapse of something essential, something as obvious and clear as the house they were standing in, the moon becoming visible when the sun sets, the taste of s'mores being sweet and hot and messy and pure.

"Ah, well, had to end sometime," Barrett said.

"I do need to get home," Joni said. "I know I'm a little—you'll get it someday, Sydney." And maybe she was talking about being a little tipsy after a day in the sun or maybe she meant something else, maybe she meant that someday Sydney would understand what it was to have someone else's husband's face touching your skin, maybe she would understand someday that everything solid was actually a little liquid, a little more movable and re-shapable than you'd always imagined.

Maybe what Joni really wanted Sydney to someday understand was that people like Joni were dangerous, were freight trains, hurricanes, whole entire oceans, impossible forces that were bigger and brighter and more beautiful than the tidy forms of Sydney and Beth Ann.

"Okay," Sydney said, not sure what she even meant by it. "Someday, I guess I'll get it."

She hugged Mae goodbye. Mae was distracted by something—fireflies or the moon or the wanting of one last bite of chocolate—but still Sydney tried to say something.

"Your mom," she said. She couldn't come up with anything to add to the sentence. "Is something going on with your mom? Is she fighting with your dad? Does she talk about my dad? Are they—I saw something." Sydney said it all in a whisper, and Mae heard it, she must have, the whisper was right against her ear, but she didn't look curious or worried.

"Did you hear that Eleanor Evans is having a birthday party and we weren't invited?" Mae said. "It's tomorrow. Why do you think we weren't invited? Did you make her mad about something? Because she and I were in art together and she was always complimenting my paintings, so I don't think it's because of me."

Sydney's brain couldn't keep up. It was still focused on Joni and her dad and whatever she saw that she couldn't identify but that looked a lot like two people doing something they weren't supposed to be doing. But Mae was somewhere else—on the infractions of sixth-grade girls and the impossible placing of themselves in the social hierarchy of their school, a map that seemed to change practically daily and that neither of them was very good at following.

"I'm talking about our parents," Sydney said. "Not Eleanor."

"I'm talking about a party that literally everyone is going to. Boys and girls. I bet Wes is going to be there. I could talk to him."

"You can talk to him at school," Sydney said.

"Mae, come on, we need to get out of here," Joni said. She was calling to Mae but looking at Sydney, at the lean of her body, trying to judge if Sydney was telling her daughter anything.

"Find out what you did to make Eleanor mad. We have to go to that party," Mae said, already turning away from Sydney, issuing a command she could have given hours before but for unknown reasons had saved for the end of the night, like it had all been leading up to exactly this the whole time.

"Girls, that's enough," Joni said, her eyes big and looking right at Sydney, begging or accusing or telegraphing something vital that Sydney both understood and did not at all understand.

"Okay," Sydney said, agreeing with that one word in that single moment both that she was at fault for the two girls not getting an invite to Eleanor Evans's party *and* that she would not tell Mae what she'd seen.

Mae and Joni both smiled, nodded, pleased with Sydney's acquiescence. Pleased to be the kind of people who decided the way forward instead of the kind of people, like Beth Ann and Sydney, who let life happen to them, who said over and over, a million times in a million different ways: *Okay. Okay. Okay.*

NOW

Sydney

SAM HAD ASKED her to put on headphones while she watched Ivy Miller's latest on her laptop. "I just can't listen to it before bed," he said. He was cracking the spine of a novel, showing off. He read novels in bed. So what. She was bettering herself. She was *becoming*. She had put in an enormous preorder for the lingerie, and she needed to be ready for when the product came. She needed to make this count. She needed the credit card bills to stop. Her heart started to pound and she gripped her laptop. She needed to listen harder. Take more notes. Be *more*.

"You'd learn a lot from it," Sydney told him instead of saying the rest of it, the jumble of nerves in her head. She'd hoped listening to the speeches in front of Sam might prove something to him.

"You'd learn a lot from *this*," Sam said, wagging the novel in her general direction.

He said it like a joke, the sort of thing married couples said lightly, tiny teases that were harmless and maybe even, under the right circumstances, erotic. And over the years, Sydney had given in to the teasing, to the asks, like this one, putting her headphones on, which felt harmless, if annoying. *Okay*, she was used to saying, and he was used to hearing, when he asked her to wear lower heels so that he could appear taller, when he asked her to do his laundry while she was doing her own, when he said it was a little silly, wasn't it, to take college classes if you were in your thirties and didn't really need a college degree anyway.

(It wasn't fair, really, that she blamed Joni's death for her not getting her degree when she was younger. But it felt like she could trace so much back to that too-sunny afternoon, the mozzarella and tomato salad, the bottle of Chardonnay she and Mae stole and drank, the sound of her mother's knees hitting the ground when Graham burst through the front door with the news.)

Regardless, pregnancy had taken all the *okay* out of her; she was too worn-out from nausea and joint pain and the insistent worry of what might go wrong to be agreeable. Sydney was wearing this new side of herself awkwardly, a bridesmaid dress that wasn't her color, that didn't quite fit.

"If you wanted some professor wife, you should have married what's her name from college," Sydney said, snide and hurting. "Someone who wasn't dealing with a traumatic death and her whole life falling apart when she was eighteen. That would be nicer, I'm sure." Anywhere Sydney went, she was asked where she'd gone to college, and somehow, though it had been nearly fifteen years of those questions, she had yet to come up with a breezy, confident answer. She always found herself oversharing about her best friend's mother, Joni, and the EpiPen and how she couldn't let go of how unusual it was for Joni to be without it, how, despite all the ways Joni was flaky, permissive, and unworried, she was diligent about her EpiPen, teaching both Sydney and Mae at a young age how to use it in case, in case; Joni afraid of almost nothing except her allergy to bees. It wasn't the sort of thing you were meant to talk about with almost-strangers, but she'd go on about how the EpiPen was found later in a bag Sydney had never seen before. How strange it was, how she just couldn't seem to define what those last hours of Joni's life looked like. It was always met with strained *I'm sorry*s and the silent begging for Sydney to shut up, move on, talk about something nicer, like where to buy the best jeans, whether she'd seen any of the movies nominated for Oscars, who had the best catering at their wedding.

Did Mae do the same thing? Did she roll the facts around in the same uncomfortable way—EpiPens, bees, purses, fathers, affairs, girlhood, motherhood? Sydney supposed that was why Mae's famous painting was so unruly. It was, undeniably, her attempt to reckon with it all, just as Sydney was doing now, was doing always.

"Okay," Sam said, rolling his eyes, missing the way she was reeling. "All right, Syd." He turned his attention back to his book, so Sydney turned hers back to the screen, something hateful and prickly clasping her insides. She recalled, though she tried not to, the time long before Joni's death when Barrett started picking up poetry books and philosophy texts at the library. He had reading glasses from the drugstore and he'd slip them on to read Neruda and Jung in the backyard. Once, he'd read a few lines aloud to Sydney. Beth Ann overheard, flew outside in a wild rage, grabbed the Neruda out of his hands, and threw it in the trash.

"That's the library's!" Barrett had said.

"Fuck the library," Beth Ann replied, her eyes narrow, the words beneath the words fire-hot and unrelenting.

Sydney wondered what had happened to that book. Had Barrett fished it out of the trash, paid to replace it, or simply ignored the overdue notices from the library until they gave up on him, prepared, perhaps, for the budgetary consequences of extramarital affairs involving poetry in translation and existential pontificating?

After Joni died, he did not read. He barely spoke.

And when he did, Sydney didn't listen. There was a night when she was home for Christmas, that first year after, when she overheard him whispering in the kitchen with her mother, who kept saying, *Don't say that, that part wasn't your fault, it wasn't.* And also, later, *Clean slate* and *A tragedy, of course, but the way it had to be,* at which point Sydney put on headphones and turned up the volume on her favorite song of the moment, Pink's "So What," a song that Mae deemed silly but that anchored Sydney in a kind of anger that felt manageable, acceptable.

Sydney did not want to hear anything else. She was tired of the weight of secrets, and it felt always like another one might land in her lap if she wasn't careful. So she was careful.

Tonight, she turned to her headphones again, missing the way a song could ground her when she was a teenager. Ivy Miller wasn't Pink, exactly, but she gave Sydney something similar.

"Get out of your own way," Ivy Miller said into the sequined microphone she always used at these events. "Get away from your cousins, your coworkers, your best friend that you see every day. You've already spoken to them about the work we do here, and either they get it or they don't. And if they don't get it, then it's time to put that relationship aside and think bigger." Sydney shifted her body the slightest bit away from Sam. Ivy Miller wasn't talking about husbands, of course; they were a whole other topic of conversation, a dozen video lectures on how to make peace with spouses' lack of support. But Sydney shifted anyway, her body preparing itself to look elsewhere.

"Have you ever been to an art museum?" Ivy Miller went on. "It's okay if you haven't. Art museums are spaces we sometimes think aren't meant for us. So we avoid them, thinking we won't understand what we see. But I want each and every one of you to go to a local art museum or gallery. Walk in like you own the place. Drape a pashmina over your shoulders and know that you belong there.

And when you're there, go way, way up close to a painting. Don't worry, you're allowed! Great artists know that the painting changes depending on where you are in relation to it. Your relationships are like that. They are works of art. And you are so used to being all up close and personal, you aren't seeing all the possibilities. Step away from that art. Step away from what is right in front of you and look wide, to people you have forgotten about, relationships that drifted away but may be worth getting back. You know who we want in LillyLou? Everyone. We want every woman to have this possibility. It is unethical *not* to do your best to make this available to the women in your life. You are holding them back by not reaching out. I want to say that again. You are not an imposition. You are holding back the women in your life if you don't call them up to talk about this huge door they could walk through, this new life they could live. Maybe you think you don't have anything in common with that former friend, that woman you used to date, that person you went to college with or worked your first job alongside. But you know what you do have in common? The desire for more. I guarantee those women want more too. And you are the Path to More. LillyLou is the Path to More. You have the map. Surprise them. Surprise yourself. Remake those old forgotten connections. Build them stronger this time. Rewrite the map, draw new paths, find new routes, new places to stop. Isn't that what it's all about, ladies? Relationships. Friendship. Empowering each other. Building something beautiful together. Finding a new way."

Whenever Ivy Miller finished a speech, she pursed her lips and shifted her weight to her heels, waiting for something—applause, maybe; adoration, definitely.

She got both from the live audience and even from those watching from home. Sydney watched the speech three times in bed next to Sam, her hand resting on her chest like she needed to monitor the beats of her heart to decide what to do. By the end of the third time, Sam was asleep, the novel still open next to him. Meanwhile Sydney was more awake than ever, sure that Ivy Miller was speaking directly to her. Commanding her to reach out to Mae, that essential bit of her past. What if reconnecting with Mae was part of her path forward? What if there was a piecing back together that could happen now that time had passed and Beth Ann and Barrett and Graham had all settled into new lives, far away from those backyard cookouts and beach vacations and basement playdates and secret moments together that were destined to un-secret themselves.

It was so simple, actually. Mae and the map they needed to reconfigure together.

If—when!—Sydney finally got to meet Ivy Miller face-to-face, maybe she'd tell her about Mae and about this moment, this decision, right here. The bills in the drawer. The sweat behind her neck, the unsold pashminas in the corner. Sam snoring and the heat of her laptop on her belly and the battling back of a craving for saltines dipped in ice cream. The unshakable quality of the memory of that Memorial Day weekend and then, later, the graduation party, and everything in between and after.

Maybe she'd mark it as the moment that changed everything, a moment when the Path to More became clearer, easier to traverse. The longer she sat with the thought, the more obvious it became that Mae was the key to something. That resolving this bit of the past would be enough to settle Sydney into her new life. The one with the baby and the business and the doting husband and the not having to worry anymore about the possibility of things falling apart. Ivy Miller talked about the past as both an obstacle and a bit of hope, and Mae was both. Mae was certainly both.

Sydney had Mae's email address and phone number, remnants from their time together, and she assumed they hadn't changed in the intervening years. Why would they? The email wasn't hooked up to a job, the phone number was a coveted 917 area code, and Sydney knew Mae would never leave the city.

She imagined Mae was trying to do her mother proud by living some life of café-dwelling and Belgian fries–eating and gallery-hopping beauty. She probably had a margarita at a hole-in-the-wall bar every Friday, as Joni had once described to them when they were sixteen and interested in things like the taste of tequila and the dark corners of Manhattan bars.

Joni had made Mae promise in a hundred different ways to move to New York. She spoke constantly of her longing for the endless pavement, the cramped apartments, the potted plants gathered on stoops, the way neighbors didn't know your name but would help you bring groceries up the stairs in a pinch, would offer you their spare umbrellas in a downpour, their arms reaching out through first-floor windows, their faces not even looking your way, just *Here, take this, you need it*, the way kindness in the city had a logic to it, had no sheen or smile or sweetness. Joni used to talk about the things strangers had done for her with practically religious reverence. "If I looked lost, someone would stop to give me directions without my even asking. If I fell down, tripped, or whatever, someone would lift me back onto my feet without even waiting for a thank-you. If I forgot my wallet and was buying coffee, the person behind me would pay for it but not want to chitchat about it. *I got it, I got it*, they'd say, rushing away, saying without saying, *We will remain strangers forever, but let's get through this mess together. Alone. But together.* It was—it was nothing like here. It was so real. You have to live there, girls. Then never leave. Okay?"

With a grip of heartache, Sydney thought about how the kindness of city strangers might have saved Joni. In New York City, you were never alone in the woods. In New York, you were always surrounded by mothers of children with allergies who certainly would have rushed forward to save a woman in anaphylaxis. In New York, the bees swarmed garbage cans and flowerpots but were otherwise avoidable, uninterested in concrete and cigarettes and oat-milk lattes and the sound strollers made bump-bump-bumping along the sidewalk, calling attention to every crack and divot and poorly paved bit of ground.

Maybe Joni was right. She never should have left.

After Joni's death, Beth Ann had had a few private sessions with Ivy Miller through her connection with HigherLife. She had emerged even more confident about the strength of her marriage, the value of staying with someone for the long haul, the beauty of forgiveness. She booked vacations with Barrett to the Florida Keys and Rome (decidedly *not* to Paris or Peru). Before Joni's death, Beth Ann had been waffling—leave Barrett, move them all to Colorado, open up her marriage, become a preschool teacher. For a time, all such ideas were on the table, and Beth Ann was scattered and spacey, scared and unsettled. Sydney had hated it. Then Joni died and Beth Ann met Ivy Miller, and then she knew how to move forward.

On the anniversary of Joni's death last year, Beth Ann had posted a simple statement on her social media: *Sometimes life gives you what you need in strange packages.*

Sydney asked Instagram to hide the post, hoping to avoid the awful feeling of a secret she shouldn't know, a revelation that would change everything. Sydney did not want to consider Beth Ann's strange contentment with the death of her former best friend.

She did long for her mother's certainty, though. That sudden knowing of what life should look like and the clarity of the steps that could make it come to be. She was desperate to know what wisdom Ivy Miller might bestow upon her.

All of which was to say, Mae was a piece of the puzzle that would eventually lead Sydney to something that felt sturdy. And she had been waiting to feel sturdy for about twenty years. And she was so close. Pregnancy, motherhood, a house in the suburbs, a reunion with her childhood best friend, a thriving business—if she could pile each of those eventualities one on top of the other, didn't they make a life? Didn't they?

Hey, Mae, Sydney began her email, straddling the space between casual and formal—she wanted this to feel intimate but official, the way Ivy Miller described the ideal correspondence. *It's been forever. You've been on my mind as a fellow strong woman who—*

No. Mae would hate that. Someone had called her strong once, their first year in New York, a person who'd just heard about Joni's death, and Mae had rolled her eyes. "Calling someone strong is just another way of saying you're glad you aren't them," she'd said later to Sydney in their living room, which was just a room with a futon Sydney's father had bought them and a coffee table they'd found on the street. "It's such bullshit to call me strong when really I just got dealt a bad hand. Meanwhile, the rest of the world is moving on and I'm stuck. It's like no one else even cared about my mom."

Sydney knew Mae was talking about her father, Graham, who had already started seeing someone. She didn't know that Barrett was hollow-eyed and fragile in the wake of Joni's death. That he called his daughter at odd times, seeming to want to say something that probably Sydney didn't want to hear.

"People cared," Sydney had said; she was about to finally, finally tell Mae about the affair, about broken Barrett, but stopped herself. "I care."

Hey, Mae, Sydney started again. *I think a lot about how you said you were dealt a bad hand, and not strong. And I wonder if your luck could change.*

She was terrible at this, truly.

Hey, Mae, I miss you. I'm pregnant. It's a girl.

Ivy Miller reminded them to always start with humanity. LillyLou, after all, was a circle of humans, a human endeavor. A business too, certainly, but more important, a web of friends, of moms, of women who were on a path together. Ivy Miller loved hiking metaphors. Climbing metaphors. Images of women in the great outdoors, wearing backpacks, handing each other water bottles, knotting ropes and looking at maps and digging holes in the ground to set up tents—the sorts of things Ivy Miller didn't do personally, she'd always say with a laugh and a swing of her salon-dried hair, but wasn't being on the Path to More just like climbing Everest, when you got right down to it? Wasn't it every bit as grueling, really?

Mae. I know we said we weren't going to talk anymore. But now I'm pregnant and I miss you and that doesn't seem quite right, does it?

It wasn't the sort of email Ivy Miller would write or even remotely approve of. There was something too raw about it, too casual and vulnerable and murky. But Mae liked vulnerable and murky; she liked people all laid bare and true.

Sydney sat at the computer, staring at the words. The last time she'd seen Mae was over ten years ago in their old apartment on Second Avenue. The place had had a mouse problem and was covered in traps that only Mae was brave enough to set up. Sydney was scared of slicing off her fingers by accident. Mae had done the mouse disposal as well, Sydney so squeamish she had to go into the bathroom, cover her eyes, turn on the water, and wait until it was done. Even now, the memory of the mouse that she'd stepped on in their dark, dusty kitchen area late one night when she was trying to get a glass of water set off her gag reflex, made her whole body retch.

She wasn't sorry exactly that she couldn't help with the mice, but she was embarrassed that Mae was hardy and durable while she was so delicate and useless. Maybe that was why Mae had moved out. Maybe she was tired of doing things like killing mice and calling plumbers and getting Sydney drunk enough to be able to flirt with the cute bartender down the street that Sydney was in love with—if love was the same as wanting, if love was the same as sitting on a stool sticky with soda and vodka and beer and wishing the handsomest person in the room would look her way. If love was the same as giving him a blow job in the bathroom, then wondering what it meant and not knowing for months upon months that it meant exactly nothing, just like every other blow job in every other bathroom before it.

But of course, none of that was the reason Mae moved out.

Remember the mice? Sydney added to the email. *I should have helped with the mice. I'm stronger now, Mae. I swear I am.*

Now that she was on a roll, Sydney didn't want to stop. She wanted to write an entire novel about the way things were and who she was today and what it all meant, and she wanted Mae to write a novel in return, a deep unpacking of their friendship, their families, and that ending, that awful ending, the day with the curtains and the blizzard and Mae's strained face, her tight way of talking, the quick, messy pace at which she gathered her things like even another hour or two with Sydney would be enough to end her.

Can I buy you a coffee? Sydney wrote. Ivy Miller always reminded them to offer something tangible, to be the one hosting the meetup, to put themselves in the leadership role in small ways. *I owe you at least that.*

Sydney wasn't sure if this was true or not. It was possible that she owed her nothing at all—Mae was the one who'd moved out without warning, leaving Sydney to scramble to figure out rent and roommates and mousetraps. It was Mae who ignored calls and texts and emails and who, she'd heard through a mutual friend a year after their falling apart, had slept with the bartender whom Sydney had been so sure she was in love with.

And it was Joni who had started it all, Joni who had been the engine behind the destruction, Joni who had taken something beautiful and made it into something ugly, the way she'd done for a while with her found artwork—finding discarded treasures on the streets, old photographs and paintings from her attic and Beth Ann's basement, and deconstructing them, painting over them, collaging and sculpting and cutting them up and piecing them back together into something unseemly and, at times, scary. Unsettling.

With Joni gone, shouldn't they be able to be friends? Joni couldn't hurt them anymore, Sydney thought, her optimism overly bright, desperate, naive.

Then Sydney felt a shiver of haunting, Joni maybe listening to her thoughts, furious that some part of Sydney was—it was awful to say, to think—glad she was gone. Sydney apologized to the air, to Joni, to any ghost that might be listening, to Mae in case she could somehow hear her ungenerous thoughts.

She put all that aside. Ivy Miller promised that reaching out was always the right thing to do. "Remember, we are helping them. We have the path forward. We have the Path to More. So we do what we have to do to get them to accept this gift. The gift of being in business together. The gift of being on the path together. It's an act of love." Ivy Miller had gestured broadly to include all of LillyLou and each and every one of them sitting in the auditorium or watching from home later.

"This is an act of love," Sydney said to herself now, a sort of mantra that she needed to hear and believe.

An act of love. Yes.

And an act of hope.

Sydney stalled for only a moment before pressing Send.

NOW

Mae

MAE'S BELLY WAS starting to blossom. She was five months along, and finally, occasionally, strangers asked when she was due or offered her a seat on the train.

"You don't look pregnant," Georgie said over pasta and garlic bread. They were in Mae's apartment, as usual, twirling the last few strands of spaghetti, dipping the bread into the remnants of the thick, creamy sauce, both of them holding on to these nights as long as possible, knowing they weren't the sorts of things that lasted forever. They were thirty-three. They knew about friendship—how it shifted, how it vanished, how the exact dimensions of it changed over time, sometimes sprawling and intimate, sometimes spare and contained. They were in the glory days, when afternoons curled into nights that sometimes pooled into mornings, Georgie sleeping regularly on Mae's couch, starting the coffee before Mae arose, asking her if she wanted to get croissants or scones or just take a walk in the park.

It wouldn't last, not just because this kind of fast and flurrying friendship never did, not in this exact form, but also because of the baby, who would come in and, Mae was sure, change everything.

"That guy. Brendan? Braden? You're seeing him tomorrow?" Mae asked, wanting a sip of the life she'd almost lived before this one here appeared.

"He's divorced. Has kids. I don't know. Not really my thing."

"Yeah. Totally," Mae said, trying to ignore the ache of joints, the swell of stomach, the relentless reminders that were pregnancy.

It felt familiar, this friendship with Georgie, had the same outlines as the time in New York with Sydney. But it was different too, even more precarious, as things are in your thirties.

Mae felt new to adulthood still and hadn't figured out grown-up friendships. The last one she'd seen was Joni and Beth Ann's, which had seemed so stable, so sure, for so long that the ending of it still took her breath away. Beth Ann could order Joni a glass of wine without asking—she wanted a friendship like that. She wanted the books they passed back and forth, the birthday presents they gave—thoughtful and emotional things wrapped in silver and gold paper: A photo album of their families. A monogrammed journal. A mug in Joni's exact favorite color, a scarf in Beth Ann's.

There was still a gripping in her chest when she considered the tight look on Beth Ann's face at the funeral. She hadn't given Mae a hug. She'd left immediately after the service, as if there were somewhere else more important she needed to be.

Barrett had hung on for hours, sitting on the window seat in their living room, eating piles of casserole and watching Mae with an intensity she still couldn't shake.

If she and Georgie got closer, Mae would tell her all of it. Finally, a place to unpack and detangle the knotted mess of it all.

A person who would listen to the story of the things that happened and maybe, somehow, help her finally make sense of it.

Not yet, though. They weren't there yet.

"Well, if you're not gonna meet up with him, you and I should go out," Mae said. She heard a desperate edge to her voice.

"I'll probably meet him," Georgie said, either not hearing or ignoring the wanting. "I can't write off absolutely everyone."

"Sure you can." Maybe the problem was marriage, not friendship, Mae thought. If Joni and Beth Ann hadn't had their husbands to contend with, maybe their friendship would have survived.

Maybe, she thought, the same gripping in her chest tightening, then releasing, Joni herself would have survived.

Georgie looked at her phone without replying, so Mae mirrored her, hoping that maybe Leo might have reached out. She wasn't sure what she wanted from him, but she wanted more than the absolute silence she'd experienced since telling him about the baby.

She opened her email, that flutter of hope annoyingly alive and well in her throat.

"Oh, shit," she said.

"Everything okay?" Georgie wasn't asking with much interest. Mae got alarmed by small things—her favorite restaurant announcing a new special, her father going in for dental surgery, a previously lost item suddenly turning up. Georgie had learned to take a beat before giving much thought to Mae's emotional responses to the world around them.

"I mean, *shit*. Shit. Seriously, what the fuck. Fuck."

"Okay, all right, you have me intrigued. What's up?"

"Sydney Sullivan. Jesus. I can't even open it."

"Sydney Sullivan?"

"Yeah." Mae didn't explain. She said the name like Georgie had heard it a hundred times, which she hadn't. It wore on Georgie, the way Mae was trying hard to make their friendship something bigger than it necessarily needed to be. She'd noticed that she sometimes waited to reply to Mae's texts. That she wasn't always that excited to come over. That she was already looking around Mae's apartment like it was a place she used to go. "God, I haven't heard from her in years and years and years. She was my best friend growing up. Her mom and my mom were best friends too. It was a whole thing."

"Oh. Okay." Georgie wasn't sure what to say or how much to care. Mae had mentioned things here and there. She knew Mae's mother had died, tragically and suddenly, in some kind of accident. But mostly they didn't talk about the past. Or the future. It was a relationship of right now.

"Read it for me?" Mae said, as if it were a question she shouldn't even have to ask. "Please? Sydney and I aren't friends anymore, obviously after everything, and I sort of can't do it myself."

"Something happened with you guys?"

"I left when we were living together, that whole thing, you know."

Georgie did not know. "Give me the phone," she said anyway because maybe the email would let her in on what she needed to understand.

Mae handed it over and Georgie read.

"Okay. It says, 'Mae. I know' —"

"Nope. Nope. Just summarize. I can't hear it word for word like that. It sounds too much like her."

"I read three words. The whole thing is like three sentences, I promise."

"No. It's just way too real. I mean, to start an email with the words *Mae, I know*. What is that? That makes no sense. I can't listen to that."

"Okay. All right, let's see. Basically, she's pregnant and she wants to buy you a coffee." Georgie didn't mention the mice, mostly because she didn't know what it meant and therefore what it would drum up in Mae.

"What?"

"Yeah, that's what it says." Georgie put down the phone. Poured more wine. Just a little.

"She's pregnant?"

"That's what this says."

"But I'm pregnant," Mae said, the two timelines impossibly colliding in her head. She was flushed, sweating a little. Her hand found its way to her stomach, like Sydney's pregnancy was a challenge to her own and now she had to protect hers.

"Yep."

"We're both pregnant." Mae grabbed the table, trying to stabilize herself. "What are the chances? I mean, that's a lot."

"Is it?" Georgie was getting tired. There had been many late nights at Mae's, and Georgie was missing the way she could see the sunset from her own bedroom. Mae moved closer to her on the couch, and Georgie tried to move her body the slightest bit away.

"She was like a sister," Mae said.

"You should see her. That would probably be—"

"And then we moved here together. And then—I don't know. We weren't meant to be. We were really, I think, just friends because of proximity. Because our moms were bored. Not because of anything particularly real. None of it was real. Maybe our moms were real? Mine was. Very real. Too real, sometimes. But also perfect? And for a while, we all were. Perfect. I mean, fuck, that's how it is, right? Something beautiful turning ugly? Always?"

All around Mae's apartment were beginnings of paintings, sketches, little notes written on receipts, on ripped-open envelopes, sometimes even on her own skin. The painting of the sisters that Georgie had always loved had been taken down and replaced by half-painted canvases in blues and greens that Mae then attacked with orange and gray. Figures of men, children, mothers, that started off one way before devolving into chaos. Georgie didn't know enough about art to have any idea what other people would think, but they made her anxious.

"Something beautiful turning ugly," Georgie repeated, agreeing somewhat. "Sometimes things stop making sense. Sometimes they're not what you thought they were."

She wanted Mae to hear something underneath the words — their incompatibility, maybe. The fact that Mae could try and try and try to make them into something but it didn't mean they would actually become that thing. Georgie wondered if this was how Mae always was, and Mae's art answered that, yes, she was always this way.

"You should meet up with her," Georgie said. "The email is nice. Familiar. Or intimate, I guess. She sounds like she knows you. And that's nice, isn't it? To be known?"

"That's the whole point," Mae said, suddenly looking Georgie square in the face. "That's all I've ever wanted. To be known in that real way. But Sydney — I mean, fuck. With you — I know you get me. You don't keep secrets. This is real. We're real. You know? We're in the same moment, together."

Georgie swallowed. Surely Mae knew that Georgie wasn't actually her best friend. Not in the forever way. And certainly not when it came to the baby and the messy, weepy sort of life Mae was about to be living. She hadn't said that to Mae, of course, but maybe this was good, maybe this was a way to hand Mae over to someone else, someone more suited to what her life was going to become.

"We're actually in sort of different moments—" Georgie tried, gesturing vaguely at Mae's belly. She thought of that day in the coffee shop when Leo was moving out. It had seemed then like they would be close. She would have liked that. But this was good too.

Mae's baby would be cute, probably, and smart. And Georgie would wave at them on the street before meeting up with a date, and that was how it was meant to be.

"You don't get it. She's—she's annoying. She's very rigid and she wanted me to be something or us to be something—she practically forced her way here. I was coming by myself and she just, like, grabbed a ride, made it all about her, it's complicated. She thought she knew everything about everything, but she doesn't, you know? She didn't."

Kids would suit Mae well, Georgie thought. They were all chaos all the time and Mae seemed to like chaos, was able to turn everything—a dresser, an email, probably even this pasta they were eating right now—into complication and mess. Mae would be able to live her fully drama-filled life, every moment more stressful than the next, what with nipple confusion and sleep training and tantrums in the playground and the seemingly fraught and fragile relationships of moms with babies the same age whom Georgie was always seeing in the park, tensely offering advice that sounded more like pale, tepid judgment to her ears.

Mae would be just fine without her.

And Georgie—well, Georgie could get back to the bedroom sunsets and the ease of not being Mae's best friend, the ease of just being oneself and not a person populating someone else's orbit.

"You need a mom friend," Georgie said. "Not that I know anything, but you see them, right? At the park? At happy hours down the street? They travel together with those backpack things around their fronts that they store their kids in, and they look all tired and they say really nice things to each other. They're all *You're so strong, you're doing so great*, and you need that. It's annoying from the outside, but I bet it's nice when you're in it. And I can't—I mean, no offense. I don't want to go to a bar at four in the afternoon and watch you breastfeed. I don't know how to tell if you're doing a good job."

Georgie hadn't even meant to broach the subject, but things came up, and they whooshed out, this Sydney Sullivan suddenly feeling like an exit, a path out of a friendship that was already turning into something bigger than Georgie had intended.

"You need support. This whole special kind that I don't—Don't get me wrong, I love this, Mae. Spaghetti and wine and everything. And I can come over and bring you a coffee and hold the baby so you can pee and maybe order takeout after she goes to bed sometimes, but I'm not—this isn't—"

It wasn't coming out right. Georgie knew it wasn't. She was trying to do something kind, make sure Mae knew what was coming, what would change when the baby arrived. Georgie didn't want it to be a shock that she wasn't going to stop by every day with a croissant and a smile and an endless amount of energy to hear about sleep training. "You're going to do the mom thing, and I don't really want to do the mom thing," Georgie said, knowing as it came out that it would hurt.

The energy in the room shifted, the way those paintings of Mae's turned from literal and understandable to erratic, desperate.

Mae looked around like there was something tangible that had made this happen. Her gaze finally settled on Georgie. She got the sense that she'd missed a moment, again. She'd missed signs that things were going awry, that the perfect construction of this friendship with Georgie had soured without her knowing. She hated this feeling—everyone else noticing a shakiness, an unstable foundation, when she was too lost in something else to know the world was turning, the universe shifting.

She wished she'd known the last time she, Sydney, Beth Ann, and Joni would eat waffles and whipped cream at Beth Ann's counter.

She wished she'd known things were ending, wished she'd known, honestly, that things *could* end.

The same with Leo. She would have liked to know, sitting across from him at the coffee shop, that he was sending messages to other girls, that he was entertaining other versions of his life while she was so busy constructing the version where they ended up happily ever after.

She was suddenly breathless at how many other people's decisions had conspired to get her here. Joni's and Beth Ann's and Barrett's, Sydney's and Leo's, even the critics' for the *Times*, the buyers' at the galleries. Even this baby, this impossible baby, was making decisions without her—what she would eat and what shape her body would take and how she felt in the morning and, apparently, who she was going to be.

Here she was, Mae Dyer, who was supposed to be strong and brilliant and talented and special but who was instead just a person always caught in the whirlwind of everyone else's whims. Trying to make art about it all like some idiot, as if paint on a canvas mattered when it was up against the force of the choices of the people around her.

No, she wouldn't be caught in that this time. There would not be a complicated oil-covered canvas of Georgie's awkward, sorry face. This was the last time Georgie would come over for pasta. Mae was not going to miss the moment, get left behind again. She did not need another mystery to spend the years unwinding.

"It's fine," Mae said. It was a tight, sharp smack of a sentence. "You should go, anyway. I've got this."

"She sounds nice, this Sydney person, and you guys are in the same boat so—"

"I've got this," Mae said again, getting up to clear their plates, snatching the bottle of wine off the table like an extra dose of punishment. "I'm gonna be some mom, and that's it, that's the whole of my life. I've made my decisions, and now I'm on this one tiny track where I can do that and be that and that's it. This is it." Mae's eyes were welling, her hand flinging itself around as if to direct Georgie's attention to her failings — the size of the apartment, the unfinished art strewn around, the overcooked pasta, the red-wine ring on the coffee table, her own body not even her own anymore, decisions made without feeling like she'd made them, as if motherhood were a gigantic domino effect, and fuck, you know, maybe it was.

She thought of Joni, ill-fitting in Sommersette, going to holiday concerts and talking to parents at soccer practice, buying jumbo Milky Ways for Halloween, out of place even in art class, where she should have thrived. Then going to the woods when she never went to those woods behind the house and the bees finding her, attacking her, and the one thing that she needed, her EpiPen that she always had with her, somehow missing, tucked into a black-and-white-striped purse that was a size Joni never used, too small to fit much of anything, lacking function, lacking the promise of a well-lived life. Joni liked enormous tote bags that could fit sudden purchases of acrylics, records, crocheted vests, croissants.

But none of it mattered; life happened to Joni, happened *at* her, really. All the way until the end.

Beth Ann and Sydney could believe what they wanted about the things Joni did or did not do, but Mae knew a bigger truth, which was that her father had brought Joni somewhere all wrong and then been surprised when she felt all wrong in it.

And now it was Mae's turn to have ended up in the wrong life. Without Joni here to help her make sense of it, to tell her how to fix it, to commiserate on the way it comes at you, like a wave, appearing one way in the distance but violent and salty and always unexpected in its force when it finally reaches you.

She missed Joni harder than she had in years, suddenly. Needing her here, knowing she was the person who would understand all of it.

"You should go," she said to Georgie, who was not that person at all, who was nothing like Joni, really.

"Thanks for the pasta," Georgie said. She looked, Mae thought, relieved. She wanted to walk away.

Which is what she did, quickly and without saying goodbye.

In the blank space of Georgie having left, Mae sat on the couch and did not turn on the TV. She laid one hand on her belly and the other gripped her phone. She pushed on whatever it was she was feeling in the absence of Georgie, wondering, idly and then deliberately, if it was how Sydney felt when Mae had left, years ago.

Back then, she'd shut the door behind her, leaving plates and scarves and half-used bottles of shampoo and body wash and hair spray, forgetting that Sydney would have to decide what to do with all those abandoned objects, some perhaps laid out on the street for strangers to pick up, some maybe still residing in Sydney's cupboards or drawers.

Mae wondered for the thousandth time what it would have been like if Sydney had told her about the affair when they were kids, years before it came to light, before it took apart her parents, before it shifted her whole world. Would her telling of the truth have been direct? Gentle? Would they have tried to solve it together somehow? Would they have told Beth Ann? Would Mae have confronted Joni? Would Mae, and Sydney too, be somewhere better now, somewhere more powerful or steady or—even just normal?

Would Joni be alive?

That question was the one that always floated to the surface, unanswerable and awful.

And impossible to know, because instead of Sydney telling Mae when she was eleven, she let it out when they were twenty-two and Joni was already gone and there was nothing to be done about any of it.

Fifteen years after Joni's death, Mae missed knowing people who'd known Joni. Her father was unwilling to talk about her, to talk about anything real, aside from the one time he'd mentioned how he wished they'd had more kids so that Mae could have a sibling to help her through, in his words, *all of this*, which she supposed meant the loss of her mother and breakdown of the life she thought they'd lived.

Mae asked why they hadn't had more kids, and he'd shaken his head and shrugged, said something about trying and it not working, and then Catherine had shushed him, muttering, "Not now, Graham," like there was more to say but it needed to be said in its own perfect moment.

There seemed to always be more to say, and those perfect times to say it never manifested.

Mae sat on the couch for a long time, considering the scraps of Georgie scattered around—sunglasses she'd left on the kitchen counter, two books Mae had borrowed but were still unread on the TV stand, a red circle on the table from the wineglass, something that would be hard to rub off, even the smell of her still in the air—peaches and sweat and tannins.

Broken relationships that were supposed to have been forever were everywhere, really, weren't they?

Mae wore Joni's wedding band on a chain around her neck, after all. A holding-on to Joni herself and even the lie of what they'd lived. The hope that maybe it hadn't been a lie, not all of it. That some of it was true.

How long, Mae wondered, had the old apartment with Sydney held on to Mae's scent?

How long after Joni and Beth Ann fell apart did Joni hang on to Beth Ann's old sweaters? Did Beth Ann ever give Joni back her Crock-Pot?

Was there a sign of Mae anywhere in Leo's place? A sock? A handmade valentine from back when she did that sort of thing?

She hoped so.

The questions made Mae sad in a new and uncomfortable and deeply lonely way.

And in that cloud of loneliness and sadness and wishing for the whole of her life to have been different, right then, for the first time ever, the baby kicked.

THE PAINTING

SHE HAD BEEN taking a semester-long course on the *Mona Lisa* when she'd started working on the girls' expressions, and that portrait filtered through onto the canvas. She painted both girls with the enigmatic almost-smiles of people who knew something no one else did, expressions that could be projected upon, faces that the viewers could make what they wanted of.

But the result angered Mae, ultimately. *Fuck them for thinking they get to decide what it all means*, she thought. She had been working on the Painting for months, and the girls were looking more and more like herself and Sydney. It had been three years since she'd left the apartment and Sydney and that whole friendship behind, but still it kept popping up.

Mae tried the faces again.

In the next version, the girls were rageful, taking on exactly what Mae was feeling. They looked like they were in some sort of argument about maybe the shade of the sky or the wildness of the waves or nothing, really, just the anger of having spent too much time together, of needing a break, of being alone on a beach with just each other.

But that wasn't right either.

Mae tried something more tense. The brunette looking away, the blonde looking at her, wanting something from her that she wasn't going to get. Yes, this was closer. Mae made the blonde's hair messy, like her own, windswept, and let the features on the girls' faces be plain and the tiniest bit lopsided.

The brunette she made undeniably pretty, the way Sydney had always been, whether she believed it or not. The tiniest upturned nose and high cheekbones and long, dark lashes that strangers stopped her in the street to comment on. They were fun to paint, the lashes—the tiny feathery mess of them a very delicate sort of work that took Mae days to get right. It was the sort of work that was frustrating for its precision, then exuberant once perfected.

Graham saw this version of the Painting on a visit with Catherine and looked astonished. Mae optimistically, stupidly, thought it was an awestruck look of pride.

"I wish you'd let that family go," Graham had said. "Sydney and all of them. It would be healthier, don't you think?"

They never spoke of the Sullivans. Graham had left Sommersette the same month that Mae herself had, as if he had a college orientation to get to as well. He'd tolerated the occasional mention of Sydney when they were living together but seemed relieved when they broke apart, like maybe he'd never have to hear of the Sullivans again.

"That's not Sydney," Mae said, because it wasn't. Sydney had never worn her hair that long, Sydney had never made that particular wistful expression, wistfulness being, Mae thought, a bit too lofty an emotion for Sydney, who tended to operate in the literal and essential rather than the romantic. The girl in this painting was wearing a long, flowing nightgown that looked like a toga or the sort of thing Wendy in *Peter Pan* would wear, not Sydney.

"That time in our lives is over," Graham said, perhaps not hearing Mae. She felt like he often didn't. "Simple as that."

The expression on Graham's face wasn't simple, though. It was the opposite of simple — a furrowed brow and a tight smile and eyes that looked several stops past sad.

Catherine raised her eyebrows like perhaps there was more to be said but it was not her place to say it.

"I know it's over," Mae said. But she didn't call it simple. It wasn't. Every memory of her time with Sydney — picking out their complementary prom dresses; making screwdrivers with Barrett's fancy vodka when their parents were out to dinner; fashioning their dolls' hair into French braids; wondering aloud if Santa Claus was real and determining at last, later than their peers, that he was not; sharing drugstore lipstick; coaching each other through the awkward discomfort of tampon usage; procuring fake IDs to use at dive bars in the city; staying out all night and eating French fries and pancakes at the diner by their apartment; making a list of New Year's resolutions a month before their falling apart, promising to try sushi and go for runs around the neighborhood and kiss at least ten people and get themselves to Europe — all that was marred by the things Sydney had known and the things Mae had not known. It was all — from the blush and blue shades of their dresses all the way to their detailed notes on Venice versus Vienna — a lie.

And if that was all a lie, Mae was not sure where that left her. She missed Sydney and hated her. Her mother was dead and also right here all the time. Mae was an artist but she could paint only one thing.

If she thought too much about any of it, her heart pounded and her ears thrummed and the walls started to close in on her just the littlest, awfullest bit.

"Your mother wouldn't like it either," Graham said; Mae and Catherine responded physically to the sudden mention of Joni, who seemed to haunt every conversation without ever being mentioned.

Catherine whispered some platitudes about art and memory and the color blue and ushered her father out of the apartment before another word could be exchanged between them.

As soon as they left, Mae got to work again on their clothing, deciding that the brunette's outfit should be more Wendy than Greek goddess, liking the oversize, awkward feel of the choice. She painted the blonde in a plaid pajama set, the sort of thing a middle-aged dad might wear on Christmas morning if he was in the holiday spirit. She painted the sleeves long, the pants bunching up around her ankles, the top three buttons undone showing the very edge of a neon-yellow bra, just like the kind she and Sydney spent their babysitting money on at Victoria's Secret, as if an overloud bra would somehow beckon one of their crushes to reach up and under it, as if a certain kind of lacy undergarment was a promise that it would soon be taken off.

Around the brunette's neck she painted a string of pearls and three chunky pieces of statement jewelry, maybe borrowed from a mother's collection.

Mae vowed to hide this painting away the next time Catherine and Graham came to visit.

But they didn't come again for a long time; New York City was suddenly somehow too far from the farm, too long a trip. Mae herself no longer worth the effort.

THEN

IT WAS OBVIOUS that it would be Joni who would take them. Beth Ann couldn't tolerate the smell of weed, the squish of bodies navigating the patchy lawn, the stumble-fall of college kids getting too drunk and crashing into each other or the ground, the distinct possibility of witnessing someone with a hand down someone else's pants, searching for the thrill of chaotic closeness.

Barrett and Graham, meanwhile, weren't up for things like concerts, especially not the ones the girls wanted to go to—Avril Lavigne and Pink and Maroon 5 and anyone else whose songs were both popular and pointed, lyrics about longing and not fitting in and falling in love in the bighearted, impossible way one does at thirteen and sixteen and twenty-one and also, even though no one had ever told Joni such a thing, as an adult, a married one who was supposed to know better but somehow, somehow didn't.

Still, Beth Ann hated how casually Barrett offered Joni up for the event. "Let Joni do it," he'd said when the girls begged and the parents were pushing the uneaten bits of dinner around on their plates, finishing the last few sips of wine, lingering in a moment that was at once common and strange, at least to Beth Ann, now that she'd seen what she'd seen, knew what she was pretty sure she knew. "Joni will actually have fun. She's basically still a teenager herself."

"Am I?" Joni asked, and it sounded newly flirtatious to Beth Ann. She kept looking at her friend for confirmation of what she had pieced together over Memorial Day weekend. Surely the plan was to eventually tell her, wasn't it? Surely Barrett and Joni were waiting for the perfect time, and in every second of every day, Beth Ann wondered if this was it, if this was the moment when she'd have to decide what to do about everything.

"You know how to have fun," Barrett said, leaving in the air the awful truth that Beth Ann did not.

"I don't want you to miss out, Beth Ann," Joni said. "First concert. Sort of a big deal. We can go together."

"No!" Beth Ann said too quickly and loudly, so she tried it softer, slower, but still the same "No."

Graham's fork scraped across his plate, and upstairs the girls sang along to something desperate and wanting. Barrett put his hand on the back of Beth Ann's chair and Joni poured a little more wine in each woman's cup, winking at Beth Ann conspiratorially, the truth that didn't need to be said: *We deserve this more than they do.*

It was a perfect, ordinary moment of which they had had approximately a thousand, but it was all marred now by the unmistakable vibrations between her husband and her best friend. She wanted to press Pause right here, where she could pretend not to know, where she could pretend this was still her life—easy and sweet and built on the simple way that Joni and Beth Ann could be together, judging and not judging each other's children, parenting choices, newly wrinkled foreheads, forever-postpartum bodies.

She looked at Graham to see if there was knowing written on his face, in his hunched shoulders. It was hard to tell. He was looking at his watch, was tapping his fork against the table, was as quiet and distant as ever. Beth Ann felt, for a moment, a wave of rage at *him*, for not being charismatic enough for Joni, for not trying hard enough, for not keeping her occupied. He was so often lost in his own thoughts, so rarely fully present at any time, not Christmas Eve parties or kindergarten graduations or even the ordinary moments of joy that parenthood promised and, on occasion, delivered. Maybe this was Graham's fault for not clapping hard enough at the ballet recitals, for not staying long enough in the pool on vacation, for not exchanging those secret glances with Joni when their kid did something mundane and spectacular and perfect.

She hated Graham for a hot, furious second.

But it was only a distraction from the rest of it, and not a very successful one. Graham was too bland to hate. And her rendering of him wasn't right, wasn't how it had always been. For years, he had been the one to play tag at the playground, the one to tell jokes that made the girls bend and bellow with laughter, the one who sat on the ground helping construct a castle out of cardboard, out of blocks, out of couch cushions. She recalled how he'd been that first Nantucket summer, gamely holding the girls' buckets, chasing them in the waves, building those same castles, always castles, out of sand. Beth Ann tried to determine when exactly he had started to check out a bit, when he'd gotten off the floor and never returned.

Her heart pounded with that new question and she begged her mind to stop wondering when it all began, what things Barrett said to Joni in bed, the color of Joni's bras, the meter of her voice when she spoke to him. Did they talk on the phone? Did they meet at hotels? Did they share secrets about Beth Ann herself, each of them knowing a slightly different side of her? Did they talk about the girls in the never-ending, drowning way that she and Barrett and she and Joni did, the nuances of Sydney and Mae's friendships and bad moods and hobbies and shared and unshared dreams always begging to be discussed, dissected, worried over.

Graham, Joni, and Barrett moved the conversation on to politics and books and the terror of having an almost-high-schooler. On their plates, things cooled, congealed, became inedible when minutes before they had been delicious or, if not delicious, at least satisfying.

Beth Ann gripped the edge of her chair.

She didn't want anything to change.

Maybe, she thought, she could pretend not to know.

Maybe, if she tried very, very hard, she could have it not matter.

Then Joni's laugh rang out and Barrett's clamored behind it, and her heart broke and broke and broke. This beautiful thing—they had risked it all. And for what?

She looked back and forth between them. Eyes alight. Torsos leaning forward, hands ecstatic in conversation. Truly, for what?

"You take them," Beth Ann said to Joni. "They'll have fun with you."

"We'd have fun together," Joni said. Beth Ann looked for the breaks in the words, the clues in her tone.

"I'm not sure we would," Beth Ann said. Joni either did not notice or chose to ignore the bite of the words.

And so it went, with Joni being the fun concertgoing mom, and Beth Ann staying home. She bought three self-help books and made a vision board. She tried a mantra. She considered church. She watched Barrett watch the news. She wondered about divorce. She hoped the girls were having fun. She missed the friendship with Joni that was somehow both totally available and completely gone. The flatness of her marriage felt even flatter now without the brilliance of that friendship filling it out.

But she would say nothing, Beth Ann thought. For the kids. For the girls. She would give up everything, for them.

* * *

Down the street, Joni knew nothing about Beth Ann's new understanding of their world. And maybe that was unfair too, another secret being kept. Its own sort of betrayal. At least, that's how Joni would view it eventually, when she needed to be a victim as well.

"What should we wear, girls?" Joni asked Sydney and Mae. She opened her closet and pulled out options for herself and the girls—bits and pieces of things she used to wear to bars when she was trying to pick up cute guys, Halloween costumes she'd hung on to because of the way they made her feel, and attempts at homemade dresses and tank tops and headbands—things that were lopsided and poorly stitched and missing a zipper here or a button there or any sort of hem but were still, in their own ways, beautiful.

"I'm good," Sydney said. She picked up and put down a leather halter top, a beaded lavender dress, a pair of denim cutoffs with white strings hanging off them like icicles from the roof in winter.

"Don't be boring," Mae said. She pulled on a tube dress, red with white polka dots, and admired herself in the mirror. Her body was just beginning to fill out—her legs and arms still wiry and breakable-looking, but the rest of her body starting to push out and over, shifting the space between herself and Sydney in delicate ways. She was twelve, which was early, or at least it was to Joni and Beth Ann, who monitored the girls' bodies as if they were bombs ready to go off, as if they were weather, storms coming, blizzards or hurricanes that would change the terrain of the world they lived in, things that required devout attention and concern.

"I don't even like Avril Lavigne," Sydney said. "You should ask someone else. Eleanor. Dana. Julia. I mean, it doesn't matter who. Someone that will like it."

"That's stupid, you love Avril," Mae said. "Plus it's our first concert, so it's, like, irrelevant how you feel about her, it's about the experience. Right, Mom?"

"Right," Joni said. "This is a moment, Syd. Let's not miss any moments, right?"

"Yeah, let's not miss moments," Mae echoed. Other girls were starting to roll their eyes at the things their moms said. Sydney, for one, often cringed at simply the sound of her mother's voice, all high and whiny and searching for the right words. But Mae was doing practically the opposite. She'd stick out her hip the way Joni did; she let her hair air-dry in the sun, hoping it would curl in the same places as Joni's, make the same pattern of baby-blond hairs weaving through the light brown strands. She liked shopping with Joni, painting with Joni, even cuddling on the couch with Joni, her head on her lap like she was six and not twelve at all.

Sydney was either jealous or disgusted; it was hard, honestly, to figure out which.

"I'm fine in what I'm wearing, then. I don't need a whole costume change," Sydney insisted. She was in flared jeans and a pink T-shirt, nothing special but nothing embarrassing either, a perfectly acceptable outfit for a concert. No one said it was mandatory that a person wear floral peasant blouses and tight silver tube tops and five layers of necklaces to listen to live music.

Joni wasn't hearing it, though. She draped a scarf around Sydney's neck, the sort of ornamental thing that doesn't keep anyone warm, that's more of a necktie than a scarf, soft and semi-sheer and super-skinny. She picked out a neon-pink crop top and a long paisley skirt for Mae and a white floor-length sundress for herself, dressing it up with dozens of bracelets and rings.

"I said no, thanks," Sydney said, practically tearing the scarf from her neck. "I don't want to look like some hippie freak show to go to a concert. That's your thing." She directed the words to Mae, but they were meant for Joni, and Joni felt them—sharp, angry, a reminder of what Sydney had seen, a proclamation that she wouldn't forget.

"Mae, get yourself dressed, Sydney and I need to get some snacks together."

"Snacks? I'm not three," Sydney said, and this time the words were pointed right at Joni.

"Sydney. Downstairs. Now."

It was usually Beth Ann who spoke sharply to the girls, Beth Ann who lost her temper and shouted, once in a while, *I can't do this anymore!* or *You are making everything impossible!* or *That's ENOUGH, I am DONE.*

When irritated, Joni was quiet and would float away like a ghost who was finished with her haunting, then emerge hours later with a half smile and nothing words: *Well, that was something.* Or *Let's have a new moment.* Or *I needed a big breath.*

But today, now, Joni was fighting a Beth Ann–like outburst, and Sydney could see it in the strain of her neck and the way she pulled her fingers through her hair like it was manual labor. Joni grabbed Sydney's elbow and took her out of the room before she could further protest. Dragged her all the way downstairs, ostensibly to gather bananas and cheese sticks and put messy sandwiches in foil for the drive to the concert, where surely they would be told no outside food was allowed in the venue. It was an obvious cover for something.

Joni was not, in spite of it all, a very good liar.

"Look. You're a kid. You don't get it. But everything is fine. It is," Joni said before a single snack had been put into a single Ziploc baggie. She turned on the water but didn't pull out a glass, just let the faucet run and run on high, an effort to drown out their voices, as if someone were listening in.

"Does my mom know?" Sydney asked. She knew she was supposed to play along with the idea that nothing had happened months before, that all she'd witnessed was her dad checking out a burn on Joni's perfect mouth instead of something else, instead of the intimacy that Sydney knew she'd seen. She didn't feel like pretending. She didn't feel like acting in some play called *Everything Is Still How It Always Was* when she knew things were starting to crumble and rupture and might even explode around her.

The previous night, she'd woken up to her mother yelling at her father about something she'd found in his pocket.

Two nights before that, she'd overheard him on the phone cooing in this awful, whisper-quiet voice about love and some hotel in the city and the way the sheets—

She'd shut out the rest. It was unbearable, the snippets of conversation that she had to hear and remember forever, the words that she had nowhere to put, the things that were happening that she was not allowed to talk about.

Joni paused—waiting, perhaps, to decide whether to go on with the imaginary life she was trying to hang on to or to stand here in the kitchen with her twelve-year-old daughter's best friend, her own best friend's child, and say the truth.

The pause wasn't long. Joni didn't agonize over even the biggest decisions. "Your mom doesn't know. My—Mae's dad doesn't know. No one knows."

Sydney had asked the question but hadn't actually wanted an answer, she realized. She was twelve, her limbs still out of proportion with the rest of her body—a little too long and skinny to fit the rest of her. She hadn't yet figured out how to properly apply eyeliner or what it meant when a boy from school asked if she knew how to give a blow job. She still didn't understand how to put in a tampon, how to get rid of acne, how to get good grades at school without everyone knowing she was getting good grades and calling her a kiss-ass. Sometimes, not often but not never, she played with the dollhouse. Not just decorating it or admiring it, but playing with the dolls, making them speak and walk around their home and have a simple life that looked like her life used to look when it was simple too.

"So, you and my dad are..." She didn't know how to end the sentence. In seventh grade they called it *going out* when two people were in a committed boyfriend-girlfriend situation. They called it *hooking up* when two people were known to make out or feel each other up or do any number of other things at a party where parents were supposed to be in the house but somehow never were. None of the phrases she knew were right for Joni and her dad and whatever it was they were doing.

"We're in love," Joni said. Maybe she hadn't meant to say as much. It hadn't been her plan, certainly, to bring Sydney to the kitchen and talk to her as if they were girlfriends, as if Sydney could help her navigate the affair, as if Sydney could maybe even give her permission to do the things she wanted to do — tell her own husband, run away with Barrett, have a new baby with him after years of trying unsuccessfully with Graham, finally start the life that she'd always imagined.

Sydney's body stilled. Upstairs, Mae was singing along with an old Indigo Girls album, one that Joni had played when Mae was a baby and then had reintroduced to her because she said they were the precursor to everything Mae and Sydney liked to listen to. Mae had taken a liking to a song called "Dead Man's Hill" that she knew the harmony to. The song unsettled Sydney always, but especially now, the tune a haunting one, heavy with nostalgia and something else — the promise of something bad to come, the memory of something bad that had already happened.

Mae had a good voice, rising up above the track itself, and Sydney was dizzy, hot.

"I hate this song," she said. "And maybe my mom doesn't know everything, but she knows something."

"You're not a kid anymore," Joni said, not seeming to hear her, plowing forward now that the damage was done. "I'm being honest because you're not a kid, really, you know?"

"I'm not?" Sydney felt like a kid. She wasn't allowed to stay up past ten and it wasn't like she could drive a car or decide what to eat for dinner or swear in front of her parents.

"You don't need to be protected," Joni said, softer.

"Oh."

"It's better if you're prepared, anyway."

For what? Sydney asked in her brain but not out loud. Joni looked out the window like she was planning something big. The neighborhood was moving along as always: Across the street Mrs. Randall was gardening, sweat slick on her forehead, dirt on her nose. A little kid was trying to ride a bike and falling down or maybe pretending to fall down the way Mae used to do when she and Sydney were learning — she'd always loved to put on a show. Sprinklers were going on and off, cars beeped and revved on other streets, sixteen-year-old beauty Laila Audon was sitting on her front stoop smoking a cigarette for the whole world to see, her mother tucked away inside, maybe drunk or just sad; it was always hard to tell. There were other secrets in Sommersette, and Sydney was only just now starting to see them peek out.

"I'm telling Mae," Sydney said. She'd meant to ask a question — *Have you told Mae?* or possibly *Can I tell Mae?* — but it got warped in her mouth and came out as a statement or maybe even, accidentally, a threat.

"Absolutely not," Joni said. Her head snapped away from the window, the whole of her back in the kitchen again, all the way present and alert.

"But you said we have to be prepared."

"You are not telling my daughter anything," Joni said. They both heard the slap of her tone, and Joni took a breath. Softened. Stepped closer to Sydney and put a hand on her shoulder. Squeezed. "I'll tell her myself when it's time for her to know, and I expect you to keep this between us, Sydney. You've always been — you're like a daughter to me, you're like a beautiful second daughter, and you've always been more... You can handle this. I know you two are the same age, but Mae is so—she's still so unpredictable and emotional, and you're my Sydney. I know you can handle this, and I know you'll be there for Mae when the time comes, and everything's going to be okay. It may be strange for a little bit, but we're all—we're all family, right? And we will keep being family and it may be bumpy but it will be okay. Okay? It's okay, Syd. It's okay. So it's just—it's okay."

Joni was starting to cry. Sydney had seen her cry before, at the end of sad movies and a few times when Mae was upset about a mean thing a boy said to her or a grade she didn't think she deserved. But never like this, never in a swirl of sentences that made no sense, never so hard and fast that she had to use the backs of her wrists to try to keep up with the flow of tears, never when it was just the two of them in a kitchen that could use a good cleaning, never because of Sydney's own dad and her clueless mom and the way their lives were clearly unraveling all around them.

"All that matters is you girls being together, okay? That's what I've worked so hard for, that's what this is all for—you girls. We can't ruin what I built here. We can't." Joni's words scared Sydney for their intensity and their strangeness, the things folded into them, the desperation.

"Okay," Sydney said, which was the exact opposite of how she felt, but she wanted the tears to stop and the conversation to end and the day to go back to being just the day of their first concert. She wanted to go back in time and never have run into the house on that one firefly-lit heady evening, never have seen what she saw. "I won't tell." And this was at least true. She didn't want to hear Mae's rage or worry that Mae might tell Beth Ann or have to sit in the dark with Mae at night, wondering what their parents were up to.

Maybe Joni would change her mind about Sydney's father—she'd notice, perhaps, that he sometimes ate with his mouth open and smelled a little like broccoli in the mornings before he brushed his teeth. She'd see — wouldn't she? — that he always left wet clothes in the washing machine and that he got short with people when he was tired. He'd called Beth Ann a monster once for forgetting that he didn't like parsley on his spaghetti. He rolled his eyes at Sydney when she was upset about something he deemed not that important. He thought she didn't notice but she did, and maybe Joni would too. Then Joni could put him aside, stay forever with sweet, soft, hundreds-of-jokes-about-cats Graham, and nothing would change.

If Sydney told Mae, that meant it was real, it was happening. If she stayed silent, things might rearrange, go back to normal. If she stayed silent, there was still hope.

"You're a good kid," Joni said. "This will all make sense to you someday. Being a grown-up is — it's more complicated than it probably seems. It's not all errands and watching CNN and setting arbitrary rules. You know?"

Sydney of course did not know. She didn't know what it was to be a grown-up or what she was doing here in this kitchen or how she was supposed to feel about Joni, who seemed right now to want a friend.

The conversation ended there, with Joni kissing the top of Sydney's head the way she had when the girls were both younger, when things were easier, when the house wasn't so heavy with body sprays and loud music and questions about boys and bras and birth control and whatever else it was that Sydney and Mae stayed up late discussing.

Hours later, at the concert, Sydney and Mae sang along with "Complicated" at the top of their lungs. Mae had a good voice, clear and on pitch, the sort of voice people would turn around to listen to. "You should be up there," a white woman with long dreadlocks said, a glittery star punctuating one cheekbone, the smell of weed emanating from her, from everyone, really. Mae shrugged and smiled and said thank you like she always did. Her ease with her own talent was always a little stunning to Sydney, who preferred to mouth the words, knowing her own limitations as intimately as she knew the sway of Mae's body, the curl of Joni's hair, the swooping melody of their favorite songs.

"This is the best day of my life," Mae said, breathless, still singing a little, really, still finding a melody even in the pause between songs. She looked at Sydney, waiting for agreement, waiting for the perfect moment she'd envisioned when they'd convinced their mothers to buy them these tickets, when they'd agreed to have Joni chaperone, when they'd wondered what it would be like and how it would feel to see eyelinered Avril in person, to be part of a crowd pulsing and shout-singing and maybe even getting a secondhand high and seeing what the older teenagers looked like when they got all drunk and messy and horny. Mae waited but Sydney said nothing. "Isn't it the best?" Mae asked eventually, the silence of her best friend making her itch, making the wonder of it all pale a little.

"Sydney? Aren't you loving it?" Joni said, inserting herself into the conversation with a little more verve than the situation called for. Her eyes narrowed; all of her narrowed, her body turning into an arrow.

"I am," Sydney said, the words coming out smooshed, something stomped on and then forgotten.

Mae held her hand as the next song's familiar chords started; this one was Sydney's favorite. "'Why should I care,'" Mae sang in her perfect voice, trying to match Avril's tortured tone.

Sydney, still, did not sing along.

Joni squeezed her shoulder, a borrowed affection now turned threatening. A something gone sour, a shift in the atmosphere that only the two of them were privy to.

Joni's shrug at the idea that Sydney was a kid made sense. The thing that had come before, childhood in all its wonder and splendor and silliness and messiness and ease—Mae was still in it, singing so hard her voice would be gone tomorrow, dancing with her shoulders and hips like she was discovering them for the first time. But it felt gone to Sydney. It felt like a place she had lived once but no longer belonged.

She would wait to belong somewhere else.

But the waiting would last. The waiting wouldn't end.

NOW

Sydney

SAM WASN'T THRILLED that Sydney had Small Group on the same night he had a company dinner.

"They expect spouses to be there," Sam said, putting on a tie, changing his mind, putting on a different one.

"I know, but I'm expected to be at Small Group," Sydney said. It always felt a little awkward, saying the phrase out loud. Sydney emphasized the first word *Small*, since there were also big group events—cruises and trips to Napa and conferences in Vegas and a dozen other things that she planned for and looked forward to and insisted she needed in order to maintain the strength of her business.

"This is important, Syd. They're looking at who to move up, who has what it takes. I'm trying to make partner. You know this."

"That's what happens at Small Group too," Sydney said. She was a business owner, whether Sam was willing to understand that or not. And LillyLou was exploding. "LillyLou is exploding," she said, seeing what the sentence in her head sounded like out loud. It sounded professional, the sort of thing those other women probably said on their phones or in their emails.

There were four more enormous boxes of product in their bedroom. They partially blocked the closet, making it hard to open the door properly, see oneself in the full-length mirror. Sam tried to move around them without acknowledging them, but it was awkward. Sydney, Sam, and LillyLou could barely live in this space together.

"Maybe when the baby comes, you'll take a step back from all of this," Sam said. His voice was kind but the words were cutting.

"This is all *for* the baby," Sydney said. Her brain played the greatest hits of the warnings Beth Ann had given over the years: *Be your own person; Don't let a man be in charge of everything; Make your own money; Take advantage of the time you've been born into and what it means to be a woman now.* This last one she always said with a certain strain to her voice, a holding on to the way things were when she was Sydney's age. It was not like Beth Ann had gotten married a hundred years ago or something, but still, she was quick to remind Sydney about how it was a *different time* back then, with different expectations. "You can have more, so take more," Beth Ann said. Sydney had thought it was Beth Ann's own phrase until last night when she heard Ivy Miller say it on a new video that had just been posted. "You can have more, so take more. LillyLou is your way to take more. LillyLou is the manifestation of everything women have been fighting for."

"I like having you there with me," Sam said. It was sweet, but it wasn't enough.

"I want more than that," Sydney said. Lately, the words she spoke felt like pairs of jeans she was trying on. And well-fitting jeans were notoriously impossible to find after you turned thirty. They never seemed to look quite right on Sydney anyway.

She kissed Sam goodbye after taking a photograph of him in his suit, which made him look trim and successful and was the sort of thing she was sure she could find a use for on her account. In yesterday's video, Ivy Miller lectured that one should be prepared at all times, should see potential in the mundane moments. She said that to be successful, you had to post a lot of content and that building up a treasure trove — her words, of course — of photos of life looking beautiful would make it easier to generate connections.

Sydney had scribbled along, furiously taking notes, and right on time, here was a moment just like the ones Ivy Miller had described. Her handsome lawyer husband, even handsomer than usual, standing in a pool of evening light.

Perfect.

Small Group always took place at Genevive Lett's apartment, which was the spare, spacious, modern sort of home that every apartment looked like in listing photos but that no apartment actually lived up to. Except this one somehow did, with its three large bedrooms and kitchen island and always freshly vacuumed light gray rugs.

"You're enormous!" Lake, big-voiced and Botoxed, said upon seeing her, the sort of greeting Sydney hated. For some reason people who kept their lips nice and zipped up on most topics — the gaining or losing of a pants size, the frizziness of hair during a particularly humid summer, the cheap quality of a dress that was meant to look sophisticated — finally let loose on pregnant women, commenting on their body changes as if the mothers-to-be were science experiments and not people anymore. It didn't matter that Sydney was in the third trimester and perfectly within her rights to be enormous and not want attention drawn to it.

"You look nice too," Sydney said, shutting Lake up rather swiftly. She sounded like Beth Ann, her hormones granting her permission to be bitchier than usual settings might allow. Besides, Lake had gotten a gorgeous new haircut and was wearing high, high heels for a casual night in, so she didn't need Sydney or anyone else to be gentle with her. She was winning.

Sydney had heard Lake's sales were good this month, and it was confirmed quickly as the meeting check-in began. Lake was selling left and right; there was probably not a box of unsold product to be seen in her home. "Trying my best to get that one-on-one time with Ivy," Lake said, a smug smile sneaking onto her face. Sydney hated her for calling Ivy Miller just Ivy and hated her even more for how she was inching closer to Sydney's goal than Sydney herself.

"Love your hustle!" Genevive said. Everyone in the room was approximately Sydney's age, give or take five years, so it wasn't age that determined status. Rather, it was the LillyLou hierarchy that ruled the group. Genevive was classified as a Gardener, which was above the members of the garden itself, Sydney and Lake and the rest of them. Sydney was a Violet, striving to be a Rose. Most of the women here, including Lake, were Tulips, a level below Sydney. If Sydney had money to bet, though, she'd put it on Lake being a Gardener soon. A person like Lake could move from Tulip to Violet to Rose to Gardener quickly.

Florist, Beth Ann's level, was above Gardener, and Vase was the final level; only a lucky few ever got that honor, which came with the privilege of being in Small Group with Ivy Miller herself.

Ivy Miller, of course, didn't need a level. She was Ivy Miller.

Sydney had talked Sam through the levels once and watched as his face contorted with concern, then judgment, then outright mocking.

"These make no sense," he'd said, laughing, shaking his head, assuming they were on the same side of this thing. "You know that, right? I mean, I get it, flowers are the, you know, theme or whatever here, but Vase is the highest level? *Vase?*"

"Vases hold flowers," Sydney said. It was the sentence that Ivy Miller had used in the slideshow where she broke it all down, but it didn't sound right coming out of Sydney. "They're, you know, containers." She wasn't going to give up. The concept was beautiful, actually. Sam would see. "So the levels aren't about being better or worse, you know? The higher up you go, the more your job is to support people. Vases support flowers, even the newest ones, the Baby's Breath. They contain them. They show them where they might be most comfortable, where they'd look and feel their best."

"And what are all of us exhausted spouses?" Sam asked. "Water? From the faucet? Just pouring out and out and out, trying to make something grow?"

"Well, yes," Sydney said. She had been waiting to reveal that detail. She loved that water was essential but not showy. It was the perfect metaphor for the support networks of the women of Lilly-Lou, their spouses and friends and family.

"You're serious?" Sam was laughing so hard, he was starting to cry a little.

"It's not funny. How'd you know that anyway? Did you read my materials?"

"No, Syd, I didn't read any of your little pamphlets. I just thought of what the most ridiculous thing would be and guessed that." His laughter paused then. He waited for her to see what he saw.

But instead Sydney got lost in the thought that maybe the worst was happening. Sam looked at her like her own father had looked at her mother. The thought, even the shadowy edge of it, made her a little bit ill. And so she watched Ivy Miller speeches instead of watching TV with Sam at night. She went to Small Group instead of his lawyerly dinners. She created a life that could not be broken by him, just as her mother had instructed her to do.

* * *

Sydney nodded and listened to the reports of her friends—because they *were* friends, or at least on their way to becoming friends. They were other women with interests like her own—Pilates and learning the difference between expensive and cheap wines and reading whatever book about sex or race everyone else was reading and babies, or the wanting of babies, or the trying to figure out the not-wanting of babies.

Holly was considering moving to the suburbs; Adrienne was starting IVF; Elyse's mom was sick and she was worried; Genevive's toddler was in physical therapy for something or other. The life updates were given after the sales reporting, a number spoken quickly but always written down by Genevive, whose job was surely to send it up the line to the Florists and Vases and maybe even, in some cases, to Ivy Miller herself.

"And how about you, Sydney?" Genevive asked. "I mean, aside from the obvious, though we're happy to hear how pregnancy is going, of course. It starts to get hard around now, right? You're thirty-two weeks?"

"About there," Sydney said. She was flustered by Genevive knowing so precisely about her pregnancy, as if she was keeping notes on it, and probably she was. Maybe that was even considered part of her job. There was a pause, everyone waiting for Sydney to fill it with something. "And I feel fine, really. So that's—that's all good. Um. I guess my news this week is that I reached out to someone from my past. An old friend."

Genevive lit up. "Well, that's *wonderful* news!" she said. "Your numbers have been—well, you've been needing to shake things up and take some risks and put yourself out there, and it sounds like you've done exactly that. Who is this connection?"

Sydney tried not to let herself hear the critical part of Genevive's sentence. "Her name is Mae," she said. "We grew up together. We were very close. Our moms were close."

"Oh, her mom's a friend of your mom's! Even better!" Genevive was practically panting. People loved Sydney's mother, or at least pretended to.

"Not exactly, not anymore. I mean, actually, her mother died years ago."

The women nodded, serious. There was an eagerness in the room, always, at the mention of tragedy. Ivy Miller didn't say it crudely, of course, but the difficult parts of life were always, in the opinion of LillyLou, worth sharing. *We want aspiration,* Ivy Miller often said, *but also inspiration. And inspiration is about overcoming. Don't shy away from the things that are painful. They are a part of your story too.*

"That is so tough," Genevive said. "Was she—if you were childhood friends, I bet she was sort of like a second mother to you."

Sydney considered the sentence. Lost her breath at both its accuracy and inaccuracy.

"She was a big part of my life," she said.

"I'd love to hear more about her someday," Genevive said, the words heavy with extra meaning.

"Right. Yes. Maybe I could—she took me to my first concert. Avril Lavigne." The women nodded again, smiling this time, remembering the stick-straight hair, the black eyeliner, the way it felt to wear your angst proudly, like a crown, rather than squirreling it away as a thing to be embarrassed by.

"I bet that's an amazing memory," Genevive said. When she was excited, she lost the art of subtlety. Sydney knew this would hold Genevive back in LillyLou. "You should post about it. Share it. I'd love to see a photo of you all decked out preteen."

Sydney nodded, not committing. "So. Anyway. When Ivy Miller talked about expanding our circle and all of that, yeah, I thought maybe Mae was someone... She's in our demographic. My age. Lives in the city. Single. Probably going to lots of weddings and events and stuff. She's an artist, so—"

"Oh, show her the prints!" Holly interrupted. "Artsy women love the prints!"

"Great point, Holly," Genevive said, her voice turning serious, pointed, ready to give the sort of sage advice she was supposed to give, that her title of Gardener required. "We don't approach every connection the same way, either in our initial contact or in what we show them of our product. Think about what *she* would like, what would fit her lifestyle. You can push her a little out of her comfort zone too, of course, we encourage that as well. But try to *see* her. Okay? Do you want me to come along on your meetup? Do you have a date set? We could all get coffee together. Or something that suits her better. Yoga? Tea?"

Genevive didn't get it at all. Mae knew how to make something boring look interesting; she knew how to fashion clothing into an outfit, how to turn words into a poem, how to make paint into art.

How to make a dollhouse into a masterpiece and then into an object so emotionally charged, it had to get taken away, for a time, by Beth Ann. Locked in a closet so the girls would stop using it to poke at each other.

"I'm waiting for her to respond still," Sydney said, not knowing how to say the rest—that actually selling Mae a gray pashmina, or even a striped one, felt sad. Because of the pashmina or Mae or the memory of their friendship or the things that Joni did to destroy it or that Joni was gone and could never be forgiven or hated properly, she couldn't say. Genevive's chair felt uncomfortable. The cheese plate looked sweaty. The others had opened a bottle of red wine, and their teeth were stained. Just thinking of Mae and how Mae would see the scene turned it all sour and wrong.

"Oh," Genevive said, the room practically filling with the imagined sound of screeching brakes. "Not much of an update, then."

"It's complicated."

"Men are complicated," Genevive said, waving a dismissive hand like Sydney had a whole lot to learn. "Friendship is easy."

Sydney burned with shame. Maybe it wasn't normal to have the sort of explosive and heartbreaking split she'd had from Mae. She hadn't built any close friendships in the intervening decade, despite how many book clubs she'd joined, how much effort she'd put into her group text replies. The rest of these women, in their well-tailored pants and freshly done hair, had real friends. Ones who stood up next to them at their weddings, who came over for coffee some mornings, who took their kids in a pinch, who knew their middle names and everything about the last arguments they'd had with their husbands and what their dreams used to be.

Sydney and Sam had decided not to have a wedding party when they got married, a fact her mother had never quite managed to let go of. "Isn't there *someone* you'd like up there with you? Wouldn't you like a bachelorette party? Something silly with the girls? I'd be happy to contribute some funds to make it special, sweetheart, just say the word," she'd said no fewer than a dozen times in the year of wedding planning. But Sydney couldn't think of a group of women that would make sense for such a thing. A cousin or two. Someone from work. Sam's sisters. A few random friends with whom she shared recipes, book recommendations, texts about *The Bachelor*, but not much more. She invited them to the wedding, sure, and they came, dutifully styled in black cocktail dresses, making small talk with one another, looking, probably, for the other friends, the main ones whom they surely assumed Sydney had.

Beth Ann was sad-eyed about the whole ordeal.

"A woman needs friends," Beth Ann said the morning of Sydney's wedding. "I hope what happened didn't—you need friends. Sam can't be your everything. Friends. Money. A life of your own. Are you listening, Syd?"

"It's my wedding day, Mom. I don't want a lecture. I'm happy."

"Mae was never supposed to be your lifelong friend anyway. You two are so different. Like me and Joni. Just from different worlds. Find friends that are more like you. Like us. Okay?"

Sydney wanted to ask what *like us* meant, was somehow both repulsed and comforted by the idea that she was like her mother. But more than continuing that conversation, she wanted to feel like the platonic ideal of a bride, so she stared at herself in the mirror, and when that didn't work she took a dozen selfies from different angles until she snapped one that fit, that made her look the way she'd hoped she'd look in her head. *There*, she thought. *Perfect.* She posted it with the caption *The happiest day of my life is right now.* This past year, she'd used it again to up business, to get more engagement, to remind people, maybe, that she had a life worth envying. *Five years ago I thought I could never be happier...then I joined LillyLou. Now I have two loves of my life!*

She wondered—while hating herself for wondering—what Mae thought when she saw that post. Mae almost never posted anything. When she did, it was something small and possibly symbolic—a bird flying in a sunsetting sky, a tangle of hair on top of a tilted head, a blurry picture of a man in an armchair sorting through records.

Stranger still was seeing on occasion other people, random ones, post the Painting on their social media with some caption about the way it moved them, what they thought it meant. It wasn't *Starry Night* or anything, but it was a known entity, an image that had taken on a life of its own, away from Mae.

As Sydney thought about it, her stomach dropped.

Emailing Mae had been a mistake. She knew that now. Mae probably had boatloads of friends, the way single girls always do. Famous ones who loved the Painting and idolized Mae. Probably they went on girls' trips to Mexico, shared clothes, spent mornings at dog parks or coffee shops comparing notes on people they'd dated, wondering at the women like Sydney with their swollen bellies, the way they waddled uncomfortably, dreading and celebrating the future with each uncertain step. The last thing Mae would want was an email from Sydney.

And honestly, Sydney didn't want Mae, did she? It had been exhausting protecting Mae, watching Mae be a kid forever while Sydney sank from the weight of adulthood. She had been jealous of Mae long before finding out about Barrett and Joni, of course she had. Mae was spirited and talented and fun in a way that Sydney wasn't. But she was even more envious in their teen years, watching Mae fret over outfit choices and awkward first kisses and failed driving tests and arguments with her dad over the acceptable length of a miniskirt. Mae got the privilege of worrying about those things while Sydney watched their lives crumble, watched as Beth Ann grew skinnier and angrier, as Joni got more brazen, touching Barrett's arm, leg, the back of his neck, when she thought no one was looking. Sydney had to watch it all, waiting to see if it would resolve or explode.

And Mae had had the gall to be mad at her all those years later for holding that responsibility alone.

Sydney should never have emailed her.

The meeting was wrapping up. Genevive passed around some photos of what the new lingerie looked like, told them it would be available to sell next month and that, no, Lake couldn't take preorders, so she'd have to do the delicate work of hanging on to the connections, checking in on them, making promises about the future but not being overbearing. "Strike that perfect tone, that in-between," Genevive said to Lake but also to all of them. "You don't need them. They need you. That's the most important thing. And don't forget that it isn't just selling them things. It's asking them to join us. It's having your own Small Group to run, right? That's the goal?" She raised her eyebrows at Lake, and Sydney knew this would be one of the last times that Lake would be here with the Flowers. Soon she'd have her own people below her to tend to and water and watch blossom.

And Sydney would still be scrambling.

Lake would win the opportunity to meet Ivy Miller. It was as clear as day.

Genevive kissed Sydney's cheek on her way out the door. "You'll figure it out," she said, maybe meaning the baby or Mae specifically, or LillyLou, or just life generally—how to live it, how to enjoy it, how to be a part of it in some perceptibly fuller way.

Sydney nodded in passive agreement and rode the elevator back to the street with Lake, who, even after two glasses of wine, smelled sweet and neutral, freshly soaped and showered, *good*.

"I have to say something," Lake said before the doors opened and the night ended and Sydney could shove away the regret she felt at going to Small Group instead of being one of the prettiest wives at dinner with her husband. At least there, she would have had a role, a place higher up in the stratosphere, a way to be admired and not pitied. "This friend? I mean, give it a shot, sure, but LillyLou isn't about fixing the past, you know? It's about moving forward and showing people the Path to More, and if this Mae person doesn't respond, then she doesn't want that. And there's no room for people who don't want more in their lives, right?"

"Right," Sydney said.

"I just don't want you wasting your time. I've had a few of those old connections that go nowhere. My college roommate? We met up and she said what we were doing was stupid. I mean, she actually said that. She was all smug, you know? She'll see, though. She'll get it when we're in Paris, putting our kids through school with our own money, taking business meetings. She'll get it then. But she doesn't deserve to get it now."

It was a lot of information for Sydney to take in at once. She barely knew Lake, and now she was supposed to understand all these details about who Lake was and what she wanted—fortune and glamour and being admired.

Sydney wanted the other thing. The quiet sureness that everything was going to work out. The knowing herself and the knowing what her life was. She didn't need Paris. Or big business meetings. She wanted simply the glow of Genevive telling her she'd hit great numbers. She wanted to sit across a table from Ivy Miller and be told what she should do next. And then she wanted to do it, simply, easily, confidently.

"Some people don't get it," Lake said. "That's their problem, not ours. But Genevive was right about posting about the loss you endured. The Avril concert, all of it. Losing a mom figure. People can relate to that. Let them in, you know?"

Then the elevator door opened and Lake strode ahead of Sydney, waving goodbye as an afterthought.

Sydney took out her phone to occupy her on the walk home. Flipped to her texts, then the news, then her email in a careless, reflexive way.

And buried beneath emails telling her about sales at J.Crew and her order being shipped from Bloomingdale's and the senator she'd donated to in a rush of political concern was an email from Mae.

I'm pregnant too, it said. *And whatever about the mice. We should meet up. Talk about breast pumps or whatever it is pregnant people talk about.*

Honestly, Syd, I could use a friend.

In spite of everything.

Love, if that's okay,

Mae.

NOW

Mae

MAE DIDN'T GET nervous easily, but she was nervous meeting Sydney. It had felt good all those years ago to simply leave, to make a clean break with the girl who had hid the biggest secrets, lived the biggest lie.

But it had been ten years, and leaving hadn't fixed Mae. Nothing fixed Mae, so she was pinning her hopes on this baby and maybe whatever might shake loose from this unlikeliest of meetings.

Sydney had chosen a small, sterile place on Sixth Avenue in Park Slope, a doable but strenuous walk from both of their homes where they served bagels and carrot bread and subpar coffee in enormous cups and asked people with laptops not to stay longer than forty-five minutes. Leo would have hated it, Mae thought, and Georgie too. She pushed the thought down. Leo and Georgie weren't here.

As soon as Mae sat down, Sydney arrived.

Mae had a moment to take her in before they locked eyes. Something in her churned, hurt, then settled.

"Wow. They're going to be close in age," Mae said when finally their eyes met.

"I'm due on the thirteenth," Sydney said.

"Twenty-eighth," Mae answered, the two of them marveling silently at how their lives could spike away from each other and then, somehow, without warning, fold back together, like they were always meant to be on top of each other in this way. They spoke quickly, trying to move through the mundane to get to something deeper. They lived a neighborhood apart from each other. Sydney was with Sam. Mae was on her own, impregnated by an ex whom she mostly hated, but she was cautiously optimistic because he had finally said that he might like to be involved in some way. Mae was getting her master's at Columbia and starting to paint again.

"Are you working?" Mae asked Sydney.

"I have my own business," Sydney said, trying to straighten her neck, lower her shoulders, embody the type of woman that Ivy Miller was always insisting she was, insisting they all were.

"Oh! Wow. Impressive," Mae said, startled. She'd pictured Sydney's life a hundred times over the years, of course she had, but in her mind, it had always been smaller than Mae's. Now it was Mae's life that felt small and silly, she in her tiny apartment, trying to push out a thesis on women and literature for some unclear purpose—a future job somewhere, she supposed, if jobs like the ones she wanted were even available to single moms who didn't have time to look for them or apply for them or figure out, even, how to move to a new city and start a new life. Paintings and mixed-media works of art sat abandoned in her closet, the biggest article about the Painting framed and hung in her living room, begging to be taken down so that she could forget all the things she had not managed to become.

"I'm fucked when the baby comes, honestly," Mae said because Sydney had known her since she was three and she needed a safe space to say out loud the things that everyone else was saying behind her back.

"Fucked?" Sydney asked, saying the word like she'd never heard it before, a verbal tic that annoyed Mae, who had of course been with her when she'd said it for the first time, when they were six and discovering cursing and trying it out on each other.

"I mean, I'm fine. There's the money from the Painting still. And I can make money, like, tutoring or something. I'm just not exactly all set up to have a baby the way you are, you business-owning married woman!" Mae cleared her throat. She sounded fake even to her own ears.

"What about your art?" Sydney asked. "That article—what did they say? 'Rising star'? 'Sure to take the art world by storm'?"

"They say that stuff all the time about everyone. Then they can feel like they were right as long as one of the people they said it about gets famous, even if the rest of us just, like, wither up and do nothing ever again."

"Oh."

Mae noted that Sydney didn't try to tell her this wasn't true. She let it stand, and it did, hovering over them for a moment before they could move on to something else.

"Maybe I'll be an art teacher," Mae said, shrugging, an idea that had never before occurred to her but suddenly felt sweet, possible, like the sort of thing she was meant for all along. "Like, with little kids. That would be fun. I've done some of that before, but maybe I should do it, like, officially."

Mae watched something happen to Sydney's face then. Sydney clearly wanted to say something but was looking for the words. Mae smiled. It was good, so good, to know someone the way she knew Sydney. There was an ease to it, a predictability. She knew what was happening without having to guess.

"The women who I work with in my business have a really great way of figuring out goals and what's next and making sure you're really living the life you want," Sydney said. Mae watched Sydney's shoulders roll back, her chin jut. She watched Sydney become someone else, a sort of simulation of Beth Ann, maybe, a person who wanted to be more adult than she was. It made Mae remember playing dress-up in Joni's closet when they were little. Joni was fine with them rummaging through old flowery dresses and beat-up leather jackets and worn-out shoes that used to thump around city streets and now just lived in haphazard piles in the back of her closet.

It was a favorite rainy-day activity, making outfits and enacting events at which they would wear such outfits. A blazer over a shiny cocktail dress from some bachelorette weekend that Joni giggled when talking about. The girls imagined themselves wearing it to their veterinary office or the opening night of their Broadway debut. A long pink ruffled dress with panels upon panels of fabric that Joni used to wear while pregnant was, on Sydney's slight frame, a ball gown for an event at a castle in England where princes chose brides. Leather pants and a fuzzy sweater became an outfit for going out to brunch with the girls, a favorite imagined setting that the girls liked to act out, with plastic waffles and Sydney's tea set and Joni or Beth Ann recruited to play waitress.

And right now, Sydney looked not unlike that six-year-old in leather pants that dragged over her feet and fell down to expose princess underwear and skinny legs. Trying to be someone she could never really be. It struck Mae that Sydney knew how to keep secrets — big ones for long years — and that it would be impossible to know the actual size and shape of Sydney's life just from the words she was now saying. Sydney had resculpted Mae's own childhood. She was certainly capable of crafting a not entirely true version of her own adulthood.

It also struck Mae that they had jumped right into the now of things, eschewing (permanently? temporarily?) their complicated past. Joni would never have let them move forward so swiftly. Would not like this moment at all, probably.

"The group is almost all moms," Sydney went on. "Or, you know, like us, expecting moms. It's people whose lives maybe feel sort of constricted in some way, and it's really about opening up instead of shutting down, you know?"

Mae did not know.

"Being empowered. That's the big thing. Opening yourself up to more." Sydney's mouth seemed to work hard on the word *more*, like it wasn't just a sound she wanted to get out, but a whole mood.

"So you own, like, a therapy business?" Mae asked. She took a long sip of coffee. Sydney was having decaf. Mae wasn't being precious about caffeine consumption, letting herself linger over a couple coffees a day.

"Oh," Sydney said, blushing a little, "no, no, nothing like that. It's not therapy. It's just that we all work together as whole people. We're not robots, you know? We're women. With needs. And we think a lot about how life and business intersect. We mostly sell pashminas? But it's a really exciting time in the company because we're about to start selling lingerie as well. Like, empowered lingerie."

Even Sydney winced at this last part, looking like someone who had not actually said the words out loud before and didn't like the way they sounded. "Lingerie that makes women feel empowered," she tried again but shook her head right after. "It's an exciting new venture," she said, losing the battle and surrendering to familiar LillyLou language.

Mae watched in wonder. Pashminas. Empowered lingerie. What the actual fuck was Sydney talking about? Had she always been this shoddy at pretending things were fine? And did that mean Mae had been willfully, shockingly obtuse for all those years?

"And here I've just been expecting my lingerie to do the bare minimum of holding up my boobs and looking at least a little bit cute. I didn't know I could ask it to empower me too!" Mae said, grinning through all the other things she was feeling about the past and the present and the fictions of both. Sydney didn't smile back, just blushed deeper and tried, it seemed, to stick her entire head into her coffee cup. Mae spoke again, kinder this time. "No, seriously, that sounds really interesting, and you seem passionate about it, which is the whole point. And, I mean, I get it. Lingerie. It's personal. It's vulnerable. I'd much rather get bras from a woman-owned business." It was true, at least, and a small kindness to pay Sydney, who looked a little broken around the edges, a little raw. "Do you want to split a cinnamon roll? They look good. I mean, they look fine, but honestly any cinnamon roll is better than no cinnamon roll, right?" Mae hoped the sharing of something sweet and cozy would shift them into a safer space, make Sydney relax a little, let them talk about doulas or what seemed scariest about labor or how they could possibly be ready to be mothers.

And when they were done talking about that, Mae wanted to know when Sydney knew and how she decided not to tell Mae and what she'd wanted to come of the whole debacle, what it felt like to watch it crumble when Mae and even Beth Ann and Graham themselves didn't know it was happening.

What was it like, Mae wondered, to have a secret with Joni? She had never shared something so intimate with her mother. In her lowest moments, she wondered if she'd ever known her at all. Then she broke, from the knowledge that she couldn't get to know her better now, not ever.

And again the idea, powerful and insistent, that maybe Joni would be here had Sydney not kept her secret. Surely Joni's walking into the woods without her EpiPen was the result of secrets and mistakes, some sort of monstrous act of distraction, a domino effect that Mae had been unable to successfully chart yet.

So if you looked at it in a certain light, Joni's death was maybe, possibly, somehow, Sydney's fault.

Just like her anger at mostly absent Leo, Mae felt a rumble and reckoning of her anger at Sydney. It crested and fell, finding the unlikely rhythm of a storm-swept ocean. She wondered if Sydney could see it rolling beneath her surface. This unsaid, enormous thing.

"I don't do sweets," Sydney said simply. Mae had nearly forgotten about the cinnamon roll, but now she needed it more than ever.

"Well. More for me, then," she said. She got up, walked in her new slow, unbalanced way to the counter, ordered, and brought it back. She brought two forks, just in case, and laid one ceremoniously in front of Sydney, who turned away from it, like if she even looked at it, she would make some mistake she couldn't undo.

It would have been unclear to casual onlookers if the cinnamon roll was a peace offering or a threat. It was absolutely drenched in frosting.

"You should come to a meeting," Sydney said, though Mae had hoped that part of the conversation was over. "I'm not good at explaining it. I know that. It's why I don't—I'm not…I'm not the most successful person ever at promoting the business, but it's amazing and it would be so good for you. You're not sure what to do and how to be a working single mom. I get that. LillyLou can help with that."

"LillyLou? That's, like, your boss?" Mae took three bites of cinnamon roll in quick succession. It was fine. Not fresh. Not gooey or in the business of bringing back childhood memories of Christmas, when Barrett would bake cinnamon rolls in the afternoon and they'd eat them in Sydney's family's living room, oohing and aahing over brand-new toy kitchens and kid-size cars.

Mae watched Sydney for signs that she was remembering the same things. Those moments were precious, and she wanted them back, but maybe they were gone forever. Or maybe, more likely, they had never existed at all.

Anger fizzed, then stalled. Mae swallowed it down.

"No, it's the company. LillyLou. Look, you're—you're having a baby on your own. Your mom—you must miss her more than ever. You're in school and you're this incredible artist who didn't manage to take advantage of the doors that opened to you a few years ago. You need time to paint and finish your master's and even date, maybe, someday, and be with your kid and be the mom I'm sure you want to be, and LillyLou is a way to get all those things."

Sydney straightened herself. She took a bite of the cinnamon roll after all.

"Barrett's were better," Mae said then, letting his name drop into conversation, a little science experiment in the midst of everything else.

"Yes," Sydney said.

"Maybe that's why my mom was so into him," Mae said. It was not in any way the *right* thing to say, but Sydney was saying so many things about Mae's life, and Mae needed something to say back, and there was that whole ocean under her skin and the pounding reality of Leo not responding to her last three texts and having seen Georgie on the sidewalk this morning and Georgie not even saying hello, and this one gold bracelet around Sydney's wrist that Mae knew used to be Beth Ann's. Somehow, that particular combination of realities made her want to say the unsaid things.

There was a farcical quality to the entire morning, honestly. Their matching swollen bellies. The whiteness of the walls of this café, the sadness of the music choices—unironic pop shit from the early 2000s. The way their parents' affair sat between them, taking on the form of a cinnamon roll that tasted like it had been wrapped in plastic for a few weeks. Sydney being some sort of businesswoman.

It was exhausting, pretending any of this was normal.

"I don't want to talk about it," Sydney said.

"So that's why you never told me? It was just something you didn't feel like talking about?" Mae thought about that snowy day when she confronted Sydney. How Sydney shrank from the truth even then. How much it hurt, hearing it when it was too late to ask Joni a single thing about it. The magnitude of the way Sydney's revelations landed after Graham's wedding, like she figured Mae's life was already so unrecognizable, what was one more thing to throw at her. *I saw your mom and my dad kiss when we were eleven...And then for years I heard and saw snippets of...It went on our whole childhood, pretty much. Until she—until graduation, maybe. I don't know...I wanted to tell you. And tried to at first. Sort of. But Joni and I—I promised her I wouldn't tell you.*

It was the secret of the affair that broke Mae, yes, but also the fact of Sydney and Joni having a secret between them. It was the whole of the thing, the way it painted over everything she'd believed about her entire life up until then.

"Maybe it just never came up? I never asked, like, *Hey, is my mom fucking your dad?*"

"Mae—" Sydney began.

"The day she died—your dad wasn't at the party either. They were both missing. You ever think about that?" It was a thing she had been waiting fifteen years to say to herself, to Sydney, to anyone who would listen. Beth Ann, Mae, and Syd sipping lemonades with fifty of their closest friends. Graham coming in, having gotten a panicked call, too late, from Joni's phone, discovering her in the woods, already gone. And Barrett—where? Mae tried to picture his face when they'd told him. Was he surprised? Upset? Or something else entirely?

"I try not to dwell on the past. Ivy Miller says the past wants to keep you—trap you. The only way the past can stay alive is if you live there. If you let it go, it stops having any meaning. Any control over you. You know?"

Mae shook her head. She would not be letting go of the past. Of Joni. She couldn't.

Beth Ann had collapsed upon hearing the news. But the way she looked at the funeral — wasn't that relief in her eyes that refused to cry? Wasn't she squeezing Barrett's hand harder than Mae had ever seen a hand being held?

Joni hated the woods behind the house because there were always so many bees.

Joni never left home without her EpiPen.

It was always in her canvas tote.

Mae shooed the thoughts away, as always. The improbability of her mother's death made her dizzy, but it had been investigated, the case closed, questions answered enough for her father to tell her it was an accident, a terrible piece of luck, the sort of thing you think won't happen to you but can and sometimes even does.

Still, there it was, the knowing that Joni must have been distracted to leave without the tote. And the discomfort of not knowing what that distraction was. It could have been Mae herself, some awful thing her teenage self said or did. Of all the awful theories Mae had, that was the worst one, but she couldn't seem to remember saying a single thing to Joni that day.

Which was its own sort of guilt.

"We don't have to be the past," Sydney said again. She took something out of her bag: a business card with her name and the Lilly-Lou website address on it. Mae watched as Sydney wrote a time and place on the back. Her script was as familiar as the rest of her. Mae had always been a bit of a calligrapher, but Sydney had never taken to it, the way she'd never truly taken to anything artistic. Still, Sydney had practiced alongside Mae, so the result was handwriting that looked like it was trying to be beautiful but was failing.

It was, Mae thought with a sudden sadness and pity, the perfect handwriting for Sydney.

"We don't feel like the past," Sydney said, and there it was again, the sadness of Sydney. Even though she was certainly the more successful friend, she was still, somehow, the one to be pitied. The one who needed Mae.

And, God, it had been a while since anyone had needed Mae.

"I'm not really a joiner, Syd," Mae said, stating the obvious.

"And how's that been serving you?" Sydney asked. Mae remembered this about Sydney. That mostly she said a bunch of fluff, then every once in a while, she'd cut through it all and say the truest thing in the simplest way.

"I guess I'm a little bit alone," Mae said, smiling to make it sound lighter than it was.

"Worth a try, then, isn't it? Come to a meeting." She handed her the business card.

Mae was sure it was not going to be worth it, to meet a bunch of pashmina-selling moms. But maybe it would be worth something, to be near Sydney again.

They were carrying girls, growing them in their own bodies. They were living in the city Joni had promised them. They were weeding through decades of memories. Their story didn't feel quite over.

She didn't have Leo to fuck or Georgie to hate-watch *The Bachelor* with or Joni to talk to about the relationship between creativity and motherhood, but here was Sydney offering, if not exactly their old friendship, then something. *Something*. She was curious, anyway, if Sydney's life was built of sturdier stuff than her own.

"If I go, know I'll be making fun of it in my head the whole time. Like when you made me go to that youth-group thing with the trust falls," Mae said.

"Better come after the baby's born. Pregnant women can't do trust falls," Sydney said, a joke that let them both take a real breath, consider a way forward together. "Why don't we start with a dinner at my place?"

Mae said yes to this and found herself hoping it was a real invitation, not one that faded away like so many other promises to get drinks, go to Pilates, start a book club, have a monthly girls' night.

They hugged on the sidewalk, their bodies awkward in an embrace—because of the years that had passed or the size and shape of their bellies, it was hard to say.

Still, it was almost nice, the parallel moments in time, the way they both laughed at the physical awkwardness of it, the unlikeliness of the timing, the semi-sweetness of seeing each other again, the hint of a dream around the edges of their little-girl selves echoing a past that was imperfect and confusing and painful but still, in spite of everything, a shared thing between them. A tiny treasure, like the kinds they used to store in jewelry boxes and dresser drawers and backpack pockets and on the railing at the beach house and sometimes—for the best bits of sea glass or mica or European coins—in the dollhouse itself.

After the walk home, Mae climbed up her stairs, huffing and puffing and replaying the coffee date in her head, and wondered, for the first time in a long time, where that dollhouse was and what had become of those treasures trapped inside.

THEN

JONI SHOWED UP with baked pasta and a tray of brownies, like a neighbor visiting after a death, and Beth Ann almost shut the door in her face.

"It's been too long," Joni said. "I missed you."

Mae pushed past Beth Ann into the house, there to do some school project with Sydney. Beth Ann had left out a bowl of grapes and a bowl of popcorn for the girls and had hidden a bottle of wine in her bedroom, something light and white that she could drink right from the bottle while the afternoon wilted away.

On the advice of the leader at HigherLife, a community of like-minded women who were navigating middle age, Beth Ann was practicing gratitude, and lately that looked like being grateful that her life had waited to fall apart until her kid was basically old enough to take care of herself.

"You can just drop Mae," Beth Ann said, not reaching for the baked pasta, the brownies, things Joni had never brought over before. "They'll entertain themselves."

"I know they will. We can hang out. Catch up."

"I was going to nap."

Joni didn't respond right away. She tried to calculate the last time she and Beth Ann had spent an afternoon together in the kitchen, gossiping while the girls played or did whatever it was that girls their age did. Months ago, maybe, even though that seemed impossible. For most of the years of the girls' lives, they had been in the kitchen together usually more than once a week. There were days with chipped coffee mugs and not enough milk to go around, the both of them tolerating the bitterness so they could continue talking, negotiating how many cookies the girls could have, how much TV. Afternoons with wine or, more than once, margaritas. Early evenings picking at abandoned pizza bagels or Kraft Macaroni and Cheese. Days when they made a salad, a vegetarian chili, sandwiches piled high with everything about to go bad from the fridge. Sometimes they were in the kitchen perched atop bar stools. In the warm months, they sat outside, commenting on the weather, forgetting sunscreen, regretting it later when their ears, their hair parts, the tops of their feet burned. Once in a while they'd be in the living room, usually in the colder months, when the light faded early and they needed the coziness of blankets and cushions and the idea of a fire in the fireplace, even though they never actually lit one.

Those memories were precious. They were everything.

Or, well, they weren't everything. But they were the unexpected beauty of being a parent here in Sommersette, the thing Joni didn't know would happen. They made her feel normal. Made everything sort of lovely and sepia-toned. Idyllic, the way it was supposed to be. The way she'd hoped for when she first located Sommersette on a map, first taken the train out here on her own to see what it looked like, how it felt, why it would make a good home.

Joni wanted those moments back. It was why she'd made pasta, sprinkling it with spinach and Parmesan, following a recipe from a cookbook someone who didn't know her very well had given her. It was why she'd given Mae the task of making brownies, which she'd done with her Mae flair, tucking bits of raspberry jam and almonds into the batter, the result either delicious or disgusting.

"I need girl time," Joni said. It was a sentence she'd heard Beth Ann say, a sentence she'd scoffed at for the way it infantilized their friendship, made it seem frivolous and small, not powerful and meaningful.

Joni invited herself in, put her signature canvas tote with almost nothing inside but an EpiPen and a world-beaten wallet on the counter. Beth Ann didn't stand in her way exactly, and then they were together again, the two of them somehow in the kitchen, Joni turning on the oven, Beth Ann considering grabbing the bottle of wine from her bedroom to bring downstairs.

Beth Ann took in the length of Joni, who looked tall in a long brown skirt. Beth Ann never wore brown. Never wore long skirts. Maybe that was the problem. Maybe that was what made Joni so alluring.

"I've missed you. You've been hard to reach," Joni said. She looked squarely at Beth Ann as if challenging her to say something real, to say the realest thing, but Beth Ann would not. Could not.

"I'm focusing on me. On bettering myself." Beth Ann's words were tight and she tried to make them sound powerful, cool. But Joni's nose scrunched and made everything in Beth Ann's life seem stupid, small, pointless.

Beth Ann tried for the hundredth time to believe something other than that Joni was involved with Barrett. It wasn't like she had hard evidence. Maybe it wasn't true. Maybe it was just a fear of Beth Ann's, as absurd as her fear of lightning, spiders, splinters. But she couldn't unthink the thought. Joni in her dust-sweeping skirt, her smirk, her impossibly tangled hair, here now in Beth Ann's kitchen, grabbing a brownie that was meant for Beth Ann. Joni ate it hungrily, uncaring if the chocolate smeared, if her hands were messy.

"That must be time-consuming," Joni said. "I thought we didn't do that stuff. I thought we were over the whole 'be your best self' hoopla."

They'd had conversations about this over the years—who hadn't?—about the way self-help preyed on moms, made them feel like they had to do more and more and more to be better, to be best. They'd rejected all that together. Joni thought they had.

Maybe it was Beth Ann who had been lying all along. Joni let the thought feed her.

"This isn't hoopla," Beth Ann said. "This isn't silly. I don't need your approval. The girls are growing up. The shape of our lives is changing. We didn't have the second kids, we didn't make those choices, we made other ones. Didn't we?"

Beth Ann's eyebrows went up. She was a curious mix of scared and sure, confident and breaking apart. Joni couldn't get a handle on it.

"I guess we did," Joni said. She'd always wanted the second kid, and she and Graham had tried. Beth Ann knew that, knew the tender pain of it, the arduous work of letting go. But today, now, Beth Ann didn't seem to care about that raw spot, the shared history of making peace with the families they had, their singleton daughters, the promise that they would grow up like sisters.

"We did. We made choices. We're living with them." Beth Ann's voice was an explosive device, tightly wound and ready to detonate. It was all there—rage, disappointment, regret, shock, grief. Joni tried to believe it was about something else, that it was for some other reason than the most obvious one.

If Beth Ann knew, if she really knew, Joni thought, she'd have shoved her out the door. If she knew, she'd have hit her straight across the face. She'd have screamed at her, moved their family away, and told the whole town.

If she knew, she would have killed her by now, surely.

"Maybe I could better myself too—" Joni began, a peace offering. She could go to some group therapy for middle-aged moms with Beth Ann. They could go forward. They could stay what they'd always been: best friends.

But Sydney entered the room before Joni could finish or Beth Ann could respond. She was a disarming mix of child and adult. Joni hadn't noticed until that very moment. She saw Beth Ann noticing too, her daughter caught in that awful early teenage purgatory. She was in a sweet khaki skirt bought on a recent shopping trip to the Gap and a striped tank top so tight they could see Sydney's ribs. A line of acne wound its way along her chin. She was beautiful and raw, innocent and ruined. She was nearly thirteen.

"Sweetheart," Beth Ann said, relieved beyond measure to have her in the room, to be spared the pressure of being alone with Joni. "You hungry? Can I get you more to eat?"

"What do we have?" Sydney asked.

"Lots of food. What were you thinking?"

Sydney shrugged.

"There are brownies. Good ones. Homemade," Joni said with a little too much pride for Beth Ann's taste. Beth Ann had things the girls liked right in the pantry—chips and hummus and popcorn, the brand that Sydney had told her to get, and two different kinds of cheese.

"I don't like brownies," Sydney said, a sentence Beth Ann knew to be a lie. Just last week Sydney had begged her for brownies. When Sydney was younger, she and Beth Ann made them together often from the box, sneaking bites of the eggy unbaked mixture, salmonella be damned. But lately Beth Ann had started saying no to things Sydney wanted to bake, to eat. Not because Sydney needed to be careful now, exactly, but she would later. Beth Ann's own body had changed over the years, rounding in places she had begged it not to, and she could practically connect the beginning of Barrett's lack of interest in her to the new way weight clung to her since her thirties began. And now she was in her forties and she wondered sometimes if he'd ever reach for her again.

Sydney needed to know what was coming for her.

"But you *do* like them," Joni said. Beth Ann watched Joni's eyebrows rise, and she also watched her daughter shrink from the look.

Sydney shook her head, petulant.

"Oh, come on, now, you told me once that brownies are the best food on earth. I made them especially for you."

Joni took another brownie, bit into it with abandon. Joni's body had changed too over the years, but the shift suited her better.

"I don't want them." Sydney was flushed, angry about something. In recent months, she had certainly gotten angry about far less than brownies, and she'd been changing her mind about all sorts of things she used to love—favorite dinners, songs Beth Ann played in the car, her own hair, which she was threatening to cut short or dye auburn or do something, anything, that would make it different from the lovely hair she'd had her whole life.

Mae came out of the living room then and joined the crowd in the kitchen. She was unaware of whatever was bubbling between Joni and Sydney, and she reached for a brownie. "Okay if I take one, Syd? I know they're your favorite."

"They're *not*," Sydney said, her voice losing anger and giving in to something else—a weepiness that had been emerging lately, something surging and hormonal and unstoppable that Beth Ann found herself feeling both sympathy for and annoyance about. Beth Ann, after all, managed to keep her own hormonal events under control. The feelings would simmer uncomfortably for a while, wanting to be let loose, of course, but Beth Ann would busy herself with cleaning or cooking or going for little runs around the neighborhood, her arms tight at her sides, her face flushing, her feet flapping against pavement.

"More for me, then!" Mae said, grabbing another brownie. Beth Ann hated her for the casual way she scooped them up, how she knew Mae would enjoy the taste and not get lost in the shame. Just like her mother. Beth Ann's broken heart raced. At HigherLife they gave her mantras—*I am here and now* and *I am better than the events around me* and *In forgiveness I am myself, in grace I am strong*—but in the clutter of her mind, each of the mantras came to her all clunky and wrong. She couldn't seem to find her breath, couldn't locate where her feet actually were, even though certainly they were on the ground.

"What's your new favorite food, then?" Joni asked Sydney, not giving up even though it was obvious she should. "Pizza? I'll order a pizza. Cupcakes? Whatever you want, Syd."

Beth Ann watched Joni's neck strain. She had never seen tension held there, or anywhere, really, on her friend. Joni was unworried, untrying, unconcerned with making people happy or proving anything to anyone. Except, suddenly, she seemed to want something from Sydney.

"I'm not hungry," Sydney said.

"You'll be hungry eventually." Joni was relentless.

"I'm not six," Sydney said. "You can't bribe me with treats." Sydney's eyes narrowed. Her breath was held.

"Please," Joni said. "Something?"

The thing happening between Sydney and Joni was strange, wrong. They were speaking in sentences that Mae and Beth Ann couldn't untangle, talking about something they weren't privy to.

"Stop." Finally, the tears pooled and Sydney's voice was soft—begging, even.

"Do you need our friends to go home, honey?" Beth Ann asked quietly at the same time Joni asked, "Why don't you and I go on a walk, Syd?"

Sydney and Joni had never gone on a walk before. The mothers and daughters never split up like that. Sometimes Joni would take both girls somewhere or Beth Ann would, but they never took each other's daughter unless there was an emergency—Joni picking Sydney up from a sleepover when Beth Ann was sick and Barrett was on a work trip, Beth Ann taking Mae to the mall to get a dress for picture day when Joni's mother had died and Joni couldn't get out of bed for a few days. But never like this. This was all wrong.

"Joni," Beth Ann said, starting a sentence she truly had no idea how to finish.

"What's going on?" Mae asked, always the one to cut through the confusion and the unsaid things. Beth Ann hoped she'd still know Mae at twenty and thirty and forty. She'd like to see what a girl like Mae turned into over time, with wisdom and heartbreak and stress and wonder, all the things packed into those decades that shaped and shifted you.

"Sydney's upset with me," Joni said. "I'm trying to make it right."

Sydney's body seemed to shrink.

"It's complicated. Right, Syd? But we're working it out."

"Upset about what?" Mae again, asking the questions that Beth Ann knew she herself should be asking, a better caretaker of her daughter than she could be in this moment.

"It's a long story," Joni said. "Right, Syd? A long story that no one needs to hear."

Sydney's tears released, dozens of them streaming down her face, more quietly than tears usually did. Beth Ann finally went to her side, wiped the tears uselessly, but more just came and came and came.

"I think you need to leave," Beth Ann said. "Joni. You should go. You shouldn't have come." She looked at her friend, at the person who used to be her friend, and hoped her voice sounded stern. Final. This wasn't appropriate, whatever was going on here; her daughter was crying and Joni was speaking in strange little sentences and even Mae was looking confused, slowing her brownie eating, furrowing her brow.

"A long story that no one needs to hear," Joni said again, and Beth Ann didn't know what to do with Joni's endless pushing, with the way she was unbothered by the awkwardness she was causing, the rules she was breaking by acting this way.

"That's enough," Beth Ann said, more annoyed than mad, even though she was both, and other things too. Curious and scared and nervous.

Joni and Mae left, barely saying goodbye, and Beth Ann and Sydney stayed in the kitchen. Sydney didn't speak and Beth Ann didn't ask her to, even though her whole body was sweating with a fear that needed to know where to land. Sydney just kept crying and crying, going through tissues and shirtsleeves and finally giving up, letting the tears and the snot and the release of it all just flood her face, the kitchen, their lives.

Hours later, Beth Ann closed all the windows and sighed at the sound of the wind. It was always loud against their walls, a strange feature of their house that would have led her away if she'd known before purchasing it but that she was instead stuck with forever.

"It's just wind, Mom," Sydney said, even though she'd always claimed to hate the noise the wind made, the way it rattled things, the way it whistled. It felt, somehow, like a betrayal, Sydney suddenly accepting the gusts, the way they banged and swooped and swept up leaves neatly piled in the yard, making a mess of everything. It wasn't just wind, and Sydney should know that. Still, Beth Ann tamped down the flare of irritation rising in her.

"Do you want to talk about what happened?" she asked her daughter. The people at HigherLife would be impressed with her restraint. Beth Ann wanted to push and insist and work herself and her daughter up into a fury. But she left it there. And for a moment Sydney hesitated, like she might really say something. But then another gust of wind hit the window, and Beth Ann locked the window latch as if the weather might lift the whole frame, remove the screen, rage inside and ruin everything.

"It's nothing," Sydney said, looking at her shoes, at the mess of mail on the kitchen counter, at the trees bending precariously outside. "A long story that no one needs to hear."

Barrett got home late, as always, but Beth Ann waited up for him, a rare occurrence. He tiptoed into their bedroom, something she realized he must do all the time but she'd never witnessed. He sighed coming in, like encountering her sleeping was a difficulty, and he seemed to have a whole system for taking off his clothing without waking her up. Maybe it was a kindness, to let her sleep, but it felt now like an avoidance, a way not to have to speak to her. She suddenly needed him to know she was awake.

"Hey," she said, and just that word said in a tight little whisper startled him into dropping his phone.

"Fuck," he said to the phone or to her or to whatever he had planned next. "Jesus. You scared me."

"I had a weird day," Beth Ann said. She kept herself from asking what was on his phone and why he was home so late.

"Okay." Barrett picked up his phone and went back to his undressing, unwinding, but without the staying-quiet precautions. He didn't ask what was so weird about it. Beth Ann supposed he must not really care.

"Sydney did too."

"All of Sydney's days are weird," Barrett said. He'd been saying some version of this since Sydney had been a hard-to-understand infant with uneven naps and messy eating habits and a way of crying that could drive anyone crazy.

"Joni came over," Beth Ann said.

"Doesn't sound weird to me."

"We haven't been seeing each other much, actually. Me and Joni." She wondered if it sounded pointed or casual.

Barrett squeezed his phone more tightly. The moon seemed to shift in the sky, the pattern of light changing in the bedroom. Beth Ann closed her eyes briefly before speaking. "Barrett. Just tell me."

She took herself by surprise with this. She knew something that she hadn't thought she'd known. But here she was, under two comforters, a heating pad, and the weight of the darkness of night, knowing it. A thing she'd known a long time and also never known before. A truth so obvious it took her breath away. She just needed him to say it.

"Tell you what?" Barrett's face scrunched.

"Tell me why Joni is being weird. Tell me why Sydney and Joni are being weird together. Tell me why my daughter has a secret with my best friend. Tell me why we are the way we are. Just tell me. Tell me."

Barrett stood still then. He was down to his boxers, fiddling with his watch. He was in a slash of light that was coming in from the streetlamp outside. It was always there—the curtains weren't quite the right size, and though Beth Ann had asked Barrett to look into getting new ones a hundred times, he never did, so they lived with this line of light that punctuated the otherwise pitch-blackness of their bedroom at night. The light cut across his stomach, which was soft and covered in hair and was in so many ways unrecognizable to Beth Ann, who hadn't taken much notice of his body in a long time, who was too scared to calculate how long it had been since she'd touched him in any way other than pushing him aside so she could open the dishwasher or the top of the coffee maker because he always made the coffee wrong.

He looked at the ground. It was a long moment when they could both just be in the before, be in their marriage the way it was, the way it had always been, Barrett and Beth Ann and their big beautiful home in

Sommersette and their lovely daughter, Sydney, who was well-behaved and well-meaning and had nice hair and pretty-enough eyes.

They were those people now and for another few seconds—three? four? fifteen?—however long Barrett could wait before saying what it was he was deciding to say. It had been nice to be those people; they were boring, sure, and a little sad, maybe, but comfortable too. Easy to explain. Beth Ann almost took it back.

"Or you don't have to—" she started, the decision having seemed so clear only moments before. But it was too late.

"We're involved," Barrett said. "Joni and I."

And there it went, gone, like so many things that seemed like they would last forever but didn't—long sleepless nights with a newborn baby, the color of your hair before grays come in, the shape of your body before you turn thirty-three, that bar on the corner, all dingy and smelling of spilled beer, that is a neighborhood stalwart until it isn't, the song you hear on the radio every day for an entire summer, with words that stay with you and a melody that doesn't leave you.

Like love and friendship and the life you thought you were living that you weren't, really, or you were for a time, until someone forgot to tell you that you weren't anymore.

Everything that seemed like forever gone.

Just—

Gone.

NOW

Sydney

"THIS IS QUITE a feast," Sam said, eyeing the shrimp scampi, the arugula salad, the garlic bread and the cheese plate, and even the tap water that Sydney had poured into a large, clear pitcher along with a handful of ice cubes. It would look better with a bottle of white wine or two on the table, but there was no need for Sam to be drinking with two pregnant women, and anyway, Sydney was nervous enough about Sam meeting Mae without introducing into the mix his propensity for slurring while drinking.

"I want it to be nice," Sydney said. Lately everything Sam said was like a pinch, an annoyance, and so she replied in kind, with a tight sort of swat back, which was perhaps not exactly fair but was the best she could do, this pregnant.

"And what's her husband's name? Does he like sports? We'll have something to talk about, right? You've met him?"

Sam had never been the world's greatest listener. Early on, sure, he had asked the right questions about her family, her job, where she went to school (a conversation she hated, slipping and sliding around the fact of her not having gone to college, like she was revealing a prior criminal conviction). Still, he had asked and had, in response to her answers, nodded his head at the appropriate times and, it seemed, remembered most of what she'd said back then.

But even when they were planning their wedding, the listening had plummeted—she'd tell him details about flowers or music or which guests she was annoyed about having to invite, and he'd nod like he heard it all, but later he'd ask questions that revealed he hadn't taken in a word of it. His eyes now were often trained on his phone, looking at news or baseball scores or who knows what else; Sydney liked to avert her eyes. It was a habit she'd gotten into after learning about Joni and Barrett—she knew now that she didn't want to know anything she wasn't supposed to, so she looked away from things like text messages and internet searches and even how Sam spoke to a woman at a work function or a wedding—just in case.

If her life was going to blow up, she didn't want it to be by accident.

Today, though, she'd have liked to take his phone right from his hand, throw it out the window.

"She's not married," Sydney said, trying not to yell. A memory burst into her mind: Giving her mother a photography book of porches, knowing how badly her mother wanted a porch to read books on, have her coffee on. And her father's blank expression at the gesture, total cluelessness about who her mother was, what she craved, what mattered to her.

Memories like these always resulted in a low-level fear, her throat closing a little, her head aching. *It's happening*, her brain shouted at her. *It's happening to you too. Of course it is.* Sydney tried to ignore it. Sam was not Barrett. And, wisely, she did not have a Joni in her life.

"Not married," Sam said. "Got it. So what's her boyfriend like?"

"She's not with anyone. Jesus, Sam. We talked about this. Look at the goddamn table. Three place settings. Three. Where are you?"

She was sounding like a certain version of Beth Ann—short, irritable, impatient with her husband's pace of understanding. She had another flash of memory of Beth Ann on a particular day when Joni had brought over brownies to try to bribe Sydney into staying quiet. Beth Ann had been tense and short, Sydney had been tired, and Joni hadn't known that she didn't need to bring brownies, didn't need to do any of the things she tried over the years—the concerts and food, the offers to let Sydney pierce her nose, drink a beer, borrow Joni's clothes.

Joni didn't need to bribe her. Sydney kept the secret for free.

Sydney tried to shake off the memory and, with it, her current irritated way of speaking to Sam.

"But she's pregnant," Sam said, not overly worried about the way Sydney's voice was winding up, readying for explosion.

"Uh-huh."

"Is it a whole sperm thing?"

"Literally what are you talking about?" Not taking after her mother was harder than it seemed, actually. Beth Ann was imprinted right inside Sydney, her worst qualities somehow constantly a little bit alive underneath her skin. The truth of it always made Sydney panic.

She took a deep breath. Ivy Miller cautioned against hanging on to the past. It seemed especially hard to do when you were having the past over for dinner.

"So there's no guy? Just a pregnant person?" Sometimes it was almost like Sam was being purposely dense. If she answered, she would scream, and Mae would be here any moment. She didn't need Mae hearing them fight. She needed Mae to see what was good, what was working in her life, so she'd want a little bit of it. She needed

Mae to wonder how Sydney got here and then ask more about LillyLou, knowing that that must be at least part of the path.

It wasn't that Sam was some dumb jock or even particularly conservative on things like premarital sex and what a family looked like. It was more that he lacked imagination, so if something didn't meet his narrow definition of How Things Are, then he couldn't seem to process its existence. It was exactly his take on LillyLou—she didn't have a yearly salary or health insurance, so it wasn't a real job. His brain simply couldn't make space for the parts of her life—of anyone's life—that were surprising in any way.

She let him sit with the stupidity of his comment. As if a pregnant person couldn't exist on her own! For a moment—a swift and strange moment—Sydney wanted to leave him. She'd move in with Mae and they'd be two pregnant people, no men in sight, no partners anywhere, and she'd watch from afar as his brain fell to pieces at the impossibility of it all. She treasured the impulse briefly, then let it go.

She barely knew Mae anymore anyway.

"Okay, so it's just your old friend and you and me?" Sam said, still slowly putting together something not even remotely complicated.

"Yes. I want you to meet her. I also think she would be a great addition to LillyLou, so I want her to see what being on the Path to More can do for someone. I want her to see what she could have."

Sam squinted. "Right," he said, but Sydney got the impression he wasn't so sure that what they had was worth showing off. The look broke her a little. She'd cleaned the house and had Sam wear something that matched, but not too closely, her dress. There were fresh flowers. The meal was impeccable. She'd gotten a blowout. Ivy Miller reminded them often about the money that had to be spent to get the life you wanted. It seemed counterintuitive, but she could see it was the only way.

She knew Sam had been holding back a comment about it. She'd promised him she would cut down on the spending, with the caveat that she had to invest in her business. Sam had bristled, she had blustered, and the conversation never really reached a conclusion. But he didn't complain about the money she spent on nights with friends, only about the money she spent on the boxes in the bedroom and the conferences in Michigan and Utah and Arizona.

The buzzer rang, and there Mae was, downstairs, on the little black-and-white screen showing them who was trying to get in. Sydney buzzed her up.

"Everything looks really nice," Sam said. He wasn't one for flowery words or exuberance. But he also didn't lie, so it was verifiably the truth. She pulled him in for a kiss.

Someday, Sydney decided, they would buy a house with an enormous front porch. A wraparound one, with rocking chairs that faced the sunset. The thought made her back straighten, her head clear. She was on the Path to More. She knew what she wanted. It would happen.

Mae knocked at the door. Sydney was shocked to realize she knew Mae's knock, which was loud at first and then, as if remembering itself, quieter, an adjustment that Sydney had seen Mae make a million times over the years. Sydney moved herself as quickly as her body would currently allow to the living room to let Mae in.

She opened the door.

The girls who were women now tried again to figure out what to do with their bodies. They leaned in for a hug that they changed, mid-course, to a kiss on the cheek, and then, feeling the formality of that, moved into a hug. Sam went into the kitchen and stirred something on the stove. Trying to make himself appear useful and legitimate and whatever else it was that Sydney needed him to be.

It was his way of loving her.

Sometimes, it was almost enough.

"Come meet Sam!" Sydney said as if moments before she had not been raging at him, wondering how they were even together.

"Sam, hi," Mae said, stepping into the space, looking around, assessing something. "Smells delicious in here. Thank you for having me. God, I should have brought something. Flowers or something. I'm sorry, that's what people do, and I just—I wasn't thinking."

Sydney silently agreed that Mae should have brought flowers, but then, that would be so adult, and Mae was not the sort of person who came into adulthood naturally. A surge of jealousy took Sydney by surprise. Maybe if she hadn't known everything, she would have stayed young and irresponsible and light like Mae. Maybe she wouldn't be in this beige apartment in a big-windowed high-rise with her nice but uninspiring husband, making a meal for her old friend. Maybe she could have been Mae, painting pictures of how things felt and never worrying much about how things actually were, never doing the work of keeping the world in line.

She pasted on a kind smile and straightened her back. "We don't need flowers," she said, and felt good about the truth of it. There were already flowers on the table. "I never expected you to bring something."

It wasn't an insult, exactly, or it wasn't meant as one. It was a truth. This was what knowing each other was like. It meant you knew why the worst parts of a person were there, and you loved even their infractions. You loved them for how much you knew about them.

"You two really are due right around the same time, huh?" Sam said, eyeing Mae's body in a way that made Sydney lurch. Mae looked down at herself.

"Oh, yeah, I guess so," she said. This was not the first impression Sydney had hoped for, on either side.

"I know I can't get you a cocktail, but how about some water?" Sam asked, and this was better, this was thoughtful, at least, the sort of thing a husband did, and Sydney looked at Mae closely to see if she'd noticed.

"Water is great and— Oh!" Mae stopped in the living room. Her hand went to her chest like she'd seen a ghost, which, Sydney supposed, she sort of had. "Wow. You kept it."

"Of course I did!" Sydney said. They were, both of them, looking at the dollhouse.

"It's— Wow. It's really right here," Mae said. She was stunned into stillness.

"I know it will be a few years until the baby will be able to play with it, but I can't wait. Sam thinks there's not enough room for it, but it's not like we'll live here forever, you know?"

"It's growing on me!" Sam called from the kitchen, a kindness he must have known she needed.

"You don't think it, like, has bad vibes?" Mae asked. The question surprised Sydney, who hadn't been expecting anything except, maybe, the old vestiges of Mae's jealousy, the last remaining glints of the way she used to look at the dollhouse, starry-eyed like she wished more than anything it could be hers. It had felt good back then to have something so clearly special, to know that someone like Mae couldn't have it and would have to pine for it forever. In so many ways, their friendship grew uneven over the years—Mae was more talented, she was funnier, she had better style and a cooler mom and an easier way of existing in the world. She wasn't as pretty as Sydney, not in the obvious ways, but it didn't matter. Boys liked her more, for her confidence and her long legs and the way she sort of twinkled, like she was made with a little bit of starlight.

But Sydney had the dollhouse.

And the secret.

And—she swallowed at the awful truth of it—she had the mother.

And now Sydney had the husband, the chandelier above the table on a dimmer, the expensive brand of maternity clothes instead of the hodgepodge of a stretchy T-shirt and an open cardigan that Mae was draped in. She'd won. Somehow, after everything, she'd come out on top. She'd kept the secret, she'd protected her best friend, she'd done what was asked of her, and she'd been given the adult life, the real things, the true Path to More.

"It has great vibes," Sydney said.

"Well, okay." Mae took one last look before Sydney announced it was time for dinner.

Sam sat at the head of the table, which felt old-fashioned to Mae and unremarkable to Sydney, who would have set the dollhouse dolls in this exact configuration were she to have them eat a lovely seafood feast.

"It's nice to meet Syd's oldest friend," Sam said as they dug in, the smell of garlic so thick it was a little oppressive, the sun setting outside and turning the whole apartment peachy pink, all of it lovely but unnatural, foreboding.

"We've known each other a long time," Mae said, but there were so many other things that needed to be said. The place was big, by city standards, but was feeling small, the history of Mae and Sydney and their moms practically crowding them out. Someday, surely, they would need to talk more about Joni and Barrett. The exchange at the coffee shop hadn't been enough, hadn't answered any real questions, had ended as things so often did with Sydney—with her saying she didn't want to talk about it anymore and the two of them pretending to move on from events that were, in fact, impossible to move on from.

Mae wanted to bring it up again, the lurking question of how exactly Joni had ended up in the woods alone that day. She couldn't stop the worry that Sydney was the keeper of even more secrets, bigger ones, that might emerge at any moment.

But Sydney ate shrimp scampi tidily and kept rubbing her swollen belly absentmindedly. She did not look like a woman protecting any lost truths. She spoke carefully around Joni and Barrett and Beth Ann and Graham today, making strange curlicue conversational paths to avoid mentioning them.

Mae felt a little like a ghost, erased from the important moments of Sydney's life. And she wanted to write herself back in somehow.

"We've known each other forever," Sydney agreed. "That's how I know what's best for you. I've known you forever. I've known every dream you've ever had. And how close you've come to making your dreams come true. Sam, did I ever show you the article about Mae's paintings?"

"Singular," Mae corrected as she always did when people said this. "One painting."

"She's an artist," Sydney told Sam, then turned back to Mae. "You're an artist. Except I can tell something has set you on the wrong path; you've gotten lost or something. And this is the moment to get, you know, found." Sydney had practiced the words in her head, or some of them, at least. She'd mouthed them in the shower, on walks around the neighborhood, in the waiting room at her doctor's.

"Wow, an artist. Very cool. What kind of stuff do you do?" Sam asked. Sydney put a hand on his arm to quiet him. She didn't want the conversation to move into some other territory. They were right where she needed them to be. She could do this.

"A painter. I just told you," Sydney said. "Anyway, having your own business frees you up to do the sort of work you were meant to do, you know? And having a supportive community. I mean, I don't know, maybe you have that, but I never had one before. Or, I mean, after you and me. We had each other. And then we didn't. And now I have the women I'm on the path with. You deserve that too."

Mae's mouth was full, a tiny bit of garlic dripping down her chin. The garlic really *was* overpowering and probably would give her heartburn later. Everything gave her heartburn at this point in her pregnancy; it was just a question of how intense it would be, how many Tums she would need to counteract it.

We had each other. And then we didn't. The words were so brief, distilling something enormous into almost nothing at all.

Mae had been waiting for a way to talk about everything, waiting for some reference to the past, and maybe this was it, but it was so thin it was hard to grasp on to. She took a brief inhale to fill herself before saying something more substantial, but Sam spoke first.

"I'm sure Mae has her own friends," he said. He had turned stern in the few seconds it took for Sydney to say what she'd said. Sydney reached out to put her hand on his arm again, but he pulled it away. She added it to the list of tiny injuries that might someday add up to something horrible in her marriage.

"I don't have any old friends like you, Sydney," Mae said, which seemed like maybe it could be the right thing to say, an honoring of what they'd had. It was also the truth. There'd been Sydney. Then a series of girls she went to parties at people's cramped apartments with. Fiona, of course. A girl named Bridget who had followed her online after the piece about her painting came out and whom she'd spent a year or two meeting up with at galleries, imagining some sort of idyllic artistic partnership. But eventually they'd run out of things to talk about and Mae had stopped painting and Bridget hadn't. Then Bridget sold some work to an important dealer and she no longer returned Mae's calls, a move that should have hurt Mae, and did, maybe, but she also understood.

Mae had been the art "it girl," that one impressive sale catapulting her into a kind of stardom and status. But it was so fleeting she couldn't expect anyone to stick around for the fallout. She wasn't the sort of person others pursued without a reason, and the reason was gone.

After Bridget, Mae threw everything she had into Leo and an occasional coffee with a fellow grad student whom she liked to gossip with about professors or other students or the department itself, the intricacies of the way an English department at a fancy university was run, who was in charge and who was *really* in charge and what was taken seriously and what wasn't and why. It wasn't friendship, exactly, at least not the kind that came with late-night texts or birthday brunches or the deep knowing of someone that she'd had once. But it was something.

Then there was Georgie. Often while Mae looked at her phone, her finger hovered over Georgie's name as she read and reread texts from her like there might be answers there about what went wrong or why something always did go wrong or why it was, exactly, that she was thirty-three and pregnant and friendless and husbandless and living in an apartment with a tiny window through which you could see a beautiful bit of Greenwood Cemetery but that had no dishwasher, no washing machine, no space on the counter for a special bottle-drying rack that the baby blogs all assured her was a necessity, though for what reason Mae couldn't pinpoint. Were bottles especially bad at drying? Did babies notoriously hate wet bottles? Or would the bottles take over her apartment like some sort of infestation she needed to adequately prepare herself for?

Sydney seemed like the sort of person who would know the answer—she had always been that sort of person because Beth Ann had always been that sort of person. If you have a mom who knows a lot about being a mom, then you become that kind of mom too, surely.

"What do you know about bottle-drying racks?" Mae asked, taking a conversational left turn, a swerve that wasn't on purpose, exactly, but here she was with Sydney and Sydney's handsome husband and Sydney's perfect bump that would be a baby girl someday soon, any day, really, and Mae didn't know who else to ask this suddenly urgent question.

"Bottle-drying racks?" Sydney had practiced a great many versions of her LillyLou pitch, but none of them had included this sort of conversational cliff jump. She glanced at Sam, but he just looked relieved.

"Or does Beth Ann know anything about them? Online, a lot of them look sort of like grass? Obviously I can't ask my mom, and honestly, even if she were still around, I don't think she'd know much about bottles. Joni wasn't much for domesticity. In a lot of ways, I guess. I'm sure you've heard about her a little, Sam. Probably mostly awful things about how she ruined all our lives. But she was fun. Took us to concerts. Got us bras. Did tie-dye with us in the backyard. She wasn't, you know, a mom in the way Beth Ann was. In the way Sydney will be. In the way I'd sort of like to be, if I'm perfectly honest, even though I think that ship probably sailed with the whole out-of-wedlock thing. But I'd like to have some Joni in me too. The good parts. There were a lot of good parts." Mae was swallowing tears, the missing of her mother still something crisp and potent. Sam said nothing. Sydney said nothing. And in that pocket of nothing, Mae simply kept talking, filling up the awkwardness with more awkwardness. "The baby's dad is a theater guy. Maybe the baby will like theater. That wouldn't be so bad. I'm not sure I'll know what to do if the baby likes, I don't know, lacrosse. I wonder if there are books for taking care of sporty babies when you hate sports?"

Mae couldn't be drunk, because she was pregnant, and Sydney knew that Mae was a lot of weird and wild things but was not a person who would get drunk in the last month of pregnancy. But she was acting drunk, or maybe just hormonal, or overwhelmed by being in this moment right now, which Sydney could understand. She was too.

She was too.

"I'll send you some links," Sydney said in her gentlest voice. "Things to get. Wraps and bassinets and whatever. Bottle-drying racks. The basics. And babies don't play lacrosse. Even the sporty ones."

"I have no idea what I'm doing," Mae said. She hadn't had anyone to say it to. Catherine would have happily listened but would've offered no real insights, no deep understanding. Maybe she would have whispered it to Leo if he'd answered her calls, come to appointments, had been generally around. Or Georgie, if Georgie still came over for pasta every third night like she used to.

It was the exact sort of thing she could have told Joni.

"We'll help each other," Sydney said. "And my group of women in the business—they can help too. You don't have to be alone. Not in your grief. Not in motherhood. Not in any of this." She smiled. She'd done it. Maybe it had been too obvious at first, too disconnected from the conversation. But this last push, she knew, was right. Mae was asking for community, for support, and Sydney was offering it up. It was simple, actually.

"Okay," Mae said, and maybe it wasn't the same as putting in a pashmina order on the spot, but it was something, it certainly was. It was something good.

NOW

Mae

IT HAPPENED JUST the way they said it would—an undeniable rush of pain that built and built, made itself known, and then told her to get herself to the hospital. Sydney had said she should pack a bag with things like a robe and baby clothes and a phone charger and socks, because hospitals were cold and socks helped. So Mae had the bag and she had her doctor's phone number, and she had the contractions and the ability to time them, sort of. But she did not have a person to call.

It was a decision she'd kept putting off. Catherine, maybe, although their relationship had never been especially intimate. Her father barely even tolerated hearing about morning sickness or ruminations on whether the baby would take after Joni's side of the family or his. Surely Georgie would come if she asked, even after everything. Leo, now that he checked in with a daily text asking how she was doing and if the baby was coming. She was simultaneously pleased and enraged by these texts. She wanted Leo involved, wanted him to care about their baby and even, maybe, about her. But how was she supposed to know when the baby was coming? She'd never done this before. And there was an urgency to the question, an annoyance, even, as if she were purposely not telling him to keep him on his toes. As if her lack of knowing was an action taken against him and not just the uncertain reality of pregnancy and, probably, motherhood in general.

She tried Leo first. He was the dad. Or at least he'd said he wanted to be the dad if they could be flexible on what exactly that meant, but maybe it could mean this — driving her to the hospital, watching her pant and scream and, she was sure, eventually get an epidural. He could help her when she was pushing, couldn't he? Hold her hand the way husbands were supposed to do, remind her to breathe, cut the cord? She tried to imagine it, but then another contraction came and Leo's phone went to voicemail and she let go of the image swiftly, knowing she would grieve it later. Right now, it didn't hurt as much as the next wave of radiating pain.

She called Georgie next, and Georgie did answer, her voice fuzzy and slurry on the other end of the line. They hadn't been much for phone calls in their short friendship, and it was past midnight, so Mae should have known, probably, that Georgie answering was a bad sign, not a good one.

"Let me guess, you're in labor." Georgie cackled. Mae could hear the buzz of nightlife in the background — clinking glasses and chatter and the occasional too-loud laugh.

"Correct," Mae said, begging the contractions to stop long enough for her to ask Georgie to come with her.

"I'm drunk," Georgie said.

"Super-drunk?" Mae asked, trying to do the calculation on just how drunk was too drunk to be her labor and delivery partner.

"You don't want me there," Georgie said. She lowered her voice. "You don't even really know me, Mae. We're not close. We haven't even talked since—you know. And it's been better for everyone. Us not talking."

Mae tried to make sense of this. She'd clung, ferociously, to the memory of Georgie holding her hand as they walked into her Leo-less apartment last year, taking in the damage with her, making it okay. Without Georgie, Mae would have climbed right back up her stairs to halt the move-out. She would have told him she wanted to give it one more chance. She would have waited for a ring; she would have lived an entirely different life.

"Should I just go alone?" Mae asked.

"Mae, I have no idea," Georgie said. "I told you—this part, it's not my thing. But I'm sure whatever you do will be fine, you know? Women do this all the time. You're strong and stuff. Okay?" The edge in Georgie's voice was unmistakable—she wanted to get back to whatever she was doing and whoever she was doing it with. "I gotta go. You're fine. But get to the hospital. I don't want to come home and hear you trying to get a baby out, okay?"

"Okay," Mae said, the pain subsiding, leaving her sweaty and wilted.

"Hospital," Georgie said again instead of goodbye.

And because Mae didn't know what else to do, she called a car and told the driver to take her to the hospital. Wisely, he didn't speak to her as she gasped and groaned in the back seat the whole way there.

Five minutes into the drive, her body startled with a newer, deeper pain. She needed Joni, who would have shown up with essential oils and a meditative playlist and probably a lot to say that Mae would have hated, but she missed even that, the things Joni did that she hated, the ways Joni was impossible and selfish and distracted.

She missed all of it — Joni's self-portraits painted on enormous canvases and the dozens of bracelets looped around her wrists and that she never let people compliment Mae without drawing attention to the ways she and Mae were similar so that the compliment could be for her too.

She called Catherine on the way, specifically using Catherine's cell and not the house's landline, but no one answered. Then she texted Sydney, who wouldn't get back to her, of course, no pregnant woman was checking text messages at two in the morning. At last she tried her father's landline, which Graham groggily answered with "What's wrong?"

"I'm having the baby," Mae said, and she could hear Graham's dissociation across the line. "I need help," she said, hoping it was a sort of password that might unlock the parental figure in him. It was funny, the way she had been so entrenched in family her entire childhood, only to be alone now, fully and truly alone.

Maybe the silence wasn't dissociation — maybe, maybe, he was missing Joni too in these bodacious, brutal moments before he became the grandparent that Joni could never be.

Mae groaned as the next wave of contractions hit her, and there was a rustle on the other end of the line, and then, finally, she heard Catherine's voice, surprisingly clear and alert for the middle of the night.

"I'm on my way," she said. "I've never done it, but I give a great massage and I'm not shy about bodily fluids, so we should be just fine."

It wasn't filled with love, exactly, but it was something. It was enough. It allowed Mae to relax in the tiny pause between contractions, knowing there would be someone the approximate size and shape of a mother with her.

* * *

It took Catherine almost two hours to arrive, and when she did, she was still in her pajamas and Mae was hooked up to machines, epidural'd, sleepy, waiting.

"Dad's in the waiting room?" Mae asked, hoping her father was just beyond the doors, pacing, purchasing balloons or teddy bears, checking in every ten minutes to see how his little girl was holding up.

"I drove myself," Catherine said carefully. "You know how he is with his sleep."

Mae waited for a promise that he would come, would be here when the baby was born, would be here to meet her as soon as he could. Those assurances did not come.

Catherine settled herself on the small couch in the room and made chitchat with the nurse who came in from time to time to look at vitals and tell Mae she wasn't dilating much. The nurse reminded Mae of Leo, her annoyance at Mae's lack of progress not unlike his, as if Mae were holding her body back from giving birth more quickly.

"Your dad is so excited," Catherine said, filling the space with words that didn't sound especially true. "Grandkids! He'll be a great granddad. He loves kids. Always wanted more, I'm sure you know that."

"Mmm," Mae said. She remembered mumblings about doctors' appointments and whispered conversations in the car when Graham and Joni thought she was asleep about how hard it had been trying for another and Joni not getting pregnant. But she didn't particularly want to discuss her parents' fertility issues or her parents at all. Now that the epidural had kicked in, she didn't want to think about much, preferred to simply exist in the liminal space that seemed to drag on endlessly, the pain not gone entirely the way she'd been promised, just dulled, still thumping in the background.

Machines beeped. Nurses and doctors left and came back. More drugs were offered—Pitocin, things that would speed the whole process up, and Mae said yes to it all.

"You would have been a great older sister," Catherine said, moments or hours after that. She was holding Mae's hand, something Mae wasn't sure she'd ever done in all their years as stepchild and stepparent. Catherine's hand was round and warm. Joni's had always been small and soft.

"Who knows," Mae said.

"Your dad thought so," Catherine said. She kept bringing Graham up, as if saying his name were enough to make his presence real, as if she could will him into caring.

"I don't know that my dad thought much about not being able to have more kids," Mae said. "It was my mom who always seemed kind of down about it."

"I think your dad thought about almost nothing else," Catherine said. She took a deep inhale, preparing herself for a story, a soliloquy of some kind that Mae hoped the epidural was strong enough to let her tune out. The air in the hospital room was tight, sterile, metallic-tasting. She waited for another nurse to come in and take her blood pressure or recommend another intervention, but none came.

Mae's father had seemed, for a time, to genuinely enjoy the basics of fatherhood—playing tag at the playground and being in charge of Sunday-morning pancakes and showing up, a little late but always there, to her recitals and concerts and art shows. He was good at all those things, until he wasn't.

After the affair, he vanished, more or less. But a lot of dads went a little bit missing during their daughters' adolescence, so it didn't necessarily stand out then. And later, when Joni was gone, the grief of losing her mother was so astonishing there wasn't much space left for Mae to long for her dad.

"Fertility issues can be so devastating," Catherine said, as if she'd heard Mae's thoughts. "I struggled too, in my first marriage. It's part of what your father and I bonded over. Our fertility struggles. But I was so jealous of him, of course, that he had you."

Flashes of memories glided through Mae's mind when she closed her eyes, half dreaming, half dreading. Finding pregnancy tests in Joni's bathroom more than once. An emphatic talk about the miracle of Mae even existing, *given the numbers.* Mae herself had dreamed from time to time about what it would be like to have a sibling in the nearly empty room next to hers, where Joni stored extra toilet paper and magazines she said she was going to read but never did. It might have been nice to knock on the wall when she was lonely, to have someone listening in when things fell apart.

"It took a lot of strength for him to talk to me about it," Catherine went on. Her voice sounded like tiptoeing, like a person entering a room she isn't entirely sure she is supposed to be in. "It really is amazing, you know, that you were even conceived. Given your father's—"

"Sorry you went through that," Mae said, hoping her voice communicated how desperately she did not want to be in this conversation. "And my dad too." She wished someone would come in and tell her it was time to push. She was thinking too hard about her father's sperm, something she'd never wanted to think about and now could not shake from her brain.

"I'm just saying, it really is shocking. That you exist at all."

"Okay," Mae said. It wasn't like Catherine to go on like this, not to know when to stop. Historically, Catherine and Mae spoke about *The Bachelor*, skin care, recipes involving lentils or chickpeas.

"I've told your father he should have this conversation with you, especially now that you're having a baby, but you know him, he keeps to himself, he doesn't always know how to have a difficult—"

"I think I just need to be quiet," Mae said. Her heart was pounding, and pain was breaking through the epidural, an awful ache in her hips and back, a promise of more to come. Catherine's words hung in the air and Mae felt the presence of a secret underneath them, something Catherine was trying to tell her or was trying to have Mae guess at without actually having to be told. An hour passed. More beeping. More nurses. And if another hour had passed, maybe Mae would have changed her mind, told Catherine to spit it out, let her in on whatever it was she was holding on to.

But another hour didn't pass.

"Okay, all right, it's go time," the next doctor to check on her said, and Mae said she wasn't ready and the doctor said she was, and a bright light was switched on over her pelvis, and she was shouted at to push and push and push and do it harder and more and to keep going. She was told the baby's hair was dark, that she just needed one more push, even though it would take at least twenty more, that she was doing great, that she couldn't give up, that she could do this, that she had to do this, that it was time, it was time, it was time.

And then there she was.

A dark-haired baby girl, screaming, taken away from her for a moment, then returned to her chest, still a little slimy, wet-haired, crying, but hers.

Hers.

"Alice," Mae said. "Her name is Alice."

"Alice?" Catherine asked. "I always thought you'd go for something more whimsical."

Catherine might have preferred the names Leo had tried to float: Ophelia. Regan. Ocean.

But Mae wanted to give her girl something Mae had never felt she had, something she wished she could have right now: A clean slate. A space in the world to make her own. She needed the name to reflect that possibility. A name that wasn't tied down to meaning or implication.

Alice.

She looked like an Alice.

THEN

SYDNEY WANTED TO name the dollhouse baby Alice. Mae wanted to name her Tallulah.

"Is that even a name?" Sydney asked, her nose wrinkled, her eyes ready to roll.

"Of course it's a name. A pretty name. You're saying you can choose any name in the world for this piece of plastic, literally any name because it's not even a person and you could change it again tomorrow, and you choose *Alice*?"

"Alice is classic. Pretty. And literary! *Alice in Wonderland.* You like *Alice in Wonderland.*"

The girls were fifteen and too old for dollhouses and *Alice in Wonderland* and arguments like this that could last an entire afternoon and often did. But still, here they were, playing with the dollhouse, renaming the baby, re-wallpapering the kitchen, rethinking what the dollhouse family might be up to, who they might be.

Lately, Sydney had been wanting to make the house nicer, more luxe. She'd started with the office, painting its walls a calming peach color, finding a new, more feminine desk and a fuzzy rug. She'd set the mom doll in there most days, with a tiny mug and a tiny muffin, and it made her feel better, like she was doing something to protect her.

Mae, of course, hated the shade of peach. Thought the room looked silly now.

It was early morning; Mae had slept over. Beth Ann looked tense lately when Mae slept over.

"Is it okay for Mae to come over?" Sydney would ask, trying to see if Beth Ann knew, trying to understand the blueprint of their families, what was ruined, what was still intact.

"It's fine," Beth Ann would say. "It's always fine." Sydney couldn't parse it. Maybe her mother knew. Or suspected. Or maybe not.

Beth Ann and Joni hadn't seen much of each other lately. A coffee last month when they talked about the latest school-board uproar over how much science was too much science for science class. A month before that they'd tried to go out to dinner at the new Thai place in town, but Beth Ann had lasted only twenty minutes and half a glass of wine before she felt the urge to say something pointed to her best friend: *Why are you sleeping with my husband and for how long and will you please stop and do you know that I know, did he tell you he admitted it and does he even care that I know and should I leave him and will you leave him and how are we here at all, why are we getting dinner together, are we friends even though you are ruining my life?* She couldn't fight back the urge, so instead of letting it spill out, she left.

Beth Ann felt a little like the dollhouse mom lately. Stuck in someone else's version of family, unable to do anything to change the familiar patterns of her life, even if others were doing their best to change them for her. Other women, she supposed, might leave right away. Might go to Joni's house and key her car. Might find

Graham in the grocery store and tell him everything their spouses were up to.

She wondered about Joni keeping the secret too. It was a strange thing they had in common, the two of them refusing to blow up their lives, maybe each of them in her own way protecting Mae and Sydney, protecting the tangled family friendship they'd created over the course of a decade, protecting something that maybe didn't entirely exist.

Beth Ann borrowed yet another book from the library on forgiving infidelity and pulled a tab from a poster at the grocery store advertising a women's group for "women navigating that next phase of their lives." The poster featured a stock image of women lifting mugs of coffee to their lips, the beginnings of smiles on their faces, a hint of pinkish light peeking in through the windows, the dawn of some new day. She'd taken the tab from the poster delicately, quickly, not wanting anyone to catch her wanting something that made her look so vulnerable. The tiny slip of paper was in her wallet. She looked at it often, promising herself every evening that she'd call the number, losing her courage every morning.

This morning, though, was different. She could hear the girls' upstairs arguing, the coffee was strong, an extra scoop having made its way in either by accident or on purpose, her subconscious knowing what this would require. It was raining outside, no perfect peachy light dappling the kitchen table. Barrett was still asleep. He'd gotten in late last night. The late nights hadn't stopped. Nothing had changed, really, since he'd admitted what he was up to.

Beth Ann dialed the number.

Upstairs in Sydney's room, Mae and Sydney wouldn't have been able to hear Beth Ann's whispering voice asking what kind of meetings the group had, how many people came, what they talked about. Mae and Sydney were in their own whispering secret space. In the early mornings, you could pretend what was happening was all a dream. You weren't, after all, really your whole self when you were in your pajamas. The girls could imagine themselves younger, simpler, not so silly for still getting lost in their dollhouse world.

"I like how weird *Alice in Wonderland* is," Mae said, perfecting a wallpapered corner. "I don't like that her name is Alice and that she's a typical pretty girl."

"Nothing wrong with being pretty," Sydney said. Lately, she had begun straightening her hair, putting on eyeliner, applying self-tanner to her legs. She asked Mae to go to the mall every weekend, but once there she'd set her eyes on a group of boys and follow them around until they eventually noticed and flirted with her and on occasion got Sydney's number. A few times she made out with them by the bathrooms, but these dalliances didn't lead to boyfriends or even, as it turned out, phone calls.

"Do you think your mom is pretty?" Mae asked. Sometimes she straightened her hair too, played with eyeliner, tried her hand at the chemical-smelling tanning lotion that stained her sheets and towels with puke-colored streaks. But it never sat quite right. Neither did the trips to the mall. She liked browsing the Borders and grabbing an Auntie Anne's cinnamon sugar pretzel; she liked the hot, buttery way it greased the napkin she held it in, the way she had to lick the sweet topping from her fingers, how it was always exactly the same as the last time.

Mae wasn't interested in boys. Not the ones at the mall, at least, with their white baseball hats and skinny arms and way of walking around like it was theirs, all of it, the mall and the people in it too. They acted like nothing mattered, Mae thought, but everything mattered to Mae, and the disparity felt too large to manage.

She made out with one once, by the fountain, but even the way he kissed seemed like he was bored, only occasionally moving his lips or tongue as if he suddenly remembered he had them, putting his hands on her butt like it was his too.

"Do I think my mom's pretty?" Sydney asked, like she'd never even considered it. "Sometimes. When she wants to be, I guess. Pretty enough. Mom-pretty."

"And my mom?" Mae asked. She'd noticed something different in both moms over the past few months and was curious if Sydney saw it too.

"I don't know." Sydney had been clamming up a lot lately when certain subjects came up: Joni, summer vacation, her own father, a plotline on *Dawson's Creek* she didn't like.

"Come on. She is, right?"

"I hate her clothes. And she should wear perfume. Her hair's always messy."

"You're not answering the question."

"She's not pretty. She's something else. People notice her."

"Sexy," Mae said. It was the word she'd sort of wanted Sydney herself to come up with for how true it felt. "You see it, right?"

"I hate this conversation, Mae."

"Okay, here's the thing, though," Mae said. She moved a miniature bowl of fruit to the center of the dolls' dining-room table. She took the dad doll and put him upstairs in the bed. She took the mom doll and put her peering out the window, looking somewhere else. "I think my mom is sexy but my dad doesn't even care." It felt good, actually, to say it out loud. "I don't think they even like each other. I don't think my dad even really likes *me*. Or the whole family thing. Not anymore, at least. He liked me when I was little. Remember when he coached soccer? He was so funny, right? I remember him being funny. But now—I don't know. Maybe he wanted a different kind of kid. Someone who likes stuff that he likes? Someone who looks like him? Do you think he'd like me more if I looked like him?"

"He's your dad," Sydney said. She was trying to set up the baby's nursery. Alice's nursery. Mae had let her do it how she wanted, with pastel pink and lacy curtains and an old-fashioned basket on a set of wobbly wheels—a baby carriage instead of a crib. It was perfect, just right.

"My mom has all these new nightgown-y things. Like, lingerie. Victoria's Secret stuff. Hot pink. Red. Not the sort of thing she'd normally wear and it's weird and they're everywhere. Just sitting there on drying racks and stuff. I mean, what is that?"

"I don't want to know about your mom's lingerie. Don't be weird." Sydney got up from the dollhouse. "Let's go to the mall. That guy, Mike whatever, said he was going today. He's hot. He said if we came by we could all get burgers at Johnny Rockets."

"I don't want to get burgers at Johnny Rockets," Mae said. She hated the fake 1950s diner, the garish jukeboxes.

"Well, obviously, it's not about the burgers," Sydney said, rolling her eyes.

Mae pulled her legs in, a sign of not wanting to go, and Sydney stood up, a challenge set out that they'd have to navigate.

Except they didn't have to navigate it today. There was a crash downstairs. Something breaking. "You piece of shit!" Beth Ann screaming—words she'd never say in a tone she'd never say them in, except here they were.

"I told you I needed space," they heard Barrett say. "You've known what was happening. I told you what was happening. I thought you'd tell me to leave but you didn't and now—"

"You packed everything? Your whole closet? Were you going to tell Sydney? Or just gallop away in the middle of the night?"

"We've talked about telling Sydney! I've been wanting to tell Sydney! She knows most of it anyway. But you just keep holding on as if—"

"You're going to just throw it all away? That's your plan? I'd forgive you if you stayed. It would take time, but wouldn't that be something? Isn't that the whole point?"

"I don't want to stay and wait for your forgiveness! I want to be happy!"

"We all want to be fucking happy, Barrett, but we're adults, my God! I'm trying to make this work! Can't you see that? I'm reading that book and I just joined a support group for women—"

"That's not what I want," Barrett said, his voice quieter, gentler, which was somehow even worse. "I don't want to work on it. I don't want to hear what some book says about how to love you."

There was a long and terrible quiet after this, both upstairs with Mae and Sydney and downstairs with Sydney's parents.

Sydney was staring at the floor like maybe there was a way to fall through it into some other, better reality. Mae watched Sydney for signs of what to do, how to feel.

"I want you to leave," Sydney said at last.

"Let's both leave," Mae said. She kept her voice gentle. This was not a competition over whose house was better and whose mom was prettier and whose life was harder. This was what having a best friend was for—someone to pull you away from the awful and ugly parts of your parents' marriage, a thing you weren't supposed to know anything about anyway. They could sit in Mae's backyard and eat Popsicles like they used to do when they were kids and something sad happened at school. They could watch a movie, an old one they'd seen a hundred times already and had a million inside jokes about. They could fix this.

Or at least put it aside for a few hours. They could survive it.

"Come over," Mae went on. "Sleep over. Your parents probably need space or whatever. They'll make up. My parents fight all the time, then the next day it's just, like, over. You want tacos? You love Mom's tacos."

"I hate her tacos," Sydney said, her voice a knife, her words a confusion to Mae, who had heard Sydney rave about Joni's tacos a hundred times. "Please leave. This isn't any of your business."

"It's not really yours either, Syd. Whatever's going on with them, I'm sure it's—"

"Shut the fuck up." Just like Beth Ann, Sydney almost never swore. It wasn't that she was against it, exactly, but it didn't suit her and she knew it. Or it didn't suit her until now.

Mae stopped trying to argue. She gathered herself up and started toward the stairs. She tiptoed, but it didn't matter. The floors at Sydney's house squeaked, the way all floors do in all houses everywhere. A predictable and unavoidable pattern of sounds that was unnerving but still cozy, familiar. And when she reached the kitchen, she saw it.

A broken coffee mug on the floor, a yellow one she knew Beth Ann loved, because she knew everything about Beth Ann, or at least everything about the things she treasured and the patterns of her days and what she would say if the girls made a mess in the living room or were wearing clothes she didn't approve of or were talking too loudly late at night. She knew Beth Ann but not this version, the one she caught sight of as soon as her eyes moved on from the coffee mug.

This Beth Ann was collapsed on the kitchen table, her arms bent, her head between them, forehead on the dark wood. Barrett was across the room, pacing like he had more to say but no one to say it to. It was the image of a broken marriage, a broken moment in a broken family that Mae was having to walk through.

"Sorry, excuse me, Syd asked me to leave," Mae said, because even in moments like this, she wanted to tell the truth, even if the truth was a little too much for everyone right now.

Beth Ann heaved a sob.

Barrett looked at her and stopped pacing. "Stay," he said to Mae. "You can stay."

"Oh. No. I'm good," Mae said, startled by the way Barrett was looking at her — intensely, like she was a part of this somehow.

"You're always welcome here," Barrett said loudly so that Beth Ann had to hear it too, and she must have, because she raised her body up like a zombie from the dead and took a blue plate, one with breakfast crumbs still clinging to it, and threw it at the space between Barrett and Mae, which wasn't a very big space at all, actually.

The plate didn't graze Mae or anything, but Beth Ann hadn't exactly purposely avoided her either. It hit the fridge and shattered on the floor.

"Beth Ann," Barrett whisper-yelled.

"Fuck you," Beth Ann said. "Both of you. All of you. She's not welcome here whenever. She's not welcome here now. Stop saying things. Stop deciding whatever you want to decide. You're leaving, so leave. I'll decide if this is a good time for Sydney to have friends over."

The plate just lay there on the ground, cracked into a dozen pieces, a thing Mae would never forget.

She walked home, banging in her front door, barely saying hi to Joni on the couch with her book and Graham in the kitchen making eggs. She didn't do much upstairs in her bedroom. Sat on the bed. Looked out the window. Squinted at the sky and then tried to forget all about what she had just seen.

Eventually, Sydney appeared, as Mae had known she would,

knocking on her bedroom door, still in her pajamas, not wanting to talk but not wanting to be at home.

"He's leaving," she said eventually when the two of them had been curled up in Mae's twin bed together for a while, watching the second half of some Saturday-morning movie they'd seen before. "He really is. He's moving out."

"Why?" Mae asked, even though the reason didn't matter as much as the thing he was doing.

Sydney looked hard at Mae, deciding and then quickly undeciding to tell her the truth. "He's really leaving," she said again.

The Saturday movie finished and another one began and eventually they looked out the window to see down the street. Barrett's car was gone from the driveway. They'd missed the moment it had all ended.

"That's it?" Mae said.

"What do divorced kids do? Get, like, pancakes with their dads on Saturdays or something? I guess that will be my life now," Sydney said. "What about your parents?"

"What about them?"

"They're fine?"

Mae thought about the scene downstairs. Neither Graham nor Joni had really said hello when she'd walked in, and they were always in decidedly different rooms, and she remembered a long time ago they used to play records on weekend mornings, not dancing around to them or anything, but swaying sometimes. Singing along. Laughing, the two of them, about something they remembered from a concert they'd attended or a time they'd heard the song at a wedding long before Mae was born. But there had been no blue plate broken on the ground. No screaming.

"They're fine," Mae said.

"Well," Sydney said. "Good for you, I guess."

The girls settled back into the bed. It was too small for them both now. It always had been probably. Their legs and elbows touched, their hair tangled together. They stayed like that for a long time. Saturday movies didn't have an end point—one after another after another played, and for once, no one was looking for them. No one was wondering where they were.

They were, they both thought to themselves, exactly where they were meant to be.

THE PAINTING

MAE PAINTS THE girls closer together. This time, she doesn't paint over the old versions of the girls; she simply paints more versions, cloning them over and over and over, trying to find their ideal form. She paints them tangled up in each other, legs on top of legs, heads on shoulders, hands knotted up and gripping hard. She paints them back to back, leaning against each other but looking in opposite directions. She paints them on far ends of the canvas, contemplating the enormous space between them.

Over the course of the month of November in her twenty-sixth year, Mae covers the canvas with a dozen versions of the girls, so that the resulting work is a strange, hectic gathering of clones.

In the evenings, Mae drinks cocktails at bars in SoHo, making friends with other artists and people who want to be close to artists, who want to have the aura of artistry without the paint under their nails, the worry of what's next wandering their minds. There is Sasha, who works with oils, Benjamin, who is a photographer, and Fiona, who is rich. She's the rich kid of rich parents, a girl who dresses all in white even in the dead of winter, even in dingy, dirty bars. A girl who majored in art history and seeming important. A girl who strides into Mae's home one night after wine and dancing and smoking cigarettes that they would both regret the next day.

"This isn't you at all," she said to the boxy apartment Mae had always lived in. "Where's the fun?"

Mae put her arms up high, an exclamation point of a gesture, grinning from the force of her own wit: "I'm right here."

Fiona smiled. "Fair enough," she said, cozying herself onto the couch, which back then was navy-blue corduroy, a relic from the seventies or eighties, a thing Graham offered up when Mae asked for help furnishing a new place after leaving the one she'd shared with Sydney. Her apartment with Sydney didn't have a couch — their two beds had taken up the whole of the studio — but in this place there was room for a bed and a couch and a tiny table that functioned as a workspace. Everything was handed down from Graham and Catherine or came from the people who'd lived here before; they left behind a few pots and a dish for baking bread and a Ziploc baggie filled with batteries and loose screws that probably belonged to furniture they had taken with them. Mae didn't have a screwdriver, but still it seemed adult to hang on to the screws, responsible to imagine a life where she might need a screw and, spectacularly, also be able to provide one.

Fiona looked at the walls, which were mostly blank. Mae was hesitant to display her artwork until it was right. And it was never right. She had, however, hung up the Painting. Not because it was done but because she needed to live with it for a while before figuring out what it needed next. Something was missing, but she didn't know what. It was stranger and wilder than anything she'd attempted before.

"Yours?" Fiona asked, pointing her chin in the direction of it.

"It's not done," Mae said.

"What is it?"

"Oil on canvas."

"No, what is it? Like, really?"

The girls both contemplated the texture of the paint, the way it rose up and out in certain moments, looked smooth and thoughtful in others. The canvas was large, wider than Mae's arm span, bigger than anything she had worked on before, and as she looked at it with Fiona, the size was especially overpowering.

"It's about friends," Mae said, and in saying it, it became true. Her heart ached, a sudden thud of longing for Sydney, for closeness, to be *in* the Painting, in the complication of it, instead of out here, observing it, creating it.

Fiona's eyes darted from side to side, trying to take in every moment of the work. She probably would have liked to take a few large strides back to see the whole of it from a better vantage, to get some space and see it as a complete, singular work and not dozens of tiny vignettes. But in Mae's cramped apartment it was impossible, so the Painting was more of an assault or a demand.

"This is a gallery piece," Fiona said. "You're good. This is good. And strange. And this little hovel you live in, it's perfect, actually. It's a whole story. You're a whole story." Fiona moved her gaze from the Painting to Mae, who was undone from the night out, mascara coming off, lipstick smudged, her patchwork dress loose around the waist, falling off her shoulders. Around her neck she wore a locket that Sydney had given her years ago, originally with a photograph of the two of them inside. Now it was empty, and it had come unhooked over the course of her partying, so its vacancy was on full display.

"I don't know about that," Mae said.

"Well, I do. I know all about it. We can make you happen."

After another drink, Fiona fell asleep on Mae's couch, and when she woke up, stripes from the fabric were imprinted on her cheek.

Mae thought perhaps the night before had been a drunken promise, a plan like so many others that would never come to be. But

Fiona, bright-eyed in the morning, desperate for the two of them to get out the door for coffee and bagels and more cigarettes, said it again, more forcefully this time.

"I'm going to make you someone. That painting. It's something. I can see it. Whatever it's about, friendship or sisterhood or girlhood or selfhood or whatever, we'll tell the story, we'll make it happen."

"Friendship," Mae said, wanting to draw a line in the sand before Fiona fully took over, before things got out of control. "It's about friendship."

Fiona shrugged. "It's about whatever they think it's about," she said, gesturing vaguely to the window, the world outside it.

And after a coffee, half a bagel, two cigarettes, and a long, frantic talk with Fiona, Mae returned to her living room that was also her bedroom and her art studio, and she took out her paints again. No matter what Fiona said, the Painting wasn't finished.

NOW

Sydney

BETH ANN WASN'T meant to be at the birth. In fact, it was written right in Sydney's birth plan, a document that she had been working on for months, using bold and italics and underlines to make sure the most important parts would be clear to whatever doctor or nurse came by to check on her during however long the whole enterprise took. Based on the women at Small Group who loved to share their birth stories even though Sydney wanted nothing less than to hear them, twenty-four hours was what to plan for. The women were always saying they had been in labor for twenty-four hours. It seemed impossible, really, but then so did pregnancy in general, and having a baby, and the rest of it too, being married and living a life and all the tiny inconveniences—running out of eggs! Cleaning the filter in the dryer! Renewing her passport! It was all, on some level, impossible.

Still, here she was, even the shape of her was absurd, the unlikeliness of carrying another human, growing one, had her awestruck and, on occasion, disbelieving.

NO OUTSIDE FAMILY. HUSBAND ONLY, the birth plan read.

But here was Beth Ann anyway, and Sydney couldn't even blame her. They'd been at lunch when Sydney went into labor, parts of her tightening and releasing in ways she couldn't fully understand but seemed familiar to Beth Ann.

"Well, here we go," Beth Ann had said, calmly calling a Lyft because she'd had wine with lunch and so was not in any condition to drive a pregnant woman to the hospital.

She'd said those exact words, as if Sydney were a laboring stranger and not her only child.

"Call Sam." Sydney must have said it a dozen times to her mother, who kept insisting it might be false labor, even though she was just days before her due date and everything she'd read about Braxton-Hicks contractions made it sound like they were more pressure than pain, and this, this was certainly pain.

"Call Sam," she said again when they put her in a wheelchair at the entrance to the hospital. But Beth Ann just shrugged.

"I will, I will," she said, and Sydney could have called Sam herself, of course, except lately by afternoon her phone was out of battery. She'd been doing her best to stay on top of her Lilly-Lou work, but that took endless time on social media, uploading photos and commenting on other people's posts and scrolling through threads to see who was up to what and watching Ivy Miller's videos and texting with her Small Group about what Ivy Miller had said and why it was brilliant and what they should take away from it.

Sydney was sent to labor and delivery triage with Beth Ann by her side, but still Sam hadn't been called, and still Beth Ann was talking for her—yes, Sydney would probably want an epidural soon, yes, the contractions were close together, yes, she knew the sex of the baby, no, she wasn't allergic to any medications.

"I'm here, I can still talk, I have a husband," Sydney whispered to her mother, wishing she could scream it.

Certain things, certain rules of How to Be, were especially difficult to let go of, and this was one of them: We do not yell. We do not make a fuss, we are not difficult women, we are the kind of women about whom, when we leave the hospital, the nurses say, *Wasn't she nice? So sweet and easy.*

"I'm sure your husband's on his way, sweetheart," the nurse with the blue earrings and husky voice said.

"I don't think anyone's called him," Sydney said, darting her eyes toward Beth Ann and then back to the nurse, trying to communicate a lifetime of incomprehensible decisions to this woman who had a whole floor of expectant mothers to care for, a hundred other more important things to do than untangle the impossible knots of Beth Ann and Sydney's relationship.

The nurse put a hand on Sydney's arm. "I'll see that he gets called," she said, and for a moment Sydney relaxed. This woman looked tough, sturdy, someone who would talk back to Beth Ann, a person who would get it done. This was the nurse to have on her side.

"Now, please," Sydney said. "My mom isn't—"

"I'm just about to!" Beth Ann interrupted. She took out her phone to show it to the nurse. "I just wanted to get my girl settled. One thing at a time, and I know how long labor goes on. He won't miss anything. They're pretty useless until the end anyway, aren't they? The husbands?" Beth Ann tilted her head and smiled at the nurse like they had some secret knowledge about husbands and birth and how it would all go. And maybe they did, because the nurse smiled back.

"I see a lot of napping men in these parts," the nurse said, laughing a little. "Sweet but a little clueless, yes."

Sydney willed her to wait and watch, to make sure that Beth Ann started dialing the number, maybe even take the phone from her and confirm she'd actually called. But the nurse chuckled and turned away to attend to someone else—someone huffing or moaning or saying in a sad, tight little voice over and over, *I can't do it, I can't do it.*

And Beth Ann put the phone back in her pocket.

"Mom," Sydney said.

"Relax," Beth Ann said, like it was nothing.

"Why won't you call him?" It was getting hard not to cry. The contractions hurt, the epidural hadn't arrived, the phone was in her mother's pocket, and the nurse had forgotten all about her dilemma.

"What if we did this, just you and I?"

"He's the dad!" Sydney said, gasping at the way her body seemed to be revolting against her.

Beth Ann grabbed her hand. "Squeeze," she said. "I can take it." And Sydney did, hard, and Beth Ann stayed solid, immovable, unbothered by the crushing of her bones, the pinching of her skin. There was so much about Beth Ann that was easy to judge, even easy to hate. But her there-ness was beautiful in its own way. She was a woman who had withstood a great deal and would, she seemed to promise, withstand even more. She was asking, in this moment, for Sydney to add that to the list of things she knew about her mother. Add it to her list of ways to be a mother.

"Today is yours," Beth Ann said in a whisper. "It's you. And your daughter. And I'll be here, and the doctors and nurses. But what if you let this be a time to show yourself you can do it alone? All of it. Just so you know, Syd. Just so you have that tucked away like a secret, like a little bit of armor against whatever happens next." It was Beth Ann now who was squeezing Sydney's hand, Beth Ann whose eyes were filling, whose breath was quickening from the importance of what she was saying.

Somewhere, Barrett was still living in Beth Ann's home, changing their light bulbs and paying their bills and being her husband, in spite of everything. Sydney had always believed they'd come back together after the separation because of love—because wasn't marriage the same thing as love? Wasn't love the reason for any difficult choice? But she could see now—maybe because of Beth Ann's voice, which had never before been this quiet, or maybe because of the hazy, destabilizing force of the pain of labor—why Beth Ann hadn't left Barrett: Because she couldn't. Because she had never proven she could do it alone. Not even when they were separated. Beth Ann was still trying to show that it was possible, but so far, it simply wasn't.

And still, here she was. Withstanding.

"You can do this," Beth Ann said, urgent. "And then you'll know."

It was hard for Sydney to think clearly. The hospital gown was a terrible beige nothing of a color and it was hanging off her awkwardly. She smelled like lunch and sweat and how much it hurt, which was a lot. She was making noises she'd never heard her own body make, was moving it in ways unfamiliar to her, like she could somehow twist away from the contractions. These were all things that were large and true and holdable in this moment; the rest of the things Beth Ann was saying, the things she was implying, were not.

Barrett's affair with Joni, though—that was real. And true. And so big it sometimes took up the whole room, even in moments like this, where there was barely space for anything but the question of how to survive this moment, and this one, and the next one too.

Sydney did not want to be a woman whose husband loved someone else. She did not want to be the less exciting person in a friendship, the solid force who stayed but was utilitarian at best. She didn't want to be Beth Ann. She didn't want to be Joni either, really, who had been more of a storm than a person.

It was the familiar conundrum she and Mae had grappled with since they were old enough to imagine themselves as future women, future moms. There was Beth Ann. There was Joni. And there was the hope of a third option. Like the dollhouse mom. A different kind of woman than these two, with their flaws and contradictions and messes.

Between contractions, Sydney reached for the third option.

"Okay," she said, not believing, really, that she was agreeing to this. "Maybe you're right. Maybe you shouldn't call Sam. Maybe he can come after."

The dollhouse mother had never given birth, of course. Her hair was plastic, so it did not get matted to her forehead; she had never groaned, all low and animalistic, from pain; she didn't have to wonder what would happen next, what a baby would mean for her marriage, her friendships, her business, her life.

Sydney was rooted in her body in these cavernous, bellowing, impossible birthing moments, but still, she wished for the simplicity of the dollhouse mom. For a hiccup of time, she even hoped for something akin to the dollhouse baby—uncrying, sweetly smiling, easy.

"Sam can come after," she said again, the words becoming a mantra, the decision easier to make than she'd have thought.

"Oh, Syd," Beth Ann said, and it felt like it had been eons since Beth Ann had been proud of Sydney in this way. Possibly she had never been so happy with her as she was in this bare, breaking instant.

And that was something, wasn't it? To have, for a breath, the clarity of her mother's love, the promise that she had, at last, done something worthy of her approval?

Things were moving quickly anyway, a serious doctor and someone he seemed to be teaching administered the epidural, and soon after, what had been so bright and vibrant and painful became quiet and dulled and cloudy, and the urgency passed. She'd call Sam or she wouldn't. The baby would come either way, and Sam would arrive eventually, and she couldn't remember why it had seemed like such a big deal. There wasn't much to watch here. There was lying around and the occasional urge to vomit and the nurses checking numbers and doctors in training reporting things she already knew about her own body. There were endless people looking between her legs, but even that seemed like nothing. It didn't feel like her body anymore; it was a machine being watched, the way she waited for the laundry to be done, peeking at the time every once in a while so she didn't accidentally miss it and leave wet clothes overnight.

The doctors were checking on her in just that same laundry-day way — perfunctory, cursory, maybe occasionally a little bit impatient but then forgetting all about her again.

"I'm like a washing machine," Sydney said to her mother, who was half asleep on the cramped chair next to the hospital bed.

"What's that, Syd? You feeling something?"

"Or maybe I'm the dirty clothes?" Sydney went on. "Am I dirty clothes, do you think?"

"No, sweetheart."

"Well, I'm something."

"You are."

There were a few conversations like that — groggy, half formed. The epidural hit people differently, but it gave Sydney a drowsy high, which was great until she was told to push. Then she had to be roused to a more suitable state for exertion, something she really wasn't up to.

"Bodies are not miracles," she said to her mother between bouts of being yelled at to push and push and push. "Bodies do not know what they're doing."

"I suppose not," Beth Ann said with a shudder.

It took two hours of this half-hearted pushing for the baby to come out, but she did, eventually, red-faced and screaming and healthy and all the things Sydney had hoped she would be.

She was wrapped up and put on Sydney, who smiled and named her Alice.

Sam missed it all. By the time he arrived, Sydney was in a floral robe and Alice in a matching floral swaddle and Beth Ann had run a brush through Sydney's hair, applied a tiny bit of blush to her cheeks.

"You're beautiful," Sam said to Sydney or maybe to Alice or to the both of them. And Beth Ann, watching, sighed with relief, smiled. "You did it," he said, a little surprised, maybe. A little put in his place, Sydney let herself hope.

She was bleeding, her legs were shaky, a smell of burned plastic and witch hazel and iron emanated from her, but still she felt the tiniest bit like the dollhouse mother, her hair neat, her robe tightly tied, her expression faraway and content.

She wanted to hang on to it.

And she knew, in the same moment, her body screaming in agony as the painkillers wore off, that she would never be able to be that kind of woman either.

NOW

Mae

MAE HAD DRESSED herself in an oversize waffle-knit lavender Henley and she'd even done her hair. Alice was three weeks old, and it wasn't that Mae had it all under control now or anything, far from it, but there was a tiny bit of rhythm to her day, a knowing of this baby, who had been such an unimaginable mystery from the moment she arrived. She'd strapped her successfully into the stroller, she'd figured out the cup-holder attachment and made her way into a coffee shop to grab a latte, and she was feeling, for the first time, like a mom. No. A *Mom*. Someone who was pulling it off. She'd put on blush! She'd remembered pads in her bra to hide the leaking! She was well enough to walk this far in spite of the injuries she was still navigating from the delivery.

She felt the way she'd hoped she'd feel — not like wound-up Beth Ann or messy Joni but like someone else, someone put together and smiling and sweet, someone wholesome and lovable and warm. She wished Joni could see her like this. She tilted her face up to the sky as if maybe somehow she could if Mae could just get the angle right.

She felt like the dollhouse mom, the one she and Sydney had spent years making tiny clothing for, creating a life for, fashioning themselves after. The dollhouse mom was always there, always home, always happy to bake dollhouse cookies or sit down and play dollhouse Monopoly. The dollhouse mom didn't ever change. She was solid and predictable, and it felt impossible that Mae—a single mom, an artist, a girl whose mother destroyed everything and then, impossibly, horrendously, died—could be so stable. But today—in her Henley, with her coffee, sliding sunglasses from her hair to her nose as the beautiful autumn sun squinted through the trees—she thought maybe she could be that kind of woman. Maybe.

Mae lifted her chin. She took a sip of latte and placed it back in the cup holder. She peeked in on Alice, who was sleeping, who was always sleeping, except when she most decidedly was *not* sleeping and was wailing and sucking at her and making noises that Mae didn't recognize mere weeks ago but now were an entire language she was expected to be fluent in.

"What a good baby," Leo had said upon meeting Alice, who was sleeping strapped to Mae's chest. He petted her head. He kissed it, which felt odd to Mae, since Alice was attached to her and it felt a little like he was kissing her too, except of course he wasn't.

Alice had slept the whole time and Leo hadn't offered to watch her at some point, hadn't come up with some plan for how their arrangement might work, hadn't defined what exactly his role would be in Alice's little life. "You've got this under control," he said to Mae on his way back home after the meetup. And Mae wasn't sure if it was meant to be encouraging or more like a warning, him telling her that she would have to continue to have it under control, alone.

This was perhaps the sort of thing she was supposed to talk to a friend about, and Sydney was maybe going to be that friend. And there she was now, across the street, waiting for Mae at the Bartel-Pritchard entrance of Prospect Park, sunlit and pushing an expensive stroller back and forth, back and forth, like she'd been doing it forever.

Mae tried to wave but Sydney wasn't looking in her direction, wasn't looking anywhere, really, as if she were just *there* and not there with a purpose, not there to meet Mae, not there to begin this new chapter of their friendship. The wave failed, so Mae just pushed the stroller until she was across the street and almost at Sydney's side, which was when the stroller's wheel hit a branch or a bump or maybe nothing at all, who could say, and the latte jumped, the cup holder tilted, and, like that, Mae was covered in light brown liquid, her lavender waffle Henley dirty and dingy and no longer the comfortable shirt of a woman who knew what she was doing but in fact the emboldened exclamation point of a person who was not meant to be a parent at all, a declaration to the world but especially to Sydney that she was going to be *this* kind of mother — the haphazard, falling-apart, harried, and covered-in-coffee kind.

She had failed so fast at being the kind of mother she'd imagined herself being.

"Hey." She announced herself to Sydney in a voice that was far cheerier than she felt. "I look like a mess but I swear it just happened. Cup holders! Who knew what a racket they were. I need a thermos, I guess."

"Huh?" Up close, Sydney looked less like a seasoned pro and more like a zombie. Flyaway hairs. A glassy-eyed gaze. An unslept look to her posture.

Mae held up her arms, showing off her shirt. "Live and learn, right?"

"Right," Sydney said, but she still seemed not to be registering the full scene.

"So this is her?" Mae asked. She leaned over Sydney's stroller and moved a draped muslin aside to see the baby. They hadn't exchanged the types of texts she imagined most new mothers shared—hospital photos of brand-new babies with names and weights and times of birth, miniature twenty-first-century birth announcements. They hadn't shared the gruesome details of labor and delivery or updated each other on the trials and tribulations of sleep patterns or breastfeeding or the special mesh underwear the hospital sends you home with and why it is so much better than any other sort of postpartum undergarment one might buy.

"Yes. Her. Alice," Sydney said. Her voice was a little dead and a little dreamy, but still Mae startled at the name.

"Alice?"

"You knew that. I've always loved the name. You know. Like the dollhouse."

"Well, fuck," Mae said. She smiled. It maybe wasn't funny. Sydney might not think it was funny. Mae herself was going to have trouble figuring out how to put into words why she had named her own child Alice when the name so clearly belonged to Sydney, Mae having quickly dismissed it years ago.

"Fuck?" Sydney repeated.

"Meet Alice," Mae said, pulling back her own light muslin blanket, patterned with tiny yellow ducklings. Why baby gear had to be so pointedly babyish was beyond her. The baby didn't know anything about yellow ducklings. The baby didn't care. The parents were the ones having to see whatever was on the blanket-swaddle-onesie-boppy-changing-table-bedsheet. Shouldn't it therefore reflect a parental sensibility and not a baby's? Mae for one had no real interest in baby ducks.

"Alice?" Sydney was a slowed-down version of herself, which wasn't surprising, exactly; the babies had been born only weeks ago, and Mae was slowed down too, unable to watch CNN or eat Thai food or listen to music over a certain decibel. She was sensitive to the world in a new way, raw. But Sydney was even further gone, a shadow person.

"I know. When we were little, I was all—I needed her to be named, like, Aphrodite or whatever, something big and strange, but when I saw her all little and wrapped up and smoosh-faced, I don't know, I wanted something familiar. Alice. I didn't know you still liked the name, obviously." Mae was blushing. It was embarrassing to be in her thirties and still in a push-pull with her old best friend over baby names and what belonged to whom. She wished she'd chosen something else. Jane. Sarah. Charlotte. There were other names that were equally wholesome, plain, that she should have used. She hadn't wanted a fancy name on top of the unknowableness of what this baby wanted and how Mae was ever supposed to deliver it to her. But she hadn't had to name her Alice. "I'm sorry," she said, still waiting for Sydney to say something, anything.

"Two Alices," Sydney said at last, it having taken full minutes for her to absorb it all. "Weird. She's cute."

"Yours too," Mae said, though really she found only her own Alice cute. All other babies had something strange about them—little gremlin faces misshapen, features startlingly mismatched. Her Alice, though, was beautiful. "We should walk, right?" Mae asked. She grabbed her mostly spilled latte from the cup holder and experimented with one-handed stroller maneuvering, something she'd seen many other mothers do.

Sydney nodded and they entered the park. There were countless groups of women with strollers, women with pregnant bellies, women in general talking, walking, making their way through the paths and trees and occasional puddles. Mae noted there were no groups of men doing the same; this was a distinctly female social activity, it seemed.

The old friends walked in silence. It was maybe the quietest they'd ever been together. The Alices were quiet too. The rest of the park was loud with birds and children and the huff-huffing of runners and the endless chatter of everyone else and, even in the center of the park, the sirens and horns of the city streets.

In the three weeks since Alice was born, Mae's life had been a mix of loud and quiet, nothing in between. Alice's hungry or sleepy or dirty-diapered screams followed always by the quiet of her napping and no one around to talk to. Graham and Catherine had come and gone the same day that Mae and Alice returned home.

"Labor sure was a lot," Catherine said. "We'll come back in a few weeks, right, honey?" She'd looked at Graham for affirmation, but he didn't give it.

"Oh," Mae said, trying to understand what it was that labor—which had felt distinctly her own, heavy on her body and no one else's—could possibly have done to Catherine or Graham. Catherine rubbed Graham's back like he was the one who needed coddling, the one whose existence had been altered.

The bloodied pads and aching nipples and general exhaustion of her entire body told Mae that *she* was in fact the one who needed to recuperate, she was the one who would never be the same, but there was no space to say that to Graham and Catherine. She hugged them goodbye, sleepy, droopy-necked Alice draped over her shoulder, and took another extra-strength Tylenol, begging it to ease the way every inch of her felt raw and cracked open and throbbing from the mire of things it had somehow accomplished.

She willed Graham to say something, anything, about Joni. That the baby resembled her. That Joni would have been proud of her. That Joni was watching from wherever Joni was. But Graham patted her back and said nothing at all.

Mae considered telling Sydney all this. About missing Joni and damaged nipples and the way the mommy blog posts warned of day-and-night confusion as if it were a thing that happened only to babies but didn't mention how it would happen to mothers too, floating through days and nights and nights and days without being able to say, really, where any of them ended or began. But it took too long for Mae to organize all these enormous thoughts and feelings and pounding, ceaseless physical sensations, so Sydney spoke first.

"Ivy Miller says that this is a time to stay connected, so I'm really trying to," Sydney said at last. "Posting as much as I can. Babies look cute on the pashminas, but I get the feeling I'm supposed to be doing more than that. Connecting with other moms and stuff. Which — this counts. We're supposed to look out for other moms with kids around the same age, make those connections, build those paths."

Sydney, Mae thought, sounded like a robot. But Mae couldn't really trust her own impressions of the world right now, in the shaky state she was in.

"Like, for a mom group? For the babies to make friends or something?" Mae tried to take a sip of the latte, but between the gulps she'd already taken and the epic spill, the cup was empty. Still, she hung on to it, bringing it to her mouth occasionally, a sort of social safety net.

"For connections," Sydney repeated, saying the word more slowly, as if maybe Mae wasn't familiar with it. "It's all about connections, you know?"

The sky was a solid white-gray; there was a damp quality to the air. What had been a beautiful day had shifted into something else, the sun suddenly impossible to locate in the dead, bleak expanse of the sky.

"You mean for your work?" Mae took another sip of air. "Don't you have maternity leave or anything? I can barely think about anything but which boob this kid ate on last and how many hours in a row she can sleep. You're, like, superhuman, thinking of work right now. She must be an easy baby." Mae smiled kindly before correcting herself. "An easy Alice. The easier Alice. No surprise there."

Maybe it wasn't so strange after all, their babies sharing the same name. Maybe it was sweet, the sort of thing that would tie them to each other in new, better ways. As was often the case, Mae started translating the way she felt about it into the idea of a painting. It would be called *Two Alices*. She peeked at Sydney's Alice to see how she looked compared to Mae's. A slimmer face, longer lashes. Less hair. Maybe it would be a whole series, Two Alices at every age. Maybe she'd watch these two grow up together, painting them anew every August or November or March—not January; too predictable. Maybe, after all this time, Sydney would become her family again.

Mae shivered. She was surprised to find even this small moment of inspiration. She wanted to grab on to it hard and not let go. She wanted to make sure the impulse to paint didn't vanish the way the desire to drink, the interest in the news, the care she used to take with her skin all had.

But Alice cried and Mae's body lurched into anxiety—that she wouldn't be able to stop the tears, that something was wrong, that she'd have to go home, that she'd have to move her clothing aside and nurse in public, which she hated. And as quickly as it had appeared, the dream of a painting slipped away. Mae was too tired to mourn it.

"Ivy Miller says there's no reason to think of work and life as two separate entities," Sydney said, ignoring the rest of Mae's words. "In a good life, in a well-lived life, you're happy enough that you don't need to compartmentalize. Your friends are your family are your business partners. You know?"

Mae did not know. She lifted the empty cup again. Mimed a long, satisfying drink from it. Maybe the sun was behind a tree? Maybe the white-gray of the sky was simply one enormous cloud? She squinted upward, searching.

"She sounds interesting, this Ivy person," Mae said. It would have been a challenge to have this conversation with all her faculties, but it was even harder in her current unslept, unthinking state. Everything Sydney said sounded stranger than it would have otherwise, and words were troublingly hard for Mae to access.

"She's amazing. You have to meet her. I mean, I have to meet her too. I haven't actually been able to meet her face-to-face yet. But there's some incentives that involve a sit-down with her that I'm working on. If I got it, you could come. I'm allowed a guest."

Mae wondered, briefly, if this was a dream. The logic felt dreamlike, Sydney talking about things Mae didn't fully understand, making plans for Mae that she had no intention of involving herself with, pushing her stroller, not seeming to hear her Alice start to cry the high-pitched cry of a hungry baby, picking at her bottom lip like something was there, looking out into the middle distance with a sort of wanting that Mae found herself frightened by.

"Are you okay, Syd?" Mae asked as gently as she could. "These days are—"

"Oh, shit, my mom," Sydney interrupted, her gaze finally landing on something, someone.

"What about your mom?"

"She's in town. Helping with the baby. I didn't tell her I'd be with you, just that I was walking and I guess maybe she thought she'd join me? Shit. *Shit.* She doesn't really know we're in touch." Sydney looked at Mae with wide eyes, like Mae could solve the problem of her own presence, as if Mae could swerve off the track into the trees, hide out until Beth Ann had come and gone. Maybe she would have if her reflexes were faster, her brain working more quickly. But Beth Ann was up ahead and closing fast; her eyes squinted when she saw Sydney. She waved. And then, unmistakably, she saw Mae.

Mae could tell, because Beth Ann stopped right there, mid–speed walk. She was too far away for Mae to see her face, but her body jumped, a shudder of surprise and fear and anger and then, oddly, determination. Sydney seemed unsure of whether to continue walking forward or possibly run in the other direction, as if she could somehow, for the rest of her life, avoid her own mother.

"She sees you. Us. So I guess she knows now," Mae said, surprised to find herself feeling sturdy in the face of Beth Ann. Sydney was wilting but Mae felt her feet heavy on the ground, her body solid; even her postpartum mind was clarifying, narrowing in on the moment, suddenly and gloriously available to her for the first time since Alice was born. Mae lifted her hand and waved.

Beth Ann paused before waving back.

"Okay," Sydney said. "Okay, she knows. Listen, just don't mention Joni, okay?"

It was an odd request. Joni had been gone for fifteen years; there wasn't exactly something new to say about her. The new thing was Alice and the way Alice made her miss Joni more intently, more sharply. And also made her angry with Joni. And pitying of Joni. And impressed with Joni. But there was no reason to say any of that to Beth Ann.

"And don't tell her you came over. That I made dinner for you and everything. That wouldn't—don't tell her that."

"Okay, Syd."

Beth Ann was close now, within hearing distance, and still Sydney was whispering rules to Mae about what not to do and say, so Mae put a hand on Sydney's shoulder, a strong one with a squeeze to shut her up.

"Hey. Beth Ann. Hi," Mae said, finding that neither Sydney nor Beth Ann was going to start the conversation. "It's really good to see you."

"And you!" Beth Ann said, her voice so enthusiastic that it circled right back around to obviously miserable. Mae winced. "What a wonderful surprise! Mae Dyer! Here with Sydney! And a baby!" Beth

Ann peered into the stroller and made a face at Alice, something strained and smiling that Alice wailed at. "It's a...girl?"

Mae nodded.

"Well, good luck to you in about thirteen years," Beth Ann said. It was the sort of thing people always said to mothers of girls. Surely not every girl was fated to be an awful teenager. Surely not every mother-daughter relationship was going to end in disaster. Mae herself didn't have evidence to support this, but she still believed it had to be true. Besides, even if she was fated to be tangled in a terrible bit of trouble with her child someday, what possible purpose did it serve to have every person telling her this? Was it an earnest warning, as if she didn't know? Or was it, as Mae suspected, something smug, the awful human instinct to hope for the worst for others, to watch her go through the same hard things they'd had to survive.

"I'm taking it day by day," Mae said, hoping that was enough to push Beth Ann to some other topic.

"Well. We'll see how long that works for you. What's her name?"

Mae looked at Sydney, who looked right back at Mae.

"It's a coincidence," Sydney said before Mae could answer. "We didn't talk about it. We've barely talked. I'm in touch with Mae because I thought she might do well in LillyLou, so that's all we've talked about."

This was, Mae realized, exactly the way Sydney had managed her childhood troubles too. She'd give Beth Ann a hundred explanations for why there was a broken plate, a missing can of beer, a boy in the house with lips that looked swollen from kissing and who knew what else. Sydney spoke quickly when she was in trouble, barely able to keep up with herself.

"What's her name?" Beth Ann asked again, breezing right past Sydney's eager list of why it needed to be okay.

"Alice," Mae answered, again feeling her solid feet, her body comfortable in the space it was taking up. She squeezed the stroller's handles, happy to have something to do with her hands.

Beth Ann blinked quickly. "Well. That's—literary, isn't it? Almost poetic. I seem to remember Sydney has loved that name for a long time, hasn't she?" Beth Ann's chin jutted out. She looked like she was holding something in and it was taking a great deal of effort.

"Yep," Mae said, treading as carefully as she could, "she's always loved that name."

"And you figured you'd just take it for yourself," Beth Ann said. Her lower lip did something. It wavered, the way Alice's did before she settled in for a big, long wail. "Guess that's what you women do now. Just see what you want and take it. Most of us weren't—well, your mom, I guess—but the rest of us..." Beth Ann shook her head like she was on the wrong track. Sydney and Mae stayed quiet, wondering how they would ever find their way out of this conversation. Maybe they'd been stuck in it for years, decades, already. "Did you know women couldn't even have their own credit cards in the early seventies? It was that recent. When I was a teenager, it was a whole new idea, women having credit cards of their own. So."

It didn't feel like a particularly relevant fact to Mae, though it was an astonishing one nonetheless. Beth Ann was looking at her as if she was supposed to connect the dots between credit cards and Joni and the Alices and this moment. Mae tried in her foggy way to detangle it.

"I'm sorry," Mae said, not making it clear if she was apologizing for Alice's name or for not thinking more about the history of credit card rights or for her mother or for all of it—the way their lives had run into one other's and changed everything. When they were little, she and Sydney loved doing watercolors, and it was one of the only kinds of art that Beth Ann would say yes to. It was messy enough to satisfy their five-year-old urges but easy to set up and easy to clean up, and sometimes the house would be filled with white paper drenched in paint and water, waiting to dry.

Mae was thinking not of the paintings, though, but of the water. Sydney always got mad when, inevitably, over the course of a few minutes, the water turned from pink to purple to gray to sludge. If Sydney was painting on her own, she'd stay in a single-color palette, just to keep the water a lovely mauve color. But Mae was always using navy blue, then dipping her paintbrush back into the water, turning it stormy and wrong.

Mae shuddered now, feeling a little like that paintbrush with too much navy blue on its tip, known for the way it ruined the prettiest things. Like friendships and marriages and now babies too.

"I'm sorry," she said again.

"LillyLou for Mae, huh?" Beth Ann said at last, like the past few moments hadn't happened at all. She looked hard at her daughter, tilting her head to get a better, or maybe just different, look.

"She's a single mom. She's an artist who isn't doing her art. And everything she's been through, with grief and... the rest of it. She needs community, and we need, you know, her unique perspective." Sydney kept glancing at Beth Ann with the particular look of a kid in her school play, checking in with her parents in the audience to see if she's getting her lines just right.

"I'm not really looking for a whole, um, business venture," Mae said. She rolled the stroller back and forth, back and forth, willing Alice to sleep.

"That's reductive, Mae," Beth Ann said.

It had been a long time since Mae had heard Beth Ann say her name. It brought her right back to being every age—three and seven and fourteen and then right now, too, thirty-three and still bleeding from birth and feeling her breasts fill with milk, an alien sensation that made her want to cry.

Beth Ann tilted her head again, a new set of thoughts seeming to dawn on her.

"LillyLou is about giving yourself a gift. Taking yourself seriously. Being your best self. And everyone deserves that. You deserve that." Beth Ann said the last bit with a tense jaw, like it was hard for her to admit but worth it too. There was something a little fragile in the way she was taking in air and maybe in the particular crossing of her arms over her chest. "You're clearly a bit lost, Mae. You were always a kid with a lot of — what was the word that came up so often on your report cards? *Verve. Spirit.* Right?"

"I guess." Mae hadn't known Beth Ann knew anything about her report cards. The time when Beth Ann and Joni were close felt like centuries ago, but also it was here, this moment, a fact between them.

"I don't see that side of you today. Taking Sydney's name for your baby. Not doing your art. And I'm sure it's hard to be doing this on your own. I can't imagine." There was something solid on the park path with them now — the fact that Beth Ann had stayed, had chosen to keep Barrett, had decided, rather definitively, that the worst thing in the world would be to be alone.

And maybe it was, Mae thought for a terrible moment, aware of her leaking breasts, her new, reckless body shape, the way every night stretched ahead of her and baby Alice, knowing no one could swoop in to save her from the wails at midnight and two and three thirty and four forty-five and six fifteen. Maybe this was, in some ways, the worst version of her life. Especially if even Beth Ann felt sorry for her.

"You're lost," Beth Ann said, sure now. "LillyLou is for people who are lost and want to be found. No, that's not right. Want to find themselves. Is that you?"

Mae glanced at Sydney, who was watching her mother with an academic concentration. Then she looked up at the trees, some mostly bare, a few still heavy with leaves, all of them truly beautiful but so often ignored. The sun was back, finally poking through again, a tiny almost yellow patch in the sky. And she looked down at Alice, mewling now, a cooing that would turn quickly to cries. The only person missing was Joni, and her absence was breathtaking, actually. The three of them were meant to be four; they were currently a puzzle put together all wrong.

Joni would have hated everything about this — the crisp air and the expensive strollers and the talk of bettering oneself and Beth Ann's haughty confidence most of all.

"Maybe?" Mae said, and the answer was an honest one. "I mean, I don't know. I guess. Maybe." It was all her sleep-deprived self could muster. Beth Ann grinned.

"Well, then, okay," Beth Ann said, and maybe she was thinking of Joni now too, with rage or forgiveness or grief or some aching mix of all three. "This is what Ivy Miller says, isn't it? Past colliding with present and creating future. This is the work. It's our most important work." Beth Ann ran a hand through her hair and tried to smile. "Let's get her to Small Group, Syd."

"Yes! And you can bring Alice. I know with single parenting, getting out of the house is probably — hard." Sydney said *single parenting* like it was some secret Mae was trying to keep from the rest of the world and not, in fact, the plain, neutral reality of her life. "I'll bring my Alice too. LillyLou is all about motherhood and working moms and mixing family and work. That's the whole thing. That you can make this money *and* be a full person, be there for your kid, pursue art, you know?"

Sydney and Beth Ann shared a look that Mae couldn't parse. Conspiratorial, but not in a way that felt bad, exactly. Almost the opposite. Mae was happy to see them in on something together.

"Okay," Mae said, because there wasn't much she *could* bring Alice to, actually, aside from story time at the library and the concerts of twee bands performing children's music in the backyards of coffee shops all over the neighborhood. Mae had tried both of these, but with a baby as young as Alice, there didn't seem to be much point, really. It took an hour to get out the door, and by that time, the baby had to eat again, so there you were, breast out, listening to a recent library-school graduate read *Goodnight Moon* to a crowd of tired parents and their cranky babies. Small Group, whatever that was, would at least be something to do, a way to cut up the long days with Alice, who was beautiful and perfect and also, at times, unbelievably boring. It was hard to imagine Joni doing any of it, although Joni had been a person who knew how to make the mundane magical, which, Mae was realizing, might be the key to motherhood after all.

"Perfect," Sydney said, or rather squealed, loudly enough to wake up her Alice, whose subsequent wail was loud and insistent, cutting the air, cutting the moment, cutting the past and present and everything between them all the way only a brand-new baby could.

"I'll leave you girls to it, then," Beth Ann said, turning to walk back to wherever she'd come from.

"You could, um, walk with us," Mae said, but Beth Ann looked back and shook her head, thankfully—the offer had been an empty one.

In the wake of Beth Ann, Sydney's energy was different. Tighter, quieter, smaller. Maybe it had always been that way. "You and your mom get along these days, it seems like," Mae said, trying to piece together the then and the now of it all.

Sydney looked stunned. "You think?" she asked. Her eyebrows furrowed and she looked temporarily lost in the calculation of her intimacy with her mother.

"You seem closer than when we were kids," Mae said, shrugging. She was relatively sure this was true.

Sydney sighed. Shot an indecipherable glance Mae's way. "How would you know?" she asked, as if Mae hadn't been there nearly every day of their childhood, as if it hadn't been a shared experience, aside from the parts Sydney kept from her.

"I mean, from just the whole, you know, best-friend thing, I guess? You know, just, that's how it seemed. When we were kids." It felt odd to have to explain something so simple and obvious to Sydney. The thing they had in common was their shared memories, the uncountable hours and hours and hours of time spent with each other's families.

"So you noticed how close I was to my mom but not anything else?" Sydney asked, her chin tense, her mouth barely opening as the words came out.

"I mean, I knew everything about you," Mae said. She paused. "Are you okay, Syd? Listen, if you come over—you could nap or something? I could probably handle the two babies for like an hour. Or I could make us some lunch? Or something?"

"You knew nothing," Sydney said, ignoring the rest of it. "You chose to know nothing. You chose to stay a little clueless kid and let the rest of us deal with real life. So don't act like you were in on some nuance. You were a kid. You stayed a kid and I—"

"You didn't tell me!" Mae was surprised how quickly a conversation could turn to yelling. She was surprised by the force of her own voice, the sound of it raw and cracking. "What the fuck, Syd, you kept a secret. You can't blame *me* for that!"

"Willful ignorance," Sydney said, like she'd been thinking this over for a long time, and maybe she had. "It was obvious. It was obvious to anyone. You fucking knew, deep down, I know you did, but you just made the rest of us deal so you could keep being Mae Dyer, child-prodigy artist and innocent kid. And then you get all the things, the college and the articles and the being a famous whatever, and seriously, fuck that. Fuck you, thinking you know what my mom and I were like back then. Fuck you, thinking you could chart our closeness like you were observing and watching and giving a shit. Seriously, fuck that."

Mae tried to think of what to say in response. Sydney was writing the history of her life—their lives—without the biggest part: The graduation-party day, her father's face twisting in confusion and pain, Beth Ann collapsing to the ground, Barrett going quiet and pale. Police officers arriving and asking questions of all of them in separate rooms, Graham throwing up in Beth Ann's bathroom.

And Mae—all of a sudden, a girl without a mom.

Were all these details lost on Sydney? Had she maybe been even the littlest bit relieved that Joni and the secrets were gone? Had Beth Ann? Had Barrett? If Mae had known at the time all the secrets Sydney and their parents were holding on to, maybe she would have been able to see something clarifying and important. But Sydney let her see it all through a false lens of their lives, and it was this madness that Mae found overwhelming, and even more so now, bleeding and blurry and brand-new.

She wanted to start with a clean slate. She wanted to understand everything that had ever happened. They were, the two of them, furious and desperate and alone and so, so deeply together.

"I think your Alice needs to eat," Mae said because her brain couldn't think with the crying of the baby reaching a fever pitch; she couldn't think, knowing there was still another long night ahead of her, another sleepless week of dirty diapers and sore breasts and wondering if she was doing everything wrong. Sydney was saying enormous things that made Mae's brain want to think enormous thoughts, but Mae couldn't remember even the name of her favorite artist, her mother's birthday, the address of the place she and Sydney had lived together, the weight Alice was when she was born, the way it felt, even, to push her out, to watch her enter the fray.

And if she couldn't remember that, she certainly couldn't remember what it felt like to be eleven and fourteen and sixteen and twenty-one. She couldn't possibly remember if there was a difference between not knowing and not wanting to know and on which side of that divide she had actually been.

Sydney took her Alice out, sat down on the side of the walking path in a patch of dry grass and, probably, hungry ants, and lifted her shirt to feed her baby. Mae sat to do the same, not because her Alice was screaming but because she felt a pull to be in that same space, to mother in the same moment as Sydney was mothering. The babies latched, and then their mothers' shoulders relaxed after that initial scream of pain still present all these weeks later. The grass tickled their ankles. The air held the words Sydney had said.

"I was just a kid," Mae said at last, thinking of herself as Alice — tiny, needy, undiscerning. She knew it was the wrong thing to say but it was also the only thing she knew for sure anymore.

"Lucky you," Sydney said.

There wasn't anything else to say, really. The babies finished eating, eventually, both of them spitting up more than seemed necessary, more than seemed possible, and both of them fussing at being put back in the strollers, the walk starting again.

When they got back to the entrance of the park, Mae lingered, trying to figure out how to leave the moment.

"So you'll come to Small Group," Sydney said like the fight between them had never happened. And she was right, it sort of hadn't.

"You really want me to?" Mae asked.

Sydney shrugged. She seemed to be weighing something, her head tilted at Mae, the two Alices, the matching strollers, Mae's stained Henley, her own soft body. They were new people, both of them. The babies, allegedly, were the ones who had been birthed, but Mae and Sydney, too, were remade in the shapes of mothers, searching for some center that wouldn't be found.

And still there was the way their bodies knew how to stand

near each other, the memorized shapes of their hands and eyes and mouths, the familiarity of closeness, the shade of memories they couldn't exactly organize or understand but that were there anyway.

They were still, at least in this patch of sunlight, in this moment, in one way or another, Sydney and Mae.

The unlikeliest of anchors.

The clumsiest ports in the swirliest of storms.

"I want you to come," Sydney said at last.

"Then I'll come," Mae agreed, her voice quiet, gentle, and at least a tiny bit hopeful.

WAY, WAY BACK THEN

EVEN ON HER wedding day, Joni had wondered if she was making a mistake. Graham was handsome and kind too, acquiescing on all sorts of details about their wedding, from serving a buffet instead of the sit-down meal he and his parents would have preferred to agreeing to a restaurant wedding with fifty guests instead of a big hotel-ballroom reception with two hundred.

Joni got dressed in a West Village restaurant's back room, where they stored canned goods and paper towels and so much alcohol that Joni figured no one would notice if she opened a twist-top bottle of white and served herself an impromptu drink. She didn't have bridesmaids per se, but she was with two friends from college who were married, had pushed Joni to get married, had said it was great, she'd love it, until of course this exact moment, when, drinking from a stolen bottle of pinot grigio, first one and then the other admitted that actually, they sort of missed being single.

"Now you tell me!" Joni said with a smirk like it was a joke, except it maybe wasn't. Her dress was tea-length and itchy. Her hair was in a low bun, and she had a daisy behind one ear. It was too late to change anything and she could hear guests chatting just past the heavy doors, voices rising up, laughing, then settling back down into whispers, maybe about the decor or any number of mistakes that Joni-the-bride had made. No one here thought Joni was made to be a bride, including Joni.

She'd meant to have only a few sips of wine, a glass at the most, but Joni and her not-bridesmaids finished off two bottles before all the guests arrived. Thus, Joni's walk down the aisle was sloppy, meandering, and the fifty guests watched Graham's smile slip, then work hard to remake itself in spite of his bride's obvious drunkenness. Joni didn't feel drunk, exactly, as much as a little bit not-here. She smiled, strangely aware of the shape the smile was making on her face. She waved to her parents. Then she waved to Graham.

"Hiiiiii," she said, shimmying her shoulders a little, raising her eyebrows.

"Hey," he said back, trying to make the moment cute and mostly succeeding.

"Let's get married!" Joni said, and everyone laughed, or at least awkwardly chuckled.

She stumbled through vows she'd written the night before, slurring the words *magnanimous* and *adoration* and *infinity* and ending finally on *you're my best friend*, which was true enough, truer than Graham's words about them being madly in love. Joni didn't feel mad for Graham. She liked him. She loved him, even, if love meant finding it nice to eat bagels in the park with him every week, and she was pretty sure it did mean that. She was pretty sure the other thing—the madness, the head over heels, the love that makes it impossible to think of anything else—didn't really exist or existed only when you were sixteen and feeling it for the first time. She had a theory that you felt it less and less with each relationship, and Graham was her seventh boyfriend, so the math wasn't exactly on her side.

The slurry vows would be a memory they fought about months later when things were rocky and Joni had plans to go out more often than she ever had before and Graham was noticing the way she forgot things like his birthday and their monthly date at the Italian place down the street.

The slurry vows were a story she'd told Barrett when she met him just two months after the wedding while waiting for a bathroom at a bar on the Lower East Side that was nothing special except that she knew the bartender, so she got every third drink free. Which was, actually, pretty special when you got right down to it.

The bar was called No Idea, which meant every time someone said, "Where should we meet?" and she said, "No Idea," there was a huge "Who's on First"–type situation, which was maybe the point of such a name but was really more annoying than amusing.

"I'm drunker than I was at my wedding," Joni said to Barrett in lieu of hello. It wasn't a pickup line; Joni was just lately in the habit of chatting up whoever was at No Idea. She had been coming on her own every Thursday night. She'd bring a sketch pad and draw the faces of people at the bar, practicing shadows and expressions and trying to find her artistic voice with the aid of liquor and bad karaoke.

"Ah, my dream woman," Barrett said with a laugh. He had a nice laugh, a big smile, a comfortable way of sitting that made Joni feel comfortable too. He was tall. Broad. Took up so much more space than slight, wiry Graham with his glasses and serious face. "My wife didn't let me get drunk at ours."

"No? You seem like a great drunk," Joni replied. She was surprisingly sharp after three drinks, or at least she thought she was.

"See, I think so too. She says I get too friendly."

"Is *friendly* code for *flirtatious?*"

"Should it be?"

"If you are in fact flirting with me," Joni said with a smile so big it hurt.

"I haven't flirted in ages."

"How does it feel?"

"Pretty good. You make it easy."

"Not the first time I've heard that."

It went on like that for a while, double entendres and insinuations and the bubbly feeling of meeting someone who makes you see yourself in a brand-new way. Because it was Joni falling in love with herself more than anything. She was falling in love with the self that appeared when Barrett was in the room, a version of her that was funny and light and mysterious too.

"You're an artist," he said, pulling her sketchbook into his lap and flipping through the pages like it was his now. "I've never met an artist. These are amazing."

Joni blushed. Beamed. Pulled the sketchbook back onto the bar, tried to draw Barrett's disarming smile.

Barrett and Joni came to No Idea every week at the same time, then twice a week, and it wasn't a plan, exactly, it wasn't a date, it was just something that happened and then kept happening, the two of them side by side at the bar, making each other laugh, watching the tail end of a game or a presidential debate or *Jeopardy!*, choosing patrons for Joni to draw, ordering drinks at an inadvisably fast pace. Occasionally playing with the cord of a pay phone while explaining to one or the other of their spouses why it was exactly that they were going to be late.

Then, after a few months of this, Joni told Barrett she was in love with him, and he said it back, seriously, darkly, like an apology for what was going to happen, which was them kissing, finally, the kiss of people who had been aching to kiss for weeks. The kiss of people who knew they were eventually going to blow up the lives they would spend years delicately constructing.

The kissing turned into sex, which turned into an affair, which turned, terribly, frighteningly, inevitably, into a pregnancy.

Joni told Barrett about the pregnancy at No Idea, a place they couldn't seem to stop going to in spite of the fact that people knew them there, knew their spouses too. Joni was always forgetting the name of Barrett's spouse—Mary Sue? Grace Belle? She knew it was two names masquerading as one. "Don't you ever call her just Beth?" she asked Barrett that night before telling him.

"That's not her name," he said. He was tired, a little, of the making fun of Beth Ann, who wasn't here to defend herself and who, for all her faults, didn't deserve the incessant nitpicking of a woman like Joni, who didn't seem to know when to stop.

"It sort of is, though," Joni said.

"If you met her, you'd get it," Barrett said. "She isn't a Beth. She's a Beth Ann."

"That's the most incriminating thing you've ever said about her," Joni said, cackling.

"I don't make fun of your husband," Barrett said. He was thinking of ending the affair, maybe. Beth Ann was pregnant with a baby girl, something he hadn't told Joni yet, and he wanted to be the kind of father who went to soccer matches, parent-teacher conferences, band performances. He didn't want to be the kind of father who was fucking someone else. Even if that someone else was Joni, with her long hair and long legs and irresistible way of talking about literature and films and coffee and religion and the economy. Joni was brilliant and artistic, and Beth Ann liked looking at paint samples for the new house they'd purchased in a suburb called Sommersette, a place Joni would never move to, a place he wasn't sure he could even tell her he'd be going to.

"That's true," Joni said. She leaned against Barrett and ordered another drink before remembering she wasn't supposed to have had even the one. "You could, though. Make fun of him. I mean, it wouldn't be kind, but it would be okay. He's a little short. He has terrible fashion sense. But it's how boring he is that gets me. He doesn't — he isn't particularly funny or sharp, and he doesn't have interests, really, aside from me and what kind of paper is in the printer at work and, I don't know, the weather. The guy just loves the weather. Talking about it. Explaining it. Watching it on TV." Joni took a deep breath. She saw an in, a way to lay the groundwork for what she had to tell Barrett, a way to make it clear. Barrett, for his part, squirmed in his seat. He looked up at the screen showing the lyrics for the person singing "Leaving on a Jet Plane" for weekly karaoke. They were okay. Not great, not one of those show-off karaoke people. But nice to listen to. On pitch. "It's why we haven't had sex in ages," Joni finished. "I can't have sex with someone who watches the Weather Channel, you know?"

Barrett startled. He looked at her, then back at the screen, then at her again. "We don't talk about this stuff," he said like he was reminding her of rules they'd both read and negotiated, but of course there was no such rule book. There was the way things began, in chaos, and the way they continued, with some predictable times and locations and methods of keeping each other secret, and all of that had felt — well, if not exactly right, then at least stable. They didn't talk about their spouses; they didn't discuss sex in particular; they tried to keep their lives untangled, their time together in a sort of bubble.

"I need you to know that. That he and I don't — we haven't been sleeping together." Joni pursed her lips. She fluffed her hair. She didn't think she needed to look sexy, exactly, for this, but she needed to look like someone he could want, someone he *would* want.

"I don't need to know that."

"Well, you do, actually," Joni said. She fluffed her hair again. Followed his gaze to the screen with the lyrics, then looked back at his face, which was a little sweaty around the mouth, a little perturbed, maybe, judging by the way he held his chin. "It's weird to just say this, but I have to just say it. I'm—Barrett, I'm pregnant." She tried to look appropriately serious for the situation, but a smile spread over her face. She laughed. It felt so good for the words to bubble up and out and see the way they were practically tangible in their ability to shift Barrett's entire body, which was now straight-backed, brow-raised, bristling.

"Joni. Come on," he said. He took a sip of his beer, and another. He wasn't much of a drinker, really, though he'd told Joni he wished that he were, he wished he could blame their whole situation on alcohol and not just himself. Joni had deflated at this comment, which had been mumbled a week ago over one of their long *Should we maybe end things* conversations that lately Barrett seemed to be initiating rather often.

"I'm pregnant," she said again, lighting up more and more, a little giddy, actually, from the realness of the situation, the magnitude of it. It felt good to have done something so monumental that it changed everything. Something that rewrote the whole future history of them.

She said that out loud, testing out the romance of it. "This is the moment," she said. "This is the rewriting of our future history."

"I don't know what that means," Barrett said, his voice finding a whisper. "I don't know what any of this means. I mean, you're not—you can't be pregnant."

"I am. I promise I am."

"Joni. We're married. To other people. I'm married. And Beth Ann—Beth Ann is—Beth Ann's pregnant. My wife. With my baby."

Oddly, Barrett reached out and grabbed Joni's knee, squeezed, the way he'd done a hundred times in bars and hotel lobbies and places they were meeting up when they shouldn't have been meeting up. The gesture made no sense in this new context, and Joni moved away from it.

"And so am I." She swallowed. The future history was getting written again, and she now was feeling silly for the opulence of the phrasing, for how romantic the words had seemed just moments before. Now this new information caused a scramble, a chaotic reorganizing of everything she'd thought would happen, which was Barrett leaving Beth Ann, Joni leaving Graham, Joni and Barrett waiting an appropriate time before getting married to each other. Having their baby. Living their life in a fifth-floor walk-up in the West Village, raising a little girl who liked museums and city sounds and squeaky swings in crowded playgrounds. Joni would paint enormous portraits of their child; Barrett would go to his nine-to-five and come home hungry for her, cooing at their baby, perfectly executing some idea of cozy, artsy, non-suburban parenthood that made Joni ache with wanting.

She watched that future history vanish, and nothing rushed in to replace it.

Barrett finished his beer. He put it down gently and turned to her, finally. "Graham is a good guy," he said. He'd never met Graham, so the certainty with which he delivered these words was confusing, startling, even. "He'll be a great dad."

"The baby isn't Graham's." This was true. It had been months since she'd slept with Graham, there was no complication to the timing, no possible way to make this baby belong to anyone but Barrett.

"But in some ways it is, Joni. And can be. And should be. You can, you know, sleep with Graham this week, and then tell him in a few weeks, and it will all be okay, it will work out the way it was supposed to with both of us—with our lives still, you know, intact."

"No," Joni said, but even then, somehow, under the no, she felt a tiny bit of yes peeking out.

"It could have been different," Barrett said, pointing in the air and then to the empty beer to order another from the harried tattooed bartender, "but this is how it is. We're star-crossed. It's actually romantic, you know? Star-crossed lovers, not able to fully be — do you really want to have some kid with me and clean up poop with me and argue about discipline strategies and get resentful about who got up more times during the night? I don't want that with you. That would ruin what this is. This is the moment when we decide to keep this thing beautiful." Anyone else in the bar would have been able to tell that Barrett was drunk. Not blackout drunk, not past some point of no return, but slurring-his-words-and-getting-all-heavy-about-the-future drunk.

"Won't you — this is your baby too," Joni said. She was struggling to get the words out; the conversation had gone somewhere she hadn't expected it to go, and here she was, in a foreign land without a map. She was looking for signposts, familiar landmarks, anything to steady herself. "You're saying I'll have this baby and you'll be fine with Graham being her father and you being some stranger? Will you meet her? Will you miss her? Will you think about her? I don't understand."

"What makes you so sure it's a girl?" Barrett said, missing the point completely, smirking like it was all a fun game, an amusement.

"Barrett. Come on."

"I don't know. I don't have an answer to all this. I don't know what it feels like to be a father to any baby — Beth Ann's, yours, I don't know. I don't know. I mean, really, I don't know."

Joni wondered if he'd heard how many times he'd just said *I don't know*, if he knew what he was saying at all. She wanted to shake him into some other kind of response, but he was stuck in this one, his eyes blurry, wandering, wistful, his mouth twitching into different smiles and frowns, the whole of him unsettled on what it all meant.

"You can't be a stranger to this baby," Joni said at last, making a decision for both of them.

"We can't keep being what we are," Barrett said, making a decision too, but not disagreeing with Joni's. She held on to that blank space where an argument could have been. Where a disagreement wasn't. He didn't say no, so that meant yes, he would know the baby, he would be a person in the baby's life, not a dad, maybe, but something, someone. Joni would make sure of it. This baby would be loved. This baby would be surrounded by love and family. She would not let this baby be wanting. She would not let Barrett abandon whoever this little child was going to be.

They stayed long enough for Barrett to have one more drink and to kiss Joni on the mouth, his hand struggling up her skirt under the bar even though he had just said they should stop. Joni let him kiss and touch and be the very thing he'd said he wouldn't be anymore.

"We're always just going to be us," Joni said into his neck. It was sweaty there, salty and warm and intimate in a way that unspooled her.

"Things are changing. The baby—"

"Babies."

"And I'm moving. A little town outside the city. I won't be able to just come here and see you. It won't be the same."

Joni pressed herself against him. "It doesn't have to be the same," she said. "We'll figure it out. What town are you moving to?"

"Sommersette," Barrett said.

The name sat in Joni's chest, glowing, orbiting, churning.

Sommersette.

NOW

Sydney and Mae

SYDNEY ASKED MAE to take a picture in front of Genevive Lett's small, black-doored brick apartment building. "You and me and our girls," she said. "We can cross-post. Babies do amazing on the algorithm. Seriously, I sold more in the week after Alice's birth than I have the whole time I've been doing LillyLou."

The look on Mae's face told Sydney that she had phrased this incorrectly, though she wasn't sure what was wrong, exactly. But she could practically see Beth Ann's disappointment. "You are so clunky," her mother had said the other day, overhearing Sydney on the phone trying to convince the neighborhood barista to join her team. "You have to work on your delivery. This is something they need. This is a favor you are doing them. The way you talk—it's not inspiring."

Sydney had tried since then to be more inspiring, to sound more successful, to frame LillyLou as an opportunity. This last thing she repeated to herself in the mirror in the mornings: *I have an opportunity for people. They are not doing me a favor.* It was supposed to feel more true the longer she repeated it, but sometimes she found herself blushing at the words, tripping over them, not quite believing them herself. She knew, of course, that Ivy Miller (and Beth Ann) would say this was the problem. "This only works," Ivy Miller had said on an Instagram Live last night, "if you stand in a place of positivity and investment. You cannot succeed if you are judging the path. You have to believe in the path." Sydney had written down the words, but it felt a little like Tinker Bell in *Peter Pan*—a speck of light that would go out if you didn't applaud it constantly, a fantastical force that lived on the hope and faith of others.

Which was fine, maybe. The best part of *Peter Pan*, which she'd seen in a community theater by the beach with Mae and their mothers when she was a kid, was the part where the audience was asked to clap and cheer to bring the flagging fairy back to life with their love and belief. There was something to be said—wasn't there?—for the energy in the theater when the tiny Tinker Bell light grew stronger and stronger as the audience's applause filled her up with purpose and confidence. Maybe that wasn't silly at all.

"So just, like, hold the babies up?" Mae asked. Of course, she'd taken a great many photos of Alice—mostly Alice on her back, swaddled first in the blue-and-pink-striped hospital blankets and then in the much easier to use Velcro swaddles recommended to her by a mom in the big-box baby store she'd wandered around mere weeks before giving birth. She'd looked, certainly, like someone who needed advice on what to buy, someone who didn't have a mom herself, a fact she was sure emanated from her powerfully at all times.

It was hard to imagine Joni buying things for a baby, but she must have done it once upon a time, perhaps with Graham by her side; he would have researched which crib was the best, which stroller, which pacifier. And eventually maybe Graham had researched the best suburb to move to, the best place for a baby to grow up. Joni had always said that she found Sommersette for them, but that seemed impossible, Joni not being the sort of mother given to admiring Victorian homes or quaint schools or neighborhood lawns, with their tall trees and manicured gardens and annual spring festivals.

There were photos of Mae as a baby in New York City, then as an older baby in front of the pre-renovation version of the Sommersette house they eventually moved into. Then photo upon photo of her in the finished home as a toddler with a set of dimples and too much hair. Even these photographs seemed decidedly unlike Joni, who wasn't much for sentimentality, who preferred abstract sketches to Polaroids.

Not long after her mother's death, Mae had found piles of Joni's art, including a sketchbook filled with drawings of people sitting at a bar looking haunted or nervous or peaceful or drunk with their martinis and beers and gin and tonics. Then the sketchbook's subject turned to a town that looked like a movie version of Sommersette, done in Joni's signature messy, thoughtful style. The two series of sketches seemed like a clue to something, an answer to a question Mae couldn't quite bring herself to ask.

"Moms and daughters," Sydney said as if she needed to remind Mae of her role, of what they were doing. "Two Alices."

Mae had not, she realized, taken photos of herself with the baby. The photos she took were largely to send to Leo, as if to remind him that Alice existed, and having herself in the frame would have complicated the message.

It turned out it didn't matter what she sent. Leo wasn't coming.

She would prefer to paint herself with the baby, anyway. So much better than a selfie. So much more honest. Her fists unclenched at the idea. She hadn't painted since Alice was born, but there was an instant of wanting that was almost as glorious as actually doing. In these early months, she'd wanted nothing but sleep and croissants and coffee.

But it was there, at last—the desire to create something more than milk and memories. She wondered if she could skip this meeting, head home, put Alice to bed, and pick up a paintbrush, even if just for a few minutes, a few strokes on the canvas, a small pencil sketch in a notebook, a list of ideas of what a painting of motherhood might look like. Maybe she could use Joni's sketches of Sommersette as inspiration or pair them with her artwork in some way that would let Mae's art and Joni's be in conversation with each other.

Sydney's voice interrupted the daydream, though, and Mae knew she'd be staying. And that by the time the meeting was over, the impulse would be gone, buried under the need for rest and *Housewives* and the nothingness of cold pizza at the kitchen counter in silence.

"They don't even need to see her face," Sydney said, positioning Mae's body and the bundle of Alice so that, with Sydney's arm outstretched and angled, they would all be in the photo looking some particular way that Sydney needed them to look. "Just the idea of the baby is enough, honestly, though if we get a peek at the face, that's even better. Smile!"

This was almost art. It was art stripped of all depth and beauty.

But Mae obeyed, smiling in that tired, automatic way one did when ordered to, and Sydney took ten photos in quick succession, tilting and shifting the phone's angle slightly each time. When she was done, Sydney looked at the screen and flipped through the series until she settled, confidently, on one and showed it to Mae. There was nothing special that Mae could see about the photo, and for a moment she wanted to call this out— *Uh, I'm the one with an art degree and this is a boring-ass photo of nothing*—but she changed her mind and smiled, nodded. Tiredness was probably the reason she'd stopped pushing back on things so voraciously lately, although maybe it was motherhood or the echo of what Georgie had said to her, the shadow of the rejection hanging over her still.

"I'll tag you," Sydney went on. "'Mothers making magic'? 'Motherhood can't stop us'? 'We actually *can* have it all'? Any of those sound good?"

It took a moment of Sydney looking all puppy-eyed for Mae to realize that Sydney did, in fact, want her opinion on the caption. "Oh. Huh. I don't know. I guess... magic? That's... I mean, I don't know exactly what you're wanting to get across?"

"Just the reality of LillyLou," Sydney said, making sure to keep her voice steady, to sound *rooted in the truth*, another phrase Ivy Miller used to describe the particular kind of casual confidence the best businesswomen perfected. "That motherhood, in this company, is an asset, not an obstacle. And that we're a great example of the way the two things can intertwine." Sydney smiled. She looked pleased with herself. Pleased and also desperate, Mae noted. Lately, Sydney was calling her every day, wanting to get the girls together as if they were actual children with hobbies and personalities and not infants who didn't know the difference between being on the floor at home or being in a stroller at the Brooklyn Museum. But Mae kept saying yes. Without these strange playdates with Sydney and Alice, there was only Catherine and Graham to talk to. Catherine kept making allusions to a *big conversation* they needed to have, and Graham had asked multiple times if she was painting. It felt like a question Joni would have asked, pointed and jabbing at something tender and raw, the worry that there wasn't room within Mae to be both a mother to a new baby and an artist too.

"Say that, I guess," Mae said, "That motherhood is an asset, not an obstacle. And fuck anyone who says otherwise."

"Fuck them." Sydney nodded, typing it out.

"I didn't actually mean to put in that last part."

"No, it's good. It's real. We have newborns. We're tired. We're angry about the way this world treats us. We want more for our children. LillyLou isn't, like, anti-obscenity. It's not some Christian company or whatever. We can be ourselves."

Sydney was getting excited. She'd forgotten that Mae was edgier than her, sharper, a little more to the point. Sydney's shiny exterior and Mae's prickly interior could be a spectacular combination if she really thought about it. They could be a dynamic duo of LillyLou. Sydney and Mae might be better together than apart. They weren't just offshoots of their parents' drama, and this felt right. It felt fated.

Sydney posted, tagging Mae and insisting that Mae immediately repost it, tagging LillyLou and, yes, Ivy Miller herself, because this was exactly the sort of risk that Ivy Miller respected. She was always telling them to push the envelope, not to be little robots, that they were individuals and that their unique view of the world was their most valuable asset. Sydney had never quite taken that in, but suddenly it made all the sense in the world—it was the missing piece to the whole enterprise, it was what would change everything. Ivy Miller's words were like this sometimes—distant and hard to digest and then, all at once, obvious and deeply true.

"*Love* the post," Genevive told Sydney and Mae as she opened the door to her apartment, which smelled of pumpkin something-or-other, the classic scent of autumnal baking. "Not your usual vibe, Syd, but soooo good."

"We're a good team," Sydney said, linking her elbow with Mae's, an unexpected physical intimacy neither was prepared for. "This is Mae Dyer. My best friend from childhood. We were practically sisters and we're reconnecting because of these little chickadees." Sydney could feel Mae's grimace through the tightness of her arm, the slight leaning away of her body. She wasn't sure which part Mae was reacting to—the nugget about their history, the reference to her as a near sister, or the word *chickadee*, which was admittedly cutesy and the sort of thing Beth Ann would have said when the girls were young.

"Oh my goodness, two little girlies," Genevive said, peering into one stroller, then the other. The babies looked different, of course, but also ultimately the same, the way all babies of a certain tiny age did. Grumpy faces and wrinkled feet and pouty lips waiting, always, for milk. "I'm so glad you brought them. They're always welcome. Working mamas, right? We need flexibility. We need our work to be our family." It was practically a copy-and-paste excerpt from the LillyLou mission statement, and Sydney watched Mae's face to see if it shifted into any sort of recognition.

It held something else—a distant smile that was neither here nor there, something practiced and removed that Sydney had never seen before.

"That's nice," Mae said, clearly not finding it nice at all.

"And your little one—what's their name?"

"Alice," Mae said with a smirk that was more familiar to Sydney.

"Alice?" Genevive's face scrunched like the babies'. "A coincidence?" she asked hopefully.

"Sort of," Sydney said, laughing it off, not wanting to explain it all. She felt like if she spoke of the dollhouse, she might suddenly find herself detailing the affair, the way Mae's and Sydney's childhoods fractured and splintered in entirely different ways. "Anyway, Mae is very special. A single mom!"

"I admire single mothers so much." Lake had been nearby, listening in and probably gathering some sort of intel that would allow her to steal Mae away from Sydney. "You do everything we do times two. You are so brave. So strong. And coming here is the best choice you could possibly make." Lake looked briefly at Genevive, the question *Did I do it right?* undeniably there on her face.

"Well," Mae said, holding back a laugh or a scoff or something else, maybe a primal postpartum scream. "Thanks." She looked like she had more to say, but she didn't say it, sinking into the roles that Sydney had given her: Childhood best friend. Single mom. LillyLou recruit.

"You deserve support," Lake said, putting a hand on Mae's stroller and another on Mae herself. "You deserve it. Okay? Every time you think you don't, remember this moment. Remind yourself that you *do*."

"Right. Yep. I'll remember this," Mae said.

"She's got support," Sydney said, even though it wasn't quite the script. "She's got me. So. She's okay."

Lake glared at Sydney for the misstep. The point, Ivy Miller was always explaining, was to make the potential team member feel hope about the future and not necessarily focused on the present. The point was to show them what they were missing and how they could find it. The point was *more*, making them believe in *more*.

"You can always use more support, though," Sydney corrected herself. She thought she saw Genevive nodding. "You'll need more support as your Alice gets older and everything. Especially since, you know, you don't have Joni. So. Here we are. We're the more."

We're the more. It sounded good, Sydney thought. It sounded like something Ivy Miller would say. She grabbed her phone to write it down in the Notes app. It would make a great caption for something. Another photo of herself and Mae. Another moment of them being an unstoppable team. *We're each other's more* or something. She'd work on getting it exactly right.

She and Mae could finally be on the same team again. They owed each other this—this coming together, this fixing of the past, this righting of the wrongs.

"We're the more," Genevive repeated, smiling at both Sydney and Mae now, and the Alices too. She ushered them into the living room proper, settled Mae onto a couch that her stroller could fit next to. Lake grabbed Sydney before she could sit down next to Mae.

"I can help you," Lake said to her quietly. "She's going to be tricky, I think. Resistant. You said she lost her mom? You need to really connect to that. And single moms can sometimes put up defenses and I'm really good at—"

"Thanks, but I think it will be okay," Sydney said. She was staring at Mae, trying to conjure the same confidence in herself that she witnessed in Mae's relaxed shoulders, her skeptical smile, the rocking of her Alice back and forth, back and forth in the stroller, not missing a beat when Alice's cries grew loud, not apologizing for the way the sound of a newborn's screams could penetrate everything, cut through every conversation, every thought, really, bringing the talk in the room to a halt. Alice did exactly this until Mae calmly took her out of the stroller and attached her immediately to her breast like it was nothing. She didn't look around to gauge the okay-ness of her decision, didn't apologize for the crying or the bared nipple, the gurgling, whining, suckling, even the spray of milk that shot onto the coffee table when Alice angrily unlatched. "We're best friends. I've got it."

"I'm here if you need me," Lake said, smiling like she knew the future already, the ways Sydney would fail. Sydney smiled back, a tight expression that made her jaw hurt, and she sat next to Mae, took her own Alice out of the stroller, held her warm body to her chest, willing her not to cry, not to need anything, actually, just to be. She willed it for herself too. Wanting just this moment—with Mae and their Alices and the cinnamony promise of Genevive's home, the hum of multiple women in one place leaning in to tell half secrets and planning a future that seemed possible, if you believed, if you could only just believe.

THE PAINTING

FIONA KNEW ANY number of gallery owners, but this one, with his white hair and deep dimples and dapper hats, was, she promised, the biggest and best one, a person who could make Mae a star.

Which was exactly what he said upon viewing the Painting, which Fiona and Mae had brought to the gallery and leaned against a stark white wall currently unadorned by other paintings, ones that would maybe have made Mae's work seem small or young or striving by comparison.

"This painting, and your package. Who you are. Yes. A star," Elvin said. The name Elvin fit him perfectly, though it also had the whisper of an invented name, an impulse Mae could understand. Parents give names to babies before even knowing them. It was an act of unbelievable hubris. If Elvin had invented his name, well, then, good for him. It made sense to be the one in charge of inventing yourself.

"You like it?" Mae asked, which was exactly the question she'd promised herself she wouldn't ask. "I mean, you like it for the gallery?" She tried to make the sentence less desperate, but Elvin wasn't listening anyway.

"Isn't it perfect?" Fiona said, an artistic wingwoman the likes of which Mae could never have imagined. "So much heartbreak and vulnerability and hope—and then the sort of...how she captures the failure to become?"

"*The Failure to Become*," Elvin said, repeating the words while miming a plaque, titling the piece without so much as looking at Mae.

"Oh, I love that," Fiona said. "I mean, it resonates. It's not small, you know? The moment is small, but the idea is big."

"Thirty under thirty," Elvin said, the two of them speaking in a code that Mae could mostly but not entirely decipher.

"Even bigger, I think," Fiona said. "Not just *ARTnews*, not just our world, but broader. The *Times*. *New York* mag. I mean, she's both, right? She's downtown in the know-art scene and she's a voice of modern girlhood, a cultural touchstone."

Elvin's eyebrows danced.

Mae stayed quiet, not wanting them to remember that she wasn't a cultural anything, that her work hadn't been seen by anyone, and that she wasn't sold, exactly, on the title *The Failure to Become*. She didn't know when to say that the Painting wasn't what they were saying it was. It was a reckoning—with herself, with Sydney, with a history she was piecing together. It was a love letter to friendship, really. But maybe that wasn't the sort of thing they could sell to the masses.

The Painting was put in a show with other young artists' work. The show itself was named *Becoming* and the other paintings were a celebration of the word—ecstatic expressions of slipping into new identities, finding love, leaving behind trauma. Their titles were joyful, poignant, heartfelt, and revolutionary.

And then there was Mae's piece. *The Failure to Become*. It occupied a wall on its own, a prized location.

"Why do I have to be the sad one?" Mae asked Fiona while her friend dressed her in something white and gauzy and asymmetrical.

"You want to be the sad one," Fiona said. "That's the whole point. We found the rest of these little Pollyannas so that you would be more serious in contrast. You are more complicated. They, like, *think* they're complicated? But you actually are."

"I am?"

"Well, your painting is."

The plan worked, anyway; critics and artists and other gallery owners came to the show—it was the sort of thing no one wanted to miss. Elvin was an excellent curator of talent, and his studio's exhibitions were known for fabulous catering and more expensive than usual champagne and the kind of buzzy, heady events that started late and ended even later and would often be attended by a celebrity or two, someone recognizable for their subtle work in indie films, or Hollywood starlets trying to rehab their images and be taken more seriously.

Everyone who came to *Becoming* lingered in front of one piece. The Painting. Mae's painting.

"Haunting," they said.

"Brutal."

"You can practically taste the artist's unease with the space she occupies in the world."

"It's so frantic. Chaos."

"But beautiful."

"Yes, yes, I meant *chaos* in the most refined sense of the word. Chaos in a way so rarely captured on canvas."

"It is a work in conflict with itself," Elvin said, slipping into conversation in a practiced, perfect way. "It is telling us so many things at once. It is begging for our help. It is refusing us. It is alive. Which is the main thing, isn't it? It is life, on canvas."

Weeks later, Mae was on the cover of the *New York Times Magazine* for an article titled "Life on Canvas." She sat somberly next to the Painting in a simple peach-and-blue-striped shift dress and beat-up brown hiking boots. She had on purple lipstick and almost no eye makeup; she was all lips and goose bumps.

The article detailed her gallery debut, her suburban upbringing, her fraught relationship with her childhood, the gruesome and untimely death of her artist mother, who would never witness her success, her studio apartment, her friendship with Fiona, and the passionate conversations *The Failure to Become* had opened up about the beauty of seeing the work on the canvas, seeing the process laid bare rather than the refined elegance of hiding it. *The Failure to Become* was messy and brilliant, the article proclaimed. It was adored because of the effort one could see in the strokes, in the layers of color evident beneath, the changes that had been made, the mistakes still visible. *The Failure to Become* was about the work of trying to understand something. *The Failure to Become* was about the impossibility of finding truth. The Painting was about Mae and her unfinished relationship with herself.

These were the words of the journalist who wrote Mae's profile.

She also wrote about how Mae took her coffee (black, with sugar), about how messy her apartment was (very), and about the decade-old mood ring she wore on her thumb. The piece ended with the lines *Mae Dyer's mother had artistic aspirations as well, unmet passions put aside to raise a child in the sunny and sublime suburban haven of Sommersette. She died on the day of Mae's high-school graduation, in her own backyard, the result of a fatal allergy to bees. You can see the grief, the horror, and the regret in Mae Dyer's work. Her mother would have been proud, although one wonders if without the death of Mae's mother, this masterpiece would even exist.*

Mae wanted to hide that final sentence away, a secret she had been keeping, poorly, all this time. Late some nights she wondered if she, too, had an awful investment in Joni being gone. She was suspect too, really, wasn't she? They all were.

Graham and Catherine called daily in the weeks after the article, reporting on all the friends and colleagues who had read it.

Sydney commented a lukewarm *Yay!* under Mae's Facebook post about it.

Beth Ann, of course, said nothing.

It was Barrett Sullivan who surprised Mae, sending her a note about how proud of her he was.

Mae hung on to the note, which was brief but swooning, strangely emotional for a man whom she hadn't seen since the days when he was fucking her mom and ruining her life.

She forgot about the note, eventually, the way all strange things fade a bit, become dreamlike, then float away, filed in the brain under Things That Don't Make Sense Exactly but Don't Quite Matter Either. Curiosities, they would be called. Whimsical moments that made life feel the tiniest bit less predictable but were much less important than all the other things one had to remember, like Social Security numbers and your mother's birthday and the names of everyone you ever thought you loved.

The note from Barrett was a forgotten curiosity.

Until it wasn't anymore.

THEN

BETH ANN PUT up a flyer at the grocery store after she'd picked up frozen mozzarella sticks and a selection of mild cheeses for Sydney's graduation party. She'd need toothpicks too. Triscuits. Napkins. A few bottles of champagne and something for the kids—soda, she supposed, though she'd have to ask Sydney what kind.

Lost? the flyer read. *We will find you. And then you will find you. And that new you will be the you that you didn't know you'd always been looking for.*

"Not exactly poets, are they?" Joni had a smirk on her face and a hand on Beth Ann's shoulder, surprising her. It had been two years since Barrett moved out, and it had been a strange time between the women, who continued to pretend, both of them, that nothing had happened. But the strain was obvious, deep. They rarely spoke aside from messages Joni left on Beth Ann's machine and the very occasional coffee after an event at school, during which Joni would chatter and after which Beth Ann would spend the rest of her day in bed, recovering from the unbelievable effort of playing pretend.

It wasn't a friendship, exactly, though they still casually referred to each other as best friends, as if their history mattered more than their present, as if the title were a permanent one, unmovable even by the most enormous of betrayals.

"I don't know much about poetry," Beth Ann said after jumping out of her skin from the suddenness of Joni. "But they've helped me a lot. And they might help other people."

"Well, I do know about poetry, and you are way better than some New You bullshit. I like the old you."

"Barrett doesn't," Beth Ann said. The words dropped hard on the ground between them, practically a grenade.

"You're still hung up on him?" Joni asked, as if Barrett were Beth Ann's high-school boyfriend and not, still, her husband who happened to be living in a condo a town away.

"He's the love of my life," Beth Ann said. She kept her voice as steady as she could, but still it shuddered. She thought she saw Joni blink extra fast. Look at the ground a beat too long. But maybe it was an optical illusion, a thing she saw because she wanted to see some flicker of shame.

"I don't feel like you guys were ever meant to be," Joni said.

Beth Ann would wonder forever if Joni knew then that Beth Ann knew. She would spend the rest of her life trying to understand the cruelty, the terribleness, of Joni saying these words. Was Joni trying to convince herself that the affair wasn't so bad? Was she testing to see if Beth Ann knew? Or was there some other explanation too horrible, too base, for Beth Ann to even dream up?

Whatever the reason, it was finally, finally a breath too far and Beth Ann's eyes welled up with tears, her fingers flying to her face to wipe away wetness, to try and try and try to be someone stronger than she really was. She wanted to be sturdy. Solid. But she wasn't those things, never had been. Whatever had been holding her together, barely, broke right there in the grocery store. A half sob erupted out of her. "Why, Joni?"

But Joni wasn't going to stop pretending until Beth Ann forced her to. "Men are such assholes," she said, like Barrett's leaving was an example of male fickleness and not, in fact, a result of her own pushiness, her prettiness, her presence here in Sommersette.

"I'm asking *you* why," Beth Ann practically screamed. A few people in the store turned to look at the women, then quickly turned away. Some of them had heard rumors of what had happened. Sommersette was small, after all, and Joni and Beth Ann were well known in town, women everyone ran into at the playground, the Italian bistro, the library, and here at the grocery store. They were the protagonists of a lovely little story people liked to tell, women who were best friends and whose daughters were also best friends, and wasn't it sweet and wasn't it idyllic, and then, also, wasn't it always a little hard to believe, a little bit suspect, actually, if you'd been paying attention? "I'm asking you why *you* did this, Joni. Because you did. You *did*."

Two years ago, when Barrett moved out, he'd told Joni that Beth Ann knew "about us." Joni asked him exactly what that meant and he'd said that she knew about the affair but not the rest of it. Joni wanted to ask what "the rest of it" meant but hadn't, because she feared it meant Mae, and she couldn't stand to think of her daughter's existence phrased in that way.

The rest of it—meaning Mae's unlikely conception and dazzling birth and toothy smile and love of watercolors and sunsets, which, even though she was eighteen years old, she pointed out still when they were especially beautiful. Mae was not an afterthought. She was not a mistake or a thing to be brushed aside and left untold.

Eventually Barrett said, "She assumed it started back when the girls were younger, some night you came over and we both talked about Peru, and I guess she'd always felt strange about that or something. I don't know."

Joni had a million questions about what Beth Ann was feeling and what Barrett intended to do and if he was expecting her to leave Graham or if he was starting over on his own, questions that she kept trying to ask and that he kept managing not to answer. They still saw each other every week or two, but that didn't help her make sense of what they were—a path into the future or an echo of past mistakes, love or lust or destiny or a thing that never should have happened. Joni wanted to somehow be with Barrett *and* protect the half sisters and their perfect friendship. She wanted them to stay together, to stay close, to be family. But she wanted a life filled with love too, she wanted it all, as impossible as having it all was. Except maybe, *maybe*, with the girls going to college, what they had been waiting for would actually come to be. They would be living together—Sydney and Mae a permanent thing, a true duo. Joni had done what she'd set out to do, and with the girls taken care of, maybe it was finally time for her and Barrett. They'd talked about moving back to the city, getting a studio in the Village, trying every Italian place in the neighborhood, spending every Wednesday afternoon at a museum, living a small and beautiful life together away from Sommersette, away from Beth Ann and Graham, away from the years of secrets and stresses and uncertainty. It was time. Maybe it really was time. Joni's life—the one she had always wanted, the one she'd left behind in order to make this one—would begin.

Sometimes Graham said he wondered what had happened to Beth Ann and Barrett. And Beth Ann sometimes invited Joni to a book club or a bake sale or to go for a walk, which she would then, inevitably, cancel on the day of. And somehow they all continued on, the truth right there but also in the shadows. The four of them looking away from it.

Except here was Beth Ann, putting up a flyer in a grocery store, asking questions, the unlikely engine moving them forward into something else. Their kids were about to leave home, and Joni felt it too, the sudden space for things other than essays on ethics and strained conversations about condoms and those occasional moments of snuggling on the couch with a body who used to live inside your own body but was now wildly its own.

This moment of time in motherhood had seemed like it was going to last forever, but now it was ending and something else was coming in, right here in the grocery store with its terrible lighting and too-cold freezer aisle.

"It had nothing to do with you," Joni said now to Beth Ann, which was the exact wrong response.

"It's my life," Beth Ann said. The tears were out now, fully unleashed and hot and fast. "Of course it has to do with me, it's my family, my best friend, my whole fucking world."

"Our friendship is totally separate from— I mean, there's the girls and there's us, and Barrett and I are this whole other—"

"Fuck you," Beth Ann interrupted before Joni could continue her desperate compartmentalizations. "Fuck you and fuck him and fuck the girls' friendship and fuck those long afternoons at my kitchen table and fuck Nantucket and early dinners and cheese plates and coffee at the playground. Fuck it all, Joni. Fuck every bit of it."

Beth Ann's voice was loud now, and everyone shopping had stopped to listen in. Perhaps in a city like New York, the world would have moved along. Joni remembered that from her days there: She could sob or scream on the streets, she could wear anything she wanted, she could sing her favorite song in the middle of the subway, and no one would even blink. In the city, no one would have thought twice about a public argument. They all would have continued buying artichokes or checking the time on their wristwatches like this was nothing, like fights and make-out sessions and celebrity sightings were all just tiny parts of life, barely worth mentioning.

But here in Sommersette, any public show of emotion was notable, and Beth Ann's voice was getting louder, her tears messier, and customers at the store slipped into the cereal aisle so that they could keep watching but not, they hoped, be seen by either woman. (Days later, these same people would call the police, offer up information on this argument, say in hushed tones, *I'd never seen Beth Ann like that before... When I heard what happened to Joni—well, it seemed worth mentioning. I'm not saying she actually—but it certainly seems like a coincidence. An awful, awful coincidence. I don't know if she was angry enough to—but she was angry. She was very angry.*)

"You're my best friend," Joni said. She was whispering, in sharp contrast to Beth Ann's yelling. Their friendship had always felt to Joni, in spite of everything, like an untouchable force, but it turned out it could be ruined just like anything else—marriage and parenthood and creativity and the rest of it, all the things you were promised could last forever. That it was Joni's fault—hers and Barrett's—was a fact that she couldn't quite stomach and so therefore mostly ignored. "Can we still be—maybe after some time? Aren't we bigger than all of this?"

Joni imagined being with Beth Ann far away from Sommersette, meeting her at the Angelika to catch an indie film or at Bloomingdale's to buy something too expensive that they both deserved. She thought they might try the cupcakes at Magnolia Bakery that people were always talking about or the scones at Alice's Tea Cup, where she'd taken the girls once. Maybe that would be their place together. Not with Barrett, of course; Beth Ann wouldn't want to see him, but after some time, she'd want Joni still, wouldn't she?

Beth Ann didn't even bother to shake her head. She looked at the flyer she'd put up with all its promises for a better life, a better self, knowing in that moment that she was the kind of woman who would forgive someone like Joni and then be hurt again, and she needed to be a different kind of woman. She put down her basket of groceries, things she needed but didn't need right this second, things that could be sacrificed. Beth Ann turned and left. The groceries, Joni, the simplicity of the life she once lived — she left it all behind.

"Don't tell Mae," Joni called after her. "I'll tell Graham eventually, I will, but Mae — don't tell Mae."

Three days later, at the graduation party, Beth Ann watched as Sydney announced to the roomful of attendees that she wouldn't be attending college after all, that she would be joining Mae in New York while Mae attended Pratt. They had found an apartment, a studio in the East Village that was probably overrun with mice, and she was going to figure it out, get a job at a coffee shop or be a temp in an office.

Beth Ann tried to hide her shock, the awkward betrayal of her child making plans without her, deciding who she would be and deciding that person would be made in the mold of the woman destroying Beth Ann's life.

Glasses were raised in a toast to Sydney's new path, and Mae's gaze kept flitting over to Beth Ann, a kind of challenge for her to question their big plan. Beth Ann knew she could tear it all apart if she wanted. She could tell Mae what Joni had done, why Barrett wasn't at this party and why Joni and Graham perhaps seemed strained around each other, why there hadn't been a joint family vacation planned for so many years now, why Joni herself was not here, an absence that felt loud to Beth Ann and, she imagined, to all the guests.

Beth Ann knew people came to the party only to be able to unpack it later, unravel its intricacies, wonder at this choice for an appetizer or that, watch the way a husband cringed at his wife's joke, the way two friends pointedly ignored each other, the way someone's kid was having a tantrum or, more recently, sneaking a drink.

Beth Ann didn't want to give them any more to look at, so she stayed away from Mae. She waited an hour, then cornered her own daughter outside the bathroom. "You can't just follow Mae around like a shadow," she said. "Being near her isn't going to magically make you special too."

She let the words land.

They weren't meant to be mean, just factual. Mae had that something that everyone wanted—talent and charisma and whatever else it was, an ability not to give a fuck. It wasn't exactly a secret that Sydney was the lesser friend, the one without the dazzle and shine. Beth Ann had maybe never said it so plainly, but Syd was an adult now, making her own adult choices, so Beth Ann could say adult things to her. Real, true things.

"I know that. I learned that from watching you with Joni," Sydney spat back. This was true too. Joni took up space in the world, and Beth Ann made herself small in it, and it was clear now which way was better, which way got you further. Still, Sydney's words undid Beth Ann, even though she had flung hurtful words first, even though teenage girls were known for saying cutting things to their mothers, even though it seemed in almost every way that things really couldn't get much worse.

"You're coming with me to HigherLife," Beth Ann said, but the command came out clunky. She tried to flip her hair, do something, anything, that would make the whole thing sound natural.

"Mom. Gross."

"We can't be pushovers anymore," Beth Ann said as if Sydney were just an extension of herself, a hand or a foot, a useful thing attached to her body with no agency of its own. "We have to find ourselves. I'm lost. I can admit it. But so are you. Keeping that woman's secret all these years. Then following her asshole daughter to some scummy city to live in trash. This isn't who I raised you to be. This isn't what was meant to happen."

It had never been said so plainly. In the years since Barrett had moved out, they hadn't spoken about the secrets Sydney had kept, the endless protection of Mae Dyer, the pact she had entered into with a woman who was both Beth Ann's best friend and greatest enemy.

It sounded strange, the sudden precision Beth Ann was using to discuss it all. As if Sydney weren't just graduating from high school but from the rest of it too — childhood, the last few breaths of innocence, the gift of pretending things were simpler than they really were. Sydney was being asked to say goodbye to all of it at once.

"Mom. It's my party. Can we not?"

"You're not going to New York. You're not living with Mae."

"I'm eighteen."

"We're done with that family."

"She's my best friend. She's my whole life. I'm not going to some empowerment whatever with you. I'm going to live my life."

Both of them noticed the distinct lack of details in this plan. Her life still an unknown entity, a mystery to them both.

Beth Ann stormed away and painted on a pretty face to say goodbye to her guests, who lingered over wine and small talk, who offered to help her clean up, who said Sydney would be fine, she was a smart girl, kids did this kind of thing all the time. Beth Ann nodded and smiled tightly at the platitudes that meant nothing, that solved nothing.

A few people straggled, and the National's "Mr. November"

began playing from a playlist Mae and Sydney had put together, a compilation of their favorite songs from different moments in their friendship. Beth Ann always tried to tune this song out, and its refrain of "I won't fuck us over, I won't fuck us over" was decidedly inappropriate to be blasting at a sweet little high-school graduation party.

"Something else, Syd, please," she said, trying to keep her tone light and new.

Maybe Sydney would have changed the track.

Beth Ann would never know.

Because at that moment, Graham walked through the door, his face cracked open in pain, head shaking, tears streaming in a way that Beth Ann could never have imagined on this mild, often distant, always kind man.

"Oh, goodness, what's wrong? What's going on? Sit down, honey," Beth Ann said, surprising herself. She'd never called him *honey*, had never used a term of endearment with any man but Barrett.

"The woods, the woods," he said. "She was in the woods. Without her... She always takes it with her but she didn't. Somehow it wasn't with her. And the bees. There were bees. Isn't bee season later? Isn't it? But there they were. She tried calling. She tried, but I don't ever answer, I don't, and she's gone, she's gone, she's gone, she tried to call but she's gone."

They fell one by one, Beth Ann first, then Mae, then Sydney. Other guests howled or gasped or stumbled, too, probably, ones who cared less, who knew less, but who understood the potency of loss, people who knew about Joni's bee allergy because they all did, because she was always bringing it up like it was a thing that made her special or tragic or needy. It was something that had always bothered Beth Ann, but there was no one she could have said that to, it was so unkind a thought, so wrong a way to view a serious medical condition. Maybe it was thoughts like this that had made Barrett stop loving her; maybe he knew the ways she was awful.

Someone must have cleaned up after the party.

Someone must have brought Beth Ann to bed, must have taken Graham and Mae home, must have let the police in.

Barrett was there, eventually, and the look on his face when Beth Ann told him would haunt her forever. It was the pain, yes, but also the love, the heartbreak. And the something else.

She told herself it wasn't guilt, it wasn't guilt, that look on his stricken, sunken face.

THEN

THE INVESTIGATION LASTED weeks, and at the end of it, Beth Ann was so wrung out she barely recognized herself. There was the funeral and the hundreds of phone calls and kindhearted visitors with banana breads and casseroles and promises that she could reach out anytime. Someone gave her a therapist's business card. People shared memories they had of Beth Ann and Joni together, laughing at some PTA event or finishing each other's sentences at some moms' night out a hundred years ago, when everything was different, when it was all better and brighter and made more sense.

None of it helped.

The police cleared them all at the end of the investigation, of course they did. It was a horrible accident, it was an unimaginable tragedy, but there was no one to blame. The bees, perhaps. Forgetfulness. But not anyone living in Sommersette. Not anyone who could be held responsible, not really.

Barrett dropped by every day with a coffee and sad eyes and said he didn't want her to be alone, didn't want to be alone himself, didn't know where else to go. So they drank coffee on the porch. They had croissants. They did crossword puzzles. They wondered what kind of bird that was there, what kind of flower was growing across the street. They didn't speak of Joni. They waited for Sydney to leave home; they watched Mae's frame shrink and shrug; they worried about her but also, truly, knew she would survive. She was Mae Dyer, she was special, she had always been so special.

There was Barrett and there were her new friends, the ones from HigherLife, which had been a thing she went to a few meetings of but gradually became a whole lifestyle, a whole way of being in the world. After Joni's death, they gathered around her and promised her a life that made more sense and had more joy, a life that belonged to her. Maybe she could have gone to a grief support group, but what she felt was something so much more tangled than grief and what she wanted was so much bigger than support for her sadness. She needed more. *More*.

There were meetups most days and Beth Ann was in need of something to fill that time. Barrett and the coffee and the porch were done by ten thirty every morning, and then what? There was just the way Joni was gone, the way Beth Ann had spent years building a whole life that had been systematically destroyed by lust and friendship and, God, somehow, by fucking *bees*, goddamn *nature*, and she couldn't just sit with that, she didn't know how.

"Come," she said to Sydney the week before Sydney was meant to leave for New York City with Mae. "See what it's all about. Maybe it will help."

"I don't need help," Sydney said, but she had acne on her chin and across her nose and kept forgetting to shower, choosing instead to swoop her formerly soft, shiny hair into a scraggly, oily bun at the top of her head. "I need to get out of here. That's what I need."

"None of us know what we need," Beth Ann said. It was, Sydney thought, one of the first true things her mother had ever said.

So she went. It was clear Beth Ann felt at home among the other ladies with their expensive engagement rings and khaki-colored jackets and use of words like *opportunity* and *strength* and *independence* and *family values*, terms that felt like code to Sydney, but she didn't know what they were code for, exactly.

An hour into the meeting, Beth Ann told Sydney she could go, take the car, she'd get a ride home with one of her new friends in pink lipstick and cutesy headbands from J.Crew that seemed made for younger women. Beth Ann wanted to stay. She enjoyed the spinach artichoke dip that someone had brought. She wrote down book recommendations and made plans to go for walks with three different women. She listened to someone in charge talk about community, making that word sound luxurious and real. She signed a sheet and handed over a check and promised to come back the next week and the next. She talked about Weight Watchers and her husband's job and her own wish to bring in an income. She talked, and they talked, and it felt like a kind of home, a place she could belong.

She did not talk about Joni other than to say she'd "lost someone important" to her and she accepted the hugs, the kind, nodding heads, the platitudes about how she wasn't alone, how loss could make you stronger, about how strong she clearly was, just look at her, here, standing, surviving, raising a beautiful daughter, doing her best.

"Who was it that you lost?" a woman named Meredith who had full cheeks and terrible taste in earrings wanted to know. She was the only one who'd asked for specifics, and Beth Ann got the sense she had been chosen for the job.

"It's a long story," Beth Ann said. She was surprised to feel the promise of tears, always shocked to feel the sadness when the anger had been so big for so long.

"Let's get coffee," Meredith said. "I have time."

Beth Ann nodded. Meredith was wearing the same jeans she herself was wearing. Her hair was in a bouncy ponytail. Her nails were rounded and shiny, newly manicured, maybe always manicured. There was nothing about Meredith that would make people in town look twice at the two of them getting coffee. She carried a black purse, wore a single coat of mascara, had a pleasant face and a way of moving her body that would never remind anyone of sex. She was safe.

Beth Ann tried to walk in perfect sync with her. Ordered her coffee the same way. Sat with her legs crossed in Meredith's direction. Settled into this new manner of being, this new life. Wrote a version of the truth in her head about Joni and Barrett and the past fifteen years; she discovered she could in fact rewrite the story she'd been letting other people write all this time.

This, Beth Ann thought, relieved to be sure of something at last, *this is the answer.*

NOW

Sydney

SYDNEY PITCHED THE shoot as a kind of art, knowing that Mae would see through it but also that she wouldn't want to say no. And she'd drawn up the paperwork, the name for their part of the LillyLou business so obvious and perfect: Two Alices. What could be sweeter than two new moms and their beautiful same-named babies? The Alices had just turned one, and everyone knew that was the cutest age. And of course, the engagement Sydney got whenever she posted about Mae and her Alice throughout all these months was astronomical. It made good sense to legitimize it. Make it official. It was good for Mae too. An income. A way forward. It was time.

"We want it to look natural," Sydney was explaining to the photographer now, a soft-shouldered and wide-hipped woman around their age with a heartbreakingly beautiful smile. "Friends in the park. And classic too. You know, autumnal and leaves and sort of idyllic, but it would be good for it not to look perfect? Like, it should be authentic."

"Idyllic and authentic," the photographer repeated, nodding. Her name was Isla, and Sydney was worried she wasn't confident enough to do the job. She'd imagined someone who would boss her around a bit, not the exact opposite. On her website, Isla had looked domineering, discerning, strong. But in person she was shorter than Sydney had expected, and her voice was light and questioning. Even her camera seemed to be too much for her, the weight of it tugging on her neck, urging her shoulders into a forward slump.

"We'd like a range: Fun. Serious. We brought outfit changes. We'd like a collection of photos we can use throughout the season. Some with our merch and some without. Right, Mae?"

Mae was sitting on the grass with her Alice, who was tugging up chunks of grass, then throwing them back on the ground and attempting to pat them into place. Mae had seemed distracted lately. She kept saying she wanted to hang out, and then when she and Sydney met up, she'd go quiet, losing herself in Alice's babbling and not really engaging in conversation.

Sydney knew she had to be casual about it, but every minute with the photographer was money she was spending, and she needed the spent money to mean something. She had to believe it would bring something bigger later on. It was easy enough to believe when she said it to herself a hundred times a day but harder when the money was not, in fact, coming back to her.

When the most recent credit card bill came in, Sam asked her to stop.

He even asked, late at night when they had both woken up and found themselves unable to fall back asleep, if she might want to think about finding a job sometime after Alice's first birthday.

Sydney spat at him that she already *had* a job, and she left the bedroom to sleep on the couch before he could determine whether she meant motherhood or LillyLou.

"Whatever you want, Syd," Mae said now, which was exactly what Mae had said about what they should split for lunch and where they should take the girls for music class and whether Mae should come to Small Group again. She let Sydney take the lead for all of it, and it was at first a welcome role reversal—Mae had picked everything when they were growing up, what they would be for Halloween and who they would go to prom with and what neighborhood they should get an apartment in.

Now Mae let Sydney post about their lives and link the posts to the scarves and bras and skimpy nightgowns. After the fight they'd had so many months ago, when the babies were brand-new, Mae had grown passive in their friendship—apologetic, almost.

It was all working out just the way it was supposed to, Sydney thought. Two Alices would take them places. Would give them both what they'd always wanted.

"Let's start with a pile of leaves and see what happens," Sydney said. "I feel like we can't go wrong with a pile of leaves."

"A classic," Isla agreed, and the women and their babies sat in a pile of fallen leaves, baby hands reaching for the oranges and reds, their bodies angled toward each other. Sydney shifted closer to Mae and leaned her head on her shoulder. She grabbed hold of both babies and put them in her lap together, the two girls giggling in unison. She made Mae laugh by throwing leaves at her like they were seven again and not thirty-four and worn down by these tiny, ravenous, joyful, screaming girls.

"Beautiful," Isla said. "Really lovely. You can feel the intimacy. You two are a couple?"

"Best friends," Sydney corrected her. "Very, very old friends."

"Wow, you can really tell. Your relationship just sparkles."

Sydney beamed. It was exactly what she wanted to get across. Last night, she had listened to Ivy Miller speak about aspirational posts and how to utilize them.

"*Aspirational* does not mean expensive cars and Paris vacations. We aren't Real Housewives. What do women really aspire to? I mean, really and truly? Men who love them even when they're no longer twenty-two. Friends who understand them. Children who adore them. And an ease with themselves. And if any of that comes with a stay at a luxury spa or the gift of a diamond tennis bracelet, well, then, fine, but I've found that connecting with our customers has more to do with showcasing our own relationships than posting about our vacations or possessions. Women want to be loved. And known. And understood. How can you show the world *that*? Because we all know that's what working for LillyLou and building your business really has to offer."

Sydney brought out some props—pashminas, yes, but also LillyLou-branded travel mugs and soft matching beanies for moms and daughters. She had thoughts on Mae's worn yellow sweater, her loose-fitting eggplant-colored pants. But she was resisting the urge to style Mae, since the ladies at Small Group assured her that Mae's eclectic and whimsical style paired well with Sydney's put-together looks.

And who was Sydney to argue? Since she'd started posting content with Mae, her business had been thriving. A dozen women had joined her team, and soon, so soon, she'd see the sales coming in, she just knew it. Even Beth Ann was impressed with her growing team, texting Sydney weekly to tell her she was proud of her but never, not once, asking how Mae was doing.

And the truth was, Mae still hadn't officially joined LillyLou despite Sydney's urging. Every once in a while she went to a Small Group meeting, but she hadn't even bought a pashmina, much less signed up to be the first in line for the undergarments coming out in just one week after a series of manufacturing delays. That was what the paperwork was for. To push things forward, to get to the next level. Sydney had it all mapped out. She'd get Mae set up in LillyLou, not in her downline but as a full partner. Unconventional, maybe, but she was positive she could do more with Mae than without her. It had been so obvious—what was more childhood-best-friends-all-grown-up than commiserating over postpartum bodies and helping each other build up their confidence in their thirties?

This photo shoot was the pinnacle, a way to make what was special more refined, more official. Sydney knew Ivy Miller would be able to see how hard she was working, how seriously she was taking the job. And then Mae would sign the papers, and they'd be in it together. Saving each other, really.

After everything.

"Why don't we take some headshots of you at the end?" Sydney suggested to Mae. "You should get something for yourself if you're really going to keep resisting your obvious calling for LillyLou. We could get some shots for you to use professionally. Oh! Or on dating apps!"

"Professionally?" Mae asked. She hadn't exactly come up with a career path yet, although Alice, at one year old, was no longer a tiny infant and it was time for Mae to have a plan.

"You said you've been working on something new. A new painting? Don't you think you should start to consider, you know, your brand?"

"I don't have a brand."

"Everyone has a brand," Sydney said. She was sure of this. And Mae's was easy. In fact, there were several options; Tragic Art-World One-Hit Wonder Due for a Comeback seemed the obvious route, but there was also Single Mom Without Her Own Mom but with a Dream, and, of course, LillyLou Prodigy BFF with a Creative Side Hustle.

"Is, like, Disaster a brand?" Mae asked, half smiling, half serious. "Or, like, Postpartum Anxiety and Insecurity? No Idea How to Be a Mom—is that a brand?"

"Some people do well with that," Sydney said, not acknowledging the self-deprecation, the joke, underneath. "You have to be sort of fearless if you go that route. Open up in the emotional way, you know? Some posts about Joni, probably. I mean, Joni would play great online. She was so—captivating. Funny could work for you too, but I think emotional would be better for an artist."

"Right," Mae said—the word a suddenly shut door on the conversation.

Isla intervened before the silence grew too unwieldy, separating the women to take individual shots as Sydney had requested. Sydney took hers with her Alice, refusing to let Mae hold her for just one shot of Sydney on her own.

"I'm not on my own," Sydney insisted, holding Alice a little tighter than was strictly necessary. "Alice is always with me. This is representative of me. I don't need a photo alone. I barely want a photo without you and your Alice. You guys are everything to me. To us." She looked at Mae the way she used to—wishing a little that they could be tied to each other in both literal and figurative ways. A ribbon around their wrists. A shared Rapunzel tower they couldn't escape. A piece of LillyLou paperwork declaring them partners.

"What about Sam?" Mae asked as she always did when Sydney got emotional about their friendship.

"It's different," Sydney answered. "Can't you feel it? I mean, Sam's my husband, he's my, you know, romantic partner. But the whole motherhood thing—I'm doing it with you. Just like we did the whole childhood thing together. And just like we would have done the whole quarter-life-crisis thing together if everything hadn't gotten all—"

"I should have a photo alone, I guess," Mae interrupted. Isla cleared her throat like she, too, wanted to skirt whatever issue it was that Sydney kept poking at. "Is my hair—well, whatever, it's my hair, it's going to be what it is. It's messy. Let it be messy."

"Art is messy," Sydney said knowingly. Isla swallowed a laugh but Sydney wasn't embarrassed. Art *was* messy. She'd seen Mae's work, and that's what it was, had been even when they were young.

She'd seen Mae's sleeves rolled up, her forearms covered in paint, her hair matted to her forehead, her lips folding and unfolding as she tried to make a decision about what to do next, about how to capture whatever her vision was.

Mae looked around for somewhere to put Alice and settled on a patch of grass. A minute later, Alice pulled up a handful and threatened to put it in her mouth. Mae had just gotten herself into a position she didn't feel too wildly uncomfortable in—leaning against a tree—but she had to immediately move to Alice before a shot could be taken. She nestled a blanket underneath her daughter, hoping that would buy her a few choking-hazard-less moments, but now Mae's distance bothered Alice, and she screamed for her.

"She's okay, just take the shot," Sydney said. Alice was crying because she missed her mother, who was a mere three feet away from her and in full view. She could be left there long enough for the photographer to take a couple of pictures, and then Mae could swoop in and pick her up, and Sydney knew that in the blink of an eye, the screams would vanish, and Alice would giggle and purr into her mother's shoulder, and it would be as if the crying never happened.

Sydney knew this. Knew how desperate it felt to miss a mother. How easily it could be solved by the simple fact of her presence.

But Mae couldn't withstand it. She leaned against the tree, but her face could do nothing but grimace, and her body tilted almost imperceptibly in the direction of Alice.

"Over here!" Isla kept reminding her over the baby's cries, which weren't even loud, just insistent, more of an ongoing whine than anything else, but still ultimately more than Mae could handle. "Look at me. Smile. Nope. Smile. With your eyes too. Think of something nice. Something relaxing."

Mae tried, but it was too much. The act of pretending to forget about Alice even for a moment was impossible.

"Think of who you were before," Sydney called out, imagining what she would need to gather herself in this situation. Mae, however, looked shocked at the advice, feeling it was either impossible or undesirable, Sydney couldn't tell.

Sydney tried to do it too, just for a hair of a moment. She put her own Alice on the grass next to Mae's Alice. She imagined herself two years ago—hair blown out and decidedly un-spit-up-on, mind thinking of things like what she and Sam should do for the weekend and why she hadn't found her calling the way the women of Lilly-Lou kept insisting she would. She tried to live in that reality for a brief moment but found it impossible. And not because that version of herself was so far from the current one. Rather, it was too close.

Motherhood was supposed to have changed Sydney in ways that were so enormous as to be almost unfathomable. It was a promise that she would be brand-new, purposeful and focused and clear on what mattered to her. Motherhood was the Great Change, the Big Shift, the Before and After of her life, except here she was, her hair messier and her body looser, wilder, but the rest of her deeply recognizable as Sydney. In fact, in some ways it seemed that motherhood had simply stripped away the easiest things about her and left her with the troubles—the questioning of purpose, the insecurities, the anxieties about doing things right, about making a life that didn't collapse or implode right in the middle as her mother's had. She had thought, maybe, that motherhood would separate her from her mother, but instead it seemed to draw her closer in, because now they were connected by this shared purpose, this same uneasy navigation.

"Did you get one?" Sydney asked Isla, desperate for Mae, at least, to be able to capture something new about herself, something central and meaningful.

"Um," Isla said, as if that one sound were a complete sentence. She turned the camera around for Sydney to see. The shots were beautifully composed, the fall colors brilliant and appealing. But

Mae looked lost in them—her eyes never leaving Alice, her body tense, ready to leap into action, the whole of her unrecognizable as the elusive and mysterious artist responsible for the Painting that all those years ago a critic at *The New Yorker* had said "not only defines but also challenges the nature of the millennial generation of women."

No, in these photos Mae was plain, unremarkable, like so many mothers before her, like so many after too, just a mom distracted by her kid, unable to do or be much of anything else.

Mae and Sydney walked home together after the photo shoot. The photos with the Alices, at least, were perfect.

"I signed us up for music class with the Alices," Sydney said, "and I'm thinking art next summer? There's cute toddler art classes across the park that are definitely worth making the trek to. And you'd love that, right? I also think we should do a spa weekend. Just you and me, of course. No Alices allowed. What do you think?" Sydney was, impressively, pushing a stroller with one hand, holding her phone and scrolling through photos to post with the other, and talking at a speed that could only be described as relentless.

"I don't know, Syd." Mae's eyes filled with tears.

"Hey. Hey, the photos are fine. Don't worry. We've got this. We're getting crazy engagement on everything I post. Seriously. So just let me sign you up as a partner, and you'll sell stuff easy-peasy. I swear. People love our story." Sydney took out the papers.

"What's our story?" Mae asked, wiping the tears away, gripping the stroller hard with both hands.

"Best friends from childhood who found each other again through our babies who we both named Alice!" Sydney had figured out the snappiest way to sum them up. She was, after all, asked about Mae constantly on LillyLou group chats and at meetups with other moms who followed her accounts and by casual acquaintances at dinner parties and in the grocery store. Whenever Sydney was asked what she herself was up to, she'd mention Mae and social media and LillyLou and the power of old friends in new motherhood.

Her work at LillyLou seemed to perplex her more casual acquaintances, but their interest in her friendship with Mae outweighed their original unease when she spoke about women-owned businesses and pashminas and lingerie and empowerment. *Wow, your best friend from childhood? How sweet. Oh, she made that painting? God, I loved that, had an image of it pasted into my journal when I was twenty-two and heartbroken. Didn't she lose her mother in some awful way? I remember the articles. And now you guys are moms together! And the babies! Both named Alice! What are the chances? You should write a book, what a story!*

Of course, they only knew the sliver of story Sydney told them, but that was enough.

"It's a simple story," Sydney concluded.

And Mae nodded. The beats of the story of their lives were familiar, but she seemed on the verge of saying more.

"Let's forget the rest of it," Sydney said. They were at her place, Sam's form visible in the window, Sydney eyeing the door like she wasn't sure she wanted to go in. "Let's just tell the simple parts, the story of our friendship. Forget about our parents. Can't we do that? For the Alices?"

Mae's whole body cringed.

"I mean, not *forget*," Sydney said. She heard the misstep. It was easy enough to write off Barrett and Beth Ann and Graham and that woman he'd married, but Joni...once someone was gone, you weren't allowed to dismiss their importance. In fact, it grew greater. Sydney knew that as well as anyone, always looking for Joni around a corner, haunted by the way things went, worrying that everything could have been different if she, Sydney, hadn't kept the secret. Or, maybe, had kept it better. Who could say.

"It's okay, I know what you mean," Mae said, but Sydney didn't believe her. They hugged, and Mae seemed to hold on longer than usual, more tightly. Sydney thought about asking if she was okay, but they weren't really ever okay anymore—motherhood was a state of uneasiness and sometimes that meant being quiet or hugging hard or getting drunk after bedtime or messaging an ex-boyfriend whom you hadn't thought about for years or lying in your kid's room after she was fast asleep just to be near the sound of her perfectly measured breathing.

So the hug was unusual but not surprising, not really, and Sydney said goodbye.

When Sydney arrived home, Sam looked strangely flustered to see her. Sydney hadn't told Mae that only a few days ago, she'd stopped by Sam's office with Alice and discovered a new woman working there, one she hadn't met before. A beautiful one. Before Sam noticed his wife there, his hand—she was sure of it—had been lingering on the small of the beautiful woman's back.

Sydney had cleared her throat and Sam's face hesitated before moving from nervous surprise to happiness. She'd filed that hesitation away as something to worry about later, and it turned out that later was now.

That same pause, the expression where discomfort and excitement met. That same sense of wrongness. Sydney collapsed a little, witnessing it.

Instead of asking him about it, she kissed him hello and posted a photograph of her and Mae and the Alices. In it, she was looking down at the soft, fuzzy top of her Alice's head. Sydney looked pretty from that angle—she looked young, the lines on her forehead and the puffiness around her throat hidden by the perfect tilt of her chin.

Motherhood is our truest self exposed, she wrote. She remembered Ivy Miller's advice that they always include an opportunity for engagement. *Which self emerges most strongly when you are mothering?*

She didn't know what the words meant, exactly, but they sounded right.

Next to her, in the photograph, Mae and her Alice were smiling at something, like they were sharing a secret. From that angle, Mae's Alice's nose looked a little like her own Alice's.

Her eyelashes were similar too—long and blond, unusual for a child with dark hair.

It made Sydney smile.

She set aside the worry about Sam again.

Things were beautiful if she stared at the photograph for long enough.

Two Alices, coming soon, Sydney wrote in the comments, a secret clue for whoever was in the mood to notice.

Before she put down her phone, a comment appeared under the post. It was from Ivy Miller herself, her name coming up like a firework, Sydney's heart exploding alongside it.

Two lovely moms making their way together. Truly the LillyLou spirit. Let's talk.

NOW

Mae

THERE WERE SEVENTEEN unread texts on Mae's chain with Sydney. There were three missed calls, and Mae was sure if she went on social media, there would be a dozen tagged posts and DMs there as well.

Catherine had called too, called most days, asking about Alice but also asking, over and over, if Mae had time to *talk*, if maybe Mae and Graham and Catherine could get lunch, that Graham had something he needed to share with her, and it was important, but also maybe the sort of thing Alice should be with a sitter for.

Mae kept saying she didn't have a sitter, didn't have time, wasn't in a place to have big conversations with anyone. And Catherine understood, or pretended to understand, then kept asking again anyway.

Mae's mind flashed back to the hospital, always. The strained things Catherine kept almost saying. The comments about Graham. About secrets.

And about Joni.

Mae could not untangle the mess of it in her mind, but there was an awful knowing in her stomach, the way she'd felt the day long ago when Barrett moved out of his family's house, the way Beth Ann had looked at her in the kitchen with the broken plate on the floor. Mae had understood something was coming ever since then.

Secrets could be kept, but the feeling of secrets in the air—that was harder to tamp down.

She felt ill. She tried to breathe, as if with enough breath, she'd understand what was going on.

Mae put her phone down and picked Alice up just as she started to fuss in the crib. But Alice was only a reminder of the way life happened at you, to you, and a reminder of families and friendships and mothers, too, and the sloppy, unsatisfying ways they all came together and into being.

She needed somewhere to put the thoughts, and that's what art was for, but she couldn't exactly make art with Alice around, she thought, with a combination of exasperation and love that seemed to mix together more frequently than she'd thought possible. But there were the beginnings of what she'd drawn of Leo, the scribble on a napkin from their outing at the bar, which was the last thing she'd done resembling art. And there was paint and a canvas, and there was Alice, who didn't know how to walk yet but knew how to hold things, how to delight in something colorful and sensory and messy. And there was not much else for Mae to do with her day but follow Alice around and try to stop her from causing too much destruction or putting herself in danger.

So Mae took out a tube of silver paint and squirted it onto a palette. She took Alice's clothing off and let her sit, diapered and chubby and buzzing her lips together in a delightful baby trill. She brought out a brush and dipped it in the silver paint, narrating the experience for her baby, then handed the brush over to Alice's grasping, eager fingers.

Mae then found a stub of a pencil and the drawing of Leo folded into a mostly empty sketchbook, and she let her hand meet the blank space.

At her feet, Alice dipped the brush in paint and slapped it against the bottom of the canvas, and a laugh exploded out of her. While Mae sketched the profile of Leo's face and the strange lines she'd made on the cocktail napkin, Alice made a smattering of silver streaks that looked like enchanted grass growing from the ground. It was strange and lovely, and Mae knew immediately it was an essential part of the work.

She handed Alice a small sponge with pale pink paint next, and Alice made prints over the silver and up into more of the canvas. There was nothing artistic about it, or, more correctly, nothing prodigious. Alice was doing what babies with paint did, that was all. But the lack of a plan, the spontaneous joy — that was art too. When she'd made the Painting a decade ago, the process became the project — the shadows of former selves hidden in the paint, the mistakes not fully erased, the canvas alive with the way she'd worked through it. She could see this new thing, whatever it was, taking shape too. This was what it was to paint in motherhood. It was never wholly your own.

She let herself paint Leo's long, curling hair. She played with what color the background might be — teal or gray or pale baby pink. She mixed colors and painted a stripe of each on the canvas, testing them out. It would take months to figure out what this painting was. Years, maybe.

Alice dipped three fingers into a smoky lavender and trailed them up, paint moving up the canvas from her messy fingers and dripping down as well. She swooped a shape that looked like a broken heart. She striped it over with a handprint. It was ecstatic. Mae felt like someone she actually recognized for the first time in a long time, her heart actually in her body.

There was knocking at her door that interrupted the magic of the moment so abruptly that she almost tripped over Alice before picking her up, paint smooshing between their two bodies, and rushing to the door, assuming a delivery of diapers or a forgotten late-night purchase of epic novels that she did not actually have any time to read.

But instead there was Sydney—sweaty as if she'd run there and looking pinched and irritable.

"I *called*," she said instead of hello.

"I'm working," Mae replied, proud of the words.

"Well, so am I, that's why I called. Things are happening. Ivy Miller is happening and I need you."

"Ivy Miller is happening?" Alice tugged at Mae's hair, leaving the smoky lavender paint streaked in it. Sydney's Alice was missing from her side, a fact that Mae took note of and hoped she would soon hear an explanation for.

"She wants us. Two Alices. She wants to make us big. To be some of the primary faces of LillyLou. This is it. It's *happening*." Sydney grabbed Mae's hand and squeezed. She looked gaunt, Mae noticed. She'd probably been looking that way for a while now, but Alice obscured her view of Sydney, was always strapped to her or reaching for her or making a noise so loud and strange, it startled Mae out of observing much of anything. Sydney's Alice was active, intense, loud. In contrast, Mae's Alice was quiet, gentle, interested in her hands and the surprising things they could do, shapes they could make, and not much interested in moving around, preferring to sit with a straight back and smiling eyes.

"I'm not in LillyLou," Mae said. "You want to come in? Have coffee? I think I have bagels in the freezer."

"We can have bagels there," Sydney said. She marched through Mae's apartment to the back room, to Mae's closet, where she started flipping through dresses, blouses, skirts Mae hadn't worn in years.

"You should wear something that's you but that's also LillyLou, you know?"

"What are you talking about? Slow down, Syd. I'm not going anywhere. Alice and I are painting."

"You can play with Alice another time. Ivy Miller is taking us to lunch." Sydney was using declarative sentences instead of questions; she was telling Mae the plan instead of suggesting one, and the tactic was familiar and unsettling. Mae was immediately flooded with memories of Beth Ann doing the same. *You're wearing blue to the prom. We're going to the ocean this weekend for a family trip. Your mother will love this scarf; you're getting it for her birthday. We don't discuss family matters outside the house. You are not inviting that girl to our home.*

"I don't want to go to lunch with Ivy Miller," Mae said. She'd tried with Beth Ann too, tried to take a stand, to speak in equally certain phrases, to be just as clear. It never worked. "I don't even know Ivy Miller. Or watch her videos or whatever. This whole thing is great for you and I'll help with the photos and stuff, I don't even care if you use the name Two Alices, but I'm not doing the whole thing. It's not—"

"You have to," Sydney said, stopping her pulling of paisley and floral dresses from Mae's closet. "Mae, I need this. There's so much going on—with Sam, and also my dad's moving out, like, my mom and dad are breaking up, and it's really sudden and also, obviously, not at all sudden on another level, but my mom sounds distraught and Sam's mad at me and this is it, this is my big chance, and I just need you. I need you."

Mae tried to process all of it—Beth Ann and Barrett finally breaking apart for good, and Sydney's frantic energy, and how it all was supposed to be solved by pashminas. Alice whined. Wailed. Settled. Mae shook her head to clear it. "That's—a lot, Syd. Your mom and dad—they made it through a lot of years. But maybe it's for the best, and you've got a great life, you've got your Alice and Sam, even if things are rocky, and me, and you know, if you like selling bras, then go for it, but you don't need to bring me to lunch with this woman, I swear to God, you don't."

Sydney sat down on the bed. "I need her help," she said, her voice smaller now, less Beth Ann and more the Sydney of days past, someone unsure of her place in the world. "I need to get to the next level."

"You don't have to prove anything to anyone," Mae said. She was here trying to be present for her friend, but she was also a little bit somewhere else, wanting to be painting, wanting to be back in that quiet space with Alice, wanting to be wholly focused on the sweetness of her daughter, the metallic smell of paint, the way it felt to spend an entire morning contemplating Leo's left cheekbone. It was nearing nap time, and that, too, was a time to be treasured, the only time every day when Alice didn't require her attention, when Mae was simply herself. Alice was starting to whimper again, alerting everyone to her readiness to sleep, but putting her down now would only encourage Sydney to stay for a while. So Mae held her daughter, bouncing her on a hip, waiting it out. "You want to talk about Beth Ann and Barrett? Have things been bad for a while, you think? Maybe it's for the best, you know? Your mom seems very—together, and I mean, I don't know how your dad's been, but he's kind of a loner, right? So maybe he'll be okay too?"

Sydney seemed to try to settle herself—swallowing, taking a deep breath, clenching and releasing her fingers.

"That might be true," she said, "about my parents. I can take that as it comes. This opportunity with Ivy Miller, though, is really... important. It's a little—I'm very invested," Sydney said. There was Beth Ann again, saying something ugly in the prettiest way possible, covering up a truth with something formal and reserved.

"Okay."

"Financially," Sydney said. Her mouth tried to take back the word, but it was too late.

Mae tilted her head. Alice swatted her in the face.

"It's the lingerie. To be on the forefront, you know, you had to commit to a certain amount of inventory, and this was kind of my chance, with things going so well with us, with our brand really starting to take shape, and Ivy Miller always says you have to invest in yourself, you have to believe in yourself, and Sam doesn't really get that, so I didn't want to have to have a whole conversation about it, we barely even have time to talk about, like, Alice's diapers or runny noses, let alone the intricacies of my business, so I just made some decisions on my own."

"On your own." Mae had learned from her father the art of repeating the last few words of what someone said to allow them to keep talking. She could almost hear him now: *In love with Barrett*, he'd surely said to Joni back then. *Not sure how to stay in the marriage.*

"Our credit card has a rather high limit. I'm in charge of paying the bills. I'm better at staying on top of monthly finances. He's better at the big-picture stuff. You know."

Mae did not know. She was in charge of everything. There was no one to split tasks with. Which also meant, she supposed, that there was no one to disappoint or anger. Sydney looked frightened, a particular kind of frightened that came, Mae was sure now, from sticking your life to someone else's. And for a moment, Mae was overwhelmed with happiness that she had never stuck herself to anyone in that way.

"It's fine," Sydney said, her voice cracking, her face still looking frightened. "I overcommitted a little to the product, but it's fine because business is about to blow up, and Ivy Miller is choosing us, and it's all coming together, but you have to come. You're a part of the package. Okay? Okay, Mae? We have to, okay?"

Sydney was near tears and Alice was fully screaming for sleep and Mae was working to understand something, many somethings, a lifetime of somethings. And in that effort to understand, she said yes. A quiet, exhausted yes. Alice would fall asleep in the stroller. She would wear blue paisley. She would eat lox and cream cheese with Ivy Miller. She would do another photo shoot.

And she would—she was sure of it, walking back through the living room, paint not entirely scrubbed from her fingers—finish the painting with Alice. It was what she was surest about, actually. She didn't understand Catherine's vague messages or Sydney's obsession with Ivy Miller or what to make of Beth Ann and Barrett breaking up after all these years or how to hold her face together in a photograph. But she knew how to make the mess of not understanding into something decipherable. Not a map, not something you could follow precisely.

But a masterpiece. Maybe.

Maybe, Mae thought, maybe she wasn't a one-hit wonder of an artist after all.

THE PAINTING

IT HUNG IN the gallery for months, Elvin brushing aside offers from buyers that Mae was desperate to take.

"Supply and demand," he'd said with a flourish. "Look it up, darling."

She didn't need to. Mae knew that the longer someone said no, the more desperately the person asking wanted the yes. She had just met Leo, who kissed her and then promptly ignored her for weeks until she was sure she was in love with him, until she would do anything to have him, even though the kiss had been subpar and she hadn't particularly liked the production of *The Marriage of Bette and Boo* that he'd directed for a small theater in Queens. The play itself was supposed to be funny, she was fairly certain, but somehow the choices Leo had made in directing it had left it hollow and strange. Oddly sad.

Later, Mae would understand how easy it was to confuse sadness with smartness.

But still Mae waited—for Elvin to sell the Painting, for Leo to want her, and in the meantime, she tried to paint other things, tiny canvases about love or Leo's stubble or the fleeting friendship of her erstwhile agent, Fiona, or the way art itself might actually be pointless. Art about the pointlessness of art. There must be something there.

But there wasn't. And she couldn't seem to happen upon another piece like the Painting, which she refused to call *The Failure to Become*.

At last she worked again on a painting of herself and Sydney, crammed into a tiny apartment, waiting for the world to crumble. But by then, Fiona was long gone and Elvin said buyers liked the story of this being the only Mae Dyer painting, a self-fulfilling prophecy of sorts. A Failure to Become.

It sold for more money than Mae could have dreamed of.

She was an artist with one perfect, brilliant, beloved painting. A promise knit into every article about her that she wouldn't paint again, a promise not to tarnish the exquisite beauty of being a one-hit wonder.

And Mae didn't know what else to do but keep that promise.

THEN

MAE AND SYDNEY were back from Graham's wedding, and Mae couldn't get over one thing her father had said: *It's so sweet you came, Sydney, after everything our family put you through.* Then he'd shaken his head like it was all a dream, the entirety of Mae's childhood, and not worth saying any more about.

It was so like Graham to forget what Mae did and did not know about her own life.

And it was so like Sydney to pretend the words hadn't been said.

Mae hung on to the words, hoping that somehow Sydney would come forward on her own, but Sydney went on as normal, making fun of Catherine's decadent hairpiece and ugly cream-colored gown, asking Mae what they should do on the weekend, if they could, please, please, please, go to B Bar again, they always met the cutest guys there.

Sydney was hanging curtains when Mae blustered in, covered in clumps of snow, two days after Graham's wedding — the fluffy kind that clings, then fades, the impossible kind that looks endless, thick, solid, until you touch it, and it melts into nothing.

Mae liked that sort of snow—liked, she was realizing, things that were bold and impermanent. She shook flurries of it from her coat, her hair, letting it snow inside their tiny apartment for a moment. An indoor blizzard. She wouldn't wipe up the wet. Why bother?

"I was thinking pink for the curtains, but I know you sort of hate pink, so I thought blue, except I already have blue sheets and that seemed like a lot, so purple, you know, is the combination, right? Is the obvious way to go?" Sydney was talking fast, which she did when she knew she'd done something wrong. Decisions like curtains were joint ones, with Mae leading the way. Except that meant that their home was turning strange and moody, like Mae herself. A black accent wall in the bathroom that Sydney had fought hard against. A strange green ottoman in the living room that seemed to be made of braided-together fabric scraps, an item Mae had refused to reveal the origins of. Mismatched plates and cups and a dark orange carpet that was soft and worn and decidedly ugly.

There were traces of Sydney around—in the framed posters on the walls featuring famous paintings that Sydney proudly knew the names of: *Starry Night; Girl with a Pearl Earring; Nighthawks*. She kept forgetting the names of the painters, especially Hopper, whom she always confused with Rockwell, much to Mae's chagrin. Sydney was also apparent in their kitchen items—so many devices, you'd think they'd raided a Williams Sonoma registry: a four-slot toaster and a slow cooker and an electric carving knife and a state-of-the-art blender.

Mae took her coat off and looked for a place to put it. There wasn't anywhere. There never was, which was why so many odds and ends and articles of clothing wound up on the small yellow table in the kitchen section of the main room—what did you call a kitchen and living room that existed on top of each other, as they seemed to do in most apartments in the East Village?

"Are you ever going to tell me what it meant, what my dad said?" Mae asked at last. She'd been working on the phrasing since the train ride home from the wedding, wanting to get it just right.

The apartment was so small, it could barely contain the girls themselves. Sydney had talked Mae into a studio apartment— *We've always loved sleeping in the same room, and if we meet any guys, we can go to their places*—and that was just one of the many, many mistakes of this cramped Second Avenue space. They were spilling up and out and over, not just their things—tampons and favorite books and cell phone chargers and going-out tops, which were more or less the same as regular tops, just shinier and slinkier— but also their hopes and dreams and histories and selves. All of it was so jumbled up, so crowded and colliding, that Mae often found herself opening up the windows even on blizzardy, bleak days like today, just in the hope of somehow making space for the two of them and their friendship.

Curtains were about the last thing they needed.

And Mae hated purple too.

"Oh my God, Mae, stop looking at me like that. These curtains are pretty. You can't always hate everything I pick. It's not easy to find something that's going to look good with orange and green. My mom's coming this weekend. If we don't have curtains, we're going to have to listen to a whole thing about curtains."

"Not *we*," Mae said.

"Come on. You can't leave me alone with her."

"I'm going to Matt's this weekend. He said he'd teach me how to make risotto."

"Matt does not know how to make risotto," Sydney said with a laugh. The curtains were hung. They looked good. Or if not good, exactly, like curtains in a home, and that was something.

"He cooks."

"What's he made you?"

"He's going to teach me to make risotto, Sydney, God. He hasn't made me dinner yet. I've known him for like five minutes. But he says he cooks, and I have no reason to doubt him."

"He doesn't look like a guy who cooks. He looks like a guy who gets girls to his house by telling them he's going to cook and then never calls them again."

Sydney never approved of any of the men Mae dated. It had been the same in high school. The boys drawn to Mae were always morose or too committed to wearing sandals in January or smoked too much weed. Sydney wanted someone solid for Mae. Someone kind and sweet and maybe a little funny but mostly just smart and normal. In fact, that was her biggest focus, the thing she said most often: *Can't you date anyone normal?* To which Mae would always reply, *Look how well that turned out for our moms*, and the conversation would be over, Mac half smiling like the end of their parents' idyllic relationships was just a huge joke, Sydney slumping with the secret of why it all happened and what it all meant.

"Anyway, the curtains. You like them?"

Mae moved her gaze to the windows. The curtains were lavender, not purple, and sheer. They looked not unlike the curtains Sydney had had in her room growing up, a fact that seemed obvious to Mae but seemed to be sliding right past Sydney.

"Sure," Mae said, unable to care about anything until the confusion in her brain could be shaken into sense.

"Okay, phew. Maybe we can grab brunch tomorrow after you're back from Matt's?" Sydney had a way of talking like she was forty even though she was twenty-two. It was, Mae thought, part of the reason why it was hard for Sydney to make friends, hard for her to find boyfriends, just hard for her in general. She sounded like Beth

Ann, held her body like Beth Ann did too — straight and tight and measured, like she'd choreographed the movements of her day ahead of time. She'd tried so hard to be someone else — moving here with Mae was a part of that — but Beth Ann was always right there under the surface of her skin, wanting her to find curtains and eat grilled fish and wear shoes that matched, perfectly, the purse she was carrying.

Ultimately, that just meant you had a lot of shoes and a lot of purses and frankly were not much fun at all.

But that wasn't Mae's problem anymore.

"Answer my question, Syd." Mae wondered how long Sydney thought she could distract her best friend with musings about home goods and brunches.

"Hmm?" Sydney pretended she hadn't heard what Mae asked moments ago, but she had.

"My dad. At the wedding. He said something to you."

"People are so weird at weddings," Sydney tried, but she was sounding weaker, more nervous. Her cheeks were pinking, her hands shaking.

"He said we did something to you. Our family. And then you — you did what you're doing now. Turned into some weirdo trembling tomato. What did he mean? What did that mean?"

"I barely even know your dad, really," Sydney said. "I mean, he wasn't always around the way our moms were... Maybe he was drunk? Like, had a few shots to get ready to go down the aisle?"

The idea was ludicrous. Graham barely ever even had a beer. Sydney knew that as well as anyone.

"What did he mean?" Mae asked.

"It was a long time ago, it doesn't matter, so much has happened since, and now we're here and we don't even live there anymore, we're not kids, we don't need to —"

"What did he mean, Sydney?"

Sydney sat on the ground. She kept wiping at her hips, like there were pools of sweat gathering there under her jeans, and maybe there were, or maybe it was just the sort of thing she did when she was nervous.

"Your mom's not even around anymore," Sydney said, her voice wavering.

Mae could have screamed. It was an absurd thing to say to Joni's heartbroken, lost, stricken daughter. "I fucking know that," she said.

"It was forever ago," Sydney said, then paused. "I saw your mom and my dad kiss when we were eleven — you knew there were rumors. I mean, you knew, like, on some level, didn't you?"

"Knew what?" It was Mae's voice shaking now. She did and she didn't know.

"They were — they had a thing. And then for years I heard and saw snippets of... It went on for years. Until she — until graduation, maybe. I don't know. Forever. It's why my dad — I mean, you knew this on some level."

"No, I didn't." It was true. Mae was pretty sure it was nearly true.

"I wanted to tell you. And tried to at first. Sort of. But Joni and I — I promised her I wouldn't tell you. She wanted to protect you from all that. And so I, you know... I did what she asked me to."

Mae's eyes widened, then shut. Her arms wrapped themselves around her waist, holding her together. But so much else had happened in these years. Joni's death, most of all. Sydney had slept in the same bed as Mae on the nights when Mae couldn't stop crying. She had reminded her of Joni's birthday every year since, going out for croissants with Mae to remember her. She'd gone to the funeral and now the wedding, and they had survived it all.

They'd fought a hundred times — a thousand — over the

years. Their longest spat had lasted a month. It began when Mae chose to go to dinner before junior-year prom with her date, just the two of them, instead of doubling with Sydney and her date, and Sydney kept asking over and over why it couldn't be the four of them, why they couldn't split a limo, why all of a sudden Mae wanted to do separately the things they had always dreamed of doing together.

They didn't speak at prom or for the whole month of end-of-year exams and beach parties that followed, but they made up when Mae's boyfriend dumped her and Sydney showed up with blondies and beers and they spent a Saturday night covertly getting drunk in the basement and watching *Armageddon*, wishing, maybe, that it really was the end of the world.

This situation would eventually blow over like that. Sydney was sure.

But, like a switch had been hit, Mae started to pack up. She didn't fold her clothes, didn't seem to have any system in place for getting everything into her suitcase and her duffel and also a garbage bag, because she was twenty-two and didn't exactly have a full set of luggage or anything, really—a plan, a room of her own, a mother. The simple truth of it stabbed; the pain then spread dully. Joni would have been great at helping Mae make a scene, at helping her find some shitty studio to live in on her own.

"Mae. Come on," Sydney said. "A garbage bag?"

"I thought we were living the same life. Like, in the same reality. But you just sat around for years knowing our lives were going to implode and you didn't tell me? What, like you thought it made you better than me, to know everything? It must have been funny to watch me thinking things were one way when you knew they were a whole other way."

"It wasn't like that at all—your mom asked me to help her, so I did, I was helping your mom and helping you, and what else was I supposed to do? Seriously, what else?"

"And then she died! You kept her secret for however long, years, apparently, and then she died and you just get to have this thing with my mom *forever*, and I have to sit with having never actually fucking known her at all! Or known you. Or me! I don't even know me!" Mae was getting louder with every sentence, like she needed to make sure everyone heard, most of all herself. She had a look on her face—Sydney couldn't find the word for it in that moment, but later, in the telling of the story to a therapist that she met with a grand total of three times before deciding therapy was not for her, she would find the word. Mae looked *incredulous*. Unbelieving of what she had learned.

"Okay, let's pause. Let's just talk about—"

"Your mom fucking sucks, so you thought you could be in cahoots with mine and then you'd be, like, her alternate daughter or something? What was the plan? To just never tell me? To meet up for drinks with my mom to discuss it behind everyone's back? I'm so sorry that didn't work out for you and she fucking died instead. I mean, seriously, what the *fuck?*"

Sydney stared at the curtains. They looked sort of sad now, like someone trying too hard to be elegant on a budget. Beth Ann had reminded her again and again that if you didn't have the funds to make something truly luxurious, just embrace the basics so that no one could see you reaching for something else. They talked about it often, watching HGTV shows together, Beth Ann wrinkling her nose, shaking her head at the cute frugal fixes the designers helped the homeowners come up with: The square of wallpaper in a cheap wooden frame. The repurposed mason jars. The mirrors hung on every wall to give the illusion of more space. "Look at them. Everyone can see their *wanting*. Everyone can see their trying. It's obscene."

The sheer purple curtains were that. A physical manifestation of everything Sydney wanted her life to be. A humiliating arrow pointing at her yearning.

"It wasn't like that at all," Sydney said in a small voice, knowing Mae wouldn't believe her. "I didn't want a secret. I didn't want to know."

"I thought we were best friends. I thought we were basically sisters."

"We are!"

"No. No. I lived in that world, and you were living in some whole other one with all this extra information, all this extra *stuff*. That's not friendship. That's not what we were supposed to have."

"I promised—"

"Then you followed me here. To—what? Just, like, taunt me with how much more you knew about my own life? My own *mom*? What are we even doing here together? Why would you want us to stay connected when your dad probably broke my dad's heart? And—oh God, was he...the day she died, where was he? Did the police know?" Mae was shivering, the whole of her trying to piece together impossible facts, terrifying new timelines. She was having trouble breathing, trouble talking. Somehow, though, she had packed up most of her side of the room in the short time they'd been having this fight, as if the rage propelled her. Her suitcase was overstuffed, her duffel unable to zip, the garbage bag straining, threatening to burst open and spill out on the New York City sidewalks, but even that, Mae thought, would be preferable to one more moment trapped up here with Sydney and all the things she'd been hiding, the empty friendship they'd been navigating.

"I came here to be with you," Sydney said. "Where else am I supposed to go? You're my whole—"

"*Your* life is fine. Your parents are still together, still alive. Things are the same, Beth Ann joining weird little self-help groups and Barrett golfing or whatever, not a care in the world, it worked the fuck out for him pretty well, didn't it? So clean and easy with my mom out of the way and you're all fine. You all get to be just fine while my dad marries some weird robot and my mom—" Mae started to cry. Awful, wrenching tears.

"Joni did this too, it's not like my dad went out to just ruin everything on his own, they *both*—". It was obviously the worst, most wrong thing to say, but Sydney had to defend her dad, had to correct the strange new history Mae was writing. As if her dad could have been involved in any way with what happened to Joni—as if he were more at fault for the affair than Mae's mother. She couldn't let those things be said or thought or—

"We're done here." Mae's tears stopped, her voice suddenly strong. "We're done." The snow stopped too, then. The friendship was done. The storm was over. The world had changed, and Sydney would just have to sit with it all, watching her purple curtains hang with a promise that wasn't kept, a life that wasn't lived. The future was always rewriting itself in ways that surprised Sydney, in ways that felt all wrong.

After Mae left, Sydney called Beth Ann to tell her the part of it that was tellable, the part that wouldn't dredge up everything that had happened over the past decade or so.

"You have to be in charge of your own life," Beth Ann said, seeming to be reading from some pamphlet, some manifesto of how to be twenty-two, even though when she herself was twenty-two, she had been wedding planning, deciding between satin and tulle dresses, asking Barrett over and over and over again how big a house they could afford and in what sorts of neighborhoods. "This is an opportunity to be better, to take up more space, to be a clearer version of yourself. Heartache is an opportunity, Sydney. Pain is the thing that happens before joy. Before fullness. *Wholeness.* Trust me. I know. I know all about it."

Sydney nodded, swallowed, said yes, her mother could send her some information on life paths and embracing change and navigating loss. When it arrived in a manila envelope, printouts of paragraphs that melted together into platitude soup, photos of happy women smiling, not brightly but calmly, Sydney read it all, looking for something to hang on to, something that felt as good as spaghetti and cookies and cheap wine and watching *The Bachelor* with Mae felt.

But the thing was, nothing felt that good. Nothing ever had.

Not even, when he came along, Sam.

NOW

Sydney

IVY MILLER HAD brought her daughter.

"Shit," Sydney said at the sight of them already at the table, waiting for Mae and Sydney. Ivy Miller's daughter was five, with curling brown hair and smart glasses and legs so skinny, it was a wonder they didn't break right off. She was coloring in a princess coloring book and seemed focused on the task while Ivy tapped away at her phone, looking rested and casual and a little bit in love with her life. "I should have brought Alice. God. Shit. Can I—I mean, she doesn't know, could your Alice be my Alice? Just for today?"

She heard her own words and knew them to be strange—panicked and awkward and wrong in a way that was deeper, maybe, than she intended. And she saw it on Mae's face too—an utter confusion that settled into pity.

"Um, I don't think so," Mae said in a gentle voice that was not Mae's at all, really. Sydney watched as she gripped the stroller a bit more firmly, hummed the beginning of a lullaby to Alice as a way to mark her territory.

"I didn't mean—I just...You don't even care about this, so I thought—"

"She knows what your Alice looks like," Mae said, the gentleness in her voice straining into something else. "They're not interchangeable."

On cue, Alice made a loud, indistinct sound—not a cry but more of a one-note off-key musical moment that lasted a beat or two longer than it felt like it should have and startled Ivy Miller into looking up.

"Mamas!" Ivy Miller exclaimed, her face lighting up, then crunching into confusion. "Oh, no, only one Alice today?"

"Yes, meet Alice Dyer," Mae said quickly and firmly.

Ivy Miller leaned in and smiled at Alice's cheeks, thighs, toothy smile. "She's perfect, isn't she?" She tilted her head, gestured at the seats Mae and Sydney were meant to occupy. At last, Ivy Miller's daughter's head popped up from her task and she eyed them both.

"I'm bored," she said, and it felt rather pointed to Sydney, who hadn't even sat down yet, who hadn't had a chance to properly fail.

"Jones. You have your coloring. You're fine," Ivy Miller said.

"Unusual name," Mae said. If she'd been a part of LillyLou, she would have known the reason behind the name—Ivy Miller's love of Counting Crows and how she'd met her husband at one of their concerts and they'd kissed during the band's most popular song and how they were seventeen at the time and promised to name their first child Jones, regardless of gender, regardless of whether or not Counting Crows held up as a band over the years, regardless of anything, a plan made as a promise that couldn't be broken, and then there she was, Jones Iris Miller, ringleted and precocious and an exact even split between the classic good looks of her mother and the soft, sweet features of her father.

Ivy Miller talked about Jones often, as a way to show what happens if you plan with specificity and purpose, if you make promises to yourself and keep them, if you believe in the life you want to live. Jones Iris Miller was a mostly average five-year-old girl living in the Jersey suburbs, coveting the dresses and castles of Elsa and Ariel and Belle. But she was also the backbone of LillyLou, the proof of Ivy Miller's enduring correctness and what they were all striving for.

"I'd love to hear the story behind the Alices," Ivy Miller said, not explaining any of this history to Mae but raising her eyebrows at Sydney in a succinct and crystal-clear way that communicated that delivering this legend of LillyLou to Mae had been Sydney's job, one she had faltered at and was expected to share immediately upon leaving this very lunch.

Sydney nodded in agreement, amazed at the things Ivy Miller's eyebrow raises and chin tilts could say.

"There's gotta be a story there." Ivy Miller meant this not just as an observation but also as an order. If there wasn't a story, there had better be one soon.

"We had a dollhouse together as kids," Sydney said, making sure she, not Mae, got to tell the story. "A beautiful one. It's actually on display in my living room now. And we named the dollhouse baby Alice. I guess when we both grew up and had our babies, we were drawn to that early dream of what it would be like. And without even knowing it, without having spoken in years, we both gave birth and named our babies Alice. And the little Alices brought us back together."

Sydney smiled, not just on the outside but inside too, having nailed the telling of this story. She'd been practicing it in her head, knowing what sorts of beats Ivy Miller would like. The story of the Alices was not unlike the story of Jones Iris Miller, really. It was about a created future, a promise made in the past that was kept in the present, proof that you could build your own future, that you could make your dreams come true.

Ivy Miller smiled back, having heard exactly what Sydney wanted her to hear.

"Beautiful," she said, nodding and taking notes in a professional-looking caramel leather notebook. "That's just beautiful."

Sydney nodded, and next to her, Mae rolled the stroller back and forth, Alice giggling at the motion that used to, when she was a newborn, put her to sleep. Now that same effort was a bit of entertainment, functional still, but different. The babies weren't really babies anymore. The Alices were becoming something new, something that Sydney didn't feel ready for, really.

"There's more to the story, though, I hear," Ivy Miller said after her breath. In a swift movement, she put a pair of purple headphones over her daughter's ears and unearthed a device that was small and square and seemed to play some sort of music or stories that made Jones Iris Miller smile contentedly, happy to leave the adult conversation she'd been forced to endure. "Beth Ann has told me about the horrible things that happened. The way your families were destroyed. That you overcame that—what a wonder. What an admirable thing. The power of female friendship—and the next generation. The power of forgiveness. The inexplicable ways our lives intersect. I think your story would resonate with so many people."

Sydney swallowed. Next to her, Mae seemed to freeze. Alice started waving at passersby on the sidewalk, a few of whom waved back, oohing and aahing at her sweetness. Time passed, and Ivy Miller was comfortable with that passage. She was not in a rush.

"I'm sorry?" Mae asked.

"The affair. Your mother—Joan, is it?"

"Joni," Sydney corrected.

"Joni. How she betrayed Beth Ann. How it tore the two of you apart. And then what happened to Joni in the aftermath. My God. How your babies brought you back together in spite of everything. There are some stories—for instance, the Smith-Pandans. You've heard of them, I'm sure? Sydney's told you? Both parents underwent chemo at the same time and their children continued the business for them while they were too ill to go on, and now they are doing so well. *So* well. And Lizzie and Sara, of course. They were in awful marriages. Abusive, really. And in helping each other leave these men, they fell in love. Adopted a very cute baby boy. They're looking to adopt a girl now too, though international adoption has gotten trickier. But people love their story. These are the stories that resonate. That build community. That fill our cups, fill our hearts, clarify the meaning in our lives. I think your story—yours and Beth Ann's—is in that arena. Two Alices. Two childhood best friends. And the new grandma Beth Ann, who finds forgiveness through this new life and this resurrected friendship."

"Beth Ann?" Mae sounded supremely baffled.

"I think we were thinking more just the two of us," Sydney interjected, surprised at the mention of her mother even though she shouldn't have been. "Or maybe just me, ultimately. My story with just, like, an assist from Mae. She's not—you know, she's interested in LillyLou but she isn't—"

"No, this is an intergenerational story. This is about vulnerability and pain and courage and forgiveness and friendship and love. It's a story of redemption for Beth Ann. Letting go of her marriage at long last but making room for you, Mae, and your Alice. Building a new future from a broken past. Your sweet baby girls fixing everything."

Mae kept shaking her head. And this made Alice shake her head. Alice liked imitating Mae—clapping when she clapped, pointing when she pointed, repeating the outlines of words that Mae used, *wow* and *up* and *tickle* and *tummy*.

"I'm really—I'm an artist," Mae said, which was clearly not all that she wanted to say but the beginning of trying to find her way out of this moment.

"We love artists. And we know all about you. The voice of your generation before you got derailed. Primed for a comeback. You're a deep thinker. You're a creative. You're someone profound and mysterious, and Sydney is someone basic and relatable, and that's what makes you so special together. This will broaden your platform. For your art. This is in service of your art."

"It honestly—it sounds more like a distraction from—and also, I mean, I can't build a brand off our past. I want to honor my mother's—"

"There's no past," Ivy Miller said. "Sydney will tell you. We don't believe in the past. We believe in the places you've been and your inevitable return to them and the growth from that return and the wholeness of you. I know your work. Your work is about the same thing. We're very much aligned."

Sydney could hear that this wasn't the right way to reach Mae, but no one could stop Ivy Miller now. She was on a roll and it would be inappropriate for Sydney to interrupt. Ivy Miller's whole self was facing Mae, all her energy directed at her. Sydney felt the way she had felt her whole life around Mae: like the indistinct echo of her friend, like a side character in a beautiful novel that wasn't about her at all. Mae was the main attraction, as ever.

"I don't think we *are* aligned, actually," Mae said. Her voice was tightening, and Alice started screeching. Mae unstrapped her from the stroller, placed her on her lap, bounced her on her knees.

"Am I late?" said a voice, and at the table, Sydney stiffened, knowing who it was before turning to see her.

Sydney startled at the fact of Beth Ann suddenly here with them, the force of her—prickly, proud, anxious—at odds with what Sydney had imagined this lunch would be. It was all unraveling so quickly; these things never actually became what she wanted them to be. Beth Ann was not so unlike Joni after all, was she? Showing up, changing what was perfect, making it ill-fitting and unexpected and wrong.

"It's been a day. Sydney's father—he's packing up his stuff from the house. It'll take him a few days. So I had to get out of there. And it's all very dramatic, you know?"

Barrett had told Sydney he was headed over to the house to get his stuff. He'd sounded wilted, conflicted, but he kept saying he was fine. That it was time. It emptied Sydney out a little, to think of him wandering around the closets, the basement, the attic. But then, Barrett often made Sydney feel something aching and hollow, and maybe his fully moving out would shift things in an unexpectedly good way. She was able to see the potential for good now because of Ivy Miller. She knew to keep her heart open and ready for it. Maybe Barrett would come alive in a space of his own. Maybe she would get closer to him, maybe they had a whole new relationship ahead of them—maybe he would be the kind of grandfather who joined them at Disney World or on Christmas morning, or helped Alice learn how to ride a bike or swim or read.

"I didn't know you were coming," Sydney said, trying to make the words sound neutral.

"You're just in time," Ivy Miller said, gesturing to a waiter to bring Beth Ann water or wine or a salad—somehow the waiter knew which, though Sydney herself couldn't begin to guess which one Beth Ann thought she should have.

Mae stopped bouncing Alice. Sat up straight. It had been about a year since they'd run into each other at the park, and that day had been shrouded in a postpartum haze, making it more tolerable than what was happening now, in the bright of the sun, in the clarity of life as the mother of a toddler.

"I think Alice has to nap," Mae said, a reflexive move that Sydney had used herself to get out of a variety of uncomfortable situations. "I should really go."

"I knew you'd be wary," Beth Ann said, smiling at Mae like it was a little bit funny, the awkwardness between them. "Even as a kid, you were never quite on board with me, were you? I remember I'd make lasagna and you'd pick the whole thing apart before digging in. Worried I was hiding vegetables in it or something, I guess."

"You were, usually," Mae said.

"I was."

"This isn't that. I eat my vegetables now. I just need to go."

"You don't need to go. I can hold the baby. You need to worry about you, Mae. Not the memory of Joni. Not Alice. Not even Sydney. Just you." Beth Ann reached her arms out, confident that Mae would immediately hand Alice over. Beth Ann had recruited dozens of women to LillyLou, all of them now recruiting their own mini-armies, selling their pashminas, peddling the new lingerie in stylized boudoir shoots or prim church shots, depending on whether they wanted to emphasize the sexiness or the functionality of the items.

Mae would do well to take the sexy shots: Single mom getting back into her groove. Famous artist embracing her sensual side postpartum. Flamboyant BFF of demure homemaker Sydney Sullivan. The path seemed both obvious and impossible.

"I've got it," Mae said. "I'm figuring it all out. This is very nice, and I'm happy to take occasional photos with Syd, but I'm not entering into a whole— I'm not a salesperson or even really a people person. Sydney is going to be a star or whatever, and she can do that without me. You can, Syd. You and your Alice and whatever story you want to craft, you know?"

"You're the story," Beth Ann said, the words hitting Sydney with an unexpected force. "This is the story. Forgiveness. Moving forward. Friendship that withstands betrayal. Moms and daughters. And sisters."

Mae and Sydney didn't take note of that last part. Didn't see the look Beth Ann gave Ivy Miller, didn't realize the things these two women knew that Mae and Sydney still did not.

"But you're not my mom," Mae said. Alice opened her mouth wide and sank her newly sprouted teeth into Mae's arm. Mae's eyebrows jumped in shock before she shifted Alice frontward with a reminder in a sweet singsongy voice not to bite Mommy.

"Your mom wasn't much of a mom to you either," Beth Ann said. She paused, surprised at hearing the words come out of her own mouth, and they certainly shocked Sydney and Mae and even Ivy Miller herself, who straightened up then, hoping perhaps that a change in her position might shepherd them more elegantly through this moment.

"I don't think that's quite the message," Ivy Miller said. "We always say there's no one idea of what a mom is, don't we. That's part of your appeal, Mae. A different kind of mom."

It was an expert repositioning of the horrible words Beth Ann had let out, but it didn't matter. Mae had swung her body toward Beth Ann and her eyes were going a bit wild.

"My mom wasn't a mom? Is that what you said? By your, what, expert calculations, she didn't fit the bill? That's so—that's so fucked up. That's so, so fucked up."

Beth Ann took a calming breath, and Sydney reached out for her best friend. "She didn't mean that, you know how she is about Joni," she said. She shot her mother a cutting glance—being near Mae again was special, was grounding and important and also an enormous business opportunity, and Beth Ann was ruining it with her temper, with the never-ending resentment toward the woman who'd slept with her husband a billion years ago and who had been dead for so long it was hard to remember the sound of her voice, the shade of her hair.

"Joni was a mom," Mae said, feeling sure about that, about at least that, in spite of everything else.

Mae's Alice picked a fork up off the table and threw it on the ground. She laughed. Picked up another, threw it too. Laughed again.

Sydney waited for Mae to do something about it, scold her child or at least shift her position so she couldn't keep at it. But Mae didn't move, and Alice picked up a spoon, a napkin, the discarded shell of a straw, a roll of bread, and chucked each object to the ground with utter delight.

For a while, Sydney had thought Mae's Alice must look a great deal like her mysterious dad, Leo Whoever. She had some of the details of Mae's face—her nose, maybe, the shape of her head perhaps—but there had always been something alien about her, something unfitting with Mae's strong features. But as Mae's Alice took pleasure in dismantling the loveliness of the lunch, as she giggled at the destruction she was causing, as she went on unchallenged by anyone who could do something about it, Sydney was sure she could see Joni in the planes of her face, the sparkle of her eyes, the exact curl of her hair.

And for a moment, even though one was not supposed to feel anything toward babies but wonder and appreciation for the size of their thighs, the plumpness of their cheeks, Sydney felt a distinct and sickening hatred for this Alice.

"Let's take a step back," Ivy Miller said. Her daughter, Jones, was now transfixed by the boring lunch turned spectacle. She watched with a great deal of focus as the grown-ups went at each other, and she would surely, before bed, maybe nestled under a quilt readying herself for a bedtime story, ask for the nuances of this fight, ask to be told the story of Mae and Sydney and Beth Ann and little baby Alice again and again and again. "This is about taking control of your story. Understanding it, truly, at last, and then making it your own."

"I understand it," Mae said. "I don't need ugly bras and cheap scarves and Beth Ann fucking Sullivan to help me understand it more."

"Beth Ann?" Ivy Miller said. She looked tired, like this conversation was supposed to have been easier. "I think you can speak your truth."

Beth Ann nodded. She had never been the one with the secret. It was still new. And awful. It was still something she herself didn't understand. But she understood it was powerful. It was true, whether or not she wanted it to be, so it might as well do something useful. That's what the girls didn't understand yet. The truth was the truth, as painful as it was. But sharing it, making it your own, letting the world hear it on your own terms—that was the only way to make it tolerable.

"As you know, I left Barrett recently," Beth Ann said, willing her voice to be steady and cool. "I accepted a lot from him. I forgave a lot. But when he heard about your Alice, Mae, he shared one last part. One last thing. He told me who you are."

For a moment, Mae almost laughed. As if Beth Ann could ever have a better sense of who she was than she herself did. As if *Barrett* knew anything about her, having been a ghost in her life for so many years.

And then, slowly, suddenly, shakily, she understood.

And she did not laugh.

Just like all those years ago in the snowy apartment, the curtains all wrong, Mae decided to leave. She got up. She knew how to walk away—right as Beth Ann was putting it into awkward, breathless words. "Barrett is your father. He and Joni met long before either of you were born. And Joni got pregnant, and I suppose figured she'd just pretend you were Graham's and move you to Sommersette so we would all be some kind of horrifying family or something, I don't know, we'll never know, your mother was—"

Mae was holding Alice, but if her hands had been free, she would have used them to cover her ears.

No, a voice in her head screamed, fighting against the way this revelation was puncturing her whole history, her whole understanding of herself. And at the same time, *Yes,* another voice, deeper down, screamed, telling her it was true.

"Graham's my father," she said, which was also its own truth. "Joni's my mother. Graham's my father." Her throat was tight, and she looked at Sydney for something, but all Sydney could offer was astonishment, and Mae had had enough of that.

Sydney was holding Alice's burp cloth and pacifier. In Sydney's purse was Alice's favorite stuffed cow and Mae's sunglasses. Somehow, all these years later, they'd gotten tangled up in each other again. Mae had listed Sydney as one of Alice's emergency contacts on the forms her pediatrician made her fill out. She'd lent her three books and Alice's travel crib. Mae couldn't believe she'd let herself get here with Sydney again.

Now Sydney was trembling a little, licking her lips with a nervous energy that wasn't how Sydney used to be. The whole of her looked too thin, too tense, too fidgety. It was new information to Sydney too, at least; Mae could see that. It wasn't another secret she had kept. It wasn't Beth Ann's secret either—the sweat on her forehead told Mae that Beth Ann herself was still trying to understand that her husband had fathered a daughter who was supposed to belong to her best friend's husband.

No, this secret belonged to Barrett. And Graham, maybe. Of this Mae was pretty sure. And Catherine, probably, who had been trying to tell her for almost a year.

And Joni, of course. Joni, unconfrontable and somehow both entirely gone and right here, right now, present, spinning them around as always, making their worlds wild and impossible and new.

And even now, even now, Mae wanted Joni. She wanted Joni's help and explanations; she wanted to be able to scream at her mother, to blame her, to forgive her. She wanted to hug her and shove her and understand her and reject her and love her again.

Everything in Mae surged with how desperately she wanted a mother.

But instead: She had two fathers. It was impossible to imagine going to either of them. She didn't know what she'd ask. What she'd say. She wasn't sure what she needed to know.

She held Alice more tightly, one hand sliding up from her back to her perfect head.

Mae grabbed the stroller and took a few steps away. For a moment, no one was looking at her. Ivy Miller was holding Beth Ann's hands and telling her she'd done the right thing. Sydney had curled into herself, and the scene was the aftermath of a disaster.

But Mae and Joni were the disaster. And little Alice too, wasn't she? The reason it all had come to light. Tiny, perfect, unlikely Alice.

Sydney was strangling her phone. Beth Ann was pulling a little at her hair, not so much anyone would notice, but Mae was looking for the fault lines, for the ways it was always going to end in this, for the brokenness of them all.

"Mama," Alice said, the word coming out clearly for the first time. "Mama. Mama. Mama." She was proud, tiny Alice, and Mae beamed at her, forgetting the rest of it. "Mama! Mama!" Alice's little legs kicked the air, her body wriggling, her mouth repeating and repeating, showing off what she had finally, miraculously learned.

"Yes, that's right," Mae said, "I'm your mama."

And without another thought, pushing the stroller with one hand and holding her perfect Alice with the other, Mae walked away.

THE PAINTING

BARRETT WAS IN the attic looking at it.

He wasn't much for art. Mae had gotten that from her mother, though Joni had never made a painting like this one. Hers had all been small, delicate little renderings of flowers and mountains and then, later, as the affair wore on, strange installations built from scraps. Garbage, really, though she called the receipts and airline liquor bottles and sea glass and smudged postcards *found objects*.

He wasn't much for art, but he didn't have to be to understand why Mae's painting was so beloved, why he'd had to spend a small fortune to buy it. There was an exquisite use of color—the whole canvas smothered in sunset hues, golds and peaches and silvery grays. And it captured so accurately the way you were never one person in one relationship, you were always becoming something new, something different, inside yourself and of course with others too.

It was, Barrett thought, that day and many other days, a true work of genius. It startled him anew, every time he glanced in its direction, that someone related to him had made it. His own daughter. One of his daughters.

It was years and years that he'd had it, and he supposed it would be moving with him to his new place now that Beth Ann had, at last, released him. She'd told him about Mae and Mae's new baby and Mae's life, and Barrett hadn't even thought about it; he'd made a call to his lawyer to make sure Mae and her baby, his granddaughter—his other granddaughter—were taken care of, would be okay. Mae and Alice should get the Painting, of course, but they should also get what Sydney and her Alice were getting. More, maybe, since Mae was alone.

He hadn't taken much care in the conversation with his lawyer. Hadn't been especially quiet. Beth Ann wasn't around much, and when she was, she wasn't listening to him, certainly. But this time she was. She'd heard. And she'd understood, without him spelling it out.

And so, so quickly, she'd left. A lifetime swimming in secrets, but this one was too hard to manage, too rocky, too deep.

People made fun of Beth Ann. He'd heard it over the years, the snarky remarks about her try-hard energy, her pushiness, that she wore lipstick and perfume to even the most casual outing—the gym, a kid's soccer game, the grocery store. Even her staying with Barrett was seemingly viewed as an indictment against Beth Ann rather than him. "I'll say this about her—she sure stays," a friend of his said once over golf, and there was generous laughter, indicating it was an ongoing, not onetime, joke.

People had made fun of her, and Barrett had dreamed, over the years, of running off with Joni just like she'd always wanted. But underneath all that was a bigger truth that he was only just now seeing.

He was the joke, not her. He was the lump who waited for life to happen. And Beth Ann was the engine who decided where to go and how fast. Even now. She'd found an apartment near Sydney in the city. She was off to change her own life, on her own terms. He had only passively let things occur. He was both the instigator of the chaos and an absolute footnote to it. He felt his ineffectualness with acuity—like it was a headache, a piece of luggage, an extra limb.

He felt it the same way he felt the guilt about what happened to Joni. It had aged him considerably, the many, many years of nightmares, worrying that he had done it to her, that he had done it on purpose.

The day the girls graduated high school, Joni had been on some high about how now was their time, the girls were leaving, they could finally be together. She was going on and on about the purse he'd given her for her birthday—a black-and-white thing that was better suited to Beth Ann, really, and that he'd bought with his wife in mind but had given to Joni because she'd made a big deal about them celebrating her birthday and he'd forgotten. But somehow the bag had meant something to her. *It's our new life,* she'd said. *That purse belongs in the city, we'll go out to dinners in Brooklyn, we'll go to the theater, it's the start of the life we have always wanted to live. I think the girls are ready to know. And Graham. He'll be okay. He'll meet someone else. Someone really nice. Beth Ann will too. It's all going to work out. We did it. We really did it.*

She was aglow.

He couldn't let her stay like that, lost in some dream he knew would never materialize. It was the start of a new chapter for all of them, and she deserved to start fresh too. They all did. He needed to tell her now, finally, that this thing between them was over. They'd made it through, yes, like she'd said. And now they could leave this messy, muddled thing they'd made. And be other people, better ones, maybe. He thought he might move down south. Or to the West Coast. He'd always liked the mountains.

He'd told Joni to meet him in the woods behind her house, interrupting her daydreams about what was coming. He told her it was urgent, and she heard even that urgency as romantic, as verification that they were embarking on something together. The woods made sense, in spite of Joni's always having disliked them, having spotted bees in there a few times, some poison ivy once. She was a city girl at heart, even though she liked to play in the rain, swim in lakes, talk about sleeping bags and cabins and coziness. City girls didn't like woods, no matter how much they liked bare feet and burnt marshmallows and freckled skin. But the woods were close by and easy to slip away to. He didn't want to go far and miss the party. He didn't want to be out in the open and risk seeing Graham or Syd or anyone else.

So it made sense, didn't it? It wasn't part of any plan; it was just a convenience. Meet in the woods to have the talk. It would have to be quick — that way she couldn't turn him around in some conversation, the kind she'd used over the years to wear away his certainty.

It needed to be now, while he had the fortitude, so he rushed her out the door; time was of the essence, Beth Ann would be mad if he was late, and suspicious, of course, of where he'd been. Joni took her time, like she knew that would bother him, and so he pressured her more, and she left without her bag, and he was so used to the ugly canvas thing hooked over her shoulder that he'd noticed its absence, but he hadn't said anything because it would slow them down, he was sure that was his only reason, because Beth Ann was a stickler for time, because he needed to break it off right this second, right now, or he never would, because he was overwhelmed by the magnitude of the moment, that was why he didn't remind her to bring her tote bag with the EpiPen that was always, always stored inside, because it seemed so much less important than the conversation they needed to have, the conversation they'd been needing to have for years. He wanted a clean break, to start his life anew somewhere else, away from Joni, away from Beth Ann. Somewhere he could have his relationship with Sydney — and maybe even Mae — away from their mothers and the ways he'd tangled himself up in them. It felt reachable, it felt possible, right now. But it had to be right now.

And surely that was why he didn't remind her to bring the bag.

They started the walk to the woods together, but he got a call from Beth Ann, and Joni hated to hear calls from Beth Ann, so he paused to talk, and she traveled on; she went farther into the woods, and he meant to follow, but he didn't.

He didn't.

He went to get the things Beth Ann told him to get — ice and prosciutto and a card for Mae, whom she'd forgotten to get anything for, and he meant to tell Joni they would talk later, of course he had meant to, but it wasn't the first time he'd left her like that, she'd done it to him too, that was part of having an affair, part of keeping this secret all these years; it wasn't unusual for them to have a plan and break it without explaining why. It was how it had always been, it wasn't on purpose, it couldn't have been on purpose.

He was so tired of those thoughts, that story he kept telling and untelling and retelling himself about the day she died and how it wasn't — it couldn't have been — his fault.

Those thoughts worked in concert with the thoughts about Mae and how he'd chosen to let Graham be her father so that he could properly be Sydney's. And now Beth Ann's feelings and opinions were in the mix, and it was all too much.

And then there was the Painting, the one last secret that no one else knew. The clamoring for it all those years ago had been intense — it wasn't an act of pity, his having bought it. Though it wasn't exactly because of his love of art either. He wanted to know he'd taken care of her. He'd seen a way to be both her father and no one at all, and he'd snatched it. He always leaped at any opportunity to be sort of someone but mostly no one.

When Mae's painting was everywhere, he thought often about Joni's paintings. Once, very late at night after more than a bottle of wine, she'd asked him if he liked her work more than Mae's. Mae had been a teenager but an obvious talent, preparing portfolios for college applications. It was the sort of question she never would have asked sober, no mother would have, but *in vino veritas*, or whatever the saying was, and the comment had angered Barrett and they'd fought about it. He'd called her jealous of her own daughter. She'd called him unsupportive and undeserving of an opinion. They'd left each other alone for a few weeks after that, but then he found himself back with her again, like always. There was an ugliness to Joni underneath all that beauty. There was to everyone, maybe, but at least with Beth Ann, the ugliness was more in check.

That memory hurt, made him want to get rid of the Painting at last, get it out of his attic that was no longer his attic anyway.

It wasn't his. It didn't matter how much he had paid for it; it didn't belong to him. He needed Mae to know that he had been a father for that moment, when he'd bought it for all that money, the money that had changed, he hoped, her life. He needed Mae to know that he had tried. And it wouldn't change the rest of it, it wouldn't make his life add up to something more solid, but he could know he did something once, something all his own, something he decided on and followed through with.

Yes. That's what he would do. He'd bring the Painting to her. He had her address; it had been in Beth Ann's book and he'd written it down, somehow knowing, maybe, that a moment such as this would occur. He'd go to her apartment. Meet his other Alice, his other granddaughter. Maybe he'd find some words to say about the man he wished he'd been. And he'd give her the Painting. She could sell it again, maybe. Or hang on to it, if that's what she wanted. Maybe it would jump-start her career. Maybe it would do something for her. Or him. Or all of them.

He'd miss it, miss visiting it. But maybe he'd see it at Mae's house from time to time. That could happen, couldn't it? A new era where Mae was in his life? Not in some profound way, but occasionally. Once a year. Maybe he would mend something. Maybe this was the start of the mending.

That was that. He would explain. He would give her the Painting. He would tell her about meeting Joni and what it was like to watch Mae grow up, to be a part of it and also outside of it. He would tell Mae. He had to. He owed it to Joni. He'd been owing it to her since the day she'd told him she was pregnant.

Determined, Barrett walked down the stairs from the attic, holding the Painting instead of the railing. The stairs were steep — they always had been — and Barrett's eyesight had deteriorated. He wasn't young anymore. He was in his late sixties and his knees had started to go a little. He'd taken a fall last winter, and his doctor had warned him of other falls. Warned him to be careful.

Beth Ann had always said to be careful on the attic stairs especially; they were steep, unstable.

She had been right about so much.

He missed a step, ankle crossing over ankle, knees giving out, body moving forward in space at the exact wrong angle; his head clunked something solid in one direction and another, his heart surging from the stress of it, and his body landed hard, head banging against the bottom stair.

Beth Ann had given him a few days to gather his things. It was the beginning of those days, and she wouldn't return until the agreed-upon time.

Which would be too late. It would be much, much too late.

THEN

BETH ANN DRESSED up for her first outing with Joni, wanting to impress the new woman who had suddenly entered her orbit. Joni and her husband had, apparently, bought their beautiful home down the street right around when Joni had gotten pregnant, but it took time to finish the basement, redo the kitchen, and ultimately find a way to leave the city they'd always assumed they'd raise their kids in. Joni talked about the city like it was a place she still lived, a place she would always live. She talked about it like Sommersette was a sort of imaginary life, a place she'd ended up by accident.

"You look nice," Barrett said upon seeing his wife on her way out the door, taking in the whole of her in an ivory off-the-shoulder sweater and a brown corduroy skirt.

"I have a new friend," Beth Ann said, testing out the way it sounded to assess if it might in fact be true.

"Well, good. A girl, right?" Barrett asked, smirking like it was impossible the answer could be anything but yes. And it was impossible. Beth Ann didn't befriend men. Barrett didn't befriend women.

Those types of relationships weren't safe. And she and Barrett were safe.

"Someone from the playground. Bought that house down the street a million years ago and finally moved in. She has a daughter, and the girls get along."

Barrett looked at her again—maybe, she hoped, looking at her body, her waist that was almost trim, the shape of her not the same as it had been before Sydney but not unrecognizable either. More like a copy of a copy of a thing that had once been beautiful. Blurry and not quite as nice as the original but essentially, in the most important ways, the same.

"Right," he said. "Right, that house that was bought but no one moved in."

Barrett had taken an interest in recent years in the real estate ups and downs of the neighborhood, so of course he'd known of the house down the street, the construction on various parts of it, the way it always seemed like the work was done, only for it to start up again.

Beth Ann went to kiss him goodbye, imagining he might grab at some part of her he hadn't grabbed at in a while. The way he'd looked at her—like she was someone beautiful again—was something she was hungry for, and the hope of it was almost too much. His hands didn't touch her body; there was only the purse of his lips and nothing else.

Two glasses of wine into her time with Joni, she was recounting the moment, hoping her new friend was experiencing the same mild neglect from her own husband. Beth Ann knew, of course, she wasn't supposed to wish her sadness onto others, but she couldn't help it. The loneliness was too great to bear, and the only thing that might help was knowing that other women's husbands were just like hers, that the tiny humiliations and heartbreaks of marriage after children were par for the course, the only possible things that could occur, really, after such a massive and unmooring change.

"Tell me about him," Joni said. Her eyes were bright, her body leaning all the way toward Beth Ann, so close Beth Ann could smell the vague smells of incense and oil paint that lingered around her at all times.

"Barrett? Oh, I don't know. He's just a guy. Nothing special. I mean, special to me. I love him. But he's—he makes a good martini. He's quiet. Sort of serious, but kind." Beth Ann shrugged. It felt like an impossible task, to put Barrett succinctly into words. He wore ties to work. He made proficient French toast on Sundays. But nothing she'd said was a personality trait exactly. None of it explained why they were together, who they were as a couple.

"Huh," Joni said. "So you guys aren't—I mean, is your marriage okay?" Her voice was a whisper and she sounded so serious, like she was investigating a crime.

"It's—yes, of course. It's good. Different than it was, I guess, before Syd. But he's there, you know? And giving us a lovely life. I could never have dreamed of living in Sommersette when I was younger. This kind of place—I mean, I'm so grateful that he works so hard."

Joni had heard women talk this way about their husbands, of course. It wasn't exactly something new, the excusing away of their emotional unavailability because of the size of their 401(k)s. But the Barrett she knew—wry and sardonic about politics, kind to bartenders at the ends of their shifts even if they'd been assholes to him, deliciously slow and deliberate in the contemplating of her body—did not sound like Beth Ann's Barrett. Even the bad parts of Barrett—the way he had raged when she first bought the house, the whole month he didn't speak to her after, the way he clammed up at any mention of Mae—were understandable to Joni. Noble, even, a sign of his fortitude.

Joni ordered another glass of wine. It was her fourth, and she'd had one before coming here, so it was actually her fifth. Her head swung a little from side to side, enjoying its own looseness. She was used to being drunk with Barrett—they still managed to meet in the city once a month at least, under the guise of a work trip for him and an artist retreat for her. They'd get wasted at No Idea and pass out on too-starchy hotel sheets before fucking in the mornings. She'd taken to ordering them coffee and eggs afterward so they could have breakfast in bed, and it was in those moments that Barrett was entirely hers—loose, witty, affectionate, thoughtful. He'd ask her advice on his daughter's tantrums and complain about his mother's incessant phone calls and ask about her art, letting her describe what it was she wanted to be making and how hard it was to line up the reality of what she'd made with that lofty ideal. For an hour once a month, they were something more than people trapped in a long-term affair, more than Barrett's occasional bursts of regret when he'd try to break things off, more than Joni's unbearable ache when he looked away from a photo of Mae, unwilling to see the way her eyes were deep-set like his, her nose just as proud, the tilt of her head just as wise. In those mornings, their hands cradling the white hotel coffee mugs like they were royal goblets, she and Barrett were together. In love. A couple.

She really was drunk now, and Beth Ann was so sweet, ordering her a water, chattering on about something cute the girls had done the day before, a song they'd sung about princesses and bees and underwater castles. Beth Ann was wonderful but all wrong for Barrett, who liked Joni's long legs and loud laugh, who said he'd like to camp under the stars in Alaska, who said he'd wanted to be a puppeteer, actually, when he was young, who had made puppets, still collected in his parents' basement, a secret he'd kept from his friends throughout school, puppets too unaligned with his football-playing, baseball-card-collecting identity.

Joni was sure that Beth Ann didn't know about the puppets.

"I have to tell you something," Joni said, her words a slur of red wine.

"I have to tell *you* something," Beth Ann said. She was drunk too, not used to anything past the second glass of wine, not used to drinking with anyone but the women of Sommersette, who preferred book clubs and cocktails on their porches to sitting at the bar of the only late-night establishment anywhere near town.

"Okay, well, the thing I have to tell you is bad. It's like—bad, bad. The bad kind. So you go first. Okay? It's bad, Beth Ann. It's like—it's like, why am I even here, you know, and how did this all happen?" Joni felt like she was telling her. She practically was, wasn't she? She took another sip of wine. She wasn't sure how they'd get home. Driving was out, but surely the bartender would have the number of a car company.

"My thing is good!" Beth Ann said. Her voice was overbright, so loud it surprised her, and she spat out a small amount of wine, then collapsed into giggles.

"I love good things," Joni said.

"Me too. The good thing is that you're my best friend. You really are. I mean, I just met you. But I know that you're my best friend. I don't do this with anyone else. And this is so great!"

"That is such a good thing," Joni said. "It makes my bad thing even badder."

"I hate bad things," Beth Ann said. "Sometimes it's like—there's so many bad things."

Joni nodded; it was true. The school had called to tell her Mae really needed to get potty-trained, and Graham kept asking if they should join the church—the church! As if she were someone entirely different than the person she was pretty sure she'd told him she was. She missed the noise of the city, the grit of it, the promise of seeing someone wearing something interesting every single day.

She missed musicians underground in the subway and those illicit glances you got of the Statue of Liberty from certain parts of Brooklyn. She missed the unexpected joy of walking all the way to the river, how you forgot you were on an island until there it was, water, all casual and in perfect opposition to the reaching gray of the buildings. She missed the version of herself that lived there—going to art classes, reading the *Times* on her fire escape, blending in with the masses.

"I might be a bad person," Joni said. "I mean, I'm not. But I might be. I don't know. But I can't be? Because good came of it? But it's also bad."

"Don't tell me," Beth Ann said. "Tell me a good thing instead." She half smiled, not even sure what she was saying, but Joni nodded like they'd reached a serious agreement on what to do about the intricate weave of their lives. It felt like Beth Ann knew. She could, couldn't she? Maybe she already knew.

"Our girls are going to be best friends. And we're going to be best friends. Those are good things," Joni said.

"Those are such good things," Beth Ann said. She put her head on the bar. "This is comfortable," she muttered.

"No matter what, right?" Joni said. They were agreeing to something here, weren't they? This was a pact they were making, not to say the things that could tear them apart. This was an understanding—Beth Ann knew something, of course she did, and Joni knew not to spell it all out, and it made sense, didn't it, to live like this, wrapped around one another, a unit of sorts, a village, a family.

"Yep, no matter what," Beth Ann said, her voice a blur, a haze, an amorphous thing without a beginning and end, without any sharp corners, consonants, exclamation points, meaning.

"It's important that the girls are close," Joni said. "Even more than us. It's everything. Let's do everything we can to keep them together. No matter what. Let's agree on that, okay?"

"Pinkie promise," Beth Ann said, hooking her pinkie to Joni's like they were the toddlers and not the grown-ups.

Joni ordered another round.

They'd figure out a car home. Beth Ann could call Barrett if they needed him. He'd pick them up. He'd drive them home. They weren't far from their houses, a ten-minute drive, and the girls were sleeping. One of the husbands could leave them for the short drive here and back, the girls' slumber uninterrupted, their moms there safe and sound in the morning, never needing to know the things that would scare them. Never needing to know the whole truth.

NOW

Sydney

THEY DID IT in the car a month later, joining a long tradition of such posts done in cars. Ivy Miller gave them a month after Beth Ann discovered Barrett's death at the home that had, for so many years, been theirs. A month, Ivy Miller said, was the perfect amount of time. Grief still fresh, but not violent, raw but not scary.

It felt scary still to Sydney. It felt violent. Maybe that was because of the very few moments a day she had to properly mourn her father, how cramped her days were with first steps and first words and dirty diapers and pink eye and knee scrapes and toys that sang songs about stars and bunnies and baby sharks. Mothering a small child was in direct conflict with grappling with the unbelievable loss of Barrett at the exact moment she had the chance to actually know him. There wasn't room for both, but both begged for her attention, both demanded the whole of her heart, the entirety of her spirit.

"I think just a short conversation in the car to let your followers in on what's happening is all you need," Ivy Miller had said. "A mother-daughter road trip where you discuss the difficult things in life. A chance to let them in on heartbreak and resolution and our story. I know it's hard. But make your grief mean something, give all this pain somewhere to go."

Ivy Miller gave them the camera for the dashboard, suggested mascara that would run, but not too much, not too messily— "People want to see reality prettied up a little bit," she said. "You're still saleswomen. You're letting people in, of course. You're connecting. But you're also aspirational. You're both."

You're both was, in fact, the new slogan for LillyLou. It was meme-able, which made it successful. Hordes of LillyLou women had taken photos of themselves dressed up in cocktail dresses and pashminas and then created a split-screen effect through the careful tutelage of Ivy Miller's social media team to show themselves in the same pose, with the same hair and makeup, the same expression, in LillyLou lingerie. This could mean anything— not every woman wanted to show off her whole undressed body, of course, and LillyLou understood this. The second pose could just show a hint of a strap of a LillyLou bra. Or you could wrap yourself in a robe—LillyLou had robes now. One rogue businesswoman in her twenties had put the bra and panties over a bodysuit, and though publicly Ivy Miller herself commented with a crying-laughing emoji, privately that woman was reprimanded for not being in the spirit of the campaign, and eventually she posted a classic spin on the meme in some of the skimpiest options in a pose that felt—at least to Sydney and some of the people on her group chat—provocative.

Sydney and Beth Ann weren't in lingerie here in the car, of course. They weren't in pashminas either, though a favorite LillyLou pattern could be seen in the background, a suggestive strategy that Beth Ann considered herself a bit of a pro at. Sydney turned on the camera and immediately dived in.

"Hi, everyone. I know it's been a while. Some of you may know a bit about why, but there's more to every story, and there's a lot more to ours. But, um, the main reason I've been MIA is...this is so hard...about a month ago, I lost my father. An accident at home. Something—he was a young, fit guy. He was—a complicated man and a good dad to me, mostly, and I'm—I'm sure many of you have lost parents. It's..." She searched for a word. She should have come up with one before pressing Record on the dashboard camera. But it had been a month and no words were coming. It was impossible to talk about Barrett. He was beyond vocabulary.

"It's been a very, very painful time," Beth Ann filled in. "Not only have we been navigating this unexpected loss, but before my husband passed he let us in on some really challenging information."

Ivy Miller had told Sydney that they needed to get specific, that they needed to really detail what happened, so she did her best to do exactly that. She also said that perhaps Sydney should be the one to explain. Beth Ann might be sitting too squarely in rage still. And rage didn't attract people the way sadness did.

"There was an affair," Sydney said. It wasn't the way she would normally talk with her mother, and that was wrong, she knew—she was supposed to sound natural. But it was hard to sound natural while delineating everything that had happened over the past few weeks and months and decades of her life. They couldn't have the air on in the car, for sound purposes, and they couldn't have the windows open either, so it was getting stuffy inside, and the conversation had barely begun. "We thought the affair had started when Mac and I were kids. I know you all got to know a bit about Mae and our two Alices over the past year. I suppose this video is my mother and me trying to explain why you won't be seeing the two Alices anymore. It will be me and my mom. And my Alice. Which is what it always should have been, right, Mom?"

"It's what it always *has* been," Beth Ann corrected, her smile gleaming, her hands below the frame of the camera practically tearing holes in her jeans. "We've always been in this together." Her smile was tight. Her voice tighter.

"Yes. Right. And now even more so. Now that we understand more about what happened. The affair that tore our family apart started before I was even born. And Mae — it turns out Mae was a product of that affair. My father — he kept it a secret for a very long time, until right before his death. So we're — all of us — reeling."

Sydney had practiced the words in the shower that morning, her Alice wailing in her crib, desperate to get out, but not as desperate as Sydney had been to take five minutes in the hot water and steam and rose-peach scent of her soap. The water was loud enough to drown out the baby's cries and she recited these words, searching for seriousness, for relatability, for some sort of warmth that Ivy Miller claimed was reachable by any of them if they would just come to the conferences and watch the talks and attend Small Group and tell their truths to one another every day. If they would invest more in their businesses — in their lives, really — then they could be successful the way the Girls were, the way the rest of the Vases were, the way Ivy Miller herself was.

Sydney took a breath. She could still smell the rose-peach. Not as much as she would have liked, but it was lingering, at least.

"It's not Mae's fault. It's huge news for her too, it's so much to grapple with, and we can't know her journey. Maybe she'll share it one day. Maybe she and I will find a way back to each other. We are — after all — sisters, it turns out. Sisters. And we've both experienced enormous loss. So we have that in common." Beth Ann put a hand on her shoulder, and Sydney tried to breathe in the word *sisters* in the hope that it would elicit something emotional and real from her. But her mind was elsewhere — in the shower still, worrying about the language, the angle of the camera, the credit card bill that Sam had set on the counter last night, after which he'd poured them each a shot of whiskey and said, with equal parts kindness and rage, "Sydney, we have to talk about this." It was as if her brain was protecting her grief, making sure she didn't show its largeness, how deeply *real* it actually was.

Ivy Miller had insisted they would reach people more authentically if they were raw. But neither of them was getting there. Not here, not now.

"It isn't Mae's fault. Or mine. Or my mother's. There is a person responsible for all this. I used to think of her as a second mom. I used to wish I could be more like her. Mae's mother. Joni Dyer. A woman who knowingly created this web of lies and let us all live in it for years. I don't want to speak ill of the dead. As most of you know, Joni passed away a long time ago. But, gosh, I'm just so happy to have *my* mother. My mom. Who has been here for everything. Who was a victim in all of this. Who taught me everything I know about business and loyalty and being a mom, now that I'm following in her footsteps there too."

"I love you, honey," Beth Ann said. Sydney's heart cramped, a hiccup of a feeling reminding her that Beth Ann had perhaps never said those words to her before today. Had Barrett? She tried to conjure up a time, a memory that she could hang on to, but it was hard to see past the way she missed him and the way she had never known him at all.

She tried a smile. It felt strange on her face, like the drawing of a smile and not the real thing.

"It all sounds like some soap opera," Beth Ann went on. "I know that. I hear it and think, *That can't be my life*. But here we are. First the news of Mae being Barrett's child and then Barrett's passing— it's awful. It's truly unbelievable. It will take us a long time to understand, even longer to forgive. And longest, perhaps, for us to manage life without Sydney's father. Sydney's and Mae's father. But in this wreckage, in this awful unveiling of the truth of what our lives have been, we want so badly to take steps forward. Follow us here as we navigate our grief, build our business, reckon with what Joni Dyer did to us, and of course raise our next generation, our little Alice."

Sydney nodded. There had been discussion about whether they should have Alice in the car for this conversation, and they had landed on no—the chance of her erupting into cries or even just being distracting by way of some adorable babbling or face-making seemed too high, and there would be plenty of opportunities to have her front and center in the future.

Beth Ann kept on driving and a silence dragged on around them, the story told. They hadn't exactly come up with a way to end it.

"So I guess that's it," Sydney said at last. "Or that's not it at all, but that's where we're at. That's our, um, catch-up. We wanted to be honest with you all, especially everyone who was so invested in me and Mae and our little Alices. We didn't want to leave you high and dry without explaining everything our family is going through. You won't be seeing Mae and her Alice on this account going forward, but, you know, the door's open. This is LillyLou, after all. The door is always open."

Sydney smiled. Beth Ann wilted suddenly, the work of performing okay-ness finally over. Sydney reached forward and turned off the video, and Beth Ann pulled off the road. She rested her head on the steering wheel and didn't say a word. They stayed like that awhile, in silence, until Beth Ann started the car up again, ready to drive Sydney home. They had orders to fill. They had comments to read and enthusiastically reply to. They had their business to build.

And Alice too. Sam had said he could watch her for a few hours, but then he needed some time alone, time to think. An appointment at the bank about their mortgage. A call with a marriage counselor his friend had recommended. And then, of course, more time to talk.

Sydney posted the video. *Only One Alice, for Now,* she called it. She added in the caption *Our family has been through a lot in the past month. A secret revealed. A huge loss. We want to share with all of you that these hardships bring us together, make us all stronger. But, boy, it's been a tough one for me and my mom.*

She knew Sam would ask, when she got home, how all this was going to sell scarves, why this would make someone buy a bra, and she would have to explain, she'd have to try again and again and again, until he understood. Until she could show him how powerful she really was.

MUCH LATER

ALICE WAS IN a mood. She'd screamed at Mae when Mae corrected her assertion that Egypt was in Europe. "Oh, no, it's in Africa, sweetheart," she'd said casually, the way she was always saying things right before her daughter exploded.

Alice then launched into a tirade about her certainty that Egypt was in Europe. Her kindergarten's unit on continents was her favorite; she sang the continent song on repeat and had taken in random facts from the picture books they read in class the way she took in nearly everything—as a complete and utter sponge, reporting on such things as the Nazca Lines and Machu Picchu after the week they spent discussing South America. Mae had wondered, more than once, if there was such a thing as being *too* precocious. Clearly, some wire had gotten crossed in the song they sang about Egypt. Alice, having just recently turned six, was almost never incorrect on factual information learned at school, so whenever she was, it was a disorienting and rageful event.

"It is *not* in Africa, it is in *Europe*, it has *pyramids*, and *pyramids* are in *Europe*." Alice was red with heat and certainty. Mae tried to gently correct her again, but it was no use. Alice just screamed her arguments about pyramids louder, angrier this time, and Mae was clueless as to what to do.

"I can't argue about reality with a six-year-old," she said to Alice, speaking to her like a peer the way she often did.

"It's in Europe!" Alice yelled, devolving, as she often did, into tears. Her rage moved swiftly into sadness, often ping-ponging back and forth at a maddening rate.

"We'll talk about it another time," Mae said. She was sweating, the force of Alice's feelings always nearly too much to bear. Alice kicked the air and then Mae's shin. Mae let out an exasperated yell and wished, for the millionth time, that there was someone she could hand Alice over to, if just for a moment, so that she could catch her breath. They were going to the ocean with Graham and Catherine. She needed to catch her breath.

Once a year, Catherine orchestrated a trip for the four of them. It was a new tradition — as new as Alice herself, who was, in spite of her expansive, unnerving vocabulary and sophisticated pronunciation of multisyllabic words, still quite new. Last year, it had been a farm. The year before, a small upstate town known for its idyllic playgrounds and ice cream parlors. Mae was good at guessing what Alice at different ages might like, a trait she felt sure she had picked up from Joni, who had been a pro at the pursuit of fun, and these trips reminded Mae of that truth, of the way that Joni had been the mother playing tag at the park, the mother putting temporary hair dye into their hair, taking them to get manicures, taking them out for enormous ice cream sundaes they couldn't possibly finish, teaching them how to put on mascara, letting them watch movies that Beth Ann had vetoed, showing them how to make every stitch of a friendship bracelet that she could recall.

It was breathtaking, actually, how many things Joni did beautifully as a mother while still being able to so magnificently, awesomely, undeniably fuck it all up.

There was something about motherhood that was this way, though, Mae was discovering. Everything you were good at as a mother, even brilliant at, was always balanced by the ways you failed, so you never got the sensation of success no matter how heroically you tried.

She had breastfed Alice for eighteen months, a feat that seemed Herculean in retrospect. She had read Alice book after book after book, taken her to story times at the library, made her Halloween costumes from scratch, remembered to compliment her intelligence instead of her (also undeniable) beauty, kept a weekly hot chocolate and croissants date with her for the past year, taking her to the neighborhood café, where they colored together on the wobbly, crowded tables, Alice with her hot chocolate, Mae with her latte, both of them in wonder at the beauty of the small but also somehow enormous ritual. She'd gotten a golden retriever and named him Noodle and he slept on the floor of Alice's room at night, always wanting to lay his chin on her folded-up socks. In this and so many other ways, she'd made a beautiful, messy life. She did it all with the help of the money Barrett left them, which supplemented the money she made teaching art to little kids who made self-portraits using pom-poms and glitter glue, who drew only rainbows, who knew how to paint a sunset better than the most exceptional gallery artist. She had not finished her master's but promised herself she would someday. It would have made Barrett proud. Or Joni. Maybe. Or perhaps not at all. She would never know. So she continued teaching the children—after all, she liked it. And without either of her biological parents around to impress, she figured she might as well do what she liked.

Graham didn't have an opinion either way. And maybe that was love, after all. Maybe that was pride.

Mae would try it all for Alice, try being every sort of mother, to cover for the way Leo wasn't a father at all. She'd let him slink off to LA, where he was surely courting young starlets with adorable pictures of the daughter he barely knew.

Letting Leo disappear was a failure of Mae's, although Catherine tried to convince her it wasn't her fault. Another failure of hers was the way she and Sydney had never spoken again. At six, Alice was begging for family beyond Mae and Graham and Catherine. Other kids, she noted, had siblings and cousins, aunts and uncles and grandparents and entire homes filled with people at holidays and on vacations. She liked her trips with her mother and grandfather and Catherine, whom she called Catherine and not Grandma, not CeeCee, not Step-Anything. Catherine was Catherine. It was easier for Mae. And in that way, Catherine showed her love too, by not insisting she be anything else to Mae and Alice.

Next month was the five-year anniversary of Barrett's death. Which was also the five-year anniversary of finding out that Barrett was her father. She noted the date every year, a place in the calendar she didn't quite know what to do with. She didn't know what to do with thoughts of Barrett in general. Sometimes she'd see his expression on her face, some squint in Alice's eyes that once, she was sure, belonged to him. And that information was unmoored, unanchorable. There was nowhere to store it, no place for it to live. Sometimes she found herself staring at the Painting, the one that made her famous and rich, sort of. For years she had dreamed of it in the home of some wealthy art enthusiast on the Upper East Side or maybe in Paris or LA. But instead, impossibly, it had been hanging in the home she'd known so well, in the attic she had played hide-and-seek in. All this time, Barrett had been her benefactor, buying and keeping her one great masterpiece. She wished she knew what he liked it about it most, which parts he stared at the longest, which parts were the ones he'd spent all that money for.

There was so, so much that Mae Dyer would simply never know.

She had tried, once, to talk to Graham about it all, but he couldn't manage it. His voice shook and broke and he searched for words that didn't come, ultimately just telling Mae he loved her and that was that.

Mae hoped she'd do better than that, talking to Alice about everything, but she hadn't tried yet. So here she was, correcting and correcting her daughter about the location of Egypt without ever telling her who she actually was.

Perhaps Mae should have let Alice believe this one faulty fact until it got corrected later, in whatever year of school they learned about continents again—first grade, maybe? Second? It wasn't like Alice would run around mislocating Egypt for the rest of her life.

But Mae couldn't resist taking out her phone, showing Alice the map of the world, forcing her to look at the square shape of Egypt and the way it fit, undeniably, onto the top of Africa.

Alice threw the phone across the room at the same instant that Catherine let herself in the apartment, an accidental witness to the terrible moment.

"*Goddamn it!*" Mae yelled. "I mean, seriously, I am so *sick* of this! All because of Egypt!"

Alice started to cry. Catherine swooped in to hug her, and Mae felt the absence of a person there to hug *her*. "It's okay, sweetheart," Catherine said. "It's okay. It's okay. Everything's okay."

Mae left the room and tucked herself into a corner of her bedroom where she often went to calm herself down in these moments. She let Catherine take the suitcases out to the car, where Graham waited in the driver's seat. Let her pack snacks while asking Alice a series of questions about Australia and Asia and the continent song, which Alice sang in a loud voice that Catherine momentarily tolerated.

When Catherine had settled everything, including strapping Alice into her car seat, Mae came out, her heart beating at a regular pace again, her throat sore from yelling, the rest of her weak with a sort of shame that overcame her, seeing Catherine glide into the role of mother in spite of never having been one herself. Mae sat in the back next to Alice, Graham driving, Catherine riding shotgun, trying to make this configuration make sense, trying to let it be okay.

After dropping Noodle off at boarding, Mae stayed quiet most of the very long drive. Alice prattled on about Mars and Pluto and her favorite colors and her classmates' favorite colors and which My Little Pony was the most like her and why. Catherine asked questions but not especially interesting ones, and Graham laughed once in a while at something especially ridiculous that Alice said.

When they arrived at the house by the beach, Graham looked back at her expectantly. "You remember?" he asked.

"Remember what?" Mae answered, going over her checklist for the trip. Sunblock? Sandals? Alice's favorite owl stuffie?

"Do you remember this place?" he asked.

And in a flash, Mae did.

"I figured — it's been almost five years. Right? Since Barrett..." He shook his head, the name still hard for him to say, painful. "I thought maybe you'd want to, I don't know, think about him. So."

Graham had never been the father cheering most loudly at soccer games or remembering the names of her favorite bands. He hadn't taken her to midnight movies or asked about what techniques she'd used on the Painting. They did not meet up on Joni's birthday to eat scallops or sourdough bread or any of her favorite foods.

Like Joni, like Mae, he was a flawed parent.

And yet.

Here they were. Exactly where she hadn't known she needed to be.

Sydney had been the one to hang on to the ashes, kept in a small, jade-colored urn. At her father's funeral almost five years ago, she'd wondered if Mae might arrive, if she might want to hang on to some part of him herself. She'd bought a second, smaller urn for just this purpose, hoping that Mae would appear and shoulder some of the grief with her.

But Mae never reached out, and Sydney never did either, and the years since Barrett's death passed in the ways all such years pass—with rockiness and spectacularly tiny joys and late nights wishing she could ask him a hundred questions, and early mornings when she got to enjoy coffee before Sam or Alice awoke, and fights with Sam that lasted entire weeks, and thousands of enthusiastic likes on her posts with Beth Ann, and a sudden influx of money, enough to pay down most of the credit cards, and a move to the suburbs, where she was always meant to be, and the listening to Alice say at first a dozen words, then a hundred, then an endless stream of sentences, so many that Sydney found herself wondering why parents were so eager for their children's first words at all.

"Is it gauche or authentic to post a photo of the urn?" Beth Ann asked. "I was thinking we could do it in the car? Or maybe just wait and take a photograph of it at the beach. And then of course, you scattering the ashes in the ocean. Maybe not showing the ashes themselves, though, I don't think people really want—It's a fine line, you know? Remember Rosie and her husband's funeral?"

Sydney could hardly have forgotten. Rosie Atberry had lost her husband to cancer last spring. Beth Ann and Sydney helped her a great deal, first with just the basics of grief, then bringing her food, sitting with her in the early mornings and late nights, helping her organize his things into piles of what would be nice to hang on to and what needed to be released—everything they had done over the past few years for their own mourning. After some time had passed and Rosie's finances became troublesome, they helped her with the rest of it too. The posts. Telling the story of the parts of the experience that would resonate with the most people. The work of tying that story into her business, letting it be a bit of connective tissue that lit people up, made them want to be a part of a business that embraced rather than rejected the vulnerable parts of life.

And it had been going well. Rosie grew her business, engagement was up, and money was sure to follow, Beth Ann assured her. Even Ivy Miller herself promised Rosie that her finances would soon reflect her new station in the LillyLou universe.

And then Rosie Atberry had posted a photograph of the hand of the corpse of her husband.

Sydney felt at fault, having just given Rosie a prolonged speech about the importance of really opening up, not shutting pieces of her life away but being a full, true, raw person. She'd told Rosie that what had helped Beth Ann and herself was real transparency, an unfiltered look at the hardest parts of their lives. People wanted to be involved with that kind of realness, she told this young widow, who was pretty and unfussy and clearly perfect for the kind of role Ivy Miller was assigning her.

Rosie Atberry had nodded and said she understood.

And then she posted the photograph, recounting the hardest moments of grieving from the past year. The hand was a horrible gray color, made even more horrible by the perfect peach of Rosie's skin against it.

It was too much and telegraphed a sort of instability about Rosie, a lack of boundaries, a misunderstanding about something very central to humanity that people couldn't name or even speak about but that was absolutely *there*. Sydney herself couldn't have explained to

Rosie why one kind of sharing was good and this other kind so obviously bad, and perhaps that was the problem with Rosie Atberry. She'd needed it explained.

Ivy Miller unfollowed Rosie and in a gentle phone call suggested that LillyLou was not, in fact, the right place for her. She kindly offered up lists of support groups and therapists, and that was that.

Still, the reminder of the infraction had stuck with Sydney, a sort of warning that she needed to constantly be making sure her posts fit neatly inside the undrawn but still very thick LillyLou lines.

Clearly, Rosie's demise had stuck with Beth Ann as well. When they arrived at the beach, Beth Ann had Sydney hold the urn to her chest, and she took a shot from behind where only the hint of its green handle could be seen. Enough to know what it was but not enough to scare anyone away.

"Should we get one with me?" Beth Ann asked Sydney. "Or one with Alice?"

Alice was busy making a mess of herself in the sand, filling up the red bucket they'd brought and flipping it over her head with a loud laugh. Sydney shuddered to think what would happen if she got hold of the urn and found a way to open it.

"I think it muddies the story," Sydney said. Over the years, she and Beth Ann had found a way to talk about what had happened without talking about what had happened. It was the story, it was this awful thing and also the incredible opportunity that had catapulted them into LillyLou fame. It had broken them and saved them. And their shared goal was to keep the story clear, consistent, easy for everyone to understand.

Barrett's death immediately after—or, really, in the same moment as—the revelation of his having fathered Mae was a difficult part of the story but a crucial one, as Ivy Miller once said. Sydney had tried to shake off that phrasing and its odd implication that Barrett's death was largely a positive. Still, at the root of things,

Ivy Miller was, in some way, right. More people followed One Alice, Beth Ann and Sydney's little piece of LillyLou, after his death than before, and there was no getting around that fact.

Sydney had been the one centered in the grieving of Barrett. Beth Ann's rage made it tricky, and Alice reminded everyone of the other Alice, who was also the granddaughter, technically speaking, of the deceased, and there were too many complications tangled up in that. It was simplest to let Beth Ann experience her rage and victimization separately while Sydney grieved in her own sphere. In this way, they could appeal to both those grieving and those aggrieved, those who were mourning loved ones and those who were raging at the way they had never truly been loved to begin with.

Beth Ann and Sydney both held these roles beautifully.

And *truthfully*, Sydney was always quick to tell herself when she questioned the public grieving. This was not a lie, this photo on the beach. This was the truth.

"He did love this place," Beth Ann said. "Our summers here were — they were beautiful." She swallowed down the other, parallel reality that they were times that Barrett and Joni surely took advantage of, moments when their affair must have progressed.

"He loved a cocktail on the beach," Sydney said. "When I turned twenty-one he made me a martini and we took it to the beach, and it sploshed around in the martini glass the whole way, so there was like a drop left, but he wanted me to drink it with my feet in the sand, watching the waves. And he was right. It was great."

"We should have brought cocktails," Beth Ann said. "I'm sorry, sweetheart."

"We can make some tomorrow."

"Of course. Tomorrow."

Sydney nodded to the dock. The plan was to walk to the edge of it, fly the ashes out into the waves, and say goodbye. Beth Ann walked over to grab Alice's hand. The girl screeched, desperate to continue to play in the sand. "We'll come right back," Beth Ann assured her. "Quick break, and then you can keep playing, okay?"

"That is *not* okay!" Alice yelled. "We had to drive all day and now I'm here and I'm playing and it is *not* okay, stop saying everything's okay!"

Beth Ann swallowed a yell back. She loved her granddaughter but struggled with the way she spoke to her, the way she called out every injustice, every mistake, every moment that misaligned with her understanding of the world. It was an exhausting quality.

It reminded her not of her own daughter but of Mae.

"Nothing's okay," Sydney said, handing Alice a lollipop bought especially for this purpose. Sydney's parenting wasn't perfect, but it was practical, and right now she needed Alice to comply, and Alice complied only when lollipops were involved. Whether or not this spoke to a larger problem, a bigger parenting task to undertake, a thing to be fixed, was not a question Sydney was interested in answering.

The three of them walked down the dock, Alice happily licking away, turning her tongue a neon shade of orange. It was a long walk, the dock impressively far into the sea.

And then they were there. Beth Ann took out her phone.

"No photos once I open the urn," Sydney said. She stared out at the ocean and thought about Barrett. Beth Ann took photographs. Alice sat on the wooden planks and splashed her feet in the water right below. At last Sydney opened the urn. It was windier than she was expecting, and Beth Ann was sighing at the force of it, warning her to be careful, sitting next to Alice and draping an arm around her as if the wind might take her away too. Beth Ann had always, always hated the wind.

Sydney had always said she did too.

She grabbed a handful of her father and let the wind pick him up and fly him away. It was nice, actually, that she didn't have to do it herself—what would she have done exactly? Thrown the ashes overhand? Underhand? As hard as she could? Lightly, like some kind of fairy dust? It would have been too much to decide.

No, she was glad for the wind today. And every day, maybe. For the way it made decisions for her. For the way it was so squarely in charge.

Handful after handful of ashes she held in her hand, and handful after handful the wind picked up and flew out to sea.

And then he was gone.

Alice's lollipop was gone too, so she ran from Beth Ann up the dock, her grandmother calling after her to slow down, to listen, to pay attention, to follow the rules, to show some respect.

But Alice would not be slowed down. Another kid was on the beach, and Alice loved other kids. She sprinted toward this one, approximately the same size and shape as Alice herself. She brought over her bucket, and the two of them began filling it up together. Sydney and Beth Ann were too far away to see much of the details, but they shared a smile over the exuberance of Alice. It was something to be prized—her friendliness, her bravery, her disregard for the proper way to do something. It was the part of her that was like Barrett, wasn't it? And in their own complicated and twisted-up ways, they both loved Barrett still.

"Let's get to the fish market. Something white and light tonight? Lemon and parsley and all that?" Beth Ann said.

"Sure," Sydney said, tempted to add something even healthier to the mix—a bed of spinach, a handful of green beans. But she stopped herself. "And let's get some ice cream too. For dessert."

It was a small thing but also, in its own way, a huge thing. Ice cream. Cookies and cream, maybe.

As they got closer to the shore, Alice and her new friend came into focus. The other kid was a girl as well, Alice's age, in a yellow one-piece with a collection of friendship bracelets making their way up her arms and three shell necklaces around her neck.

Alice waved to her mother and grandmother. And the other girl waved somewhere off in the distance at whoever her grown-up was. As Sydney got closer, she looked for who the other girl belonged to. The child was blond. Pretty. Laughing with a wide-open mouth, then whispering something in Alice's ear, a secret. Sydney smiled at how eagerly Alice received it, how quickly childhood friendships could come to be.

Sydney shaded her eyes. Yep, there were the girl's grown-ups, not far off now. Two women and one man. One of the women had an easel set up in front of her. The older one behind her—drinking something out of what appeared to be a thermos—had short-clipped hair. The man had his arms crossed and kept shifting his weight.

But the one at the easel—she had long, thick, waving hair. It kept getting in her face.

Sydney took a few more steps forward. Squinted harder. The younger woman held the paintbrush with confidence, like she was almost never without it. Like she had been holding a paintbrush since she was three years old, painting rainbows and butterflies and princesses with rainbow-butterfly crowns with her best friend so many decades ago it felt like another lifetime. But it wasn't.

It was this lifetime.

Sydney stopped. The woman with the paintbrush lifted her eyes, looked out over the painting for her daughter, and found Sydney instead.

Sydney raised a hand.

She waved.

The woman with the paintbrush paused. Squinted. Recognized Sydney.

And in those precious moments, before Graham or Beth Ann could say a thing about it, before Beth Ann could ask pointed questions about what Mae and Graham and Graham's dollhouse-doll wife were doing here, before she could say something cutting and cruel about Joni or even Barrett himself, before Graham could pull his family away and pretend the whole thing hadn't happened, before any more of the history Mae and Sydney didn't choose could roar in the face of their friendship, while their daughters forged something new and undeniable right there in the wettest sand—Mae raised her hand, smiled, and waved right back.

ACKNOWLEDGMENTS

Thank you to my agent, Victoria Marini, for believing so ferociously in this book for so long. I would never have finished writing it without your encouragement, and it never would have found a home without your certainty.

Thank you to my editor, Sally Kim, for your thoughtful, precise, and incredibly meaningful work on this book. I am so beyond grateful to have your insights and understanding, and I am thrilled with every way you helped me deepen, elevate, and ground this story. What a beautiful process it has been!

Thank you to the Little, Brown team for everything you've given this book. It is incredible the diverse range of skills, ideas, dedication, and inspiration that goes into turning a manuscript into an actual book finding actual readers. I have been in awe of the hard work and creative energy of everyone who put their time and hearts into *Mothers and Other Strangers*. A special thank-you to Lauren Denney for so many things along the way. Thank you to this wonderful team: Kayleigh George, Elizabeth Garriga, Darcy Glastonbury, Sabrina Callahan, Michael Barrs, Megan Cunningham, and Laura Mamelok. And for the beautiful production: Keith Hayes, Sebastian Blanck, Ben Allen, Erin Cain, Betsy Uhrig, Marie Mundaca, Tracy Roe, and Pamela Marshall.

ACKNOWLEDGMENTS

Special thank-yous to Sarah Branham, Sara Zarr, Chloe Thompson, and Julia Furlan. Thank you Katie Cotugno, Jess Verdi, Caela Carter, Amy Ewing, Anica Rissi, Alex Arnold, Steven Brezenoff, Tara Altebrando, Bryan Bliss, and Dan Kraus.

To Mom, Dad, Andy, and the whole of my extremely supportive book-loving family.

A special thank-you to Dana Mittelman, whose lifelong friendship has inspired so many big and little things in my writing life. How lucky to know you forever.

And, of course, thank you to Frank, Fia, and Thisbe. You are my whole world. Thank you for all the ways you help me write stories, and all the things you do to make me believe I should keep on writing them.

ABOUT THE AUTHOR

Corey Ann Haydu is the author of several titles for children and young adults and is a professor in the Vermont College of Fine Arts creative writing for children program. She lives in Brooklyn with her husband and, of course, her two daughters. *Mothers and Other Strangers* is her adult debut.

RAISING READERS
Books Build Bright Futures

Thank you for reading this book and for being a reader of books in general. We are so grateful to share being part of a community of readers with you, and we hope you will join us in passing our love of books on to the next generation of readers.

Did you know that reading for enjoyment is the single biggest predictor of a child's future happiness and success?

More than family circumstances, parents' educational background, or income, reading impacts a child's future academic performance, emotional well-being, communication skills, economic security, ambition, and happiness.

Studies show that kids reading for enjoyment in the US is in rapid decline:

- In 2012, 53% of 9-year-olds read almost every day. Just 10 years later, in 2022, the number had fallen to 39%.
- In 2012, 27% of 13-year-olds read for fun daily. By 2023, that number was just 14%.

Together, we can commit to **Raising Readers** and change this trend. How?

- Read to children in your life daily.
- Model reading as a fun activity.
- Reduce screen time.
- Start a family, school, or community book club.
- Visit bookstores and libraries regularly.
- Listen to audiobooks.
- Read the book before you see the movie.
- Encourage your child to read aloud to a pet or stuffed animal.
- Give books as gifts.
- Donate books to families and communities in need.

Books build bright futures, and **Raising Readers** is our shared responsibility.

For more information, visit **JoinRaisingReaders.com**

Sources: National Endowment for the Arts, National Assessment of Educational Progress, WorldBookDay.com, Nielsen BookData's 2023 "Understanding the Children's Book Consumer"